No Need to Apologize

K.J. Serafin

ISBN 979-8-9865454-0-0 (Paperback)
ISBN 979-8-9865454-1-7 (E-book)

Cover design by K.J. Serafin

Prologue

Gray smoke coiled above the orange blaze until a wintry breeze swept it across the patio. Given a choice of either ingesting wood ash or awaiting the next cloud of second-hand pot smoke—I didn't stifle my inhale. Once the joint made a full circuit around the fire bowl and conversation amongst the five members calmed to giggling whispers, I signaled for everyone's attention.

"You're all familiar with headlines noting the rise and fall of Jared Libby, the boy from Canard. During the police investigation, a portion of his family's property was dug up. Twenty-seven bodies were unearthed: two raccoons, one opossum, one fisher, two goats, a number of squirrels, three cats, six dogs, and two deer. The dogs and cats were not microchipped and were considered strays. No matter. The court concerned itself with proving damage to property and for keeping weapons he wasn't licensed to own. For that, he received a three-year sentence.

"No one truly cared he shot a slew of forest creatures and buried them under his mother's azaleas. Little was made of the improper burials, the shallowness of the graves. He had valid permits to 'harvest' wildlife in season. Due to the degraded condition of the corpses, it was impossible to prove *when* he killed them. So, also, not a problem. The pet snuff videos were picked apart for one reason or another to bolster his claim he faked them. The jury had doubts. It was enough. All in all, a clusterfuck of an animal cruelty case."

"Tell them about Cassandra. The girlfriend," Monica said.

Folding chairs creaked as bodies leaned forward. Time and circumstance had worn grooves into their foreheads and wrinkled flesh under their eyes. The endless fight for a cause relatively few others believed in often did that to people.

"Separate, but related," I said. "She hung herself from a door in the psych unit a few weeks before his trial began. Most would agree that's when the Libby family's real trouble began."

I angled my chair to face the back wall of the cottage. Earlier, Monica and I had draped a white bedsheet over the siding to serve as a screen for viewing the torture videos from my laptop. All eleven of them. The others knew they weren't invited here for a party. This was another call to action.

"The key to solving Ella's murder," I began, "could be in what they recorded—intentional or otherwise. We just need to find it."

Chapter 1

Y ou can't stuff nasty things into a mouth and expect it to belch out beauty. My family was proof of that. The strategy for surviving this dinner with soul intact was to turn it into a solitary game of wits.

Two Sundays ago, I focused on animal assignments and got all four before finishing the salad course. This evening, I mentally scoured a produce aisle for fruits and vegetables. Time was of the essence. Cheryl adheres to a strict dinner schedule to ensure her motherly duties are in no way impinged upon. The moment she rose to remove the chicken carcass from the table, I declared success. Louis is a parsnip. Cheryl, a red onion. Anthony, a blue Hubbard squash. Carrie could be likened to an unripe persimmon: perfect in appearance; bitterly tannic on the inside. Despite her two-year engagement to Louis, I knew precious little about the woman destined to marry my stepfather. I knew more than I cared to about the others.

Coffee, liquors, and grievances accompanied dessert. Cheryl's modern kitchen produced a New York-style cheesecake baked in Boston and pilfered from Anthony's restaurant. I contributed a carrot cake garnished with candied walnuts. The cake was as welcome as my vegetable lasagna. I'd be dining well on leftovers this week. Tableside conversation meandered through petty complaints. Anthony went silent gathering energy for a harangue. At last, his gray eyes fixed on me.

"The specials menu is a bust. I said this would happen. The restaurant lost money hand over fist. Big mistake bringing you in on this, Danni."

Cheryl stood behind her husband's chair, rubbing his back, soothing the angry child in him. My lack of sympathy showed. Louis stared blankly, crestfallen; his perpetual state of being. Carrie sighed into her third glass of wine. She'd request an Irish coffee next to keep her momentum going.

I honestly don't know why I continue to accept these dinner invites. The whole of the evening was inevitably spent ignoring the invisible feathered imp perched on my shoulder. It would repeatedly nip my ear lobe and pluck at my hair offering criticisms and ultimatums I could never voice aloud. Tonight, I struggled mightily to silence it.

"Anthony. You asked for my help and I gave it," I began. "The items on the specials menu are easy to prepare and rely on ingredients stocked in the kitchen. The cooks take what you already have and make it prettier on a plate. Customers are merely choosing different entrees. I don't understand how you lost money."

"You wouldn't, would you?" Cheryl's face pinched in aggrievement. "Tony went to Johnson and Wales. When have you ever managed a restaurant? When have you ever managed anything on your own? Successfully—I mean."

Another solitary game sprang to mind. This one a bit more enjoyable than the first. *Hashtag 'broken record'. Hashtag 'jealous much?' Hashtag 'self-entitled'.*

"Throw out the inserts," Carrie said. "A well-intentioned, bad idea."

Louis turned his hangdog face to me. "That okay, sweetheart?"

I sucked on candied walnuts and continued playing the game, this time with Anthony in my sights. *Hashtag 'man-child'. Hashtag 'crook'.*

Anthony was far from finished. He lamented, Cheryl soothed, and Louis and Carrie commiserated. Fifteen minutes of whiny gibberish. This was a special corner of my personal Hell. Listening to them, one would think my sole purpose in life was to make them miserable by devising clever ways to impoverish them. I wished they would all just shut up. The imp screeched.

Cutlery bounced when my palms hit the table. "The changes cost you nothing! Any dip in revenue is due to mismanagement. You can't serve meals without skilled waitstaff. Your employees are impatient. Most are untrained. It shows every time a customer is dissatisfied with an order, which I assume happens frequently or you wouldn't have debased yourself asking for my help. People come to your restaurant for cheap beer and the oil-rich delicacies of your fryolator, not innovative cuisine. A reminder, cash goes in the register. The IRS expects you to underreport only so much."

One way to clear the table. Thirty-seven minutes ahead of schedule.

Anthony stomped out with Louis in attendance for moral support. Carrie clattered stacked dishes off the table. Cheryl blew out the pillar candles spewing hot wax everywhere. The carrot cake and lasagna, minus one serving each, were pushed next to my plate. I lingered alone at the table stubbornly determined to finish eating a second slice of cake I had no appetite for.

The knot gathering in my chest migrated to my throat. A hard lump lodged there causing an airless gasp.

I can't breathe.

Stay calm.

I . . . can't . . .

Anthony puttered in the kitchen rinsing dishes for the dishwasher. Louis and Carrie haggled in the living room for control of the television remote. Cheryl paced the second-floor hall shushing her hyperactive children.

Remain calm.

Rising on shaking legs, I made a two-handed fist and drove it into my diaphragm. Once, twice, thrice. Dislodged, a sticky glob of walnuts flew over my dessert plate to plink into a glass of water. The ridiculous hilarity of it made my eyes water. I barked out a raspy chuckle.

Anthony stepped into the dining room with a dirty plate balanced on one palm. "Christ sake, Danni. Keep it down. Cheryl's trying to put the kids to sleep." He raised a dark eyebrow at my startled expression and returned to the dishwasher.

I'd warble if I attempted words. Best to save them for when I knew whom to direct them at.

Spitballs of snow bounced off the windshield. They became hypnotic flashes of white in the headlights. Every trace of this freak storm would evaporate by tomorrow afternoon. My anger too, I supposed. The unappreciated lasagna and cake sat on the passenger seat. If food is love, my love has been rejected countless times. Despite outwardly accepting this, my psyche craved multiple helpings of indignation on the short drive home. I fed brilliant comebacks to their grimacing faces and uncharitably wished each of them had choked on the dead bird they were devouring. When my brain quieted, the imp, mercifully, withdrew its claws from my shoulder. In a flash of bent feathers, my imaginary fiend perched atop the lidded dishes. I always fancied it a busted-up juvenile Cooper's hawk, yet none living possessed such striking opalescence in the whites of their chest feathers. My imp was mine alone.

Swirls of sparkling white dusted the drab properties lining Dolly Road. I drove backward in history from slab ranches to bungalows to the antique colonial I called home. Snow drifts on the steep deck stairs leading up to my second-floor flat made for a cautious climb with the heavy dishes. An ominous hump covered the welcome mat. I gripped the dishes tighter and tapped the mound with my shoe. Icy granules rolled off revealing the gray blade of a plastic shovel. A gust of wind had knocked it over.

Dark thoughts often recede in my happy space, the kitchen. The bedazzled chandelier cast miniature rainbows on white cabinetry and yellow walls. The glazed Majolica platters Mother brought over from England leaned on floating shelves adding watery splashes of turquoise and brown. Regrettably, a handsome cabbage leaf pattern reminded me of an appetizer on Anthony's specials menu and transported me back to the disagreement. I knew I'd spoken out of turn and might not have if Cheryl and Louis hadn't first detailed flaws in my character. The daisy chain of insults flung over crystal stemware hung heavy from my neck. Even now.

I busied myself packaging leftovers. The cake and lasagna were portioned into lunch servings, sealed into tubs, and wedged into the freezer compartment next to the frozen cat. I fetched the laundry basket from the backseat of my Highlander and sorted it out on the kitchen table. Were I to move to a flat with washer and dryer hookups, I'd see less of my family. Cheryl's children would sprout up inches between visits. My opinions were unwelcome. My sympathy was tolerated as proof of inclusion in the family. Who knew washing clothes could be so angst-ridden?

Time to slip into a different mood. I declared the office off-limits. Nothing worse than revenge tweeting. The living room held the promise of escape. Sinking into the couch, I thumbed the remote and groused why the television screen wasn't larger. My gaze routinely slipped off its edges to the bar niche on the left and the hall door on the right. I hit the mute button to listen to Mr. Peebles' voice one flight below. Whether he was talking to himself, his television, or to another human being was increasingly difficult to tell nowadays. Another depressing development, my landlord's evident dementia. Which circled me back to dinner. Anthony's about-face hadn't caused my current funk. It merely exasperated one brought on Thursday evening when our pet store protest ended in a fisticuff. At some point, I'd have to respond to messages piling up on various devices. I dreaded removing my cell phone from the sock drawer.

The little red light on the answering machine flashed like a panicked heart. Somewhere within the crowd of telemarketers offering low-interest mortgages or winter vacation packages would be the terrified squeal of a pig made by a mentally corrupted human. I've heard worse sounds but wasn't prepared to go there tonight.

I readied myself for bed and hunkered down under Grandma Tilly's star quilt with a magazine. The hipster publication offered false-positive articles on mindful living. The inanity of it fed my burgeoning sense of disappointment. I flung it off the bed in a full-on snit. The living room phone rang and I lunged to answer it.

"Listen, you sick bastard. I'm going to find out who you are and—"

"Oh, God. Oh, no. I've called and called."

"Monica? Hey, sorry, what's the matter? Shhhh. Deep breaths. Tell me what's wrong."

"She's dead." Monica sobbed louder.

"Who's dead? Shhhh. It's okay. Monica, who's dead?"

"Ella. They killed her."

Snow had rendered the familiar route to Monica's carriage house surreal, an alien landscape of black and white under a clouded night sky that tasted of aluminum. The prospect of Ella murdered, the outrageousness of it, made me dizzy with fear. My car didn't hesitate for stop signs and careened around bends. I crossed into Northborough and skirted its main drag. More than once a horn blared and headlights flashed. Monica's ramblings created pressure inside my skull which only lessened when my nose and eyes began to leak and wet my collar.

I eased off the gas pedal for a turn onto Ardam Lane and rolled up the drive of a stately tan colonial. Every window was a rectangle of black. Behind it, a converted carriage house glowed yellow. I slid from my car sensing movement in a line of shrubs, a passing grayness.

"Monica. I'm here," I called from the kitchen door. "Nosferatu's snooping around outside. Are your shades drawn?"

Monica emerged from the bathroom in black pajamas dotted with green Frankenstein heads. A messy knot of black hair crowned her head. The pupils of her swollen eyes were dime-sized.

"You didn't have to come. No one said it was her."

"Of course. Certainly. We would've read about it in the paper. This happened yesterday?"

"Yeah. I think."

We flopped into separate corners of the living room couch. Our get-together Friday evening with a few of her other friends was still imprinted on the space: accent pillows wedged under the coffee table; the armchair crammed into the dining niche; the carpet redolent of spilled cumin and sriracha sauce. Monica added a soggy tissue to a pile on the coffee table. The television played a soundless loop of news stories. A meteorologist spider-walked her fingers over a map of Northeast states chasing cartoon snowflakes into the Atlantic Ocean. Monica studied the weather map. I studied her. The dizzying story she had related over the telephone involved a Jehovah's Witness, Ella's two rat terriers, Clyde and Reno, and a robbery gone wrong. Monica cried throughout rendering parts of the story nonsensical.

A dark-eyed junco trilled from my cell phone. I fiddled with its buttons to silence it. "I haven't returned calls since Thursday evening. Claire goes nutty and two hundred CL members ring me up. You know I regret the fistfight. 'Stop, drop, and run' should be our mantra."

Monica stared at her hands not recognizing them. When I touched her sleeve, her head swung up to the television. Neither of us restored the volume.

The scene shifted from a reporter in a beige puff coat to blue jacketed men entering and exiting the front door of Ella's Ives Street home in Framingham.

Midafternoon sun winked off a bank of windows set in chisel-cut brownstone. Yellow tape flapped from its iron stair railings. A video clip played of the chief of police at a podium flanked by a clutch of stern men in gray suits. A publicity shot of Ella taken two years ago filled the screen next. Posed seductively in a red wrap dress, she held a fuchsia-colored smoothie. Her blue and green ombre ponytail created a shawl over one shoulder. The broadcast shifted to three studio news anchors and the next story.

"Ella asked me to watch her dogs. She canceled it. She said not to come." Monica caught a newly emerging tear with a fingertip and flicked it away. She sucked in a stuttering breath letting it all back out verbally. "I called Reese. Jerk was drunk. He said Gordon said, 'Ella's dead.' And Reese was like, 'what are you talking about?' 'Joe, the neighbor, found her'. A Jehovah's Witness saw something weird in the window. You know? The neighbor's checking it out before he calls the cops. Right? Reese said it was the dog. It was a dog. A dog. Gordon found her. In the basement."

Every bit of me trembled. A dead woman discovered in Ella's home. Ella's whereabouts, presumably, unknown.

"Why did Gordon go to the basement?"

"I don't know."

"Why did Joe Dorvee call Gordon?"

"I don't know."

"Gordon called the police after he found her?"

"I don't know."

"Did Gordon think someone broke into her home?"

Monica screamed.

Chapter 2

E ven if today wasn't Veteran's Day, I wouldn't have clocked in at work. I stayed with Monica till nearly midnight. Once home I upped my nightly dose of antihistamine to two tablets and was rewarded with eleven hours of sleep without the ugliness of life invading my dreams. Bleary-eyed, I poured orange juice into the coffee maker and had to start over. My quivering stomach refused breakfast. I tugged on a running suit and vaulted over the deck railing to spring off the lid of the rubbish bin. It had the right amount of flexibility to make it fun.

The holiday reduced traffic on the slush-coated roads around my home. Neighbors driving by didn't honk as I wasn't wearing one of my more flamboyant outfits. The pine green stretch knits hugged my curves and could take a cartwheel and a split without flashing my cooch to the world. My new parkour routine involved a post office mailbox, a concrete retaining wall, a maple tree, and a chained link fence conveniently grouped on the corner of Wenton Street. Challenges keep the mind and body sharp. The tree trunk offered eight vertical feet for a run-up and flip. The fence mesh offered hand and toe holds for scaling. The mailbox was a stable object for a two-handed vault. The smooth-topped retaining wall allowed for walking handstands. Stringing the movements together with graceful transitions was the challenge.

I started with the tree and ended with the mailbox. Too clumsy. I altered the sequence in three more attempts. All wrong.

The owner of the chain-linked fence opened his front door. "Hey, asshole! Get off my fence! Go play in your own yard."

The interruption shook my concentration. I landed on the outside of my right foot. A twinge accompanied my, "Sorry. My bad." I limped home and into the real world.

An early lunch of smashed chickpea salad on crusty bread with lettuce and tomato paired well with a chilled IPA. I refilled the tank of my e-cigarette with a mellow tobacco-flavored oil and sank into the couch cushions with the tablet on my lap. Try as I might, I couldn't resist the lure of the daily paper unread since Saturday morning when I sought news of our pet store protest. Finding no mention of it, I went about my weekend content to ignore messages presumably from folks eager to gossip about what transpired. Before I could invent a reason to procrastinate any longer, I opened yesterday's Framingham Recorder and found a news brief.

Woman found slain in Framingham home
By Trudy Babcock

Framingham — Authorities are investigating the death of a woman found inside a home on Ives Street Saturday afternoon. Middlesex District Attorney, Mildred Guyner, has not released the identity of the victim. "The investigation has just begun. We're in the process of locating the homeowner."

The property belongs to Ella DeMarco, a former photojournalist at Recreational Times and co-founder of NPK (Nitrogen Phosphorus Potassium), a digital publication known for its controversial philosophies on modern living.

Framingham police responded to a call made by a neighbor, Joseph Dorvee, around 3:00 p.m. Saturday. A delivery man approached him in his home expressing concern for Ms. DeMarco's dogs as seen through a window. Officers found an unidentified woman inside the home with suspicious trauma to her body. She was pronounced dead at the scene. Framingham Police Chief, David Waite, has not released details of the crime at present. He issued an advisory to neighborhood residents to take extra security precautions and report any suspicious activity immediately.

In Monica's version of the discovery, both Joe and Gordon saw the body. Poor Joe. He and his wife Donna have flitted in and out of Ella's home for the past seven years. Gordon Fahey managed her career for the last five. Neither could identify the woman on sight. My immediate relief was tempered by budding outrage and deep sympathy. Murder is a heinous crime. A life cruelly cut short. The victim had family and friends. Clearly, the woman was an acquaintance of Ella's. Why else would she place her dogs in the woman's care? A handful of people qualified for such responsibility and the trust it implied. Those folks were my friends too.

Pressure built inside my head. It pressed against my eardrums. Today's edition of the much larger Globe newspaper was one tap away. I fetched my cell phone from its nest in the sock drawer. One hundred and forty-three unread messages across three platforms. I shoved the device under a couch cushion, tapped the Globe icon on my tablet, and commenced swiping.

A five-column article in the MetroWest section included a photo of Ella. Last night, Reese DeMarco positively identified the murdered woman as his younger sister. My world flipped upside down.

Lucky me. I managed to flip the toilet seat before vomiting up lunch. It tasted much better the first time. Vigorous teeth brushing, mouthwash, and four antiacids afterward didn't produce the hoped-for results. The computer in my office was closer to the toilet. A better spot to finish reading the online article.

Chief Medical Examiner, Gary Persse, released a statement estimating Ella's time of death as "occurring early Saturday morning" and determined the manner of death as "multiple blunt force trauma". Framingham's chief of police speculated Ella interrupted a robbery in progress after retiring to bed. The Globe reporter disregarded Ella's business acumen and prize-winning photojournalism career in the article. Of all her many interests and achievements, the reporter chose to rehash a failed petition we co-authored after forming our activist group, Twin Sister. We simply asked that plant milk be made available to all students of public schools and not only to those with animal milk allergies and a doctor's note. The focus on our failure made me frown.

The bungled robbery theory perplexed me for several reasons. Most burglaries occurred during morning or early afternoon hours when homes were likely to be vacant. Ella's four-year-old Malibu, presumably, was stationed in the driveway. Her revamped sixty-year-old ranch was in keeping with the socioeconomic level of the neighborhood, which is to say, middle-income. Why target her home when far grander properties existed in Flanders Estates a quarter-mile away? Ella outfitted her home with an electronic security system, an unnecessary accessory as her neighbors routinely opened doors and lifted blinds to glare at unfamiliar vehicles and pedestrians. Better home security came on four legs. Clyde and Reno, though small in size, were big in attitude. Their ear-splitting barks generated seismic waves. So, why her?

Others wondered the same. News of her murder generated a hailstorm of condolences and conspiracy theories on Twin Sister's social media account.

Sophie Ditz: Cried myself to sleep. They're shutting down the truth. Guilty consciences.

IttyBetty: Heartbroken. The world will never be the same. Someone should've helped her.

Mark Brower: WTF. Seriously, WTF. Big Ag has spoken.

Sweetpeas: OMG. Break-in my a**. Ella was silenced. Does anyone know anything about her third book? Was it investigative work? Animals? Drugs? Our criminal government?

Coconut Milk Maiden: &*%#! Submit ideas to my home page. Let's figure this out together. The official investigation will be bogus. A cover-up. You know the drill.

Comments on Compassion Lives' social media page originated from folks with dual memberships in both organizations and were only marginally less crazy. Both achieved a level of ridiculousness not normally witnessed outside of political groups. I called Monica but couldn't think of what to say after, "Hello."

She whispered, "Sorry." A phlegmy cough barked in the background followed by the shush of boxes dragged over a floor. Monica was at her desk at her uncle's plumbing supply shop.

"Why are you working on a bank holiday?"

"Uncle Ned needs me to eyeball stock numbers. We're inventorying pipes and fittings. You know he's like a hundred and two and can't see for shit."

"Have you logged onto Compassion Lives' ShowMe page?"

"Last night. Kind of. I was blotto. Why, that bad?"

My face scrunched of its own accord. "Rife with conspiracy theories. String together Satan, pedophilia, vaccines, the government and you capture the hearts and minds of the less observant. That aside, I do find the reported story of her discovery deeply troubling. The police can be led astray and there's a fair amount of prejudice in our judicial system." A flicker of movement on the street below my window. A truck bucked in and out of a pothole. The clap of its rear gate echoed like a gunshot. "Reese told you Gordon found her. The papers claim Joe Dorvee called the police. How many people were inside her home before the police arrived? Why was Gordon there?"

"You don't trust him."

"Not even a little."

"He's a sleazoid. He turned Ella into a zombie. Maybe she was tired of hawking cookbooks at carnivals. Maybe she wanted out and he said no. Maybe he killed her."

Three pigeons alighted on a cable strung from the house to a utility pole outside my office window. One pigeon sat apart; its feathers ruffled.

"Ella's business relationship with Gordon was built on trust and understanding he and I never achieved." I tapped the window glass. The pigeons took flight. "Why would Reese fabricate a story that throws suspicion on Gordon?"

Monica sniffed. "Why would Reese talk to me? I'm the lady who watches his sister's dogs."

"Good point. Oh, and please, don't delete the text Ella sent. It could be important. If nothing else, it's the last time she communicated with you."

Zips, creaks, and clangs indicated Monica left her desk. After the squawk of a door, she slurped on a freshly lit cigarette. "What if Ella was killed because of something she did with Twin Sister? Remember the nasty letters she got? Maybe Spanky wrote them. What if he's the reason everything got moved west?"

I flattened a spontaneous grin. Adrian was the first in my group to name our stalker after his presumed favorite pastime, masturbation. "We have little reason to believe Spanky went after Twin Sister members. They haven't posted any accounts of vandalism."

"Use your noggin. Twisters were bitching about the letters last year. What else has this freak been doing? How many stiff kitties or smutty messages did he leave for Ella? We don't know because nobody's saying. They don't want more people to panic and leave the group like they did when Ella went crazy."

"The letters could be love-sick ramblings from a fan. Relocating Twin Sister's headquarters to Bette's home in Barre made practical sense when she replaced me as their bookkeeper. I hosted member meetings in my home. Ella refused to do that and it would've been expected of her. All of it settled well before Spanky began stalking us. They're not related."

"Doesn't prove he didn't send the letters," Monica persisted.

"Correct. But it in no way ties him to them. I understand Ella's desire for secrecy regarding the letters. Few people know of the heinous messages I've received. But how does one keep public harassment secret? We couldn't. Spanky disrupted our vigils and protests in front of dozens of witnesses. Everyone loves conflict. Everyone posts pictures. You know yourself how extremely difficult it can be to squelch those little fires. If Twin Sister faced the same level of sabotage and vandalism as Compassion Lives, we would've heard about it."

"Doug Cosselman and his lame-ass cousin, Peter, got blamed for pulling all kinds of pranks. Maybe you should talk to him. Sort it out." Monica was on the move again. Feet stomped over a concrete floor to the echo of country music. "I bet Spanky didn't go there to steal those glass doohickeys of hers. He wanted something more valuable."

"Such as?"

"Notes on the early days."

"For what purpose?"

"Places. Dates. Accomplices. You two broke into a bunch of slaughterhouses and Ella took photos. You wrote a manifesto and sold it at Vegfests. Saying you did something bad-ass for the cause gets people's attention. Showing them unidentifiable photos gets you fans. Waving a handwritten confession under a cop's nose is jail time. Doesn't matter Gordon cut out all the illegal stuff for the cookbook."

I thumbed the raised ridge of a scar on my spine, a souvenir from a long-ago adventure with Ella. "The statute of limitations applies."

"Ya think? How long were you guys active? For real."

Nine years.

Memories, stacked like flashcards, blew apart to rain down in a heap of shifting color and sound. How many times had Ella and I launched aerial drones over poisonous manure lakes in defiance of ag-gag orders or applied bolt cutters to locks and wire fencing belonging to the worse offenders? We've trespassed into dank, fetid spaces for panoramic camera views of sore-ridden sows imprisoned in coffin-sized gestation crates and the piglets crushed beneath them. How often had we risked lung infections to document warehouses crammed with featherless, feces-covered chickens? Mutilated beaks, wrenched off toes, lice-infested wounds. How many hours of illegally obtained footage had we sent to sympathetic lawmakers and to others who were attempting to dismantle the public's cognitive dissonance? Much could be said and done to discredit the value of our more conventional work.

"I don't necessarily agree any of it is incriminating," I said at last. "I will say the only way to disprove it is to search her house. To see what's been taken. Right now, the only people getting in and out are police officers."

Monica sighed. "They'll be gone soon. I have a key."

My willingness to enter the epicenter of a murder investigation didn't offend my conscience. In the social circles I belonged to, a crazy idea was ranked doable or not based on whether it was an infraction, a misdemeanor, or a felony. Felonious acts create bad karma. My subconscious concluded the house key in Monica's possession was a Do-Not-Go-To-Jail card. Empirical knowledge assured me it was better instead to have a Do-Not-Get-Caught plan. On that, Monica left the details to me despite knowing I inherited my father's penchant for overthinking.

The more I thought, the more anxious I became. Investigating officers are currently focused on finding a stranger. A random thief. Unless they get lucky quickly the investigation will turn inward to members of Twin Sister. None of them needed another reason to distrust the police. Some knew the harsh reality of pepper spray blindness and the blunt trauma of a baton rammed into a solar plexus. My usual faith in the process was thus tempered by knowing individual officers couldn't be trusted to innately understand who the bad guys really were.

A proper investigation—if this is what I was committing to—required interviews. I left messages for Reese DeMarco and Gordon Fahey and was looking up contact information for several of Ella's relatives when my phone sounded with the squeaky scold of a black-capped chickadee.

"Danni? Sweetie. It's Muriel Nadler. How are you? How are you holding up?"

"Auntie M. So good to hear from you. It is . . . uh . . ." My throat swelled up and my eyes felt heavy.

"I know. It'll be okay. Everything will be okay. We're going to get through this. We will because we have to."

"I miss you," I whispered.

"She lived a meaningful life. Did what she loved every step of the way. The world is a better place. Enriched. Aware. Do you remember . . ."

I lay on the office rug listening to Muriel reminisce about our shared history of precious, ordinary moments. Me. Ella. Muriel. How we shuffled outside in bathrobes to gather pink tulips and purple muscari to set the breakfast table. How we listened to the buzz of insects shimmering over her herb garden on summer afternoons. Muriel spoke of bike rides through Northampton's town center and impromptu games of badminton over the clothesline. She recounted Ella's and my excited chatter of new course enrollments at Smith College. I was reminded of the Christmas the three of us took up crocheting to make ugly sweaters for each other, unintentionally. I laughed through tears and a snuffed-up nose. My heart ached with the unadorned beauty of our time together, the three of us.

As Muriel chatted on, I silently vowed to avenge Ella's murder. Compassion would play no role in it.

The gas gauge read two tick marks above empty. I didn't stop for a fill-up. The gas station has surveillance cameras and Monica just dropped a verbal grenade into my lap.

She'd been full of assurances earlier when we planned our entrance and exit strategies from Ella's home. The question-and-answer session during our late dinner gave me a headache. We haggled over what constituted a sensitive document worth stealing. We agreed the primary purpose of the mission was to protect Twin Sister and Compassion Lives members from public censure. Many relied on a mask and a nickname to remain anonymous. Harsh criticism from loved ones could be psychologically debilitating. Condemnation from co-workers could end a career. Of this, I was acutely aware.

Five minutes after midnight, as we approached a gas station, Monica said, "I'm not sure I know where the key is. Ella hides it on the patio. She's paranoid I'll blab, so she changes the spot and tells me right before I'm supposed to show up."

"We have to search her patio for a key with flashlights? Seriously?" I circled the block afraid if I opened my mouth again too soon, I'd say something regrettable.

Residents had long since tucked into bed for the evening. Here and there, solitary spotlights lit shrubs and gave shape to vehicles in driveways. We cruised to the corner of Ives and Jenkins coming upon Ella's ranch house.

Monica slapped the dashboard. "See that car? It's a cop. Keep going."

The black sedan barely registered in my peripheral vision. "Are you positive you saw someone in the car?"

"Yup. A baseball cap. Who else is going to be out this late freezing their ass off?"

A complication. The only way to reach Ella's patio unseen from the vehicle on Ives Street was to cross neighboring yards on Jenkins and scale Ella's stockade fence. I made a U-turn and rolled to stop under the bare overhang of a honey locust. We were safer in the shadows than inside the car and left it quickly. An innocent explanation for our head-to-toe black attire would meet with skepticism should anyone encounter us. We cut through the side lawn of a split-level home and steered around patio furniture in two adjacent yards. I bridged my hands to receive Monica's foot and hoisted her over the fence.

Ella's narrow stone patio ran the length of the house with a side gate at one end and a built-in cooking station at the other. Teak furniture, glazed planters, rugs, and assorted statuary provided hundreds of crannies in which to hide a sliver of metal. We divided the patio in half and began the search. Frosty night air and mounting frustration sapped my energy. I was formulating an alternate plan when Monica waved the flashlight over her palm. A key glittered.

"Bedroom slider, not the kitchen," she said, adding, "Ella never used the alarm much."

"Please check anyway. Someone else may have set it."

Monica cupped her eyes against the kitchen door glass to search out the tell-tale glow of the alarm panel near the refrigerator. Against her right cheek, a crude wood patch covered a busted glass mullion. An 'all-clear' thumbs-up and a penlight guided us down the patio and into the master bedroom where we paused for a moment of inner reflection, ironically, observing our own dark forms in the dresser mirror. We agreed to leave all interior lights off. Besides reducing any shocks to our psyches—neither of us knew how messy this crime scene was—keeping the house dark would avoid alerting the man in the sedan to our presence. The eight casement windows lining the corridor to the kitchen meant the wall was practically transparent.

"Should we crawl under them?" Monica asked.

"Yes."

"Totally joking."

"I'm not."

We split up. I crawled into Ella's office and shut the door. The last time I was in this room Ella and I argued. The book she threw left a blue mark on the wall above the horse painting. I found it with my penlight, then directed the beam over the desk. Ella's laptop, the first item on my Borrow List, was missing. She downloaded all her photos onto it. I had hoped to find something intriguing within those images. The desk's drawers were locked leaving me to search the file cabinets. I loaded my backpack with a variety of folders and financial reports and eyed her camera cases still heavy with the equipment stored within. Four lidded boxes stacked below the horse painting were labeled, Save For Danielle Mowrey. These would remain.

The blinds were partly drawn at the other end of the house where the kitchen merged with the dining room and great room at a 90-degree angle. All of it a hundred shades of gray in ambient light seeping in from the yard. I walked two laps around the dining table trying to reimagine sounds and smells from dinners past. Monica did likewise in the living room.

"I remember it from before," I said. "The orange plaid wallpaper. Hideous shag carpet. Low ceiling."

"A butt ugly house." Monica ran a fingertip over a Chihuly glass bowl on the sofa table, then froze. "Something's missing."

Peering into the hazy shadows behind her, I noted one had separated itself from a shrub outside a front-facing window. "Get down," I hissed. "Now."

We dropped to our knees in an instant. Monica curled into a tight ball behind the couch. I scuttled backward to hide amid wooden legs in the dining area.

A broad beam of cold white sliced the space in half above our heads. It toured the walls stopping to illuminate the alarm panel, the blocked mullion, a mounted flat screen television, and the costly glass vases. Monica's police officer could in fact be the burglar come to finish the job. A thrill of anticipation raced over my scalp. What were the odds of me catching Ella's killer tonight?

Catching a killer . . .

Monica snuffled. A small noise. One produced by a runny nose or tears. It shook up my sensibilities. I'd defend us against attack, but I wouldn't be the aggressor. Not with her here.

The man stepped back from the window. The front door knob rattled. He was testing the lock. Monica gasped, another snuffle. I couldn't speak to her without alerting him to my presence. A brief period of silence, then the knob of the kitchen door squeaked as gently as a mouse but held fast. The bedroom slider was unlocked. Should he think to go there next, a confrontation was inevitable. I closed my eyes willing us both the power of invisibility.

I've experienced every emotion known to man. The absolute worst is fearing for the safety of a loved one. Ella never gave me cause to fear for her. I'll always regret it.

The next sound was made by Monica uncurling with a sigh. "He left. Car's gone."

I stretched cramped arms and legs. "Are you all right?"

"Yeah, yeah. I figured out what's missing. The rug."

Monica snapped her wrist and a circle of light scurried bug-like over ceramic tiles normally hidden under a seagrass rug. Smears of rusty brown had pooled in grout lines leading to the basement door. The beam bounced upward to reflect off a shiny yellow X. POLICE LINE DO NOT CROSS.

Monica took several long strides across the floor.

"Leave it!" My voice rattled China in the dining room hutch.

"How will we know? None of this feels real."

"It will. In time."

A car thumping with music braked hard to make the turn onto Ives, then sped off. A moment's distraction. I looked up to see yellow tape drifting down upon my shoulder. My gasp came a moment after Monica's.

Gold carpeted stairs, and the white walls that framed them, were streaked with blood. Round, muddy red stains puddled into a manhole-sized circle on the lower landing. Ella let go of life there. Overlapping odors of spilled bodily fluids, cigarettes, and dog shit triggered my gag reflex. Monica stood catatonic except for a slow hiss of air leaving her lungs. I punched her arm rocking her sideways. She blinked, chest heaving. Her knuckles slammed my shoulder forcing me back two steps.

"Thanks," I said, rubbing the bruise. "You good?"

She nodded, rubbing her bruise.

We abandoned stealth, grabbed the backpacks, and ran to the master bedroom. Monica relocked the sliders with shaking hands. We wrenched open the patio side gate and made for the sidewalk with Monica leading by eight paces. My mind's eye superimposed a vision of the basement stairwell everywhere. A mark had been traced in blood on the wall above the brown circle. An attempt to name her killer?

"We should return to the car, Monica. We look suspicious."

Monica continued walking until we were both out of breath. She collapsed on a grassy margin under a street sign. "What was it like for Ella? In the end."

Kindness came easily. "Trauma induces shock. She would have floated away into nothingness." I tighten my jaw waiting for her to contradict me.

"O-okay." This, perhaps, was her kindness.

With my senses in overdrive, I reached outward in every direction absorbing the whoosh of distant traffic, the twinkle of an airplane in the black sky, the smell of must and decay in autumn leaves. Our sneakers scuffed damp pavement on the long walk back to my car. Something in Monica's backpack clacked.

Chapter 3

Another antihistamine-induced sleep removed all traces of the nightmares I probably experienced and made me deaf to the alarm clock. I scurried into work attire tugging on tights, a short-pleated skirt, and a bulky sweater. A crude Dutch braid subdued my hair in twenty seconds. I raced out the door with laces flapping on my Doc Martens.

Few free parking slots remained in the annex lot a block away from B.C. Wethers' stucco monolith. Arriving later than my coworkers worked in my favor. All were gone from the first-floor cafeteria when I stopped to fill up on free coffee. I wouldn't be exposed to Angel squirting ketchup on an artery-clogging bacon, egg, and cheese sandwich, or Trudy's endless complaints about her drop-out son, or the noxious floral fumes Bryana used to cover her morning bowel movements. My Accounts Payable job was incredibly dull and so were my coworkers.

The second floor the office was scarcely peopled. A department meeting is in the works. As they'd become increasingly grim, I wasn't inclined to seek it out. Bryana's fading perfume reached me before she did. Fair, freckled, and leggy: Bryana resembled a giraffe. She often stuck her head over the wall separating our desks to feed on my discontent.

"Lydia called a meeting for this morning," she said. "We were in the big conference room on three. Check your email for the memo."

"Sent late on Friday?" I guessed. "What was the meeting about?"

Bryana surveyed my cubicle. Bowls of cacti crowded the top of the file cabinet. Harvard Business Review magazines jutted from a wall shelf. Photographs of lost loves curled from the corkboard. My workspace also included a much-coveted window overlooking the main parking lot and an ergonomically designed desk chair not yet embedded with dust. Her eyes lingered on the chair.

"Changing terms by manual overrides. Net thirty to net sixty. Only with vendors who won't cut us off. Five hundred and up. There's a list. We start with Friday's check run."

"Doesn't bode well for the annual Christmas party in the cafeteria, does it?"

"It is what it is. We're facing fierce competition from China. They've undercut our pricing by flooding the market with inferior fasteners."

Sometimes Bryana's gullibility embarrassed even me. I credit B.C.'s publicity team and Bonnie Wethers' divorce lawyer. "Have you seen Claire Steele?"

"In the bathroom. Crying." Bryana snickered. "It's always boyfriend issues with her."

I cut through the maze of unpopulated heather gray cubicles to reach the reception area. By New Year, some of these miniature offices will be well and truly devoid of humans. Claire's desk hid behind a hedge of silk bamboo cemented into fishbowl pots. In another hour its surface would be covered in newspaper clippings to be cobbled into a newsletter for the more prestigious folk on the third floor. Currently, she frowned at her monitor with one forearm soaking up ink from a stack of newspapers.

"Good morning, Claire. How are you? Bryana said . . . you have a cold."

Claire's face was puffy and pallid from recent tears. The flowered headband taming her brown frizzy hair slumped forward. She pinched snot from her nose and wiped the stickiness on her brown corduroy skirt. "Did you hear what happened to Ella DeMarco?"

"I did. Yes."

Claire's lips got wavy. Another bout of tears was imminent. Too easy to forget she's only four years younger than me. I've known eighteen-year-olds with more composure. On her monitor, slogans and cartoon animals filled in a chalked outline of a prone woman. The social media post garnered nearly three hundred comments.

"You're a member of Twin Sister as well?" I asked.

"Aren't you? You started the group."

I forced a half-smile. I was tired of explaining why I left to start a new group with the same mission. The corridor door squeaked open. Lydia Ferguson strode in wearing her usual costume, a snug skirt and jacket that overemphasized her figure. Her hair, brittle from bleaching, formed a misappropriated golden halo.

"You missed this morning's update."

I feigned chagrin. "The email was sent after hours on Friday."

"You didn't think to check messages over the weekend?"

"I did not."

Lydia headed into her office and sharply closed the door.

The rest of the day passed as expected. I gazed out the window frequently imagining a world of possibilities and plotted little paths toward happiness. Lydia returned glassy-eyed from lunch and was padding around shoeless when I ambled into her office at two-thirty. The coffee cup on her desk had a forty-proof aroma making it a tad more pleasant than the tired loafers under the desk or the bagged Chinese food on the credenza.

"Bryana briefed me on the new terms. I process service agreements. Trash pickup, grounds maintenance, bottled water. I pay the caterer who operates out of our cafeteria. Have we renegotiated with them?"

Lydia plucked yellow leaves off a potted philodendron on the window sill. The radiator supported her swaying hip. "I know your job, Danni. I hired you. Follow instructions."

"I haven't received any instructions."

Lydia glanced at the travel brochures in her in-bin. "I'll send you the slide presentation. Is that all?"

"Yes. Thank you."

The exchange disappointed. Lydia's lunch had been infinitely more interesting than mine. One needn't be an expert on String Theory to understand what was happening. Why I stayed until five to dust down my cubicle, reorganize desk supplies, and wait on an email of PowerPoint slides destined to never arrive was beyond me. But I fully understood why I wrote to Peter Bradt, our CFO.

Mr. Peebles' Pathfinder blocked the mouth of the driveway diagonally. I drove around it not quite clearing the house. The passenger side mirror creased the siding transferring a thin line of gold paint below Mr. Peebles' living room window. Our vehicles are close in color. He might think he did it. Since he raises the rent every year without making repairs, I won't disabuse him of the notion.

Lydia's passive-aggressive management style continued to annoy me. I carried the vexation into my flat like dog shit on my shoe. The woman is notoriously self-serving. Our last departmental review granted two percent pay increases. She bought a new vehicle with her bonus. Perhaps I was to be sacrificed for new seat covers come Christmas.

I kicked off my boots and relaxed long enough to open a bottle of hard cider before attending to Compassion Lives business at my desk. The QuickBooks journal entries took four minutes. My group calendar now included a reminder to contact Alice at the Gazette a week before the highway billboard installation in January. *Why Love One But Eat The Other?* featured a composite image of a half-dog, half-calf face. That should turn a few human heads. Judicious use of the Delete key emptied the inboxes of my multiple email accounts. Sympathetic writings from long-time members regarding Ella's death proved too difficult to read and respond to. Sometime soon I'd post a condolence letter for both groups, preferably when I could do it without hiccupping tears. Yesterday, Compassion Lives' social media page was awash in conspiracy theories spilling over from Twin Sister. Today, the horror of Ella's death had been supplanted by fresh atrocities occurring everywhere else on the planet: roadside zoos, dogfighting networks, wet markets, hog farms, vivisection labs, and commercial fishing nets. Many of the posts breached group etiquette rules. I reached for my cell phone.

"Monica, it's your job to monitor our page. I don't like what I'm seeing."

"Danni? Oh, hi. So, my day? Glad you asked. Totally beat by our shenanigans last night. How about you?"

On the monitor, a smocked cook dumped a bowl of squirming shrimp into a sizzling wok. The camera zoomed in on twitching bodies turning pink amid a bubbling sauce. A lone shrimp clutched the lip of the pan with a tiny claw while holding its body away from the deadly steam. It waved a larger claw defiantly in defense of its life. The chef laughed at the tiny creature's audacity and knocked it into the sauce.

"I'm not asking anyone to fake happiness. But we have rules against engaging by enraging and inspiring by inflaming."

Monica grunted. The *plop! plop! plop!* of bubble gum explosions explained what else she was doing with her jaws.

My fingers cramped on the neck of the cider bottle. "Gore posts become petitions, which become requests for donations."

"They're bonding over a common cause. The glue that holds us together."

"I'm not up for the challenge of protecting members from scammers, especially at holiday time."

"So don't, Mommy Dearest." *Plop!* "Most of us are grown up. Except Doug. Definitely, not Doug."

"Right, until someone donates fifty dollars to an unheard-of sanctuary, later reads of an arrest warrant issued for the property owner, and cries foul. Loudly. At length. Ultimately, I'm liable for the content."

"When has that ever happened?"

"August. Lab rabbit sanctuary. September. Surgery for a pony. October. Returning sea turtles to the beach they hatched from."

"So, we're due for November." *Plop!*

"Don't be flippant. I'm reposting our guidelines. Next go-round, I'll cut loose members. The vibe of the group has turned bleak. And not in a fun, rainbow zombie way. Everyone is depressed, on a mood stabilizer, or wearing black lipstick. When did we all start channeling The Cure?"

"He wears red lipstick and doesn't hate people, just hairbrushes." *Plop!*

"Thank you for missing the point."

"Sometimes *you* miss the point," she snapped. "We post dish pics. Supermarket finds. Cute baby otters. We're totally all about refuse, reduce, reuse, and recycle. We understand Earth is undergoing its sixth mass extinction event. Holy hell. What isn't there to be depressed about? Venting is good for the soul. Equalizes the pressure between our ears. Anger is empowering."

My own words used against me. Brava. After a beat, I thought of something new. "But Anger's sister, Depression, is not."

Plop! Plop! Plop! "What happened to the Wall of Shame? Maybe we should start our own version."

"Create more 'Uglies'? What a depressing notion. Any backlash from Thursday's dumbfuckery?"

"Like a YouTube video? I can check."

"If you do find something, please ask the poster to remove it."

"Why? What's the big deal all of a sudden?"

"We should tread lightly until more is known about Ella's investigation. The person who vandalized our cars recognized them in packed parking lots. He shows up prepared and avoids detection. We should consider the unthinkable. Spanky might be one of us and he might be connected to her death."

"Lots of cra-cra in CL. But that's a whole new level of batshit crazy."

"Agreed. Speaking of insanity, I'm meeting with Reese DeMarco this evening. You know how he makes my hands sweat."

"Don't hit him."

"Easier said than done."

Much of what Shrewsbury has to offer visitors can be found straddling Route 9 in its congested retail district. Shopaholics are treated to long views of Lake Quinsigamond from a bridge not named after a legendary documentarian, much to my dismay. The Clapper Street neighborhood where Reese resides runs parallel to the lake with property values assigned accordingly. A white knee wall marked the entrance to Derborn Estates. I cruised to number 23, a modern, slate blue colonial. Landscape lighting gleamed off a clump of river birch and four red rockers on a white farmer's porch. Another fixture lit up a large holiday wreath tacked above the garage doors. Nadine's Ford Escape sat in the driveway. It looked better new, five years ago, when I wrote I MARRIED A PERVERT in black China markers all over its pristine white paint.

On the fourth chime, the red front door opened. A fluffy-haired boy in blue striped pajamas squinted up at me

"Marc, who's there?" Nadine called out from the second-floor landing.

I boldly stepped inside. "Good evening, Nadine. Reese's expecting me."

Time greatly diminished the similarities in our general pleasantness of features. Thirteen years of activism honed my edges while two pregnancies added forty-five pounds to Nadine's. My purple highlights and multiple ear piercings added another level of separation.

I tried to shrink the gap by spouting niceties. "Marc's grown. He's a handsome boy. How old now? Six? And your daughter, Wendy. Does she still love penguins and pufferfish?"

"I'll let Reese know you're here." End of small talk.

"Thank you."

While Reese and Nadine spoke in hoarse whispers at the top of the staircase, I nosed around. The living room paid tribute to *Better Homes and Gardens* with floral Chintz upholstery centered on a hooked rug. The mahogany dining room set could've been plucked whole from a showroom floor. All of it felt a smidge dated like their car in the driveway. No evidence of Ella's dogs, Clyde and Reno. None of Reese's children either. Nadine cleaned diligently to remove the messiness of day-to-day living. And yet, Reese came with a lot of baggage. I wondered where she found room to hide all of it.

Reese descended the stairs with freshly combed hair and more wrinkles than I remembered. Long ago I pronounced him the male version of Ella had she stopped developing at age sixteen. Same reddish-blonde hair, fair complexion, and youthful athletic build but without emotional maturity.

"Let's talk in the dining room," he said. "Life's been good? You look good."

I grinned, joyless, to acknowledge the compliment.

He closed the French doors and sat opposite me at the table. "What do you know about what's happening?"

"The police haven't spoken with me," I said. "You tell me. What's happening?"

"I didn't see the body. The police identified her by fingerprints. I told them about the scar on her thigh."

That raised my eyebrows. "You actually admitted to someone outside of the family you struck her with a claw hammer? I find that difficult to believe."

Reese's expression didn't change. "A detective named Charles Boynton's in charge of the investigation. He sent a car on Saturday and asked me to walk through after they took her away. Gordon thought she might be missing jewelry and other valuables. I couldn't tell. I haven't been inside since she started remodeling."

"Did the house *look* burglarized?"

"Nothing I saw, but the cops can't find her cell phone or laptop."

"Why was Gordon there?" I folded my hands. My palms were heating up.

"The neighbor was instructed to get ahold of him if anything happened while she was away. She was booked to open a delicatessen in Palmer. Gordon said she wasn't coming back till Sunday. The cops think she was killed early Saturday morning."

A thousand questions danced on my tongue. I wanted to see the photos of the house as the police found it. Did anyone report hearing the dogs bark? Did Joe know about the patio key? Why would Ella *want* Gordon inside her house?

"Gordon will make all the arrangements for the funeral once the police give him the green light. Ella was a business. In a big way. Over three hundred thousand subscribers on her YouTube channel. Something like one hundred thousand on Twitter. I'm impressed. Nadine too." Reese's eyes slid to the pantry doorway. "My parents are flying up from Costa Rica. The will is straightforward. We should be able to get through everything pretty quick."

I wiped my palms on my jeans. "Nice to see you have your priorities straight. Bury her ASAP. Wouldn't want her murder to interfere with your weekend plans."

"Hey. Don't be like that."

"Why did you agree to meet with me tonight?"

"Not obvious? You were the executor of her will. Over the summer she drew up a new one and knocked you off the list of beneficiaries. I wouldn't make any big plans if I were you." Reese smiled exposing two slightly mismatched front teeth.

The half-moon scar on my knuckle flared white. "I'm here because of Ella's money? Are you kidding me?"

"Don't judge." Ruddy circles bloomed on his pale cheeks. "I have a business and a family to support. I could be next in line to take over the company. Ella could've saddled me with a boatload of debt."

"What have you done with her dogs?"

"What was I supposed to do with them? I took them to a shelter."

In my head, my fist connected with his throat. The crunch of cartilage was deeply satisfying. "She loved those dogs more than anything. I would have gladly taken them. You were well aware of that. Which shelter?"

Reese clamped his jaws shut.

"Which shelter?"

The corner of his mouth curled upward into a smirk.

"You're a douchebag."

"Language!" Nadine said from her spy hole in the pantry.

"And you're pathetic too, Nadine!"

I didn't slam the front door on the way out. I did, however, *accidentally* run over a spotlight when driving over his lawn.

The second nicely appointed home appeared a half-hour later. Two dozen candy cane lights made the driveway Santa's runway. The contemporary house with Tudor stylings didn't entirely resemble his workshop, but a sleigh pulled by eight reindeer would fit in the great room. A motion sensor alerted Cheryl to my presence. Backlit by a stylish Joss and Main lamp, she was the light to my dark and blonde like her father, Louis. Baggy, high-waisted jeans and a snowflake embroidered sweater succinctly separated our lifestyles.

"Uh-oh." She gave me a brisk hug. *All is forgiven.* "You know where the bar is. Help yourself. I sent the kids to bed a little while ago. I'll be right back."

A tent city of couch pillows and bedsheets stretched over the floor of the great room. I navigated around it on a direct course to the corner bar in the dining room. Sunday's mishap with the candied walnuts seemed so very long ago. Unrestricted access to Anthony's liquor appealed as just compensation. The crystal decanters glittered like cut gemstones inside the mirrored cabinet. My first experiment produced an inedible three-layered drink. Undeterred, I helped myself to juices from the refrigerator, lined up five glasses, and went about concocting more. Four were pretty. One was drinkable. I savored it while reassembling the sectional couch. Cheryl strolled in after pouring herself a snifter of cognac.

"I kept hoping it was a mistake. Danni, I'm so sorry."

"Me too."

"What'd you think of the robbery idea? I mean—you knew her best. There must be something to it. The police spoke to Reese. Does he have any ideas?"

"His interest is limited to his inheritance."

Cheryl tensed. "What a jerk. I'm glad he and I were never friendly."

I finished my cocktail and stared greedily at Cheryl's glass. "Monica agreed to dog sit over the weekend. Ella sent a text late Friday evening telling her not to come. After talking with Reese, I'm convinced Ella never sent it. Her killer did. What little I do know doesn't add up. Ella wouldn't have planned an overnight trip for Palmer. It's only an hour away. Her neighbor could've let the dogs in and out to cover her absence. He's done it before. The missing phone troubles me. The killer has contact information for all of us."

Cheryl drew her knees up onto the couch and snugged the snowflake sweater around them. "Do you know for certain he has it?"

"No. But that's not the worst of it. A crackpot has been targeting Compassion Lives members for the past few months. Keyed our cars. Stole props. Wedged glass bottles under car tires. Once, he dropped stink bombs on us from a second-story window. He might be connected to her death."

"Cripes, Danni. The guy sounds like a nut. You should talk to the police. What if someone got seriously hurt?"

We locked eyes.

Cheryl uncurled herself and disappeared into the kitchen. I cupped my face losing the battle to hold back tears. Cheryl found me whimpering on the couch when she returned with two wine glasses and a sealed envelope.

"Open it when you're in a better frame of mind. For your sake."

Chapter 4

S witching to cognac after the white wine proved a colossal mistake. Coconut water, aspirins, and a cool compress dulled the drums beating between my ears and steadied the vertigo. Going into the office today was an impossibility. I didn't trust myself not to cry. Effective leaders don't have public breakdowns. I left a voice message for Lydia. Postnasal drip lent legitimacy to my complaint of a head cold. Tea and toast got me through morning talk shows I never watch. Seeing others overcome obstacles they created themselves did little to reduce my anxiety.

To jump-start my lackluster day, I examined the news articles from Cheryl. One recapped Joe Dorvee's account of a presumed burglary and included a photograph of police officers stationed on Ella's front lawn. The second came from a Boston e-zine. Lifestyle columnist Natalie Budka interviewed Reese DeMarco and Gordon Fahey. Reese bore the brunt of questions pertaining to the investigation and side-stepped all saying some variation of "she's only been dead a day". Gordon blathered on promoting NPK's online health coaching services. An advertisement wrapped with a ribbon of grief. Twin Sister wasn't mentioned despite it being a significant part of Ella's life.

My mind drifted. A ghostly rendition of me hovered above Ella's open casket studying her quiet repose. Unaware of her latest hair styling, I gave her the ombre ponytail she favored. Her cheeks dimpled slightly in restrained amusement, a child pretending to sleep for a watchful mother. Organ music, at first bland, then increasingly eerie, wormed into my ears. The veritable garden of roses and gladioli surrounding her casket winked out in a sudden shift to a wintry cemetery scene. The casket, now closed, lay in a snug hole framed by gray carpet. Shovelfuls of dirt went *shtick, shtick, shtick* on the lid. Mourners in drab winter jackets with turned-up collars wept and embraced. *I'm so sorry. I'm so sorry. I'm so sorry.*

". . . missed your call. Please leave your message at the sound of the beep. Thank you."

"Hel-lo-ho! Karen Putnam here. I know this is a shitty time for you, but we real-ly got to talk."

I knocked the teacup to the carpet fumbling to reach the phone. "Hello! Karen? Your name is Karen?"

"Thank goodness you're at home. In case, you know, I got it wrong and you don't who the hell I am or Ella was."

"Actually, I don't know who the hell you are."

Karen laughed throaty, cheerful. "I can be a bit much. It's what she loved about me. God, I miss her already and it's too soon. Really too soon."

"Is this about NPK? If so, you should speak with Gordon Fahey, her business manager."

"Gosh, no. I'm not into matcha or yoga. Not that that's a bad thing just not *my* thing. I'm the de facto admin gal for the Twisters. By the by, your book is fab-u-lous! How it all came together. Should be Twin Sisters. With an 's'. That's you two! Am I right? Of course, I'm right. I'm not calling about them. I am, but I'm not. I'm a lousy admin. I only took the job because Ella thought her bookkeeper lady, Betty, was slacking. Noooo. What's being said about her. The rumors."

"Rumors?"

"Historic hissy fit?" Karen gasped for emphasis. "Good gawd thank heavens I didn't bear witness to her temper tantrum in real-time. I would've shouted, 'Slow down, missy. Step away from the keyboard. They have pills for that!' I do believe hearing she was rewarded with threats of bodily harm. A poison pen pal?"

"Everyone's entitled to their opinions. People disagree passionately all the time. Rarely do they resort to murder to remove an opposing view. If you believe you have information helpful to the investigation, please contact the police directly."

"Not for all the champions on Superbowl day. I don't mix well with men packing heat other than what's between their legs. This is my public service announcement. You watched her spin out of control in front of her disciples and didn't lift a pinkie. Somebody else did. The guilt must be eating you alive."

The woman's affected southern drawl irritated like a blister. Her critique of my relationship with Ella was an affront. An uncomfortable chill tingled the hairs on my arms.

"You're correct in that I didn't act. Though you're wrong to believe I should've. *Flowering Foods* was our last collaborative effort. The last time she sought my opinion. I quit the group the year before her rant."

Karen sniffed. "You can't ever quit loving your baby. Be a hero! Take a big ole interest in who was flinging poo back then. See who's been up in her face. Some grudges never go away."

Under no circumstance would I admit to this creature I was investigating Ella's murder.

"Hel-lo-ho! Are you snoozing? Did you hear me?"

"Why should I involve myself? The police are hard at work."

"'Cause you're the only one who can kick up dirt without scuffing your shoes. The police are only going to use this as a statistic to ask for more pepper spray and SWAT cars. We lost one of our own. If we don't get real answers fast there's plenty who'll make them up as they go."

Members were inclined to do that. Appealing to their inner wisdom was a soul-crushing task. An easier route to reshaping dialog is to control the dialog. "I must have administrator status for your social media page."

"Good golly, that was easy. Glad I didn't have to get all mopey and wring out tears. I'll do it when I get home." Karen issued a noisy air kiss. "You're a doll."

"Karen. How did you get my telephone number?"

Karen hung up.

Something lumbered in the front hall. Footfalls on the stairs. The wince of the banister. Mr. Peebles locked out of his flat and in want of help, no doubt.

"Coming!" I flung open the door to find a barreled-chested man in a black trench coat and a navy-jacketed man wearing a grim expression. Surprise trumped fear. "Can I help you?"

"Danielle Mowery?"

"Yes."

"Detective Charles Boynton and Detective Ray Sollecito. May we come in?"

Three pairs of eyes fixed on my purple, glow-in-the-dark, werewolf pajamas.

"We won't take up too much of your valuable time."

An examination of credentials was unnecessary. The men appeared in Sunday's broadcast on Channel 5. Detective Sollecito was fortyish, of medium built, and as forgettable as any of my high school teachers. Detective Boynton stood half a head taller and a few shoulder widths wider. The thick goatee framing his mouth resembled a sleeping chinchilla.

We sat at the tiny kitchen table with our feet touching.

"Miss Mowrey, I'm interested in your relationship with Miss DeMarco."

"I doubt you're here because you're a fan of my work."

Boynton's lips thinned. "We'll get to that. You and she knew each other for a while. If there was something—"

"Or someone," inserted Detective Sollecito.

". . . bothering her, she'd tell you. Right? Did she ever mention a boyfriend? A girlfriend? Someone special in her life."

"I doubt Ella had time for romantic involvements. Her business manager dictated her schedule. Every moment accounted for."

"Did she ever mention someone who frightened her?"

"Everyone loved Ella."

"Tell us why you ended your business relationship with Miss DeMarco and Mr. Fahey."

Having anticipated the question, I had a ready response. I delivered it slowly so as not to give the impression I had reason to rehearse such a thing. "Ella met Gordon shortly after we self-published *A Dear Choice*, an activist manifesto written as a fund-raiser for Gray Birch Sanctuary. Looking back it was clearly the last stop of an ego trip for two overly idealistic young women. Under Gordon's direction, we sought out a traditional publisher and revamped the work for a wider audience as a cookbook. Something it was never intended to be. He pressured us to quit our day jobs and devote ourselves to promoting it while he supposedly worked deals on our behalf. Nearly all of the proceeds from the sale of the revised book went to paying his salary and that of his wife Loretta, whom he brought on as our accountant. In short, he's a con man."

"You stayed on for a second book and created an online magazine together. NPK. Couldn't have been unbearable."

"I was slow to come to my senses." A phantom pain seized my right shoulder. The imp had sunk its talons deep. "NPK was already in existence. Gordon should never receive credit for creating it."

"Miss DeMarco went on to become quite successful. Did you ever regret your decision to leave? Hold it against her? That could've been your success."

"We agreed I would step back. Ella and Gordon worked out their own arrangement. I said my goodbyes and wished them well."

"But you weren't happy. You felt pushed out. Left behind?"

"Not at all. I've always wanted the best for her."

Boynton consulted a tiny notepad. He rattled off eleven names of Wall of Shame alumni. "What are your thoughts on these people?"

"I haven't kept in touch. I actually don't remember them in great detail. Whoever did this is an outsider. A stranger." Rolled right off my tongue. I pushed away from the table to open the freezer. The cat was heavy and slippery. It hit the table with the force of a bowling ball. I peeled back layers of plastic to reveal white and gray fur and the floppy blue bow around its neck. The men registered the Sphinx-posed corpse with a tiny flutter of eyelids. The cat's face had more expression. When neither asked, I explained how I came by the animal last Thursday evening and recited the story of the black cat delivered two months before wearing a pink bow.

"Did Miss DeMarco receive similar gifts?" Boynton asked.

"I wouldn't know. We haven't communicated directly in months. I followed her activities online. Accounts written by others."

"When was the last time you were inside her home?"

"Two years ago?" Lying is easier the more you do it.

"The cat problem may be yours alone," Boynton said. "Did you file a police report?"

"I've never found the police to be particularly sympathetic to animals dead or alive. They can't resuscitate her." I rehoused the cat in the freezer.

"What sort of drugs did Miss DeMarco do?"

"Pot, pills, coke?" interjected Detective Sollecito.

My left eyebrow shot up causing my right eye to squint. "No, no, and no. And if her doctor prescribed medication, she would've sought a natural alternative before filling the prescription. I'd like you to leave. Right now."

The detectives shared a look before standing. "One last question, Miss Mowrey," Boynton said. "Where were you on the night of November ninth? Say, between ten and three the next day. Approximately."

The words, and all they implied, delivered by an officer the size of a heifer, did not strike with the force of a head butt. Boynton reminded me of Chuckles, a French Charolais bull kept at Morning Glories Sanctuary. Half-blind, Chuckles developed a reputation for being impatient with caretakers. I was never troubled by his swinging horns because I made my presence known and never, ever, showed fear.

"Last Friday I was a guest in Monica Jinks' home in Northborough with three other friends—hers, not mine. We drank beer, ate enchiladas, and binge-watched episodes of *Umbrella Academy* on Netflix. I drove straight home."

"Can anyone confirm your time of arrival?"

"At one in the morning? How truly odd for me to awaken my elderly landlord or place a call at that time."

Boynton grunted.

Nervous energy propelled me off the couch. I donned rain boots and a quilted jacket, pulled Misty the cat from the freezer, and brought her outside. The garden shovel was nowhere to be found. I searched under a row of privet, toed a moldering pile of mulch, trudged through clumps of windblown leaves, and glanced into neighboring yards. The snow shovel would have to do. I selected a spot under the pine tree beside the deck. The first cat, dubbed 'Pinky', was buried here under a gargoyle figurine Monica bought as its headstone. The shovel blade scraped frosty ground removing shavings of soil. Frustration drove me to dig deeper. The blade cracked, cracked more, and then a large piece broke off. The hole measured two feet long by three inches deep. Plenty deep for marigold seeds. The weight of the morning fell on my shoulders sapping my strength. I dropped to my knees. Mr. Peebles found me mud-soaked and petting Misty a few minutes later.

"For the love of Jimmy. Leave roadkill where you find it. This isn't a pet cemetery. Might draw skunks. I gave you a pass on the first one."

"I broke my shovel," I whined.

The old gent set down two grocery bags and squatted with some effort. His polyester pants and plaid wool coat dated to the 1970s. His bulbous nose and sagging jowls placed him in his late seventies.

"I can put it in the trash barrel for you," he said kindlier. "The cat's past caring."

"She was a loved family member. You don't dump them in the trash when they pass."

Mr. Peebles rubbed warmth into his chapped fingers. "Don't people get their pets chipped? In case they run off. The town dog catcher has a thingamajig for that. Bring the cat to him. Let its family dig a hole in their backyard."

My mother's ghostly hand pinched thumb to forefinger and gently flicked the back of my head. *Silly rabbit.* "That's an excellent idea. I'll do that. I'll fix the hole too."

He scooped up the grocery bags and ambled inside the house.

I smoothed out the scrapings and lugged Misty up to the deck. After photographing her from several angles, I set her in a cooler of ice cubes. Beyond the pine's drooping branches, a clear view into a neighbor's parlor window brought an idea. I pressed the phone to one ear and leaned over the railing waving my free hand.

"Byron, hello. It's Danni from next door. Look out your window."

A tall shape materialized behind the parlor window. "How's it going over there? Are you wearing pajamas?"

"I am. Thank you for asking. Question. Someone left a package for me on Thursday evening. I'm trying to track that person down. Any chance you saw someone on my deck then?"

"Er, yeah. Not on the deck. I saw a guy sneaking a smoke behind the shed."

"Do you remember what time?"

"Nine-thirty? I was taking out trash and recycling. Didn't seem weird 'cause I don't let anybody smoke around my kids either." The shape in the window moved. "Now that I'm telling you this it does seem weird."

"Can you describe him?"

"Lighting out there isn't the best. Head level with the shed window? White guy? Dark hair. Maybe a dark hat? Hard to tell."

"Did he do anything else?"

"I saw the cigarette first, then the guy, emptied the garbage pail, and went back inside. When I came back out, he was gone."

"Could he have been a neighbor cutting through the yard?"

"I don't think so. Oh, I saw a white car. Idiot parked in front of a fire hydrant. Somebody on the street wouldn't do that. They ticket around here."

"Thank you. This is helpful."

"Isn't it too cold outside for pajamas?"

"Yes. It is."

Sidling up to the tool shed, my mood turned glum. Glummer. A neighbor saw a strange person lurking in my backyard and didn't think to warn me. "We're all going to Hell in a handbasket," Mother would say. Indeed. Eyeing the shed window, I estimated the stranger's height to be about five-eleven. Give or take for a hat. My hunt for the shovel didn't include the locked shed so any fresh footprints belonged to the stranger. The weedy ground hadn't recorded his tracks, but it didn't hide his two cigarette butts either. I pocketed them.

I vented extensively in the shower over the decline of civilization and managed, somehow, to form a plan of action for the day. I'd discover the whereabouts of Ella's dogs, Clyde and Reno, and bring Misty along for possible identification. Reese wouldn't have traveled far to be rid of the dogs. His was a lazy sort of spitefulness. I slipped into work attire for respectability selecting a sweater, short skirt, patterned tights, thick-soled boots, and fashioned a loose French braid. Calls to three shelters resulted in three dead ends. No one answered my call at the fourth shelter, Biscuits and Bows. Its director and I are mired in a stormy relationship over their penchant for holding barbeque fundraisers. With any luck, she'd be out when I arrived.

Originally a single-family home, Biscuits and Bows' building extended to include a wire mesh cattery on one side and a row of dog kennels on the other. The low-ceilinged reception area reeked of dog breath and bleach. A tower of donated dog beds and six, fifty-pound bags of dry food made the space cramped. I tapped the desk bell and read the ingredient list on a bag. Somewhere in the beehive of first-floor rooms, dogs yipped excitedly. A girl burst through a doorway. Her cocoa cheeks were shiny with dog slobber and clumps of fur drifted off her red sweater.

"Welcome to Biscuits and Bows! How may I help you!"

"Good afternoon. I'd like to speak with Melinda Ault."

"Melinda isn't here. Can I help you?"

"Do you have a microchip scanner . . .?"

"Violet," she said, filling in the blank. "We do, but I think it's broken. Why?"

"I found a dead cat. She could be chipped."

Violet made a sad face pushing out her lower lip. "Animal Control has one. I'll get you their number."

I moved down the long, scratched counter to a bulletin board. Photos of new arrivals with jolly descriptions enticed visitors. My breath quickened. One picture showed two small dogs with wiry white and brown coats fixated on a treat held above their heads. The shelter's yellow foam tags dangled off their collars. "These two. They came in on Sunday. Can I see them?"

"Sorry. Both are with a foster family for assessment. Are you interested in adopting a pet?"

"They belonged to a friend of mine who recently died. Clyde and Reno. In truth, they were never well-behaved."

"Aww. That'll make placing them that much harder."

Violet's wrinkled brow told me she knew more about the dogs. I took a chance and recounted a sanitized version of Ella's death and the aftermath with Reese. The story created the desired effect.

"Oh my gosh. I . . . I can't . . . wow." Violet paused to calm herself. "I was here when the pups were surrendered." Her voice dropped to a half-whisper. "Melinda never told us whose blood it was."

Violet circled the counter and held out her arms to embrace me. I knew right away we were going to be friends. We swapped biographies, mine a bit longer than hers. I was greatly encouraged by her line of study at a local community college, Environmental Sciences. Violet was a work in progress moving in the right direction.

I asked, "Can I schedule a visit with the dogs?"

"Melinda will probably say, 'Wait a couple of weeks'. That's where she went. House visit."

Round Two. "I'd like to show you something."

The cooler made swooshing sounds coming out of my car. I stopped short of the shelter door to turn the spigot and drain melted ice. Violet backpedaled into the counter when I pried off the lid and explained how the cat came to be in my possession.

"What kind of crazy person would do something like that?"

"If she's microchipped, she can be identified. I'd like your vet to determine the cause of death. I'll pay any fees charged."

Violet looked pained. "I don't know . . ."

I held up a hand. "It'll be fine. Please tell Melinda when she gets back. She'll know how to handle it. We're old friends."

Turning onto the highway, I pictured Melinda's likely reaction to the cat and barked out a dark laugh. *Tag, you're it.*

To appease the lingering ache of this morning's hangover; I opened a lactose-free coffee stout, gathered up the ill-gotten paperwork, and sprawled out on the couch with a cold compress. Productivity always made me feel better. A detailed look at the files taken from Ella's office might provide insight into the last year of her life. History assured me her personal check registers wouldn't match her bank statements and transfers into Twin Sister's account would play a role. Many of the organization's monthly financial reports prepared by Bette were still in the original sealed envelopes. Was Ella overwhelmed or unconcerned? I'd like to think Ella and Bette developed a friendship built on trust. Since Karen had yet to grant me special access to Twin Sister's social media page, perhaps I should find out.

"Hallo."

"Good evening. I'd like to speak with Bette Hornick."

"Cop or reporter?"

"Danni Mowrey."

"Danni! My brain turned to mush." Bette let out a hoarse laugh. "I didn't recognize your voice. Long time, no hear."

"I hope I'm not interrupting dinner. I could call back later."

"This is fine. Forget it. No, forget that. Nothing's fine. It's a friggin nightmare. Reporters started in on me Sunday. Yesterday I came home from shopping and there's a TV van in my driveway. I couldn't get in my own God-damn house. State police called this morning. I don't want them here. I want to be left alone."

"Is there somewhere else you'd rather be? Any arrangements I could make for you?"

"Won't do any good. The police said they have to talk to me. For what? I don't know what she gets up out your way. That doesn't involve me."

I thought it a curious thing to say but moved on. "Karen Putnam contacted me this morning. She claims rumors are circulating and implied they were related to Ella's breakdown in the spring. Do you know anything about it?"

"Some people find problems everywhere. Me? I don't look for misery. I don't pay attention to the griping. I do my job and I'm a happy person at the end of the day. Karen signed up to be their nanny in October. More power to him. My job is bookkeeping and event planning. I don't gossip on ShowMe."

"What do you know of Karen Putnam?"

"Nothing. Ella called and said he-she-whatever agreed to be the administrator for the Twisters. Not my job, so why should I care?"

"Sure. Tell me about your conversation with the police. Did they single out any members? Discuss incidents that had drawn their attention?"

"Now you sound like a cop. I'll tell you what I told them. I don't do ShowMe."

"Has Gordon contacted you?"

"Twice. On Saturday he was worried because she hadn't shown up at Cutting Board for a ribbon-cutting ceremony. On Sunday he called telling me not to talk to the press. I didn't know what he was going on about. I didn't know she was dead."

"When did he call on Saturday?"

"Uh. Late morning. The ceremony was at one-thirty. They were supposed to go over her speech. He couldn't reach her and got worried. Gordon's lawyer for NPK is supposed to handle things at this end. It's all about protecting *his* business. I don't know what we're going to do without her. She was our everything."

I swallowed back rising emotion. "I'd like to help. Can you grant me administrative privileges on Twin Sister's social media account on ShowMe?"

"Why? We already have someone doing that. Whatshisface."

"Karen. Yes. We've talked. Hmm. Think of me as damage control. Like NPK's lawyer only more agreeable and on *our* side."

"I'm thinking we need all the help we can get. Hey-hey. You should come for Thanksgiving. Stay with us. Let me show you around. Might be a good way to drum up new members. Some of the old-timers still remember you."

I hadn't been gone long enough for this to be a compliment.

"You're kind of famous too. Ya know?" Bette coughed away from the receiver and muttered something to a person in the room with her.

I pressed a finger to one ear. A young female voice responded sarcastically— if her tone was indicative of intent. All at once, I envisioned a hazy little house with café curtains yellowed by nicotine and a driveway strewn with grandchildren's toys. A "no" was forthcoming, yet I held off. If I backdated the invite, it'd excuse me from attending Thursday's family dinner at Cheryl's house.

"I'd enjoy that. Tell me where and when and I'll be there."

Five administrative tabs popped up on the right side of the computer screen. I clicked on one labeled "Wall of Shame" and perused the spreadsheet. Names of repeat offenders were highlighted in red, capital letters. Fierce advocates with short fuses required the occasional reprimand to keep them in line and out of jail. Most offended with generalized obnoxiousness like arguing in public while wearing a Twin Sister tee shirt. A few had been goaded into raising fists. Fewer still had landed punches. I printed the two-page spreadsheet, slipped it into a blue folder, and then deleted it from the site. Detective Boynton already knew their names.

Karen Putnam's claim of new rumors centered on old rants seemed unfounded. No one resurrected Ella's responses to a vaccine meme created by someone claiming to be a naturopathic doctor. The details returned to me as I traveled backward through months of written dialog. Quite a few members were active online the night of her ultimate rant. Many weighed in on something they would've ignored a day or two later in favor of newer posts. The debate rapidly developed claws and fangs to feed off righteous indignation. Ella antagonized while claiming neutrality. She rallied against everyone in a manic stream of pros and cons mind-bending in their gyrations. The reports, statistics, anecdotal material, and interviews she shared derided everyone regardless of their stance. Hardly surprising activists fled in droves to the more civilized community of Compassion Lives.

"Why do anything," Ella had said, "if not to move the conversation along? To test assumptions. To widen perspectives."

My response had been something along the lines of, "You're neither an idiot nor a schizophrenic. The correct answer includes the name, Gordon Fahey. The follow-up question being: Why did he ask that of you?"

Ella contributed little else to the conversation and hung up.

Looking back, I'm still not convinced she committed social media suicide to seize the riches promised by NPK. Something far more profound had occurred.

Chapter 5

T hough scarcely acquainted by her own admission, Claire claimed Ella's death was the cause of her grief and inability to function. This morning I rerouted a host of misdirected mail and apologized profusely to vendors whose calls were terminated rather than transferred. I assumed Claire's duty of covering the lunch break of the Design and Manufacturing secretary because Claire refused to leave the toilet. Ostentatious displays of emotion struck me as dishonest. They too easily became vehicles for self-aggrandizement. Claire was not above that.

Angel delivered a cup of coffee to my desk and pocketed his reward, an almond cookie. He pointed to the thumbnail pictures on my monitor. "What's NPK?"

"Nitrogen, phosphorus, and potassium. They help plants grow and plants help humans grow."

The young man blinked, uncomprehending. He avoided green food altogether.

"Years back, a friend and I created it as an educational blog. We reported on health initiatives, environmental issues, political wrongdoings, positive and negative consumer trends. We adopted a humanistic approach to solving world problems. Change begins with the individual. Accept responsibility for your choices, yes?"

Angel slouched against the cubicle wall. For once, a thoughtful look graced his face. Returning to his messy desk wasn't a priority.

I added, "I wrote articles and opinion pieces. My friend, Ella DeMarco, illustrated them with photographs. To reach a wider audience, we hired a promoter. A horrible man named Gordon Fahey. I tolerated him until he began excising hard truths from my work. 'More flies with honey.' He transformed NPK into a monthly, lifestyle e-zine for readers with large wallets. We promoted recipes and products rather than our philosophy. A degradation of our work. It's quite popular."

I clicked the mouse to expand a picture of artfully posed food. "Beautiful, tasty, nutritious. These photos were styled after the works of Jan Davidsz de Heem. Baroque floral arrangements with a vibrant, dream-like quality. As a painter, he could achieve any effect he chose. Sometimes, a Herculean feat for a camera to replicate."

Angel studied the purple highlights in my bangs. "They have apps for that. You could've made the plants purple if you want."

"Ella never faked a photo. A purist. She was masterful with the right lens and lighting."

"You put the flowers there on purpose?" Angel bit into the cookie. Crumbs tumbled down the front of his shirt, a gray oxford neatly ironed by his mother.

"The faux meat pie features walnuts. We made props of the broken shells and nutcrackers."

"The flowers?"

"Thyme. You are aware fruits, vegetables, and herbs come from flowering plants?"

Angel cast a wide glance over the office bullpen hoping someone else would answer for him.

The cursor spiraled to another picture. "This one's a favorite. A fruit salsa. The butterfly is real, captured in the yard, and coaxed to stay on the mint flowers with a few drops of sugar water. The rumpled satin tablecloth under the sliced peaches and watermelon was actually the lining of a ball gown flipped inside out. The color matched the butterfly's wings."

"Cool. Scroll down. Down. Stop. That caterpillar is real? The snail?"

I nodded, delighted. "Neither were thrilled by the experience. Kept inching away. They dined on the lettuce and cabbage scraps in the compost bin after."

"Where'd all this stuff go?" he asked. "The thing Claire showed me didn't have pictures."

"Claire has the first edition of *A Dear Choice*. A spiral-bound manifesto with black and white photos and a dozen starter recipes. That book began our journey into publishing. It's also where Gordon and *his* literary agent upended our lives. Our self-published call-to-arms was distilled into a ten-page introduction for a cookbook featuring recipes pulled from the blog. That got us a publisher and an ISBN. These photos were taken for our second book, *Flowering Foods*. Ella and I were equal parts ambitious and insane."

"They're in the flower book?"

"Regrettably, no. Gordon, now our business manager, claimed the photos were elitist. He hired a blasé photographer to reshoot everything. Manny Soto. Three months of my life I'll never get back. The original photos were relegated to a dusty corner of NPK. People are still finding them and commenting. Look." I hovered the cursor over a comment dated a month ago.

Angel gnawed the edge of a fingernail, saw the look on my face, and clasped his hands behind his back. "These pictures and all that. Wow. What happened to you? Why'd you come here? You went to college. You could be doing Bryana's job."

I toggled to a spreadsheet and fluffed the papers in my inbox. "How did I wind up at Wethers? We all have to eat, don't we? Thank you for the coffee."

My exploration of NPK continued in stealth mode until quitting time. Contributors of recent articles included guest chefs, yogis, fashion influencers, and doctors hawking vitamins. Monetized links to affiliates had proliferated at an alarming rate. My Fresh Perspective column critiquing new technologies had morphed into podcast infomercials featuring Gordon's wife Loretta and middling representatives of lesser-known retail brands. All calls for social justice and equality were smothered under a fire blanket of commercial utterings. Even Ella's editorials were tempered into lifeless essays on widely known, minor facts. My chest felt hollow.

In a different corner of the internet, NPK's cooking channel stumbled along without personality. A pair of female hands measured ingredients into bowls. Captions explained the process. Dog paws doing the work would boost views more. I should suggest that to Gordon. Ella's social media accounts showed scant activity over the past two months. As of September, she relied entirely on Twin Sister's calendar page and NPK press releases to notify members and fans of her upcoming engagements. I scrolled further back before her March Twister rant. Something extraordinary popped up. A secret admirer.

A person using the handle JoYz654 wrote fawning messages punctuated with heart and smile emojis. He claimed to be divorced without children and in a mid-level management position. Ella responded with kindness rather than encouragement.

Unrequited love is a powerful catalyst.

The phone rang. I abruptly switched screens. All work, all day, that's me.

"Accounts Payable. Danni Mowrey. How can I help you?"

"Hel-lo-ho."

"Karen? I'm at work," I whispered.

Karen chuckled. "I know. I called you. I've been thinking."

I sat down after a quick look over the cubicle wall. Bryana's chair was empty. "So have I. I didn't find any rumors. No one's resurrecting old grudges."

"Oh that. You won't find it on the internet."

"You specifically stated—"

"Don't be so literal. I have another story. Ready? We finished filming and were soaking up a good, long drink at Emerald Dragon when someone says Ella's drunk. Shit-your-pants drunk and making a fuss in the coatroom. One hot mess. We're all dead tired and I am not babysitting. I really can't say when she left the party. Had I bet a fifty on Manny I would've been right and richer."

"Manny Soto? NPK's videographer."

"What's he doing when she's getting doped up on sleeping pills? That's my question."

"Drunk? That sounds like Claire, not Ella. Also, Ella doesn't take sleeping pills."

"That's what I'm talking about, darlin'. The panic. Don't be. Ella gobbled a few after Manny dropped her off and Gordo panicked when he couldn't reach her in the morning. Hauled her to a hospital. How embarrassing. I never believed it."

My thoughts were as layered as any Jackson Pollock painting. "None of that sounds true."

"Attempted suicide? I never said that. Booze and pills do not mix. I'm horrible at retelling stories, aren't I? Didn't I say that before? Shame it's raising its ugly head again. That's what I was saying all along. Gordo knew and did nothing. He made this bed and didn't tighten the corners!"

I wondered whether Karen was seeing a therapist and, if not, whether I should suggest it.

"Did I mention I started drinking again?"

There it is. "Sorry to hear that, Karen. Is there anything I can do to help?" While she pondered the state of her health, I asked, "What, exactly, have you heard about Ella receiving threatening notes?"

"Who writes letters? Everyone tweets. I think all roads lead back to her hissy fit. I'm confused myself. Which came first? Curveball. Where are you from?"

"Pardon? Framingham. And you?"

"Aw, honey. You ain't no Yankee. You sound like Masterpiece Theater. One of those uppity Brit hosts."

The question bored me. Posed as polite curiosity, it often descended into a mash-up of idiotic comparisons. New England versus Old England. "Yankee? Never. Red Sox. Always."

"Har-har. Before Framingham, princess."

"Ipswich. England. We adored your town labeling and so relocated to Massachusetts when I was a child. Imitation is a form of flattery."

Stung by my tone or perplexed by my witticism, Karen said goodbye and hung up. I stared at the handset for a full minute grappling with the gibberish offloaded before jotting down what seemed relevant. Bryana was seated quietly at her desk when I left my cubicle. At some point soon I'll be forced to gift her my desk chair in exchange for her discretion.

After work, I plunged headfirst into the files taken from Ella's home office. Karen's mention of drug use and a suicide attempt couldn't be dismissed out of hand. A brochure for a Worcester rehabilitation center was amongst Ella's papers. It pained me to think she may have been in crisis without me there to support her. I also found art doodles of Fanny, the sow she rescued from a truck rollover last fall. The pig died unexpectedly a month later at Gray Birch Sanctuary. Ella wrote her name repeatedly in blocky print tearing the paper with the point of a magenta pen.

Ella's record-keeping hadn't improved. Her check registers showed eight-font handwriting squeezing in missed entries. The twice-monthly payments to her house cleaner, Svetlana Ustinova, added the young Russian woman to my interview list. Three sizable checks written to Joan Doyle for Gray Birch hadn't been reimbursed by the group. Ella's personal donations. Other notable checks could be payments to contractors for home renovation work. There was little here to indicate where she went outside of her publicized schedule.

The blue 'murder' folder had grown appreciably thicker. Earlier today I included a newly published opinion piece authored by Gordon Fahey.

Manager Blames Radicals for Celebrity's Death

I was disheartened to read your incomplete coverage of the untimely death of Ella DeMarco. As a close personal friend, I knew Ella DeMarco's greatest strengths became her greatest weakness in the months before her death. Blinded by tradition, she was trapped in feel-good demagoguery that brought her immense pain. With my expert guidance, she broke barriers and excelled where others couldn't. Her entire career at NPK was an uphill battle against detractors, who said it shouldn't be done. The continuing success of the company proved them wrong. The passion that fueled her rise to stardom also stirred discontent. Her kinder, gentler approach drew anger from long-standing advocates she worked with earlier in her career. Those who wave the flag of compassion can make a deadly spear of it if it suits their agenda. History will show Ms. DeMarco was often on the receiving end of their sword. Others will remember her unique style and immeasurable charm which can be found imprinted on all manner of things she came in contact with and offered to the public through NPK. A thorough investigation could and should start where the voices were loudest. Only then will the real truth be known. Revolutionary ideas come from the gifted. Radicals belong in a jail cell.

G. Fahey
Editor-In-Chief, NPK Enterprises

Gordon had assumed the title of Editor-in-Chief. What level of dumbfuckery drove him to do that? On a scale of one to ten, he'd get a two for creativity and zero for honesty. His call to action was part censure, part advertising script, and death to the nonprofit organization Ella and I founded before he incorporated us. The newspaper published this poorly written tirade to be provocative or timely. Whatever their motive, it was unseemly.

My cell phone trilled. I snapped, "Yes, Dill. How can I improve your life?"

"I need a ride from Taco Bell. My mom's gone crazy. You are not gonna believe this. I did it! Open rescue. My mom's going ape shit."

"Aw, man." A sentiment I repeated a short while later when entering the restaurant.

Dill sat at a table having a lively discussion with his school backpack. I guessed he was practicing a conversation he would soon be having with his mother. The lanky sixteen-year-old sprouted over the summer developing a rash of acne and an Adam's apple. His hormone-laced brain had yet to take a leap forward. A figure behind the service counter watched me as I watched Dill.

"Hello, Toby. How goes the battle?"

Toby stooped behind the cash register. His taupe locks and sinewy back were recognizable to every female member of our group and a few of the men.

"I know you're there, Toby. An order of rice and beans with lettuce and tomato in a wrap. Salsa and guacamole on the side."

His jaw shifted with the inner workings of his brain. I waved off an explanation he seemed ready to supply. "I don't care where you work. We all have bills to pay."

Toby was scarcely older than Dill. Twenty—a good guess. In life experience, he was years ahead though not any more successful in getting his shit together. Toby supplied group members with pot. An argument for another day.

"I do this on the side. Extra cash. I'll be quitting this job any day."

"Please reconsider."

The meal I slid across the table ended Dill's conversation with his school supplies. "Eat dinner and tell me what happened."

Dill dug into the sandwich sprinkling the table with bits of wilted lettuce and rice. Once his fingers were licked clean, he told the tale of a raid two evenings ago on a Framingham farm. He refused to give the exact location and claimed not to know the people who drove him there. A goat, two turkeys, and two piglets are being housed in his pool shed. His mother discovered the animals after he boarded the school bus and called him to express her anger. The plan he outlined required me to take credit for the rescue, rehome the animals, and deal with his mother.

I toyed with the idea of calling the police and turning him in myself.

"Compassion Lives follows state laws. First, we report. Then, we monitor. Open rescue is a last resort when all else fails."

Dill's blonde eyebrows shot up. "I did it for us. What the hell. People got my back on this."

"Thank you for not getting caught. How's that?" A miracle in itself. Dill had trouble tying his sneaker laces. I flattened my palms on the table so as not to deliver a forceful love tap to his scalp. "A better way to handle it would've been a discussion with the farmer expressing your concerns. Put him on notice if he didn't meet state standards for care, you'd report him."

"They're all gonna die. Don't *you* care anymore?"

"We are all going to die, Dill. That's the burden of living." I brought the tray to a trash receptacle and overheard Dill mutter, "Dumb ass." That stung more than I'll admit to Monica later when complaining bitterly she was the one who convinced Dill to join our happy band of misfits.

"Will we see you on Sunday for the holiday potluck, Toby?"

Toby leaned in from the drive-thru window. "I have to work."

"Dill, come," I said over my shoulder. "You lead. I've never been to your house before."

The Schaffer residence was conveniently located a quarter-mile from the restaurant on a leafy side street. Dill pointed out a neat blue cape with white trim and an attached garage painted bus yellow. He began to squirm when my headlights flashed on his mother's Buick in the driveway.

We walked around the garage passing an oval above-ground pool connected to the house by a narrow deck. Dill led us to a six-by-nine windowless shed. He pried open its latch with the aid of my penlight. Pool vacuum hoses, jugs of chemicals, and deflated floating toys spilled off shallow shelves onto its floor. The scent of urine and a chemical rodent repellent drove needles into my sinuses.

A dead piglet with eyes half-open lay under one of the hoses. I retrieved the stiff, little body—one barely larger than a loaf of bread—and cradled him in my arms.

"I see you," I told the piglet, caressing his brow. "Dill, what happened to the other animals?"

"My mom must've done something with them."

A few dreadful thoughts surfaced eroding my sympathy for Dill's mother. I carried the dead baby to the pool deck. Locked sliders forced Dill to backtrack to the front of the house. Interior lights snapped on one by one. A murmur of voices inside the house became two people yelling. I set the piglet on the deck and rapped my knuckles on the glass.

"Dill? Mrs. Schaffer?"

The elder Schaffer, dressed in a maroon pantsuit, came to the door. Her face puckered at the sight of the piglet. "Leave or I'll call the police. Take that with you. Dill's in enough trouble."

I held up my cell phone. "I'll call them myself. They could be here in a few minutes accompanied by Child Services."

The slider whisked open. "Make it quick."

The house had a 1990s vibe with rosebud wallpaper, Anne Geddes prints, eucalyptus swags, and fringed lampshades. Hard to imagine Mr. Schaffer agreeing to boudoir décor in the dining room.

"Good evening, Mrs. Schaffer. My name is Danni Mowrey. Dill called me a short while ago asking for a ride home. He explained he recently stole several farm animals." I cast a glance at the piglet on the deck. "Where are the others?"

"I told him to stay away from you. This is your fault. Putting stupid ideas in his head."

"No one from Compassion Lives would've helped him with this."

"Those animals didn't drive themselves here."

"You should be having that conversation with your son. He refused to tell me."

"Why should he tell you anything?"

"Good point. He can confess the theft to the police." I raised my cell phone.

Mrs. Schaffer tightened her hold on a dining chair to keep from swaying. "They were knocking things down in the shed. Someone would hear and report us." Her panicked voice sounded girlish. "I put them in the garage."

Five strides across the linoleum brought me to the garage door, a dismal space unfit for a vehicle let alone a living creature. Black mold bloomed on unpainted drywall. A jumble of yard furniture and paint cans clung to the perimeter. The animals were far from content. A white goat with greasy fur chewed on a paint stick between raspy coughs. Two black turkeys roosted atop a doorless refrigerator in a cloud of black fluff. The second piglet shivered and twitched on a towel inside a cardboard box. I suppressed a scream retrieving an open packet of mouse poison from a window sill and I brought the shivering piglet inside setting the box beside a heat vent. I fed the animals produce seized from the refrigerator.

Mrs. Schaffer relaxed. Someone else was dealing with her problem. "I'm Paula. By the way." She seemed pleased she told me. "I did the best I could. Dill doesn't talk anymore. He yells. He's always angry."

"Any particular reason?"

She laughed, dryly. "Today it's one thing. Tomorrow it'll be something else. Life sucks because he's a teenager. Dill's doing this to get back at me. He's angry I divorced his dad."

"I'm sorry to hear that."

"He doesn't talk about school or what's happening at work. He has a wise-guy comment for everything. I threatened to make him quit his job if his grades didn't improve. He broke down and cried." Paula hung her head. "I only knew of you because I check his phone. The pictures are scary. Awful. Everyone's pedaling anger and getting all worked up. Dill can find plenty by himself to get upset over."

"You have access to his phone? Whoever drove him to the farm probably communicated that way. If I knew who that person was, I'd make sure this never happened again."

Paula left and returned with Dill's backpack. She keyed a passcode into his phone.

"May I? Please?" I reached for the device.

Dill sent coded messages to people numbered, rather than named, in his address book. "Do you know any of his friends?"

Paula shook her head. "He didn't have friends until he started working at the trampoline park."

Chapter 6

M y shift at B.C. Wethers passed as a blur of boredom enlivened by bouts of anxiety. Rainy weather and fluorescent lighting leached marrow from my bones. Last year at this time, Compassion Lives welcomed in a period of merriment with fancy dress parties offering sugar-rimmed cocktails, rum cakes, and charcuterie boards. Orange embers crackled in fireplaces and jazzy music flowed through rooms. Party favors of rosehip tea and homemade chocolates were in everyone's pockets. A string of festive events beginning at Halloween and ending with Valentine's Day relieved the monotony of milky twilights and bitter cold nights. We canceled our Halloween party fearing Spanky would smash windows and spray paint cars. No guarantee the Friendsgiving potluck wouldn't end in misery.

A red bull's eye sign flared against the starry night sky marking my destination. Monica was wiping down the dashboard of her green Mazda when I approached. The car's rear left door was still deeply dimpled and beginning to rust. We presumed Spanky used a hammer on it.

"You're on time, which is early for you," I said. "Let's get Gordon where it hurts."

"Crush his balls?"

"Threaten his wallet."

The Starbucks café at the store's entrance gave us a wide view of everyone entering and existing. Monica ordered coconut milk cappuccinos while I secured a table. When she returned, I handed her an envelope.

"We should discuss the fallout from last Thursday's protest."

Monica slurped the foam off her coffee. "I shut down the crazies. Nothing worth saving." She pulled the news articles from the envelope while I crowd-watched.

High schoolers in saggy pants and earbuds dashed around moms pleading with crying children. Middle-aged men loosened their ties and hung red baskets off their elbows. Grim-faced, elderly women shuffled behind crumpled men in wheelchairs. A snapshot of middle-income America in a discount department store no one was embarrassed to be seen in.

The envelope skittered my way. "They're morons," Monica said. "Made us out to be loonies. All they had to do was say nice things about her."

"Deep breath."

"I'm fine. Police aren't buying it. Nobody was trucked down to the police station and waterboarded."

"Detective Boynton came to see me on Wednesday evening. He asked about the Twisters, specifically, those on the Wall of Shame. I predicted this would happen. Have you ever heard of Karen Putnam, the Twisters' new social media administrator?"

"Nope."

"She contacted me twice. Claims to know about Ella's rant and the fall-out. Much of what she said was ridiculous."

"Ella's gone. This Karen person is looking for a top spot. Brash trash."

"Uh-oh. We may be in for a PowerPoint presentation."

Outside, a rigid man in a slim wool suit yelled at a blue sedan and swatted it with an attaché case. Inside the store, a robotic floor cleaner backed him into a display of cheese puffs. He danced a jig around it bumping a teenage boy into a rack of shopping baskets. The boy raised a middle finger and mouthed, "Asshole."

Gordon set the case on our table. I immediately covered it with a photocopy of his opinion piece. "I went too far. Loretta wasn't happy either. Emotions are running high in our house. Ella leaves behind many unfinished projects. We're at a loss trying to hold it together."

I knocked knees with Monica, a signal for her to remain silent. "Strange way to grieve. Your comments were especially hurtful. Did it never occur to you that many of her NPK fans are motivated by something far greater than their waistlines? What's the point of extending your own life when the planet beneath your feet is dying? Don't denigrate the messenger."

Gordon chewed on his upper lip in a ghoulish show of crooked lower teeth. "I wasn't aware I was doing that."

"Really? A public apology. The sooner, the better."

"Can we hit the rewind button? Ella broadcast uplifting messages. No blame, no shame. We didn't play those games." He held up his hands when I scowled. "What I'd like to do is find a middle ground for us. Ways we can help each other." Gordon tugged the laptop from the case. I shook my head. He settled for a piece of paper from an outside pocket.

"NPK is bigger than all of us. We have a chance to do something great here. Last month we had a record forty-nine hundred paid subscribers for our wellness program. People are finding value in what we have to offer. We run articles on avoiding high blood pressure and controlling type 2 diabetes. Diets to prevent childhood obesity. In September we sponsored a 10K run in Providence to raise money for breast cancer research. In March we purchased supplies for Doctors Without Boundaries."

Neither Monica nor I applauded, so he continued.

"Ella told us in August she planned to resign. We brought in more guest writers. Hired a hand model for the cooking videos. The health coaching became formulas."

"I knew it!" Monica said. "I knew those weren't her hands."

Questions rattled my skull. Aloud I said, "What motivated her to resign?"

"Ella said it was time to start her own sanctuary. Isn't that the dream you all have? Saving livestock one meal at a time and owning a gentle farm?" The words were delivered like a punchline. Ridicule. "I pushed her too hard. In hindsight, we should've left the original arrangement in place. Ella providing photos and you writing the articles. Ella was better with a camera than a keyboard."

The paper pressed into my hand was a screenshot of NPK's web channel. Yellow markings highlighted crude comments posted under a cooking video. All were authored by Wall of Shame alumni. Gordon shoved his phone under my chin. On the screen, a photo of Thursday's anti-protestor sprawled on the sidewalk at my feet clutching his face. My right leg was bent back to steady me, but it appeared as though I was winding up to kick him.

"You have a fabulous right cross."

"How did you get—"

"Proving a point. You're not invincible. Both you and I are easily damaged by negative publicity." Gordon shouldered the case. "I'll save this for another day. Call off your goons. It's in everyone's best interest that NPK remains successful. Spoiler alert—we'd like to hire you back to fill the void. Working together we can change the course of the company. Take it in new directions. Everyone comes out a winner with something to show for it. I'll call to discuss the details."

Something curdled in my stomach. *Why did the neighbor call you and not me?*

Chapter 7

S coop, sprinkle, drop. Scoop, sprinkle, drop. I jiggled the handle of the muckrake sprinkling pine shavings over the concrete barn floor. Open windows created a welcomed cross-breeze blowing out stale smells while making my cheeks rosy. The mechanics of familiar tasks put me in a Zen state. My brain skipped ahead to the speech I'd deliver tomorrow afternoon at the Friendsgiving potluck.

Stop what you are doing. Drop your sign. Run to your car. Detentions can lead to arrests. Guilty until proven innocent. Compassion Lives does not have the funds to post bail or to provide for a private lawyer. A public defender rarely defends. They'll plead Continuance Without a Finding to whatever the charge: trespass, public disturbance, assault, theft. Probation ends your activism because another offense leads to jail.

Hardly inspiring. An irritated mother berating a wayward child.

I pushed the wheelbarrow outside the green barn, around the tractor gazebo, and to the compost pile. Frost-blackened squash vines seized its axle. Every summer the cooler edges of the pile became a passive garden, which is only delightful when it's producing food. I worked bare fingers around wood and metal to tear out slimy strips of vegetation and noted the mound should be turned to aerate it. The key to the John Deere was inside a cupboard in Joan's farmhouse. With her ill mother now residing at the sanctuary, I wasn't comfortable entering the house without express permission.

Locating Joan within Gray Birch's thirty-nine acres required Mike's help. Joan lost her first cell phone to an overly curious donkey and the second to a goat. She refused to carry the third around the property making tracking her movements difficult. Rolling pastures, treed slopes, and multiple structures blocked long-distance views. Yet Mike always knew where to find his mother and I knew where to find him. As today's volunteer leader, he'd task them with cleaning the henhouse. The birds tend to scatter quickly when approached making them ideal for nervous helpers who had a tremendous desire to touch every animal within reach even when they shouldn't.

A footpath cut around the farmhouse to the henhouse, which was already neatly raked. A feed pan brimmed with apple slices, grapes, and hunks of lettuce. A dozen Rhode Island Reds dust bathed and eyed me with suspicion. "Good morning, ladies and gents."

A rocky trail sloped downward from the coup to the corral behind the smaller red barn. Four white bristled pigs rooted for sweet potatoes in a fresh pile of straw. Olive, the largest of the Yorkshires at more than five hundred pounds, winked her clear blue eyes in recognition. She had a secure grip on my heart, which she was currently breaking by dying of cancer. I squatted down to reach through the boards to scratch her massive belly. Olive oinked contentedly when I hummed the melody of *Cheek to Cheek,* one of my grandmother's favorite songs.

Voices echoed from a grassy plateau behind the green barn. Mike and his charges relaxed at the picnic table for a water break. I caught his eye and mimicked a woman cradling an infant. A bit of pointing here and there and he understood I was asking about his mother, Joan. Mike's arms shot up, fingers splayed apart. *Orchard.* I marched through the fenced lower pasture and crossed the meadow. The apple orchard stretched upward bordered by pumpkin and corn fields. Mike had mowed around the base of each tree and left tall, native vegetation everywhere else. Viewed from afar, the hill resembled a checkerboard filled with pieces. Joan's crimson jacket placed her in the fifth tree of the fourth row, sprawled on a low limb with her thin legs dangling like a leopard's.

"Isn't that done in the spring?" I asked, nodding at the Felco pruners in her hand.

"I felt like talking to Jonathan. He had no patience for the lazy. When I'm out here, I can hear birds and bees talk. That's my Jonathan."

"Yes, ma'am."

"Broke my soul in two hearing about Ella. She was a fine young woman. She's with Jonathan now. Where all the good people go. They're at peace watching over us."

"I hope so."

Joan handed me the pruners and eased off the limb. Her long, once-beautiful fingers were twisted with arthritis. She gave me a brisk hug. "Any problems this morning? Anything I should know about?"

"The surrender went smoothly. Mrs. Schaffer was eager to help load them into the back of my car. Mike examined the piglet as soon as we arrived. Fingers crossed it'll survive. I appreciate you taking them in." I dug into the front pocket of my jeans and handed her a check.

"Let's get this up to the house."

We followed a tractor path along a field dotted orange with pumpkins left for wildlife. The white flash of a deer's tail disappeared behind a tree. Crows hopped amongst the dried vines.

"How's your mother faring? Mike said she took a tumble the other day."

Joan winced. "A miracle she didn't break her hip. This farm is a dangerous place for someone too feisty for her own good. Mom doesn't want to leave. Took her all this time to settle in. But . . . I can't see a way to make it work. I don't wish these worries on anybody."

We stopped beside the black and scaly husk of the burned-out garage, the past home of a scrappy tractor, and a pickup truck full of field mouse nests. The fire last winter burned with such intensity nothing could be salvaged. When a breeze ruffles the cinders, the fragrance of melted rubber still hangs in the air.

Eyeing the destruction darkened my mood. "Someone left another cat on my doorstep."

"Heaven help us. Not again."

"Tomorrow's potluck is going as planned. We've asked everyone to follow commonsense safety rules. I can't shake the feeling this goes well beyond one disgruntled person. He's too organized and undetectable."

Joan kicked at a shard of charcoaled wood. "If you're saying the garage fire—"

"I am not. Wet hay combusted. He had no reason to start here with you."

Joan seemed pensive. "Where's this going?"

"I don't know. A crazy person is harassing me and a crazier person killed my best friend. Are they linked? Is it one person or multiple people?"

"Sweetie, I don't have the answers. I wish I did."

"You have insight. Most of us have volunteered here. You've spoken to them. Overheard conversations. You're more objective than I am and I value your opinion."

"Oh, dear. I see." Joan tucked silvered curls behind her ears and stuffed her hands into jacket pockets. "The volunteers you send my way don't strike me as the kind who would do anything like that. Not the most cheerful people, for sure, though not the kind who'd do more than get crabby pants and talk big. The world's not changing fast enough. That's enough to make anybody angry and frustrated. Taking it out on your own seems downright dumb. Could it be something in her past that got ahead of her? Who was that boy sent to jail for the dogs? God awful business. You all pride yourselves on getting into good trouble. That was anything but. Tore the town in half."

I stopped walking. The sun blazed brighter. "Jared Libby. His name is Jared Libby."

Jared's hometown of Canard was a mere five miles out of my way on the hour drive home. Its downtown was divided by five streets converging like spokes on a wheel. At the very center, a bandstand on a diminutive circle of lawn served as the hub. The town itself still paid tribute to early wealth founded in the manufacture of leather shoes, umbrellas, and gun stocks. Those industries folded during the Great Depression leaving behind red brick buildings bearing the names of factory owners in bold relief. I read the names when entering the rotary and veered onto Haskill Street to park opposite Sammi's Smoke Shop. At the time of Jared's trial, this two-story building housed a Brazilian bakery that served honey cakes and coconut custards. The smoke shop retained its predecessor's white facade trimmed in green, yellow, and blue. Perhaps no one told them the history of the building. An alley between the bakery and the next building, a math academy, led to an open utility area in the rear. A wood fence once separated this space from the municipal parking lot. Jared's coconspirator, Cassandra Scott, lived above an insurance agency one street over in a flat she shared with friends. The rear wall of the bakery behind the fence could be seen from the fire escape outside her bedroom window. According to a published interview, Cassandra claimed to be inspired by errant staghorn sumac growing against the building. The shrub's fuzzy, red fruits above feathery leaves presented as gashes of blood against the white wall. To her, anyway. Until she partnered with Jared, her cat kill videos were made anonymously. This very spot was chosen for two of the four short films she brazenly produced. Today it smelled like wet asphalt and gasoline. Back then it may have smelled of cocoa powder and milk cake.

I crouched behind the building, pressed my palms against the brickwork, and pushed back the veil of time to remember dark details of their collaborations here. The first victim, a senior Golden Retriever, had been taken from the yard of a retired school teacher. The second, a beagle puppy, belonged to the nine-year-old son of an outdoorsman. Bound and beaten, the dogs were used as living props to display Jared's ongoing training with a saw-tooth hunting knife. He joked on film about warm blood stimulating his erections and posed bloody-fisted for crotch shots. Like bulls in the ring, the dogs lost their ears and tails. Rewards to the butcher. It was later reported passersby heard Jared and Cassandra laughing behind the fence when filming the puppy. They veered away so as not to intrude on the lovers' privacy.

Jared went to prison. His sixteen-year-old accomplice never made it that far. When Cassandra hung herself from a hospital door, I wept for her.

My kitchen door was ajar with the knob in the locked position. Everything was as orderly as I left it. Breakfast dishes in the sink, sunscreen on the bathroom counter, loose notes beside the computer keyboard, my party dress draped across the bed. In the outer front hall, a coat rack with an empty backpack and a heavy raincoat. In the lower hall, a Christmas gift for one of Cheryl's children sat on the doormat.

I descended the stairs to knock on Mr. Peebles' door. Cutlery clinked on a plate, the *fit-fit-fit-fit* of sliding paper, slippers scuffing carpet. The elderly gent answered in a brown robe, his skeletal legs encased in yellowing long johns. Both robe and face needed a shave. Behind him, a toppled tower of mail under the coffee table, and lunch on a tray beside the recliner. A smell akin to cat urine thickened the air.

"Sorry to disturb your meal, Mr. Peebles. Would you happen to know whether anyone came to the house today while I was away?"

"A delivery. You get a lot of boxes. Are you running an import business? Your rent doesn't cover a business."

"I purchase holiday gifts for my family." I frowned. We've discussed this before. "Can you describe the delivery person? Male or female? Tall, short? Ethnicity?"

Mr. Peebles climbed into the reclining chair and yanked the lever for the footrest. Once comfortable, he pushed a creamed soup into his mouth with a slice of bread. Much of it dribbled down his chin to hang like infant vomit. Creamed chicken, I presumed.

"No eyebrows. How's that? Damnedest thing."

"Mr. Peebles," I said a bit louder to draw his attention away from a game show on the television. "Someone may have broken into my flat."

"What's missing?"

"I don't know."

"Then it isn't a problem." The old gent commenced slopping soup on his chin.

"Has Bethany called or come to visit?"

"My Bethany has children."

"Bethany's children have children of their own. You're a great-grandfather."

On some level, he must be aware his daughter Bethany inflated her childcare duties to excuse her neglect of him. I jotted my interpretation of this encounter in the red notebook kept in the China hutch, retrieved a pile of envelopes bearing my name from under the coffee table, and wished him a good day.

I unloaded the box and mail onto the kitchen table and stepped into the shower swapping the scent of manure for the delightful fragrance of grapefruit. Commonsense also calmed my nerves. I reasoned the deck door was ajar because I failed to shut it tightly when leaving this morning. I should be more mindful. Toweled dry and swaddled in terrycloth, I played messages recorded on the machine. Two hang-ups and a voice from my past.

"Hey, Manny here. Fahey's a moron. I'm not your favorite person. He ain't mine. He's going to make big problems for everyone. A real shit-show. I got to see you tonight. Meet me at my place. We'll go to her favorite grub hole, Sliders. Eight o'clock. Don't make me wait."

If I hadn't just left the shower, I'd step back in and scrub down with surgical precision. I deleted the message.

I strongly believe music has charms to soothe the savage breast and the way to a man's heart is through his stomach. I endeavored to hit all the right notes humming the melody of *La Vie en Rose* while crafting a mushroom Wellington with cranberry-quince sauce and a French apple tart. I prepared the fillings and set them to cool. Tomorrow I'd assemble both and finish them in the double ovens in the church rectory's kitchen. I mentally high-fived myself all the way to the bedroom to dress in stretchy khakis and a slouchy white sweater. Like Joan, I preferred a productive day and it was only a smidge after four-thirty.

Cheryl answered my call with, "Hey, baby."

"Hello, dear. Can I use your laundry? The dress I selected for the holiday party is streaked with deodorant."

"No problem. Anthony has the weekend off and is out bonding with the kids. Movie and a meal. He wanted romance. I wanted a babysitter. Yay me."

"Fabulous. See you soon."

I gathered up my clothes and slid into the car thinking I should devise a better strategy for dealing with Cheryl's children. Every holiday season they careened through my living room mashing sugar cookies into the carpet and flicking expensive crystal ornaments off the tree. The little darlings have uprooted poinsettias and hidden plates of food under the couch. A level of malcontent only acceptable from a cat. Cheryl's suggestion of vigorous childproofing didn't appeal to me. It was, after all, *my* home.

Fifteen minutes later I landed in her driveway determined to bribe her children into respectful behavior with a plethora of exceptional gifts. The laundry basket preceded me into the house, a shield not necessary as Anthony and the children weren't home.

"Cheryl! Hello! It's me and my unmentionables."

"You know where everything is!" she yelled back from the floor above.

Once my delicates were gently swishing in the washer, I completed a circuit of the basement admiring anew the extensive renovations that forced me to patronize a decrepit laundromat for several weeks in September. New drywall, radiant heat floor tile, and built-in shelving graced Cheryl's craft room. The neutral color scheme was reminiscent of walnut, coconut, and banana milks. A quilting project sprawled piecemeal on a custom cutting table. Its shallow drawers popped open with the touch of a finger revealing fabric squares and pattern books. One entire drawer preserved paper targets. They were riddled from use at a gun range—presumably. I shuffled the papers noting accuracy. Anthony had nothing to brag about.

Loud scuffling overhead told of the return of the Vincent family. The kitchen television blared cartoons. Cheryl and Anthony's progeny were kneeling on chairs, reaching across the round oak table to swap energy bars, yogurts, and juice boxes. Michelle helped little Cora tear open the wrapper on a granola bar. Brody smeared yogurt on his lips and pantomimed a monkey screeching. Their pubescent years will drive Cheryl to a therapist.

"Where's your mother?"

Michelle straightened into her full eight-year-old height and said, "Daddy said we don't have to talk to you."

"Your mother said I didn't have to buy you Christmas presents, but I did."

Brody snapped into peacemaker mode. "She's upstairs with daddy doing laundry."

The second floor didn't have a washer or a dryer. "When your mother is done with laundry, please tell her I'm in the basement doing mine."

Watching clothes wash and tumble dry was slightly more intriguing than watching paint dry. As my exercise regime could use a boost, I hustled to the weight room. The stability ball, resistant bands, and dumbbells paired with a weigh bench unkinked the knots set by Gray Birch's ergonomically incorrect hand tools. I was coated with a sheen of sweat by the time Cheryl yelled down from the top of the stairs.

"There you are. They've gone." Bedhead hair and swollen lips explained her silly smile.

"Uh-huh."

"Shut up, goofball. He took them out for dinner. We have the house to ourselves. We can have food delivered or do something a little crazy. I'd like a little crazy."

"Hmm. I don't know. I did get another dinner invite," I teased. "Decisions, decisions."

"Wheee! Tell me all about it." Cheryl charged up the stairs. A pitcher of sangria and two thick glasses were on the oak table. She poured generously and raised her glass for a toast. "Yay. You're finally getting some."

I clinked glasses with her. "Henry wasn't that long ago."

"Long enough. Jeez. I could've popped out another kid by now."

I swallowed quickly so as not to spew sangria. "Why must you measure time as it relates to pregnancy?"

"Have three kids and you'll do it too. I had one kind of life before getting pregnant with Michelle. Another kind of life after Brody. I think in grades too: before Cora goes to first grade; before Michelle enters middle school. A schedule for getting things done."

I nodded, amused, and noted the kitchen chandelier picked out strands of silver in Cheryl's straw-colored hair. Being two years older, I'd never tease her. She'd point out my purple highlights and claim she, at least, wasn't living in denial. Pictures of her birth mother, Robin, showed Cheryl would go entirely gray by forty.

"Back to Henry. Our relationship was unhealthy. He put me off dating."

"Henry was a nice guy. Could it be you hanging out with lunatics put *him* off? Look at Forever Halloween."

Four seconds elapsed before I understood the reference. "Monica has a Bachelor's degree in zoology."

"Nobody sees that when she's sitting behind the desk in her uncle's dumpy store. How about that butchy old woman from the pizza place? The guy who looks like Shaggy-met-Waldo. The lady you work with who dresses like Holly Hobbie. You need a better class of friends to land a decent guy. I'm saying this because I love you and want to see you happy."

Lee Anne. Adrian. Claire. I inhaled the sangria and poured myself another. "Wow. Tough love."

"Tell me about your date."

"It's not a date. Manny Soto wants to discuss sabotaging whatever Gordon's latest plans are."

"I wouldn't call him attractive, but he has a certain style. Sort of cool, right?"

"Not even a little."

"You haven't had a date in eons. It might be fun."

"He's an example of all that is wrong with NPK. Gordon hired him because he works cheaply. Ella kept him out of pity. I tolerated him far too long because he made her look stunning in front of the camera."

"Manny flirted with you."

"Sexual harassment," I corrected, setting the glass down so as not to crack the stem between my fingers. "He leered at my breasts during production meetings. Eventually, I confronted him. 'Beautiful women deserve to be admired,' he said. Up until then, he was polite and professional. I haven't a clue why that changed."

"Maybe he's trying to be a better person."

"Unlikely. Manny hates Gordon and fears getting fired. He's trying to assess whether I'll step in and come to his rescue."

Cheryl refilled her glass and plucked orange rind from a lower tooth. "Let him buy you dinner first. If he hates Gordon that much, he might let you in on something worth knowing."

Bungling Gordon's plans did sound enticing, but I'm not the sort who threatens anyone with exposure of illicit plans. Oh wait, I actually am. I checked my watch. "Dang. I'd be cutting it close."

Cheryl reached over the sink counter. In doing so, she pushed aside a bottle of window cleaner. She set my cell phone on the table.

"Your children removed it from my jacket pocket?"

Cheryl assessed my mood with sisterly eyes. "I'll get your laundry." She sprinted down the basement stairs faster than a greyhound.

My phone was slightly sticky and the power button revealed a new background photo of Michelle, Brody, and Cora with faces crammed together. Their protruding tongues lashed out to lick the screen. Perusing two photo albums, I realized pictures in which I appeared had been removed. Far worse, I had amassed a sizable collection of applications and couldn't immediately discern if any were missing. Horrible misjudgment giving Cheryl my passcode. "Shit. Shit. Shit."

Cheryl set the basket of folded laundry on the floor. "I mean, it's not like they broke it."

"That's the bar you set for your children? Okay if it isn't broken. They deleted photos. A deliberately mean act."

"Please. It's only a couple of pictures."

I did a slow blink. "How do you know that's all that they did? They could've changed settings. Deleted applications. Contacted someone in my address book inappropriately. How do *you* know?"

"Why are you making a big deal of it?"

"I don't make the rules in your house. That's me being respectful. Cora writing on my pocketbook and tearing my checks in half—that's not being respectful."

Cheryl's brown eyes dropped to the sangria pitcher. "That happened a long time ago. She's four years old. Seriously, Danni. How mature of you to bring it up. When was the last time you used a check?"

"It's not about the checks, Cheryl. This is you not being respectful. Not defending me when your husband denigrates me in front of your children. In your own separate ways, you give them permission to act out. You reinforce their vindictiveness."

Cheryl's face stretched in disbelief. I had poked the bear. "Anthony's not even here. Now it's his fault? Paranoid much? You need to work on that, sweetie. Guess what? We all listen to you. We *have* to. Do you have any idea how difficult that is? Oh, and stop with the depressing picture books! I agree with Anthony. You're going to traumatize my kids. It's hard enough to get them to eat without you ruining hot dogs and hamburgers."

I held up two fingers. "Age-appropriate. Award-winning."

"Who gives a flying fork! I threw them out and told the kids not to pay attention to their crazy Aunt Danni. You got a few screws loose."

My stomach flew into my throat. I left before I could choke on it. Cheryl would not Heimlich me.

Chapter 8

F ederal Hill in Providence is rich in triple-deckers, small businesses, and more crime than one would expect with a dozen churches offering all-day repenting. Many thanks to Buddy Cianci, a two-time mayor and convicted felon, who disbanded the local mafia before going to prison himself for racketeering. Residents back then were willing to overlook his shortcomings as he spearheaded the beautification of this "Little Italy" making it a tourist destination for authentic Italian cuisine, none of which I ate.

I turned onto Lindenberry Street and sought out a frosty white two-family dwelling. An exterior door separated two windows on its second floor. A remanent of a missing porch. Leaky gutters and inadequate flashing often lead to such surgical interventions. The *tap, tap, tap* of rain inside my bedroom closet came to mind.

Manny answered the downstairs door dressed in shredded jeans, a plaid button-up, and his signature porkpie hat. "Welcome to the wild side."

The living room doubled as a workspace. Large framed prints from a home décor store were wedged between a glass coffee table and a denim couch. Empty frames leaned between a pair of designer sling-back chairs and an overflowing plastic pail of crumpled art posters.

"You park out front? Good. Let's roll." He held up a finger for me to wait and retreated further inside the flat.

Perverse curiosity drew me into his kitchen. My ego would be deeply bruised if a part-time employee of NPK enjoyed finer digs than me, a one-time principal. Pine cabinets, gray vinyl tiles, dingy white appliances—all of it hard used by a chain of tenants. The refrigerator chilled a trove of gooey condiment jars and expired leftovers. All major chains were represented in soggy wrappers and syrup-stained cups except for the brown and green box of brittle donut holes from Murray's Bakery. I quieted an urge to empty the shelves into the trash bin. The grungy kitchen was oddly comforting.

Manny joined me at the door wearing a striped ski jacket not sold outside of thrift stores.

"Sliders is blocks away. It's thirty-eight degrees outside. You should zip up your jacket. Gloves?"

Manny's face split in two under the dark fuzz of his upper lip. "Ah-ha-ha. You never change. Always pick, pick, pick. Vamos."

We race-walked with Manny setting the pace. Multi-family dwellings separated by alleys became boxy cottages with short driveways. He visibly shook from the cold but didn't slow his step. We turned into the driveway of a beige triple-decker. All three flats were fully dark. The sole car in the side yard sank on two punctured tires. Manny jogged into the darkness shrouding the back of the building. I leaned against a telephone pole to fiddle with my phone and confirmed my mental map of the area. We weren't heading in the right direction. A black sedan with tinted glass rolled under the rays of the street lamp. It idled for several seconds before speeding off. When Manny returned to the sidewalk, I didn't mention the sedan fearing it might've been whomever he was searching for.

On the next street, he loped up onto the covered porch of a blue, two-family house. Silhouettes and music vibrated behind thin curtains. A fog of smoke curled out the door when he entered. I sat on the steps with my hood up, dodging the wind and texting friends, until Manny lightly toed me with his sneaker.

"Come on. I'm hungry. I know a pizza joint around the corner." He snorted and pinched his nose.

"Brilliant. You certainly know how to show a girl a good time."

"There's a lot you don't know."

The restaurant, Super Bad Pizzeria, was aptly named. Silver duct tape sealed cracks in the front window making a crude tree shape. Rippled posters of Greece, orange bench seats striped with black tape, and a rumbling soda cooler set expectations. Saturday evening and the only other person here was a chubby teen in a dirty apron knuckling his nose behind the counter. I continued texting Monica from an untapped bench while Manny ordered at the counter.

Monica: Want me to call Doug? Have him get you out of there?
Danni: Thanks, no. I'll call for a car. Waste of time.
Monica: U sure? This guy a major perv? Needs enlightenment?
Danni: I can handle it. I'm leaving soon.

Manny shimmied between the table and the bench and posed plastic utensils above a saucy calzone he must've pre-ordered at our last stop. The letters Y, A, R, P, E, V, O, L were inked in black below his finger knuckles. He commissioned the design after winning a high school wrestling competition. Both he and the tattooist were soaring high. As the story goes, he kept the poorly executed tattoo because it kept him humble. Failures on both accounts.

"Why did you call me? Other than to drag me around town while you scored some dope."

"Can't go to the other place. Got kicked out of there. Food's over-priced anyway. Order a salad."

I eyed two desiccated house flies coated in dust on the window sill. "What did you mean by 'shit show'."

Manny speared a hunk of dough and licked the sauce dribbling down his fork. "Everybody's saying Ella was some kind of hero because she got killed. Not everybody who dies is a saint." Hands in motion. Chew, chew, chew. "She didn't give two shits about me being out of work. Gordo hired a hand model for the videos. Fired my ass and replaced me with a guy who takes kiddie pics at elementary schools."

The hero comment hurt. The idea Ella would be memorialized for the manner of her death rather than the totality of her life's work created a new kind of depression. "Gordon and I spoke. He said nothing of firing you. I'm sorry that happened. Ella gave notice. Why was she leaving?"

"Six hundred reasons. Pick one. They argued all the time. I think Gordo had her killed." A glob of cheese stuck to Manny's two-day-old stubble.

"They argued before and still worked together. What changed?"

Manny picked stringy cheese off his lip, examined it, and pushed it into his mouth. "He wanted credit in the book she was doing. Co-author. Fucking joke. Ella'd talk about some kind of project and he'd say, 'Is it trending?' Like what the fuck does he know? They had a big argument in August because she wanted to stick her name on a fundraiser and he said no. She wouldn't take his calls. Gordo shit cantaloupes until she did."

Part of me was thrilled Ella asserted herself. The other part worried her defiance proved sufficient motive for Gordon to have her murdered. "I recently heard disturbing news. A rumor. Is it true Ella attempted suicide last winter and you were there when it happened?"

Manny gulped from a soda bottle and belched. "April. No, March. We had a party for the crew. Appetizers were lousy, but you couldn't beat the price on pitchers of beer. That's why I picked the place. Anyway, the girls got stupid on martinis. I told Ella to go home. Gordo ripped me a new asshole for letting her drive. He didn't do squat either. He was there."

"Who was at this party?"

Manny's eyelids closed by half. The illicit pill or powder he ingested might've kicked in. "Ella had *friends*. People you don't know. Gordon, Leslie, Sonya, Kevan, er . . . what's his face . . . Bruce. People you don't know."

"I thought this was an NPK affair."

"Did I say that? Eh. Something else you don't know. Yeah, yeah. You shared diapers when you were kids. Did stupid things to get arrested—"

"We met in eighth grade. Misdemeanors and fines." I waved it off. No need to explain.

"No jail time. Doesn't change jack shit. You got nothing. How's those superior values working out for you? Gordo only wants money. He's stupid too. I *got* Ella."

For the first time in a long time, I was interested in what he had to say and none of it made any sense. "You're right. I am stupid. I'm sitting in this shithole conversing with you when I could be comfortably dining at home. Educate me. Tell me something about Ella I don't know."

Manny responded by yanking a DVD case from a jacket pocket. "Don't say I never gave you anything."

Vipers of Redemption. A label identified the video as library property. A group of men in short-sleeved shirts gathered on the cover. All gazed longingly at a thick wood cross hung above an unadorned altar.

"Gee. Thank you. I'll return it to the library. Can we return to discussing Ella?"

"I'll go one better. I'll introduce you to some of her *other* friends." Manny crammed the last of the calzone into his mouth and left the table for the order counter. He and the young man in the dirty apron spoke in whispers and shook hands twice in a weird crisscross of arms.

On the next street, we hurried past a line of mundane businesses: a newsstand, a uniform supplier, a nail salon, and an Italian deli. Chain-linked fencing enclosed white utility vehicles in a wide, dark lot. Music thumped from the windowless facade of a tavern where smokers comingled on the sidewalk. We were blocks away from Federal Hill with its upscale restaurants and hookah bars serving house-made liqueurs. Manny ducked under a purple neon sign, Righteous Roy's Tattoos. An illustration board propped in its glass window advertised tattoos for the timid, small designs easy to conceal. Plenty in my social circle were imprinted with leaping bunnies and cartoon livestock. Until Every Cage Is Empty and Not Your Mum Not Your Milk were popular inked slogans. Ella had a stud in her tongue and multiple ear piercings. Her first tattoo was a bumblebee on one ankle, which led to a ladybug on the other. She mentioned wanting to get a barcode on the back of her neck. The board showed all three.

A cursory inspection from the sidewalk revealed plump reclining chairs and a gallery of framed tattoo art mounted on raspberry purple walls. One chair was in use by a bearded artist in a plain black tee shirt that exposed vibrant sleeve tattoos of the cyborg variety. The man applied a needle to the forearm of a chubby, jean-clad woman while a younger version of her with the same curly black hair clutched her free hand. The women's presence seemed coincidental despite the Super Bad Pizzeria box on a bench.

"I'm going home."

"You can't go. I want to introduce you to Roy."

Roy, the whiskered artist, dabbed a swirl of pink off the woman's upper arm.

"Roy looks very busy. Another time. I'll call for a car."

"Come inside to wait. Fucking cold out here. I can't feel my ears."

"Fine." My nose hairs had frosted over during the walk.

The heated atmosphere of the shop thawed my extremities. I unzipped my black puffy coat and dropped onto a wood bench. A stack of art flyers on a side table briefly caught my attention. The cover photo had a familiar quality to it.

The artist winked at me and said to Manny, "A little young for you, Bud."

Manny sneered, "Shut the fuck up, dude."

The artist wrapped the woman's arm in plastic film. The daughter bounced on her heels, full of compliments for her mother's braveness.

Manny shuffled to the rear of the shop a few times. Perhaps the gooey calzone was exploding in his gut and the toilet door was locked. This evening might end on a high note.

A crow cawed announcing incoming instructions from the rideshare driver. I zipped up and gave everyone the Queen's wave. "This is me leaving. Manny, never ever contact me again."

At the curb, a white Escort flashed its lights. The YARP hand intercepted my reach for the door handle.

"Here's something you don't know," Manny said. "I'm not a creep and you aren't that pretty."

"Always a pleasure to be in your company."

"The cow eyes weren't my idea. Ella made me do it to piss you off. Get under your skin. She wanted you gone. Like, out of the company."

His words struck like a slap and something pinched my scalp with stunning intensity. The hawk imp hunkered down on my head to pluck at my bangs with its sharp beak. Each tug threatened to bring tears to my eyes. "This whole night has been about you making me trot after you like a groupie. I'm not interested, Manny. Grow up."

"You kidding? Who's laughing? We both got the shitty end of the stick."

"If it wasn't for Ella, Gordon would've fired you long ago."

"He did fire me. Only because it was her idea. I would've told everybody. I should've. I only did what I had to do to make it work. You should be asking why she did it. You should be asking about the movie."

"Don't ever call me again." The car door gave a satisfying *tunk* when slammed shut. Manny stood on the sidewalk until the neon sign for Righteous Roy's faded from the rearview mirror.

I waited until I was calmer, had willed the imp away, and was behind the wheel of my car driving north on Interstate 95 before rehashing the ruined evening. Manny's reference to movie-making puzzled me. Had Ella starred in a feature-length film, NPK's marketing team or an outside agency would've launched a press junket, which they hadn't to my knowledge. Ella did, however, film public service announcements with little fanfare. Manny may have directed one and was puffing out his chest. A perfectly good Saturday evening wasted.

To prove he hadn't wormed his way into my psyche, I threw myself into cooking dinner back at my flat. Yellow and green squash noodles topped with miso marinaded seitan. Sliders may have retro décor and rainbow cocktails, but it didn't have a dedicated kitchen.

Once bedtime rituals were complete, I snuggled under Grandma Tilly's quilt to examine the sign-up sheets I *borrowed* from a barn cupboard at Gray Birch. Taken as a whole they showed patterns of behavior, friendships, and which recruitment campaigns had been successful. Roughly twenty-five percent of the people listed were Compassion Lives members. Another five percent belonged to East Coast Herbivores whose membership pulled heavily from Rhode Island. Peter Ortell and three others from New Hampshire-based White Mountain VSN spent afternoons here on multiple occasions. Oddly, not a single Twister volunteered again after Ella's rant caught fire.

A female voice flavored by a north London accent guided me west into Northborough. Last Sunday's snowfall signaled a premature end to autumn. Judging by the number of floppy Christmas inflatables pooling on lawns, few people were dwelling on it. I arrived at the Unitarian church later than expected, which was right on time for Monica.

She rapped rhythmically on the driver's window until I lowered it. "Happy holidays! Whoa. Why the pouty puss?"

"Daydreaming."

"Panda? Wood chipper? Nachos? How many guesses do I get?"

I pulled a letter from my handbag and handed it to Monica. "This was buried in the mail Mr. Peebles stole from my mailbox. I am now in possession of *the* threatening letters. Originals. Ms. Scott blamed Ella for her daughter's suicide and demanded money as restitution. Muriel Nadler sent them to me."

Dearest Danni,

I'm giving you these letters because Ella would have wanted that. Marlene Scott wrote them after Ella visited her in prison. I made Ella take them to the police in May. Her car had been broken into and badly scratched. Before that, someone was poisoning plants in her yard. The police were concerned because of the damage to her car. It didn't last long. They called us back and made us wait for hours in the lobby. (!!!) They said Marlene died in a car accident last year. End of story. Ella told them she never paid her and never received another letter, but someone else might be after her because of Marlene and Cassandra. One officer accused us of faking the car break-in for publicity and told Ella she could be arrested for filing a false police report. We walked out of there feeling like criminals. They were terrible. Ella hired a private detective to look into a couple of people after that. She never said who but told me his report was the end of it because she didn't want to pay him to follow people around. Maybe you can find him and get him to talk to you.

Love,
Aunt Muriel

"I can name several people worthy of investigating," I said.

Monica squinted, lost in thought. Smoke from her cigarette drifted into my car moving me to raise the window and hop out.

"Where are the letters from the crazy lady?" Monica asked.

"At home. A curious read, each of them. A caged, demented bird screaming. I'll study them, apply a little brain power, and ask for help if necessary." I brightened my expression. "Enough of that. Help me carry the food?"

"Do you have our security deposit?"

"Sutter Home four packs in the way-back. One bottle of wine per guest while guarding our vehicles. It's sure to be a hit with smokers who'll congregate outside."

Monica swiveled toward approaching guests. "Zoie! Doug, my man! Yo, Lenny!" A hoochie-coochie dance showed off her orange-streaked hair and black jacket embellished with tiny gears and chains. I stood in stark contrast. The ruched red dress under my black velvet coat was reminiscent of a Christmas bow.

We set to work inside the rectory dressing tables with mini pumpkins and taping garlands of autumn leaves to buffet tables. Members soon arrived to fill the space with holiday well-wishing and trays of food. A few folks, former members of Twin Sister, offered quiet condolences for Ella's passing. Monica held court on the other side of the room. An elderly couple in matching ruby red cardigans occupied her. The stout gentleman was the minister, Mr. Mussen, and the reedy woman his wife. Monica warmly clasped hands with both before wending her way through the crowd toward me.

"Eighty-two. Decent turnout," she said.

"I'm glad you're mingling. Did you, by any chance, invite the minister and his wife to dine with us?"

Monica vigorously nodded *yes*.

The minister presented sermons on social responsibility too. Unlike me, he wouldn't insinuate police officers would neglect their duties, nor would he suggest his audience play junior detective as a countermeasure. Should my motivational speech alienate him, we could lose the church as a venue. I went outside to mull things over with a mini wine bottle and called Muriel.

"Good afternoon, Auntie M. I received the package. Thank you."

Muriel breathed heavily. "Laundry," she explained. A series of sounds crossed the wire. Muriel kicked off her shoes and thumped into a chair to open a can of something fizzy. "What do you think of the letters?"

"I think too much. Thank you for asking. Why did Ella visit Marlene Scott in prison?"

Muriel swallowed twice, set the can down, and released a delighted sigh. "The lady reached out to her. Said she was going to be released in the fall—this was last year—and had nothing to live for with Cassandra gone. Wanted a hand up, not a handout."

"Marlene abandoned Cassandra when she was a toddler. How could she claim to be devastated by her death?"

"All BS to wind up Ella before asking for fifty grand."

I sipped and puffed and watched the air carry away swirls of white vapor. "Why weren't the papers redacted by prison officials? Why didn't Ella end it by confronting her?"

"My doing. I told her to walk away quietly. Who do you complain to? That's why she's in prison. Right?"

"I'm flabbergasted Ella trusted Marlene with her home address."

"She didn't. The letters were mailed to Bette Hornick. Marlene was too close for comfort in the Framingham lock-up. Drugs, prostitution, robbery. I think Ella was trying to win good karma points by promising to find her a job."

The tiny wine bottle held one last swallow. I eyed a second bottle. "How did Bette Hornick feel about Marlene Scott having her address? The danger of an unwelcome encounter still existed."

"Bette's a retired state worker. She was used to dealing with the mentally ill. She even wrote a couple of opinion pieces about Jared's trial arguing for an expansion of mental health services. I'm sure she has complaints a mile long."

"I had no idea what her former career was. It was never openly discussed. At the time, it mattered little to me. Tell me about the private detective."

"Ray Semple. He looked into five people. That's all Ella would say. She didn't want me meddling. You should come for a weekend and go talk to him."

"Let me think on it." I wished her well and disconnected.

Inside the rectory, guests helped themselves along both sides of the buffet tables. Utensils were in constant motion dipping in and out of large tins and bowls. I stood in line with an empty plate and a head full of observations. Some incited redactions to the speech, some colored my perceptions of those who approached me for conversation. I blindly picked a vacant seat to pick at my meal. What had I learned about Amanda in the crotched blue sweater other than she likes my food photos and explained four times in two minutes she eats gluten-free? Sam laughs online at nearly all of Monica's lame jokes and admitted, shyly, that he wears a baseball cap to hide his bald spot. Eric and

Andrea post every tongue-filled kiss and every mediocre misunderstanding and yet refuse to say what either does for a living despite my obvious interest. Bucky brought his mother, a steakhouse waitress. She praised Heifer's mission while loading up on baked macaroni and cheese. The food isn't what she thinks it is. Self-doubt crushed my enthusiasm. What did I really know about these people? Was I foolish giving a speech asking for their help?

"Yes," Monica said.

I looked up from a half-eaten plate of food. My tablemates were in line for second helpings and a chubby blonde had wandered over from elsewhere to sit at my table and play a game on her cell phone. "Come again?"

"A geek god has come in answer to my prayers." Monica waggled her eyebrows.

We shared similar preferences in men so it was easy to scan the room and spot the object of her desire as the dark-haired man seated next to Adrian. Crisp white shirt, red paisley tie, silver-framed glasses, and side-swept hair marked him as a retro yuppy. He flashed a smile to Adrian. My nerve endings lit up.

"I know him. That's Russell, Adrian's older brother."

"Do tell."

"We met at a rally in Boston three years ago. Any idea where he's been hiding all this time?"

"New Jersey. Says he's a money manager." Monica wrinkled her nose. "Don't ask him to explain. Darla wanted his number for a tumble and got a lesson in finance instead. Said she's giving up clipping coupons because it's a scam. Laugh riot."

Monica detailed her plan of flirtation. I've heard it a hundred times before. I withheld my usual critiques lest I slip. After the Boston rally, a handful of us wandered Boston Public Garden until sunset, then landed in a pub. We dispersed a few hours later in high spirits. Everyone scurried off in separate directions including my boyfriend, Henry. Russell followed me home at a discreet distance and left at dawn and continued to do so, on and off, for five weeks before vanishing from my life.

Monica nudged my shoulder. "What do you think? Sound good?"

"Go for it." I hadn't heard a word of it. I was studying the brothers. From this distance, their only point of commonality was chestnut hair. Adrian was taller in stature, the pleasantness of his face obscured by a wiry beard and a grungy, knotted scarf. Cheryl fittingly described him as Shaggy-met-Waldo. Russell was smooth-cheeked and straight-shouldered. A young Steve Jobs with better hair. He was also a relative stranger like so many others. My brain somersaulted. The earlier dilemma resolved itself.

"I'm not going to give a speech. I'll call a meeting tonight after we finish here. Do you think Mr. Mussen would oblige? Address everyone as kindred spirits. He certainly made a positive impression on you."

Monica's expression shifted from mischievous to thoughtful. "Okey-dokey." Off she went, practically skipping, a happy little steampunk vampire in search of the minister.

Chapter 9

G uests began trickling out of the church rectory at four o'clock. Table talk had devolved into platitudes and folks were scooping up leftovers for to-go plates. I exploited a weather prediction of snow to leave early, intending to restock my refrigerator for tonight's meeting. The sign for Leavitt Brothers Market was viewable from a church window making it a quick detour that didn't require the pull and snap of a seatbelt.

Market customers bustled within purchasing toilet paper, milk, eggs, and bread they didn't need for this blip in the weather. I twirled around the organic produce section joyfully filling two canvas bags with every color imaginable and gladly paid for such brilliance at the register. The artificial daylight of the store's sunny confines abruptly ended at the door. Outside, a blustery night had quickly set in and snow sifted down from the heavens. I turned up my collar to brave the wind and charged across the lot in the general direction of my car. The *glug-glug-glug-glug* of an old engine dogged my steps to the end of the aisle. To my ear, it seemed very near. Too close, even. Instinctively, I sidestepped left nearly bumping a shin on a truck trailer hitch.

The bag in my right hand flew upward end over end raining broccoli, red bell peppers, an eggplant, and clementines onto the pavement. Momentum spun me around. I caught the top rail of an empty cart rack and guided a fall between its long metal bars. My black velour coat opened like a book. The red dress rode up my thighs. I had stepped out of a shoe. Surprise switched to fear at the scream of brakes and a boom of collision. The car had reversed forcefully into the rack. Gaseous exhaust fanned my hair. A tire pinned down the edge of my coat. I clung to the frame as the vehicle lurched forward dragging the rack, gouging asphalt. A stab of pain in my twisted shoulder forced me to let go. The side rails passed over my body. A jerk on the car's steering wheel freed its bumper allowing for a speedy exit out onto the street.

Gray sedan. Four doors. No license plate. Hooded driver.

A moment passed before I peeled myself off the pavement.

A series of musical knocks identified who stood on my deck. Monica had changed into jeans and washed the orange colorant from her hair. Trundling in with a six-pack of beer and a boxed pizza, she dropped onto the couch. Claire, Emma, Alicia, and Megan followed in quick succession bringing cookies scrounged from the potluck. A commotion at the downstairs front door with Toby Berrigan and Dill Schaffer jostling each other to mount the stairs. Toby emanated fryolator oil. Dill was an uninvited guest. I stepped into the front hall intending to fling some verbal arrows at him when Emma and Megan jointly shrieked announcing more guests at the kitchen door. Adrian brought Russell, who hadn't been invited either. Before I could vent my frustration at Dill, the bottom hall door opened to admit a stately woman in a periwinkle blue trench coat.

"All hail the new arrival, darlings! Let the party begin!"

Gobsmacked by the familiar voice, I shooed Dill inside my flat. Karen Putnam's auburn wig and pancake makeup did little to disguise the fact that she was truly a he. High heels and a short skirt paired with the sinewy legs of a rugby player made for a startling visual.

"Karen?"

"Were you expecting Mickey Rourke?"

"Welcome?"

The roar of voices abruptly ceased when Karen glided into the living room. The only unflappable individual was Russell seated on the arm of the couch. He raised a beer bottle in salute. "Good evening."

Claire threw herself into Karen's arms. "You made it!"

Karen patted Claire's head with a giant paw and draped the long coat over her arm. "Thank heavens. A friendly face. Hang on to that would you, dear? Gracious! You call this a party?"

I guided Karen by the elbow into the kitchen. "How did you know where to find me? How do you know Claire?"

Karen pouted. "I thought you'd be thrilled. We have oodles to talk about. I wanted to see with my own big brown eyes what you've done with the juicy-delicious gossip I gave you."

"We'll talk soon. Tonight is not a good night. This isn't a party. It's a Compassion Lives group meeting with an agenda. You'd be bored silly."

Monica sailed into the kitchen to embrace Karen from behind in an awkward hug. "So awesome you could make it to the party." She swung open the refrigerator door. "You've been holding out on us." Monica removed the charcuterie platter I assembled from the salvage groceries and carried it into the living room.

"Mmm. That looks fa-bu-lous. I'll take my chances with boredom." Karen kicked her heels off under the kitchen table dropping three inches and joined the others.

I hid in the unlit pantry clutching the shelves for support. The meeting hadn't started and already I'd lost control of the situation. Russell was a distraction. Dill, a disagreement. Karen, a disaster. The door creaked open letting in slanted light.

"We need crackers," Monica said, not at all surprised to find me there in the dark.

I handed her a box. "That's what I was getting."

"Hey. You thinking what I'm thinking?"

"Probably not."

"Claire invited her boyfriend to the potluck. Nobody showed up. I asked around. Twenty bucks says Karen is Claire's boyfriend. Makes sense. Am I right? Holy Hell. What an effing riot. I am so loving this."

"Sure," I mumbled. "Let's start the meeting."

I poured a glass of wine, dragged out a stool from the closet bar, and instructed everyone to kindly shut up. Seats were taken, glasses were replenished, crackers were topped. I had their attention.

"A week ago, we lost Ella DeMarco. Most of you are familiar with her early work capturing images of cruelty and swaths of pollution in agricultural settings. Later, she inspired thousands to adopt more healthful living through a popular online magazine, NPK. I'm sure some of you have heard me speak about it. Ella and I started the magazine together. Best friends since childhood. Business disputes—"

Karen raised a hand.

"No." *I will not yield the floor.* "The last nineteen months of her life have come to me largely as gossip and press releases. I'm telling you this because I don't believe the official account of her death. Something happened during that time that better explains it. I need your help to figure out what that is. Police see us as rabble-rousers. I doubt many are eager to lavish limited resources on an activist who spent the whole of her adult life creating mountains of paperwork for them.

"The detective leading the investigation, Charles Boynton, interviewed me a few days ago. He struck me as an old-school cop. When he finally abandons robbery as a motive, he'll draw a straight line to her activism. Possible victim-blaming ahead. Either way, it's premeditated, not random."

Karen's wig bounced. "This is getting juicy."

Three hands shot up including Karen's. I relented and pointed to her.

"Tell them what I told you. Go on, go on," Karen said. "This is good. You all have to hear it." She patty-caked her hands excitedly.

"Too far ahead." The next raised hand belonged to Toby. "Yes?"

"I gotta whiz."

"You know where the toilet is."

Toby extracted himself from the couch and from Megan and Alicia, who were cross-legged on the floor practically hugging his legs. The girls cooed when he stepped over them.

Alicia lowered her hand and fidgeted on the floor. She rarely voiced an opinion during meetings. I assumed she felt outnumbered being the only Black member to attend regularly.

"Alicia, please, your thoughts."

"The police have to prove it was burglary. What was stolen? Were any locks broken? Credit card purchases made? I've been following the story. They're not saying much. The detective could be your window. He's using you for information. You could use him right back."

Russell slid off the couch arm and dusted invisible crumbs from his chinos. Up to that moment, I kept him in my peripheral view. When everyone was hustling for a seat Monica elbowed Karen out of the way to place herself next to him. Her body moved in and out of view. I think she was leaning in to sniff his cologne.

"Thanks for the beer." He shook the empty bottle. "We have to leave. Early day tomorrow. Adrian?"

Adrian tensed. A gherkin disappeared into his mouth. He worked furiously over the platter of snacks to assemble two cracker sandwiches and stuffed a cluster of grapes into one shirt pocket and a handful of nuts into the other.

"Wait. Adrian. I want to hear from you. Can someone give him a ride back to the dormitory after the meeting so his brother can leave? Speak up. The university is here in town. A few of you will be driving near it to get home yourselves."

Heads swiveled, each waiting on the other. Megan slapped her cheek and let the hand slide down to her chin in exasperation. "Adrian, we're all bummed your car got hosed by Spanky. But, bro, you only paid a couple hundred for it and it was one speed bump away from dropping the transmission. Pony up a couple bucks and get another junker for Christ's sake." Nodding heads approved of the message.

Toby spoke up. "I can take him. It's not far from where I drop Dill."

"Thank you. Much appreciated." I extended a hand to Russell. "Nice seeing you again. Safe travels."

Russell slid his fingers over mine in the gentlest of caresses. Golden-brown eyes fixed on my lips. One deep breath and I could taste the cinnamon spice aroma emanating from his collar. I nearly swooned.

Sensing a break to stretch legs, everyone began to stir. Monica and Adrian walked Russell out. Karen and Megan lunged simultaneously for the pizza box. Emma and Alicia busied themselves replenishing wine glasses while Claire flirted with Toby. I motioned for Dill to follow me. He propped his ankles on the coffee table in a show of defiance. Karen mouthed, *Go.* Dill flinched at her sizable presence and moved sloth-like off the couch dragging his oversized sneakers with enough friction to spark the carpet.

We descended the hall stairs seeking privacy. "Dill, I understand you strive to be an active participant in this group. We do appreciate your passion. However, your mother made it quite clear she doesn't approve. You stole animals and hid them in your home. A punishable offense. Compassion Lives does not condone criminal behavior." I stiffened when his eyes narrowed, and clarified by adding, "Any longer."

His sleepy expression hardened into something unsavory. Distain.

"I won't force you from the group. Neither will I encourage you to stay. I *will* limit your level of participation, though. You can socialize with group members all you like, but you're not welcome at protests or meetings. Understood?"

Dill unclenched his jaw. He expected a screaming match and received a terse lecture instead.

"Others were left to deal with the animals. One of which died from your negligence."

"Sorry?"

"I'm not inclined to pay for carpet cleaning. Consider it a consequence of what you did."

"'kay."

"No curiosity as to where the animals went?"

"Yeah."

"Gray Birch Sanctuary in Rutland. You volunteered for an afternoon last August."

"'kay."

In our brief absence, a real party took shape involving the stereo, the blender, and liquor bottles pulled from the closet bar. Emma and Megan were dancing. Toby and Adrian huddled in conversation on the couch. The others had crammed into the tiny kitchen to eat, drink, and wait to use the toilet. Monica's bedazzled jean butt bounced in time to the music as she dug through the contents of the freezer. I snatched a Gardein roast from her hands.

"Why are you still eating? You sampled everything at the potluck. Twice!"

Claire emerged from the toilet distressed. "It won't flush. I put towels on the floor. It's not going down."

"Oh, for the love of Gandhi."

Plunging the toilet embarrassed me more than Claire. The ceiling fan hadn't worked properly in ages. I was obliged to swab the porcelain with a bleach solution to camouflage the ugliness. I fully expected my jeans and navy sweater to be splotched white in the aftermath.

Karen flopped into a kitchen chair with my spiral-bound copy of *A Dear Choice*. The chair creaked ominously. A flash of light in the driveway had her parting the curtains. "Expecting someone? Whose truck?"

"Aw, shit. Shit. Shit. Shit."

Mr. Peebles allowed visitors as long as they were quiet and he didn't have to walk more than ten paces to reach the front door. The driveway was chock full of vehicles and nearly an inch of snow. I scooped up keys and my jacket for a round of musical cars moving my Highlander and Monica's Mazda to the curb and offering Mr. Peebles my elbow over the snowy driveway. Cheerful inquiries as to his day were met with upward glances at my living room windows. I led him into his flat and pledged to keep the noise to a minimum. He shed his coat on the recliner and worked the television remote. With the speakers set to his preferred volume, he squinted at the ceiling and said, "Lower." Indeed, a veritable train station overhead.

I bumped into Monica in the upstairs hall. Her black, death-metal band tee shirt reeked of burnt herbs. "Have you been smoking pot?"

Monica's face curled upwards in a massive smile.

The pungent scent lingered along the curve of the banister. "Good grief, Monica. My landlord is forgetful, not an idiot."

Karen filled the doorway behind us. "Do I sense a problem, ladies?" She bared her teeth, made claws of press-on turquoise fingernails, and silently mimed a catfight.

My nose led me up one flight to the abandoned attic studio. If anyone mucked with my exercise equipment or the storage boxes I kept there, there'd be hell to pay. A seam of light outlined the door at the top of the staircase. Inside the studio, voices mumbled in the bathroom. The tiny pink space housed a rusted clawfoot tub bookended by a rusted sink and a rust-stained toilet. Toby and Adrian were wedged into the tub, knee to knee, sharing a joint.

"Why am I not surprised?"

"What's up, Chief?" Toby asked.

"Tonight's meeting is off the rails. I'm going to reschedule when I have a better grasp on how to proceed."

"With what?" Adrian squeaked, his voice straining with the effort of holding in smoke.

"Our investigation into Ella's death. Were you not listening?"

Toby untangled his legs from Adrian's and climbed out holding a beer bottle. "I'm good to go. Working the breakfast shift tomorrow. I'll get these clowns home to bed."

Adrian threw a playful punch at Toby's butt. Startled, the young man pitched forward sending a geyser of beer into my face. I gasped like a landed fish, shocked and suffocating, and banged my wrenched shoulder on the door frame.

"Party's over. Out! Go home! Everyone. Go home!"

One flight below, I repeated the same just as emphatically. My beer-slicked scowl kept the grumbling to a minimum. Monica, the force behind the merriment, herded everyone out the back door with terse good-byes, then apologized on a dull loop until the last of the glasses and dishes were stacked in the sink.

"Monica, all is forgiven. I've chased the boys out of the studio before. My only complaint is that I didn't speak with Karen before you booted her out. The extent of her relationship with Claire concerns me. That aside, I'd rather discuss an incident at the market this afternoon. Something horrifically weird happened."

The story of the accident, relived with car sound effects and body contortions, failed to elicit the level of sympathy it deserved. "Ruined my tights," I pouted, hiking up a pant leg to expose a bruise darkening my right knee.

Monica pushed her whole face into a frown. "Welcome to winter in New England. We all wear black coats the size of mattresses. We're camouflaged at night. The guy didn't know what he hit."

"This felt deliberate," I insisted.

"Somebody's teenager could've been driving."

"You're not treating this seriously."

"Do I believe some moron clipped you in a parking lot? Yes. Do I believe that moron tried to kill you? No. Freaking dark out and you're all wrapped up like a Smartie. In black!"

A sinister thought swirled between my ears. "You had exit duty. Who left the potluck early, right before or right after me?"

Monica rested her chin on her hand in a thinker pose. "The Kenneys. Tick-tock. Babysitter on the clock. Michelle Jones and her boyfriend. Gary Frazer and his boyfriend. The whole Capparello clan. Five of those. Most stayed for the basket raffle at four-thirty."

A parade of faces and personalities came to mind. None fit my impression of the assailant. "I volunteered at Gray Birch yesterday. Joan Doyle suggested someone from Ella's past. Jared Libby."

Monica tsked. "That asshat? He doesn't have the balls for it. I'll bet Joan does. I can think of a few reasons. Just sayin'.'"

"It's been settled. Don't say that."

"Has it? Open your eyes, Danni."

That Monica has been quietly discouraging members from volunteering at Gray Birch was an open secret. A fight for another day. I watched her pull something from her pocket. "What are you playing with?"

Monica stuffed her fingers into a brown billfold. "I found it between the couch cushions. Jackpot. It's Russell's."

I snatched it away. "Did you pick his pocket?"

"No. Swear to God and little baby Jesus."

My face told her I didn't believe her.

"What the heck. His ass was right there. I might've poked it. Accidentally."

The billfold went into *my* pocket. "Now I'm obliged to call Adrian and figure out a way to return it. This is mortifying."

"I didn't steal his wallet."

"You said five seconds ago you pried it from his pocket."

Her face pinched. "Poked. I don't pry."

That was debatable given her tendency to be garrulous and intrusive when flirting with men. "Did you, by any chance, get Russell's number?"

A slight toss of her head, then, "Struck out. Little brother was running interference. I think Russell's gay."

I massaged the wrinkles creasing my forehead. "Please get the hell out and I mean that in the nicest possible way."

Unless my thoughts are translated into doable action items for others, I'll be investigating Ella's death solo. "Many hands make light work" only holds true if my A-team is competent. Claire's awkward in her own skin. Alicia, Emma, and Megan have numerous family commitments. Toby isn't reliable with more than a two-step plan. Zoie and Lenny were on the outs of their relationship and eager to draw others into their misery. Monica, Adrian, and Doug smoke too much weed. Their deliberate forgetfulness stopped being humorous long ago. Going it alone might be the only reasonable option.

A rattan basket in the bedroom closet held reminders of memorable moments from a decade-plus of activism. Creased copies of a Recreational Times magazine and a Washington Post newspaper sat proudly on top of the mementos. Honor by association. Ella had been sent by Recreational Times to cover a women's backpacking tour in Grand Teton National Park. A conversation overheard in a Wyoming laundromat inspired her to seek out investigative reporter Margaret Rosen. Ella abandoned her assignment and the pair drove to North Dakota. They co-authored an expose on the rise of kidnapping and murder cases involving indigenous women since fracking created the 2005 Bakken oil boom. Ella lost her job documenting leisure activities in America and won a Walkley award. I was more than proud she was my friend.

I dug out three lanyards with flash drives that I hoped never to touch again. A disgruntled soul from Ella's past was likely the culprit behind everything. The obscene messages. The vandalism. The disruptions at our protests. And now, Ella's murder. I could think of a dozen folks who had openly threatened us. Though, none struck me as capable of murdering another human being to avenge their pride. Not even Jared Libby as Joan suggested.

The most intriguing, unanswered question raised by investigators at his trial was whether he and Cassandra received help creating the eleven videos posted to his channel. Video quality improved substantially after the third installment netting the young man a thousand subscribers as deplorable as himself.

Cassandra stood at his side in the eighth through eleventh installments. Prosecutors suggested she manned the equipment for the first seven. No one knows who stood behind the camera when the pair were carrying out their dirty work in front of the lens.

I dredged from memory what I knew to be true. Ella identified a turquoise dome in the background of the two bakery videos as being Canard's water tower. Armed with still shots from the videos, White Mountain VSN members canvassed stores in its downtown area. Several cashiers recognized Cassandra as an unrepentant shoplifter, who lived somewhere near the center of town. Jared's presumed age made him a recent high school graduate. Canard's police lieutenant refused to search them out. Later, he would state he sought to prevent a vigilante situation, which occurred anyway. Had the police acted decisively when informed, Cassandra might've received psychiatric help rather than publicity. By the time Jared went to court to face charges, Cassandra was lying on a table in the morgue. No one claimed her body. Jared's family disowned him.

A sharp rap on the front door had me tumbling out of bed and into the present time. Decent of Peebles to wait until after my guests had departed before delivering a lecture on the evils of everything.

"Coming Mr. Peebles!" I swung the door open to stand face to face with Russell Kristel.

Chapter 10

Freshly showered, Russell carried the scent of foamy ocean waves, briny seaweed, and sunlit quartz. Recalling the icy chill of the Atlantic, I eyed the fleecy comfort of his dark green hoodie and imagined a white tee shirt underneath pressing against his skin. I wanted to be that tee shirt.

"Sorry to disturb you. Adrian called saying you have my wallet."

I led him to the kitchen table and pointed. He stuffed the wallet into a pocket. The corner of his mouth tilted in a crooked smile. The smile deepened with the length of my stare until I wore a crooked smile too.

"Someone found it on the couch," I said.

Russell studied the cushion I pointed to as one would a Pieter de Hooch masterpiece, something familiar, yet intriguing. A truck rumbled along Dolly Road. Mr. Peebles' television burbled through the floorboards. The humidifier in the bedroom gurgled. Somewhere, a baseboard pinged. One of us needed to speak before the tension in my gut crush my innards.

"Tomorrow's a workday—" I began.

"Big couch," Russell blurted. "Where I'm staying, small couch. Hard to get comfortable."

"Oh. Where are you staying?"

"With Billy Purtell. He's a friend of Adrian's from school. He's renting a house in Sudbury with three other classmates. Cost-saving measure. I'm on a futon in the basement." He shrugged his eyebrows. "Job interviews in Boston."

My turn to act intrigued, though my attention had shifted to a hum in my lower regions. "Smart move. Boston's expensive."

"I wake up stiff in the morning." Russell's arms went wide to stretch shoulder muscles and an elbow grazed my breast.

My appendix, wherever it was, was going to explode. I said what I hoped we both were thinking. "You're welcome to sleep here on the couch."

"Wow. Yeah. Absolutely." Russell flashed a smile. "If it's not a hassle."

A tingle of energy radiated between my shoulder blades. Any more and my hair would float with static electricity. I fled to the linen closet in my office. The door jammed on a bedsheet. Nearly all the stacked towels and sheets were askew. *Odd.* I gathered up bedding and a pillow and decided in a nanosecond that my sanity was best preserved by ending the conversation before I began gabbling like a flirtatious high schooler.

I saw to Russell's comfort in the living room before retiring to the bedroom. Residual thoughts of the botched meeting and vile videos were swallowed up in waves of giddiness. The air felt electrified. Russell, in a state of undress, on the other side of the wall. Given he lived in New Jersey, his current proximity was hardly a recommendation for a repeat of what we once had. Still, I couldn't quiet my brain for sleep. The novel on my tablet, a romantic comedy, urged me in a certain direction, page after page after page.

Had he meant to touch my breast? Couldn't he have waited until morning to search out his wallet? Adrian has my number on his phone. This late-night visit wasn't truly necessary. No amount of reasoning could prevent me from opening the door that separated us.

Russell lay sprawled on the couch tapping on his smartphone. The golden glow of the side lamp shined on his dark locks and highlighted the tip of his nose.

"Russell?" I tip-toed forward.

He set the phone down. The crooked smile reappeared.

"I, er . . ." A half-formed question fizzled on my tongue.

Russell flipped back the quilt and patted the couch cushion. Tee shirt and boxers. My toes curled in excitement and carried me across the carpet.

The quilt tented us in his body heat. We connected with a kiss, tentative at first, then an all-consuming dive into something deeper. Warm hands explored curves. Fingers trailed, then massaged. I tried in vain to gracefully shed my pajamas without falling off the couch or elbowing him in the ribs. Russell laughed, nuzzling my collarbone, and slowed me with another kiss. The smell of him. The taste of him. I was ravenous and he was just as hungry. Harmonized by a string of moans and gentle coaxing, the clock spun backward three years. The couch springs were sorely tested.

When we could speak without gasping, Russell whispered, "Talk to me."

Lapsing into familiar vowel sounds happened I grew excited. An embarrassment to my Americanized self. "There's hardly a trace left."

"Say anything."

I sighed twice and returned his gaze. His interest didn't wane. My finger quit twirling his chest hairs. Was he requesting family history in the midst of love-making? Ridiculous. My life was under constant scrutiny as it was. I saw no reason to voluntarily educate him. Even Monica was kept mostly ignorant of the details of my father's unusual death and the ugly aftermath. Yet, those eyes . . .

"My youth was spent in England. We lived with my mother's family. A dreary lot addicted to KFC and pantomiming the prime minister. When the time came to expand Father's business, we relocated here and lived with his parents. They were elderly and in want of company. Out of college, I worked for my father's company. Fresh bagels and muffins every morning. Woo hoo. The end."

"Say something you haven't said before."

In the spirit of openness—given my state of undress—I knew I should say something more. A clever distraction, rather than a revelation.

"What do you find fascinating about industrial adhesives?" I batted my eyelashes.

"Nothing, really. It's how you shape words with your mouth." Russell traced a fingertip over my lips. It tickled and thrilled. "I like hearing you talk."

Oh, riiiiight. Me, overthinking again. "Kiss me. No more pillow talk."

And he did.

Monday is not my least favorite day at B.C. Wethers. Fair to say, that every day is my least favorite. Today was not an exception. I went three rounds with the file carousel before giving up. A hastily repaired mechanism responsible for its rotation was to blame. The gnash of metal upon metal echoed over cubicles far and wide. I returned to my desk refusing to make eye contact with equally frustrated coworkers.

I did manage one small accomplishment before the end of the workday. I deciphered most of Dill's communication codes. Most letter groupings were popular abbreviations: TMI, IDK, IDC, BRB, MYOB. A few were knowable by context, CWOT being "Complete waste of time" and OMW for "On my way". Others required quick online searches. CTA meant "Call to action". RTB for "Return to base" had military connotations. A kid-friendly way of telling Dill to go home. Many were used as verbal uhm's. Two references to WakeUp Farm troubled me. Dill's animals had come from there. So had Lily and Lilac. Ella and I made it very clear the farmer willingly gave us the sickly, twin calves. Knowing the farmer did it to save two bullets and the labor of digging a hole was beside the point. What was Dill playing at?

The navigator's red push pin indicated the general proximity of Svetlana Ustinova's residence. A prior conversation with the cleaner informed me her parents leased a townhouse in Hudson for their family of five. Communal living. Safety in numbers. Dependency. That fit with her projected image. Svetlana was savvier than she let on liberally using her heritage and accent to enhance her supposed naivete. A police blotter report in the Globe a year ago announced the arrest of Kiryl Ustinov for attempted theft at a lumber yard. The stain never spread to his sister who continued to clean Ella's home unsupervised. Upon entering the housing complex, I thought, perhaps, Kiryl's venture into crime could've been altruistic. An attempt to repair his community? Tattered bits of asphalt shingles and crumpled soda bottles sparkled under property lights. The dumpster enclosures were tagged with spray paint. Signage for each building was either vandalized or missing. Hence, I arrived a few minutes late after cruising between five buildings to read door numbers.

Svetlana was dressed for clubbing though it was 6:30 on a Monday evening. Long sandy curls pinned to the top of her head, a tight Demin jumpsuit, and heavily applied make-up distracted from her plain features by drawing attention to her curves. After a curt hello she instructed me to walk around the exterior of the building to the concrete pad that was their patio. A cut-through from inside her unit wasn't offered. Svetlana had never been overly friendly. A woman of few words, she often kept them to herself. I reckoned I'd be granted five minutes before being asked to leave.

Afternoon rain dissolved yesterday's snow making the ground linking patios spongy with mud. I mourned my boots and searched the dark for vague outlines of yard furniture to avoid bumping into them. The odor of fresh dog shit accompanied me to an orange dot that was Svetlana smoking a cigarette on a lawn chair. I'd have to stomp through a puddle before getting inside my car.

I yanked a plastic chair from a nestled stack. "You're aware of what happened to Ella?"

Svetlana moved closer to a window and into the weak rays of a dining room chandelier. A faux fur blanket swaddled her body. Seeing her in the gloom at a distance of five paces, I could trick myself into seeing Ella.

"Much evil in this world."

"Do you believe what the police suppose happened? A burglary."

"They have their reasons."

"Had things gone missing from Ella's home previously?"

"No theft." Svetlana shook her shoulders as though to rid herself of a spider. "Still you think they wrong, tell them. I am nobody."

"I will once I know more. That's why I asked to meet with you. You cleaned her home twice a month. You may have heard or seen things most others hadn't."

Cigarette smoke grayed the air between us.

"Not when she die. October come. Pouf. All done."

"You quit? Why?"

"Time is up. I go. I not her cleaner."

I waited. She didn't elaborate. "Did Ella have a boyfriend? Did she ever mention feeling frightened?"

Svetlana shook her head and flicked the cigarette stub into the yard.

"Monica Jinks babysat Clyde and Reno on occasion. Who else had access to the house?"

The question had her groping under the blanket for another cigarette. "People. Many people. Not only me—see? Boy from store with food. Old people next door. Manuel bring people. In, out. All day."

"Did you see any evidence of drug use in the house?"

Svetlana blew a raspberry. "You talk stupid. Ella not take headache pills."

"Do you know why she stopped filming in her house?"

"Maybe she do other things."

"Such as?"

"Go to friends in Holden."

"A boyfriend?"

"Boyfriend. Girlfriend. People. Who am I to say?"

"What key did you use to get inside her house?"

"Same key she leave me." The blanket billowed and flapped open. Svetlana sprang to her feet. "I say enough. Hey, listen. Police make trouble for me and family. I know nothing. I like Ella. She very kind. I think she love you, yes?"

"Yes."

"Like you, I sorry she die."

"Yes." I thanked her and returned to my car. Despite Svetlana's attempt to create a smoke screen, I recognized Ella's perfume on her.

Papers from the blue murder folder covered the coffee table. Beer bottle sweat rings glued them to the wood. Nothing learned over the past week disproved the police's theory. Svetlana's claim of friends in Holden could be an assumption. That Ella trusted in her should've been enough for me to do likewise, but I couldn't.

I microwaved two frozen burritos for a late supper. Opening and closing the freezer door brought to mind the unfinished business of the dead cat. I called Biscuits and Bows Animal Shelter.

The director, Melinda Ault, answered. "If I didn't know you better, I'd have you arrested."

"Nice speaking with you too, Melinda. Happy holidays."

"Before we get into it let me say I'm sorry about Ella. She was a royal pain in my ass, but I'm going to miss her."

"Thank you. Heart-warming. I mean that with all due sincerity." I hoped she heard the smile in my voice.

"Yeah, well, Violet placed the cooler in the shed and I didn't find it until Friday. Don't ask. I scanned the cat myself. Piffles. Four years old. Reported missing from a Marlboro family three weeks ago. His gum color is odd making me think he died of suffocation. An autopsy might tell. You aren't going to get one. The cat was wired to maintain the position. It'd show up on an X-ray. I don't want to be asked any weird questions I can't answer."

"Excuse me. Wired?"

"Taxidermy. Which is not the same as embalming. You do it to delay the decay of parts put on display like hides, antlers, heads, and paws. The rest of the carcass, if it isn't edible, is discarded. Piffles is unusual because he's intact. Full of guts and fat and his last meal. I had to refreeze him. He's a biohazard."

"So, whoever did this didn't know what he was doing?"

"Not necessarily. Piffles looks like a practice piece. He thawed enough for me to feel the wire. Galvanized. The sort taxidermists use for small mounts."

"Okay. I'm looking for the crazy person who did this at a taxidermist's shop. Hay in a haystack." This made me laugh. Melinda didn't see the humor.

"Professionals often work out of their homes. Many buy supplies online. It's not illegal to mount a domestic. Can I ask where you got the cat?"

"Special delivery. Left on my deck."

"Not a trophy. A message. Like the props you brought to our barbecue fundraiser. Only this one's real. Ever think of giving up your hobby of pissing people off?"

"Ever think of giving up the animal cruelty on your plate?" We'll never get over this. Best to go around it. "Where are Ella's dogs?"

Silence, then, "I placed them with a foster family for assessment. They were anxious and aggressive on arrival. They're doing much better. Less reactive."

"I'd appreciate knowing when they're adopted. They deserve a good home."

"They all do. In the meantime, I have to notify Piffles' owner. What do I tell them? Someone dropped their cat off and ran away?"

"Lots of crazies in this world," I said. "Any chance I could get Piffles' street address?"

"Planning another protest?"

"They didn't kill him. A deranged neighbor could be responsible."

"That's not for me to say. Do you want your cooler back?"

"You keep it."
"Are you going to crash our holiday meat raffle?"
"Not this year."

Chapter 11

A full twenty-four hours had passed since Russell and I kissed goodbye after breakfast. The text sent to him remained unanswered. I reexamined my every word and gesture in his presence. Was I expecting too much after confessing not to have any expectations? It followed suit that my shift at B.C. Wethers would be highly unsatisfying. I was remorseful to the point of distraction. And then angry because I couldn't find a reason for it. Followed by sad because I could feel such things and Ella no longer could.

I began my corporate workday hooking my black tights on an open cabinet drawer and tearing a V in the left leg. The gap drew attention to my shoes, one black, and one navy blue in slightly different styles. By late morning I'd developed a fixed, glazed look when engaged in conversation longer than three minutes. Claire quietly asked if I was stoned. I ventured to the first-floor cafeteria to replace my forgotten lunch. Trudy from Marketing chose that moment to sidle up to the counter and shake out her drab brown hair to reset a ponytail. I discovered brown strands crisscrossing my pasta bowl when leaving. Heads at six tables watched me frisbee the plate into a trash bin. Bryana caught me sleeping on my keyboard at three o'clock. In fairness, my work was done and I was bored. The nap bought me unexpected sympathy from Lydia, who graciously allowed me to leave early. The head cold excuse was getting stale. I reminded myself to move on to H1N1. 'Tis the season.

A proper nap on my living room couch swaddled in the quilt scented by Russell proved restorative. A cup of extra-strength coffee sharpened my wits enabling me to politely extract today's missing mail from Mr. Peebles' coffee table without losing my patience. In with the catalogs and solicitations, I found a sunny yellow envelope. The card inside featured an Easter rabbit hopping out of a painted egg. Slashes of bold red print obscured the bunny's original cordial message.

No peace without justice. The princess is dead.
Look to the reigning royals. They've bankrupted the nation.

Such drama. The neatly written return address belonged to my bank. Extra points to the sender for knowing that. I dropped the card and envelope into the recycling bin. One melodramatic soul is feeling ignored.

I rang up Detective Boynton and proposed exchanging ideas. He agreed to a tete-a-tete. Joe Dorvee had earlier agreed to speak with me regarding his brief mention in the newspaper. Monica was entrusted with confirming our later meeting with Wall of Shame alumni, the Uglies. Of my three scheduled appearances tonight, the last generated the most angst. Being a compulsive planner marked me as Shay Mowrey's daughter. I role-played question and answer sessions with each of my interviewees referencing my notes. Marlene Scott's letters slipped out of the blue folder in a shift of paperwork.

Penned in chunky script on the blank sides of her trial transcript, all were signed in elementary school cursive. The first letter, introductory in nature, mentioned Jared's upcoming parole hearing. It expressed hope of better things to come upon her release from prison and included what could pass for a sincere apology. Marlene called herself a "bad mom" to Cassandra and accepted the "sins of her crimes" promising never to "do stupid shit" again. The names of those supporting her reentry into society were not mentioned. The letter ended with a plea for Ella to correspond with her.

In another letter, Marlene thanked Ella for her interest and went on to worry about her future outside of prison walls. Employment, housing assistance, and outpatient treatment were offered, not guaranteed. Past experiences working with advocacy organizations embittered her to the process. The words "blame" and "sorry" were repeated but not in reference to herself. The letter ended with a plea for Ella to write back. What she was to respond to wasn't entirely clear.

The third letter amounted to a four-page rant. "Blame", "hate", "crying", and "fucking with" liberally peppered each page. Marlene judged her chances for a normal life woefully inadequate and included calculations for a settlement figure. All her frustrations and fears rested on Ella's slim shoulders.

People like you don't do squat for people like me. You look away.
You don't want to see us. Sleeping under bridges. Freezing in doorways.
All rolled up in cardboard. A pair of socks and a sandwich don't cut
it. I deserve more. Cassy should have had more. Because of you my little
girl is dead. You should of looked the other away and let it go.

The fourth letter included revised math upping the payout to fifty thousand dollars, which Marlene deemed sufficient for a new start in life.

I got a guy who'll take you out for 500 bucks. I make the call and you
can't make it to your car. To your house. Nowhere to hide. Selfish bitch.
You put the sheet around my baby's neck and murdered my little girl.

Marlene neglected to outline how Ella would deliver the payment. Presumably, she expected the conversation to continue and details would be determined later. I doubted Ella would've ignored such a threat.

The Dorvee's ranch house on Ives Street was typical of homes in this blue-collar neighborhood. Its brown painted clapboard had faded and the brick skirt required repointing. Most homes here dated to the 1960s and fit neatly onto small lots. Except Ella's. The L ranch had been lengthened for a spacious master bedroom and the attached garage became a living room with a cathedral ceiling. These new dimensions overwhelmed the yard despite a sizeable landscape budget to reshape every inch of it. Ella could certainly afford a much grander residence before the renovations were complete. High regard for Joe and Donna Dorvee as de facto parents might've been one reason for staying.

Joe came to the door in khaki pants and an argyle vest. Reading glasses reflected off his bald spot. Though he quit work at a mattress outlet, he hadn't retired the outfits that coordinated with the store's tan, green and red logo.

"Welcome. Come on in. Why'd you stay away so long?" My hello was muffled by a hug that reeked of salted peanuts.

We sat in the paneled living room, me on a scratchy couch, and Joe in a fretwork of grooves worn into a brown leather recliner. Everything was as I remembered it: polished oak tables; flower basket prints; an abundance of shelves holding Donna's historical novels, and Joe's spy thrillers.

"Where's the Mrs.?" I asked.

"Shopping for celery and onion. You know Donna," he chuckled, "she'll come home with a big bag of groceries and a whacky plan for dinner."

My friendly inquiries about his retirement turned him garrulous. As much as I enjoy sharing a pleasant chat with this kind man I was on a tight schedule. A request for water broke his rhythm. I fetched it myself and lingered at the kitchen sink window. The breadth of Ella's patio was clearly visible from here.

"Joe, I've come because of what happened to Ella. I find the official explanation troubling."

"Came here as newlyweds thirty-five years ago. Never seen anything like it. Shouldn't have to. It's a crying shame. How're her folks doing?"

"I don't know. They retired to Costa Rica. I did meet with her older brother Reese. He's handling it as well as can be expected." Though I truly did expect more.

"We're going to miss her cooking," Joe said. "We were her official tasters. Me and Donna. Ain't that something?" Emotion trembled his voice.

I clasped his hand on the arm of the chair and received a tender squeeze in return. "Ella asked you to watch the dogs that weekend, didn't she? You enjoy having Clyde and Reno here. Why didn't you watch them?"

"Aw, well. Stacy's having problems at home. It happens. We took the kids on Friday so she and Rob could talk it out. The dogs would be underfoot."

"Sorry to hear that. Stacy's a fantastic mother. I wish her the best." A lie. My sympathies rested fully with long-suffering Rob. "Did you see or hear anything out of the ordinary on Friday? Any strangers spotted in the neighborhood during the week?"

"Same as always. Grocery deliveries. The cleaner and the reiki guy came on Tuesday. Clyde and Reno have two appointments a month. Supposed to settle them down. Never did that I could tell."

"The same cleaning woman as before? Yes? So, nothing unusual to report?"

"We leave that up to Evelyn Pallotta." Joe pointed out a window to the peapod green house on the opposite corner. The breezeway to a two-car garage made it a rarity in this neighborhood. "Old Eagle Eyes knows everybody's business at this end of the street. Gets herself invited to card games that way. Gossip is better than pocket change."

I wondered if Joe said the same to Detective Boynton. "What time did you retire to bed on Friday?"

"Regular time. Going on eleven. Donna was already sleeping. Ella's car was parked in the driveway. We thought everything was all right."

The west wall of Joe's living room abutted the garage and was without windows. Ella's new driveway ran on the other side of it out of view. "Did Ella explain why you were to contact Gordon Fahey?"

"For emergencies."

"How did you know there was an emergency?"

"The guy that rang my doorbell said one of the dogs was hurt. Clyde's knocked down the trash before. Chewed on couch cushions. Both dogs are high strung."

"Ella would've hired a dog sitter after you said no. Why not wait until the sitter arrived and let that person clean up the mess?"

Joe struggled out of the chair. "Excuse me." Water gushed in the kitchen sink. He shuffled back to his seat wringing his hands. "Clyde didn't look good from the window. I did what she told me to do. Mr. Fahey came with the key. We went back over and found her."

"What time did you call Gordon?"

Joe closed his eyes, thinking. "After two. I called the police around three. They have a record of it."

"You entered through the front door. Yes? What happened then?"

"We checked the rooms. Found broken glass. One of those fancy bowls of hers. We thought Clyde cut his foot. There were stains on the rug. Mr. Fahey told me to take the dogs home and leave the glass for the police."

"He said that *before* opening the basement door? You didn't consider that premature? One of the dogs could've knocked it down."

Joe's eyes bulged. He exploded. "Why do you have to know everything! What can you do? It's too late! We can't fix it! This is horrible, horrible . . . I'm done with it."

The shockwave of his outburst dulled my hearing. With both of us stunned, we studied the carpet for a long, uncomfortable moment.

In a gentler voice, I asked, "Did the house appear burgled? Appliances missing. Her office rifled through. That sort of thing?"

Joe closed his eyes and settled his breathing. "Open drawers in the kitchen. The office torn apart. Everything pushed off her desk. A whole closet of clothes was thrown on the bedroom floor. What a mess."

"Did you see an overnight bag?"

Joe nodded. "In the bedroom. Under other stuff."

"What happened after Gordon shut the basement door?"

"I called 911 from here. We waited by the street." Joe searched out the wall clock. A request to leave was coming.

"Did Gordon return to his car at any point?"

"I don't know. I wasn't paying attention to him."

I smiled benignly. "Thank you so much for speaking with me. I can appreciate how difficult it's been for you and for Donna. Before I leave, can I trouble you for your cell number? In case something comes up and we need to get in touch."

"I guess that'd be okay." Joe groped a trouser pocket for his smartphone.

We exchanged contact information and goodbyes. Joe was lying and it wasn't apparent why.

The brick facade of the Framingham Police Station with its arched windows and crenelated trim imitated a castle. A rather dull one. Despite an expansion of its footprint in recent years, it hardly rated as imposing as the Parthenon-styled Memorial Building nearby. That structure housed City Hall and anchored a rotary from which converging streets spun vehicles into the business district of the old downtown. I eased the Highlander into the car park between the keepers of the law and the minders of civic duty and reviewed my plan. I'd offer Boynton opinions and theories in exchange for facts. I'd charm him into revealing points of interest and suspects being followed. I'd ask to see photos taken of Ella's home. A sudden fit of giggles overcame me. My plan wasn't grounded in reality.

I walked down Union Ave to a cozy Indian restaurant. Turmeric walls and cayenne-hued tablecloths warmed me on sight. Ella and I had occasionally eaten lunch here. Four diners, all Indian men in business suits, barely registered my presence. A waiter clothed in shapeless, hand-dyed cotton pointed me to a minuscule table with a view of the rotary. I settled in and called Boynton.

"Detective Charles Boynton. How may I be of service?" he answered.

"Good evening, detective. This is Danni Mowrey. Change of venue for our chat. I'm famished. Light-headed because of it. You can find me at Coriander Kitchen. When can I expect you?

He harrumphed. "Give me five."

"Great. See you then."

Fifteen was more likely, given the distance and his waddle, leaving me free to watch people hurrying in and out of stores, business offices, and medical practices. The waiter took my order bringing a bowl of papadum crackers with dipping sauces for noshing. Just in time. Boynton's voluminous black coat blotted out an extended view of the sidewalk. Indeed, a hulk of a man, aged beyond his fifty-some-odd years. I Googled him in anticipation of this meeting. An average officer plugging along. The greater disappointment being he wasn't presently carrying a briefcase full of notes.

"I'm here. Now what?" he said gruffly, sidling up to my table.

"We talk. You tell me something I don't know and I'll do the same. We both want Ella's killer found. We're on the same team."

Boynton bumped the table when sitting jostling the ice in my glass. The walk made his face flush and shiny. "I'm a police detective. You may be a suspect in a murder investigation. If you have something important to say, say it."

"You should verify my activities on the night of Ella's murder so you won't consider me a suspect." I unfolded a slip of paper containing contact information for everyone at Monica's house that Friday evening.

Boynton pulled a vinyl notepad from a breast pocket and patted elsewhere for a pen.

"The host, Monica Jinks, received a text from Ella canceling her pet-sitting gig for Clyde and Reno, Ella's two terriers. I'm inclined to think the killer sent it. I advised Monica not to delete it. Do you have Ella's devices in your possession?"

"If I did, we might not be having this great conversation."

"I'm sure you're working hard on securing the data by other means. Do criminals really kill for such paltry goods?"

"Might depend on what was on them."

"Certainly not state secrets." I grinned. "She kept her home locked and alarmed. No ostentatious displays of wealth. Why her?"

"Maybe only a friend would know." Boynton eyed the water glass. I pushed it toward him.

"Meaning what? The killer was a friend and the motive something else."

The waiter delivered my meal and poured another glass of water. I inhaled the heady aroma of chana masala, made room on my plate for two scoops of brown rice, and allowed myself three bites before saying, "I believe the dead cat is related to Ella's murder. Someone has been hassling my group at protests. Sabotage. Theft. Vandalism. Grotesque messages left on my answering machine. Two days ago, someone tried to run me over in the parking lot of Leavitt Brothers Market."

Boynton looked stricken. "Did you report any of this?"

I swirled a chunk of naan in chutney. "I've never found the police to be particularly helpful."

"Then why are we talking?" Boynton tugged off his coat blanketing the chair. I ate while he scratched a pen over clean white pages.

"How did Ella die?"

The detective swapped the pen for a napkin and patted sweat from his neck. "She didn't suffer."

The food on my tongue turned to paste. *All that blood required open wounds and a pumping heart.* Calling him out as a liar would require admitting I had trespassed into her home. I accepted it for what it was, an act of kindness. Boynton wasn't as crude as he presented.

"Just so you know, Reese DeMarco and Gordon Fahey are unreliable. Reese bullied Ella mercilessly during childhood. His current concern is assessing the value of her estate." I helped myself to the sauce bowl at his elbow and a sizable shard of cracker. "Gordon's a liar. Ella would never designate him as her emergency contact. They fought constantly. No love there. Many others were more suitable for the task."

Boynton consulted prior notes in the pad. "You and she fought quite a bit too, I'm told. You remained friends. How's that?"

"We argued as siblings would. All is forgiven at the end of the day."

"Reese DeMarco's her brother."

"Reese is an asshole."

Boynton suppressed a smile.

"What, exactly, was taken from her home?" I chewed quietly wanting to catch his every word.

"I'm not at liberty to say."

"She drove a Chevy Malibu," I said as if that somehow explained everything. "You didn't happen to bring the photos taken of her home?"

"Sorry. Left 'em at the office." Boynton pinched the last cracker from the bowl. "How about I ask you some questions? Why'd you leave NPK?"

"I already answered that. Gordon's a liar."

"How so?"

"The retelling would take all evening. I don't have the time."

"Why two organizations? The first one was doing okay. Had a certain reputation. The second one, the one you started solo, wasn't much different. Same complaints. Same doings. Some of the same people. How many vegans can there be? You and Ms. DeMarco ever argue over limited resources? Too many fingers in the same pie?"

"It's 'veegan', not 'vejan'. The prevailing attitude is the more the merrier. It has to be. Our world is at stake. Read *A Dear Choice*. The original book."

"That doesn't explain why you had to go it alone."

"It does, actually."

The waiter arrived with my bill. The detective had been surprisingly unhelpful, whereas, I'd given him plenty to ponder. The city of Framingham should pay for my meal. I rummaged in my purse for assorted bills while the detective wrote a single word on a fresh page. LIAR.

An overwhelming desire to explain worked my tongue. "I started Compassion Lives when I was still deeply involved in both NPK and Twin Sister. Ella understood my concerns."

"Concerns?"

"Fahey is hellbent on devouring all that Ella and I created together except Twin Sister, which lacks commercial appeal. Ella devoted too many unbillable hours to it. By his reckoning, the organization was an expensive hobby *he* disproportionately financed. He convinced us to relocate Twin Sister's base of operations westward, closer to the sanctuary that inspired it, Gray Birch in Rutland. Out of sight, out of mind. Ella was agreeable, seeing it as a way to bring the action closer to long-time members who joined early on."

"You came up with the idea at Smith College."

"Yes. Northampton. I acquiesced having already begun a sideways slide into Compassion Lives, an organization Gordon couldn't touch. The hiring of Bette Hornick as my replacement met with a bit of acrimony from others beyond myself. Perhaps you should have a chat with her. Ask her what her connection to Fahey really is."

I scraped the chair under the table and headed for the door forcing Boynton to scramble to keep up. He stopped me on the sidewalk.

"Sounds like she was pushing you out of successful businesses you helped build. Couldn't have been easy for you. Getting bumped from the spotlight. Office lackey in the end. Must have made you angry. Resentful."

Amusement expanded my face. "I fear you're a bit confused on the facts, detective. Twin Sister doesn't belong to anyone. I can't own the embodiment of a philosophy any more than you can claim to own a church of your religion. NPK, as a for-profit business, was designed as a vehicle for Ella's success. Never mine. It succeeded brilliantly. I take great pride in that."

Boynton harrumphed.

Chapter 12

G obbledygook. Yesterday, Monica and I agreed to meet with the Twisters in a shopping mall in Millbury. Minutes from an I-90 exit, the uninspired location suited convenience. A fresh reminder of the logistical insanity inherent in bringing far-flung people together. My prior suggestion of beer and billiards in Worcester met with her disapproval.

> *Monica: Don't be stupid. Beer bottles + cue sticks = weapons.*
> *We need a BIG place. Lots of witnesses.*

The chaos of recent days left me mentally unprepared to provide a rebuttal wrapped in lengthy explanations. My nit picky mental processes forced me to attempt it later in the day when we were both leaving work. We walked to our cars in separate towns shouldering our phones.

"The Twisters won't be disagreeable," I told her. "I'm sure they'll help in any way possible."

"Whatever. I'm cool with pool. What do I care?"

Just like that, she stuck a pin in my ballooning ideas. I rarely win by default. Rather than quietly relishing the moment, I felt compelled to educate her and explained how the administrative badge for Twin Sister's page allowed keyword searches for evidence of malicious intent in the weeks before Ella's death. Seeking repetitions of "cunt", "twat", and "bitch" proved fruitless. Skipping back to September of last year, I followed toothier threads forward. Ella's infamous spring rant had been her fourth and final verbal barrage. Zoo conservation programs, genetic engineering, and zoonotic diseases preceded it.

Other than chastising Ella for her wrongheadedness, I had never paused in the months since to analyze the fallout.

"Smell-o-vision! Smoke coming out of your ears. This is the part where you tell me what you found," Monica said.

So, I did. The remaining members resumed sharing prohibited content. They raged, criticized, and apologized. Some became philosophical. Others were relentlessly challenged to employ critical thinking. Crude language and violent imagery became hackneyed. Memes touting self-pity and depression lost all applause. Messages of universal well-being, forgiveness, and unity multiplied. By June, the remaining Twisters had established a code of civility previously absent. Ella's costly social experiment succeeded. Assuming that had been her intention. I had absolute faith it wasn't. Ella was orchestrating her exit.

"Gobbledygook," Monica said. She arrived at her driveway with a squeal of brakes. "We need a mall." To which I readily suggested the one in Millbury.

She won after all.

My entire sad, angry, bored, sleepy day could well be described as gobbledygook. Though I added a page for suspects to the murder folder, I couldn't imagine penciling in Joe Dorvee at the top of it. Boynton definitely should've paid for my dinner.

A green sign for Gloria's Garden Florist on the corner of the mall road inspired me to abandon the old moniker, The Uglies, and adopt The Glories instead with hope of a successful collaboration. Wall of Shame regulars were indeed a vainglorious bunch, who still favored energy-efficient cars. Several of their compact vehicles were parked near Monica's brilliant green Mazda, a poison dart frog in a murky puddle of silver-toned SUVs.

The closest entrance placed me inside JC Penney. Boxed cookware sets, tables of children's board games, and racks of women's crimson lingerie crowded the aisles. A sharp left turn brought me to the beauty counter for a quick spritz of cologne. My aromatic dinner was scrumptious. Boynton's tuna breath tainted its memory. Jingly Christmas music put a bounce in my jog up the escalator to the food court. Despondent, semi-retired adults in sweaty smocks manned counters scalloped with red garlands. Silver and green foil bells bobbed on strings dangling under hissing air vents. Everywhere, the smell of cinnamon sugar, tomato sauce, fryolators, and ground-up cow. I should've doubled up on the cologne.

The Glories arranged themselves around two tiny tables in the center of the atrium. A soft baked pretzel stand provided a lookout from which to observe them unseen. Eight invites. Four no-shows. Alba Caruso was absent. The Yulin clips she posted indelibly scarred my psyche. I couldn't rid my mind of the shriveled old man stepping on the head of a trussed dog at a public water fountain. He smiled toothless, grotesque, above the flash of a knife hacking at white fascia beneath the animal's skin. A hammer blow to my heart to see the dog blinking despite knowing dog meat enthusiasts claim the animal's flesh is tenderized by prolonged suffering. Alba's absence didn't pain me.

Those present were guilty of similar offenses best not reflected upon. Lee Anne Germain assumed the role of a white-haired matriarch to many Twisters. Built like an oak bookcase, she wore army surplus without any of Monica's arty flourishes. She gestured wildly over the table. Comical. The only thing Italian about Lee Anne was the food she prepared at her ex-husband's pizzeria. Rachel Opalka, seated beside her, cocooned herself in a pink hoodie with *Vegan A F* emblazoned on the back. With reddish hair and elfin features, she was often mistaken for a teen. The attribute contributed to the success of her ear-piercing kiosk in this very mall. John Rochler, looking dapper in a gray pinstriped shirt with black slacks, came straight from the Honda dealership. Something in his posture and attentiveness suggested he was more clear-eyed than usual. Curtis Whiting, the finest heating and cooling technician our vocational school system has ever produced, had shed his coveralls for charcoal gray slacks and a white oxford. I sensed an upward move into water heater sales. Two years since we all last met up and it could've been yesterday.

Monica dawdled at the ladies room sink.

"Did any of them see you?" I asked.

"They wouldn't know me if they did." Monica sported a rat's nest hairdo, gold eyelids, and a chain of tiny pink-haired troll dolls from the neckline of a 2XL desert jacket.

"Uh-huh." Not that my humdrum looks instilled confidence. French braid, short pleated skirt, opaque tights—forever mine. "Let's do this."

The Glories were dividing two roasted vegetable pizzas when Lee Anne spotted us and rose to her feet. A blunt hand shot out to grasp mine seconds before she pulled me into a bear hug.

"How ya doing, Sunshine? Still rocking it?"

"Every chance I get. Good to see you."

"Sorry about Ella. Hands down, one of the best. I hope they get the bastard that did it. Should have his nuts ripped off with pliers and rammed up his ass."

"Indeed. This remarkable young woman is Monica Jinks. Second in command for Compassion Lives. Her witticisms keep me sane."

"I prefer dogs to most people," Monica confessed. "Ella got me interested in NPK. Then I met this weirdo," she said pointing at me, "and opened my life up to insults and abuse from strangers."

That provoked an enthusiastic round of laughter from the group. Rachel dragged another table over. Lee Anne sent John to pilfer cups and lids from the coffee station. She served us spiked, coconut milk nog from a tall thermos. My hope of regaining their trust rose with each passing moment. Lee Anne called for everyone's attention once the pizza boxes hit the trash can.

"Danni wanted us here tonight to talk about what happened to Ella."

"What are we supposed to do?" Rachel added another turn to the hoodies' sleeves and planted her bony elbows on the table. "The cops are all over it, and, you know, we got history."

"The lead detective, Charles Boynton, is open to exploring motives other than robbery," I explained. "Though, there is a caveat."

"Caviar?" Rachel said. "Eww."

"A cah-vee-ott," Lee Anne said. "Screw your ears on right. Danni, don't mind her. Go on."

"I'll be as brief as possible and begin with an invitation to join Compassion Lives. I value your fearless devotion, your reckless disregard for personal safety, and your connections. I need your help to find Ella's killer."

All eyes narrowed for a punchline. John determined that was it and laughed. Curtis joined in only his outburst was a hacking cough and Rachel, obligingly, pounded gently on his back.

"Twin Sister's future is in jeopardy without Ella. There are plenty of other groups you could join. I won't dissuade you. I will say Compassion Lives is a better fit. We're incredibly active. Many opportunities to socialize and be a part of something meaningful."

Curtis made puppets of both hands and mimed *talk-talk-talk-talk.*

"Consider this. Who else will have you given your reputations for being major fuckups?"

The table erupted in laughter. Napkins were doled out to stanch tears and snot. I should have led with that.

"Great. I hope that's been decided. Moving on. Ella's manager, Gordon Fahey, publicly accused Twin Sister of harboring her murderer. Not a punchline. A punch in the face. He alleged NPK's commercial success tremendously upset members of her activist organization. He wrote that in a letter to the editor of a major newspaper. I tallied public response via two hundred and ninety-three comments posted."

"We're in the shitter," John said.

I nodded. "A shit quicksand and we're drowning. Gordon's tirade could unduly influence the investigation. Bette Hornick complained of journalists camped out in her driveway. Karen Putnam, your new ShowMe administrator, contacted me regarding rumors spreading within the group."

"What rumors?" Lee Anne asked.

"Isn't it all rumors?" Rachel said. "Who fact checks before they post or share?"

"Still haven't said what we're supposed to do." Curtis looked up with red-rimmed eyes.

"Anybody thinking *why us?*" John asked no one in particular.

Monica distributed copies of the screen shot Gordon had given me. Their names were highlighted in yellow in the comments section.

"All right. I see how it looks," Lee Anne said. "We got a little rowdy. Ella knew we were joking. Everyone hated the crunchy parts of the pasta salad. We told her not to do the cooking video."

Monica cleared her throat theatrically and read aloud from the paper. "'Tastes as good as gut rot feels.' 'We'll remember to serve it at your funeral in memory of.' 'Don't quit your night job at the piano bar.'"

I glared at John, who had authored the last bit. "Since when do you take part in this nonsense?"

John's head shrank into his shoulders. "Inside joke. Lots of other people laughed about it."

"None of those are funny or clever. Mean, idiotic comments left under your real names. Gordon linked you to Twin Sister and devised his own conspiracy theory. You've ruined the credibility of the organization, yet again."

Monica said, "Wall of Shame."

Lee Anne obsessively rubbed a chin hair. "Somebody going to start it up again? Put us on the naughty list."

"Who would do that? Does anyone even know who Karen Putnam is?"

Curtis barked out a cough and kicked John under the table making him flinch. "Ask Johnny-Boy here. He and Putnam had it all going on," Curtis wiggled his fingers over an invisible keyboard, "until he got a good look at her."

"Shut it, asshole." John crumpled the paper in front of him and pitched it at Curtis' head.

"Has Detective Boynton questioned any of you?" I asked. "No? Well, expect him too."

Knees vibrated under the tables.

"All of you make insidious posts that receive far too much attention. You each attract a certain type of follower, people who freely share opinions and experiences, and then some. I wish to reconstruct the last year of Ella's life to uncover a motive for her death. Your gossipy connections could be quite useful. Place your gadgets on the table. I'm going to dictate instructions on what you can do to help. Consider it part and parcel of your redemption."

The mall parking lot was full of motion. People dragged pouting children or swung colorful shopping bags in the aisles. Cars queued up inching toward the exit. Sounds coming from every direction implied safety. Despite the padded coat and heavy scarf, I felt an icy shiver race over my ribcage. I fought the urge to look over my shoulder just as a firm hand clamped down on it. I yelped loudly and dropped my car keys.

"About what you said, can we talk?"

"Cripes, John! Holy crow."

John jerked his head around, nervous too.

I unlocked my car mumbling, "Please, hop in," and hoped my embarrassment wasn't obvious.

"That Boynton guy's an asshole. He got to all of us. Lee Anne, Rachel, Curtis, Alba. Others. If anybody says different, they're full of it."

"You've met?"

"Three days after it happened. He showed up at the dealership. I don't know what he said to my boss. Everybody's acting like I'm a suspect. Nobody says hi. The mechanics won't even look at me. Boynton's got security camera pictures of a bunch of us at East Bay. The time we stopped the trucks to give the pigs water. He laid down some old New York City Kapparot pics of just you. He acted like it was a crime for you to be there documenting what they were doing. On a city street. Crazy. Jerk's trying to scare me for answers I don't have."

The initial shock of learning Boynton approached the Glories immediately after Ella's death and was actively investigating my doings wore off quickly. "John, I'm sorry to hear that. Is there anything I can do to help?"

"I doubt it. I'll work it out. Got to. I wanted you to know me and him already talked. Fahey put him onto us right from the get-go. I told him the razzing was an inside joke. Ella tested a few recipes at our summer picnic cookout. Healthy eating. Tasted awful. We did her a favor. Her new book's going to bomb if someone isn't honest with her. We weren't trying to be jerks."

To my credit, I didn't laugh. "Epic fail, John."

"Yeah, I get that," he snapped. "Boynton asked me who she'd been spending time with."

"Who was she spending time with?"

"I don't know. Bette had one simple job: keep track of Ella's schedule and update the event calendar on ShowMe. All that lady ever did was screw up. Ella was usually a no-show for our events and Bette never knew where to find her. I think she was lying. Covering up something."

"How did Ella explain her absences to the group?"

"I don't think she ever did."

I let that go. Now was not the time to discuss Ella's exit strategy with John. "Tell me more about Detective Boynton's questions."

"Someone told him I had the hots for Ella. They set me up. *Every* guy had the hots for her. She was interviewed for an article last year. What was it called? Something about the politics of the food industry. Problems with sourcing. Magazine's out of Hartford. Eh. It'll come to me. The pictures of her bending over a shopping cart holding cantaloupes and zucchini. Whoa."

I cringed, remembering. The photoshoot included several shots of Ella posing provocatively with fruits and vegetables. Gordon's idea. My objections were weak, nearly nonexistent. It was a men's lifestyle magazine and Ella's interview answers came from prior research I had completed. The article got the word out to a new audience.

John reached for the door handle. "Maybe somebody who read it liked more than just the pictures."

Another unsatisfactory day at the office. It began with a grunt and ended on a whimper with a plethora of ughs in between. Vendor invoices, purchase orders, and check copies piled up on the corner of my desk. I didn't look busy, I looked buried. Relocating them to the file carousel was soul-draining work.

Elevator up, elevator down, chink-chink-squawk—elevator stuck. I notified the Maintenance Department. "Hi. This is Danni Mowrey in Payables. Can you send Jeff up to pound on the carousel? It's acting up. Thank you."

Elevator up, elevator down, elevator up, chink-chink-squawk. "Hi. Danni again. I know, fun, right? Is Jeff around? Sorry, can you ask him to come back up? It stuck again. Thank you."

Elevator up, elevator down, elevator up, elevator down, chink-chink-screech. "No, this isn't funny. I think it's really broken this time. I heard metal grinding. Everyone heard metal grinding. Yes, I'll hold." I hung up.

After lunch, Monica called to abuse me. Detectives Boynton and Sollecito ambushed one of her backdoor cigarette breaks at Nate's Plumbing and Heating. She hyperventilated into the phone.

"I told him I lost it. No way are they getting my phone. I took pictures of the rash in case it comes back. For comparison. You know, *that* rash. Nate nearly had a seizure. Boynton's bigger than he is and nearly as mean. Sheesh."

No Need to Apologize

While I talked Monica out of a cliff jump, Bryana silenced the ringer on her telephone console to eavesdrop. As fate would have it, Cheryl called immediately afterward to remind me of her Thanksgiving invite. I stood up to stretch my legs and glimpsed Bryana with her forehead pressed to her side of the cubicle wall. She was tracking my transgressions. I ended the call with Cheryl quickly.

My frustration with everyone and everything was temporarily pounded out of existence on the emergency stairwells of Wethers' three-story building. When Bryana questioned my heavy breathing and damp hair, I told her I might've contracted the flu. Later, when Bryana went to the ladies restroom, I packed a wad of chewed gum under a wheel on her desk chair. Somehow, it transferred to the sole of her shoe. The high point of my day was not my proudest moment.

Evelyn Pallotta's ranch home did its part to contribute to light pollution. Every bulb inside and outside the home burned intensely. A veritable bonfire on the street corner. Astronauts orbiting the earth knew her address. Stranger still, I was quite certain this was a recent development. I would've noted it before.

A slim, sixty-ish woman opened the door. The neat lavender bob tucked behind her ears matched her lavender contact lenses. The lips that smiled back were a complimentary shade of mauve. The effect was mesmerizing.

"I get that a lot," she said in a slightly nasal voice.

"Sorry. Good evening. My name is Danni Mowrey. I'm a longtime friend of Ella DeMarco. Joe Dorvee said that I should speak with you. I wonder if we could chat for a few minutes."

Evelyn's purple eyes sparkled over my work coordinates and didn't find me to be mugger material. She let me into a home reminiscent of a Florida boutique hotel. Anchors, sea stars, and pelicans decorated drapes and upholstery.

"Sit here," she said, directing me to a chair covered in frolicking seahorses and lit by a lamp shaped as nautical pilings.

"The police interviewed residents of the street. Detective Charles Boynton is in charge of the investigation and he isn't the talkative type. Ella's father is coming to town soon. I feel obliged to offer him information of some sort."

Mrs. Pallotta's unwavering gaze shifted. "We all thought it neat having a celebrity on the street. At first. Malibu is not a flashy car and she wasn't glammed up like you'd expect." Evelyn tapped her nose.

My gut clenched like an angry fist. Three years ago, Gordon suggested Ella have rhinoplasty to minimize her strong nose. Ella refused and I wrote an article for our Fresh Perspectives column condemning body shaming.

Evelyn continued, "Having her here attracted personalities to the corner. Arty people in drag dragging equipment up the street. Parties on her patio. Their cars blocked our driveways. We could all hear them. The music. We never complained."

"Ella hosted late-night parties?"

"Nine, ten o'clock. We never complained. Ever."

I mouthed a small O. "Joe Dorvee said you keep a watchful eye on the corner."

"My grandchildren play outside. Cars race down Jenkins every single day. It's a death trap. I started a petition to get a stop sign installed on Jenkins."

"How good of you. Had you seen any odd people around Ella's home in the weeks before her death?"

"They're all oddballs. That's what I'm saying."

"A stranger. An unfamiliar vehicle in an unexpected spot."

Evelyn narrowed her eyes. "I recognize your face from the website. You were a contributor. I'm sure I've read something you wrote. Every month there's a story about a diet or depression. Click on it once and ninety-two ads for melatonin show up in your inbox."

"I no longer work for the magazine. Feel free to contact Gordon Fahey and let him know your thoughts. They love hearing from readers." Siccing Evelyn Pallotta on Gordon cheered me. "Getting back to Ella. She stopped producing videos in the fall. Things would've quieted down a bit. How did Ella seem then? Did you detect anything different in her routines?"

"Please, everything's a commercial. Use this potato peeler. Buy this flour. Why do car ads pop up when I'm reading a recipe? Adult diaper ads. Jewelry made out of coins."

I needed to rein Evelyn in. I consulted my mental questionnaire. Evelyn studied my mouth. A weird reflective gesture to nibble on one's lips. Stranger still to be gawked at for it.

"Where were you the night Ella died?"

"In bed. Sleeping."

"You didn't hear an argument earlier in the evening or see a car drive off quickly?"

"I have a question for you. How well do you know the company big shots?"

"I'm not certain I know what you mean."

Evelyn tsked. "I'm asking if you're in good with the owners. Do they seem like reasonable people? Open to suggestions. Taking the long view."

"I suppose."

"You don't seem so sure. Employee? Long-time friend?"

"Ella and I didn't discuss the business after I left."

"That's hard to believe. It was her whole life. Always on the go. Always cooking something new. I watched a few of her recipe videos. She could do a TV show and have guests. I've seen worse."

"Interesting idea."

"With all those ads and clickbait, the company has to be chasing after profit. A TV show would put them on top. Could there be a DPO on the horizon?" Evelyn's eyes widened. Spooky.

My face twisted. At least, I think it did. "I wouldn't know anything about that." *Why is she interrogating me?*

Evelyn flicked her eyes away, disappointed. "Oh, look at the time. Hubby will be home soon. Dinner's defrosting." She ushered me to the door.

"Thank you kindly for speaking with me. Have a lovely evening."

I couldn't hop inside my car fast enough. Evelyn, the gossip monger, must be a humdinger on Bridge night.

Chapter 13

A nother premature dusting of snow occurred overnight. Enough stark whiteness accumulated on the blasted rock faces and roadside trees of the Massachusetts Turnpike by late morning to evoke a festive mood. Bette's holiday rituals and sentiments were a mystery. We correspondence primarily via email during her short training period as Twin Sister's new bookkeeper. We could think of no reason to necessitate meeting in person. Newspaper clippings in my backpack contained what little else I knew of her. She addressed the fallout of Jared's trial in a regional newspaper. The writings were eloquent and compassionate and drew upon years of empirical knowledge. Perhaps Ella found a reason to value her judgment and confide in her.

I dodged potholes on the exit ramp and continue to do so for another mile until I reached the address on the navigator. A post and rail fence guarded desiccated flowers in the yard of the small white house. Winter color came from plastic bird feeders, fairy village groupings haphazardly placed on a brown lawn, and a young woman with neon red hair who stepped out of the house to light a cigarette.

"Good afternoon," I said with both hands gripping a roasting pan.

The woman walked away leaving a trail of smoke. I seem to have that effect on strangers.

I let myself into a living room crammed with boxy furniture. The inexpensive art and sagging cushions were unpretentious, sun-bleached and outdated. In the snug kitchen, five adults slumped against blue cabinetry drinking soda and conversing lively. An oak table set with brown melamine dishes dominated the space. Open pots bubbled on an old gas stove. The room smelled of starchy potatoes, mushy green beans, and something sinister. No point looking in the oven window.

"Danni! You're here!" Bette's short dark curls, medium build, and twenty years advantage defined my expectations. She lifted the roasting pan from my arms, scanned the crowded counter for space, and set it on the lid of the garbage pail.

"Happy holidays. It's lovely to finally meet you, Bette."

"I always said you should've come out sooner. Better late than never!" Bette returned to the stove to stir a pot of gravy.

With no introductions offered, I did it myself. The worn, seventy-ish couple were neighbors Mick and Dorothy Bellows. Both wore wispy hair, thick waists, and orthopedic shoes. A stocky, young woman in a linty brown sweater said her name was Aggie, "short for Aggressive." Another young woman, who bore a striking resemblance to Bette, studied my extended hand and said, "Arielle". Arielle channeled a full-figured Madonna circa 1985 with a polka dot headband, heavy eyebrows, and five pounds of plastic jewelry bouncing against her chest. A tight shirt and capri pants encased her abundance poorly. The ensemble screamed show-time rather than dinner-time. The red-haired smoker rounded out the dinner guests. Arielle introduced her as Grace. Grace refused to speak and narrowed her eyes at me. The room felt decidedly chilly.

Bette rummaged loudly in a utensil drawer. "I got to finish up in here if we're going to eat. Everybody, go in the parlor."

"Can I help? Slice bread. Mash potatoes. Toss a salad?"

"Shoo. I got it. Why don't you grab some wine from the frig. I can reheat that," she said of the soy roast, "once I get the turkey out."

Goblet in hand, I wandered into the parlor. My entrance stopped the flow of conversation. This coldness, no doubt, stemmed from fear I'd spoil the meal with a generous serving of guilt. I wandered into the adjacent dining room. The table supported a monitor, speakers, a keyboard, and a printer. The credenza held bins of paperwork and stationery supplies. A pyramid of lidded boxes of the same type in Ella's office rested between the front windows. I recognized half of the boxes as ones I had filled. I occupied myself rifling through the others. With fingers knuckle deep in a pile of invoices, I felt the subtle shift of air behind me and heard the tinkling of plastic jewelry. I continued studying the invoices as though I had permission to do so.

"Arielle. Hi. Could you please show me to my room? I don't want to disturb your mother while she's busy cooking."

Arielle's brows soothed into thick dashes. She pointed to the closed door at the foot of the table. "In there."

My expectations were low and remained so. The tiny room had storm gray walls, bent plastic blinds, and a twin bed.

"You should change that," Arielle said, aiming a finger at the bed. "My mom doesn't come in here much. No one does. It's a spare room. Sheets are in the basement."

Which is where I would've headed had Bette not called everyone to the table.

Bette served the bird from the stovetop and I ate what I brought. The reheating vandalized it. The chicken-style seitan roast had developed an unappealing burnt umber color under the broiler. The medley of root vegetables resembled stones plucked from a garden. I smiled graciously when handed my plate and added generous helpings of bread and discs of jellied cranberry sauce.

Halfway through the meal talk around the table became a competitive badminton match. Sentences were lobbed and volleyed until a new participant picked up the topic and altered its course. Aggie blamed her poor grades at Holyoke Community College on rising tuition fees. Grace complained of disenchantment with her boyfriend Moe, an unemployed blacksmith with high standards. Arielle complained of tedious job hunting at the Southampton mall all for the want of minimum wage employment. I played a dinner game to amuse myself. *Animal, vegetable, mineral . . .*

"Do you believe in God, Miss Mowery?" asked Mrs. Bellows. The question was not altogether surprising given the dainty cross resting on her sternum. "Don't you believe everything was put here for a purpose? For better use. Why be difficult and ungracious? All those starving children in Ethiopia would weep to see this table."

Bette smiled broadly at the compliment to her largesse.

I spit a chewy piece of roast into my napkin. "No human should go hungry. Globally, we produce more than enough food to feed everyone."

Mrs. Bellows dissected a slab of muscle from the turkey thigh on her plate and forked it onto mine. "There. I'm feeding you. Food is God's love. Isn't that so? Enjoy."

Roasted flesh of a brutalized animal . . . on my plate.

I immediately lost all desire to be agreeable. Blame the wine or the guests not of my choosing. My holiday meal was charcoaled chunks and slabs of liquified fruit. What, exactly, was I celebrating? Self-flagellation?

"Define 'purpose', Mrs. Bellows," I said.

"To serve man as God intended. There can be no greater purpose."

I debated the wisdom of engaging in enlightenment. A flash of iridescent feathers ended my internal debate. The hawk-imp clawed its way into my hair and bit my left ear. It would screech with my voice if I didn't begin first, politely.

"You speak as though man exists beyond the boundaries of nature. How would you explain the seven extinct species of 'man' that came before? Were they God's mistakes? As for predestination of animals to servitude—we have more than four hundred thousand described species of beetle. For what human purpose do they exist? Why do complex ecosystems exist in environments inhospitable to man? What is the logic of anything existing outside the realm of human involvement? And yet so much of it did and still does."

A hush fell over the table. Somewhere outside a jay screamed.

"God works in mysterious ways." Mrs. Bellows would not be made to think.

"There are more than four thousand documented religions. Not all have gods. Some involve alien lifeforms. One worships spaghetti. If you're going to ascribe to a religion, why choose a god and a belief system infamous for its dualities? Love and cruelty? Ignorance and charity? Why not choose a wholly compassionate life instead? A life free of exploitation in which all creatures, great and small, are respected. Their only purpose is merely to be."

Mr. and Mrs. Bellows dripped turkey grease from open mouths.

I gulped from my goblet. "This is quite tasty. Who brought the red wine?"

Bette refused my offer to help parcel out leftovers in the kitchen. Whether done as a courtesy to me or protection for them, I wasn't certain. This afforded me another opportunity to slyly search for anything extraordinary within the house. I noted incoming calls on the telephone console and finished shifting through the invoice piles. Of the stacked boxes, most were half full of miscellaneous items removed from the credenza. One held a musty pair of ice skates. The sheer volume of invoices Bette processed struck me as odd until I considered Ella's desire to support small businesses. Most of the purchases were well under one hundred dollars and the paperwork seemed in order. If departing guests objected to my browsing, they kept it to themselves.

The smell of fresh-brewed coffee lured me to the kitchen. Bette stood at the sink; a tower of upturned pots dripped water onto the floor at her elbow.

"Please, sit," I said, "You must be exhausted. Allow me to serve the coffee." I ventured into unfamiliar cupboards for coffee mugs and accouterments.

"Arielle's not the brightest bulb in the sky—if you know what I'm saying. I asked her to help clean the house for company and she acts like she doesn't know where things go. I'm pretty sure she does it so I won't ask again."

"Arielle sounds like a typical teenager. How old is she?"

"Twenty-four. How was your roast?"

"Fine." If not for the wine, I would've wailed over my scorched meal.

Bette nudged a plate of cookies toward me. "No one's going kick you out of the club if you do. I won't tell." Her tone was conspiratorial. The making of a naughty little secret between us. "Dorothy made them. They're really good."

I shook my head.

"Your loss." Bette stuffed a cookie into her mouth and made a comical expression of ecstasy.

Copying her tone, I said, "Now that it's just you and me perhaps we can get to know each other better. I regret not maintaining an interest in Twin Sister after I organized my own group."

"How's that going? Things working out for you?"

"Compassion Lives has grown beyond my expectations. We're nearly eight thousand strong. Online—that is."

"That's great. Maybe we can bring everybody together like one, big, happy family. Cover more ground. We're doing all the same stuff. We got our own meals-on-wheels sort of program. Ella got it up and going in September. Worcester County Cares for Seniors."

"This is the first I've heard of it. It wasn't mentioned on your ShowMe page." Nor represented by paperwork in Bette's workspace other than a collection of grocery receipts. "If memory serves correct there are more than sixty towns in this county. The largest in the state."

"I don't know much about it because I don't sit in on those meetings." Bette wedged another cookie in her mouth and chewed thoughtfully. "So, uhm, you going take the job? Be our celebrity. Bring the whole shebang under one roof? Athletes do it all the time. I see them on TV. One day they're playing football. The next day they're selling foot cream."

I thought of the calls logged in the telephone's memory. "When I was with NPK, Gordon held production meetings in the store room of Wilfred Draperies. The curtain shop Loretta Fahey's family owns. Have you ever been there?"

"I was never invited."

I refilled our mugs. My thoughts were leapfrogging all over the place. The coffee must be caffeinated. "You previously said Gordon contacted you before Ella's body was discovered. Can you provide a little more detail?"

"Heh? Oh, I got it wrong. He called Friday. I told him she wasn't coming till Saturday. I didn't hear from him again until Monday. Then it was all cops and lawyers and reporters. He didn't want me to speak to anybody."

The room shimmied. "I thought you said you spoke to Gordon on Saturday and he told you she had missed the store opening."

"Did I? The reporters were driving us cuckoo. Grace took a swing at one because he stuck a mic in her face."

"Gordon didn't ring you at all on Saturday?"

"Nope. I saw the whole thing on the ten o'clock news Sunday."

"Earlier you said you'd just returned from grocery shopping. You hadn't been informed yet of her death. What did you think of the reporters in your driveway?"

Bette froze, unblinking. I counted to four and she still hadn't recovered. The question short-circuited her.

"Never mind. What can you tell me about Karen Putnam? Ella assigned her the task of monitoring Twister posts. Have you and she been in contact?"

Bette blinked with the change of topic. "The he-she with the hairy legs? Not my first pick. Wouldn't be my last. That was Gordon's idea because a couple of idiots insulted Ella's videos. He found out they were Twisters."

"Gordon chose Karen? Not Ella."

"I don't know who did, but they agreed on it. More power to him."

The guest bed would best be served by a blow torch. Overlapping urine stains on the mattress created flower patterns under the thin fitted sheet. I snooped inside the reach-in closet, not for clean bedding but because I could. Rock band tee shirts balled up on the floor hid creased shoes and cracked leather belts. Bland, oversized clothing dripping off hangers. Artist sketchpads protruded from the upper shelf. Pages of screaming faces, mutant animals, and fantastic vehicles spoke of teenage angst. The last pages of the third pad were devoted to penis drawings. None of the sketches were signed. A few had dates. Arielle would've been twelve or thirteen. This might explain her choice of friends. Possibly the pee stains too, which I planned to double wrap for my protection.

The low, exposed joists of the basement ceiling would induce claustrophobia in even the hardiest of folk. A vinyl tablecloth covered a busted freezer chest by the stairs. Bald car tires flanked the bulkhead door. Auto parts and hand tools collected rust on crude plywood shelves and furnishings of yesteryears attracted mold elsewhere. The box the ice skates were originally packaged in found an eternal home here. I made for the laundry area at the other end of the basement and helped myself to two sets of sheets.

With the bed freshly made twice over, I indulged in a vape break while waiting to speak with Monica. Uncle Ned and Aunt Ethel were hosting this year. Monica promised not to spray paint her hair or wear pasta necklaces. Right about now, she'd be feeling naked, alone, and completely out of sorts.

Sticky chewing sounds and a burble of laughter hit my ear.

"Am I interrupting your meal? I could call back."

"Food's done. Fat and happy on the couch. How's it going with Betty Boop?"

I summarized the contents of the opinion pieces I had tracked down. "The Elizabeth Hornick who wrote of deficiencies in state-run mental health programs had a certain presence of mind this Bette seems incapable of. Also, Bette doesn't share our values. She served turkey."

"How do you not know that after all this time?"

I offered a weak excuse for my oversight. "We exchanged emails during her settling-in period. We were never chatty. She seemed adequate. My mind was elsewhere and, frankly, I couldn't have cared less whether she worked out or not. Instinct assures me Ella wouldn't have hired her. I believe Gordon did because she'd readily report back to him on Ella's doings. Quite a few calls from Wilfred Draperies have come in since Ella's death."

"Wouldn't it be kind of weird if Fahey wasn't calling her? Everyone's trying to figure out what comes next."

"Bette and Gordon played push-pull with Ella's schedule. Ella didn't have a boyfriend, by the way. She created a separate organization that delivers meals to the elderly. Worcester County Cares for Seniors."

"An animal protection league that serves humans?"

"They're not Twisters."

"Okay. Find the kitchen and you'll find her new besties. What'd Bette have to say about psycho boy? The kid with the camera."

"Jared Libby? I'll ask once I hang up. Have any of the Glories sent the pictures I requested? It was horrifying to learn at our meet-up they were harassed before us. If we can link the same individual to sabotaged events for both groups, it might confirm a face."

"Speaking of new faces, what's up with Ms. Putnam? Still can't get her and Claire as a couple out of my head. Eww."

"Bette claims not to know her. How Karen knew of the threats Ella received is a mystery. On a different note, Manny Soto remains a terrible person. He claimed Ella made a movie in the spring. The story's a bit convoluted. A work-related party, Ella getting extremely drunk, and a possible suicide attempt."

"Whoa."

"Manny has low self-esteem and is prone to exaggerate. He could've fabricated a tale to draw attention away from his involvement in a drug-related incident. The retelling by others then transformed it into something vulgar. Ella might've filmed a public service announcement. I'd believe that. Humane

Society? Karen also mentioned filming. What are the odds both would choose to mention it as part of idle chit-chat?"

"We should find that commercial," Monica said.

"Can you put Adrian on it? A way to share the workload. Have him search January through June of this year."

"Adrian? I thought we weren't letting Compats in on this." Monica snickered. "Aww. I see. You got the hots for his brother too. Say no more." When I didn't say anything more, she added somewhat sarcastically, "Will you post pics of your holiday dinner?"

Chapter 14

M y mood, as well as my empty stomach, soured over beers and German
Whist. Despite claiming unfamiliarity, Bette picked up it easily with a
few practice hands and minimal follow-up questions. When I maneuvered our
conversation to Jared's current whereabouts, she won a trick to claim a trump
card.

"Everybody knows what he did was wrong. But somebody's gotta cut the kid
a break. How many people you know are all that smart when they're teenagers?
Jail isn't exactly a picnic. I know you shouldn't blame the parents, but where
the shoe fits. That girl had trouble written all over her. Mom in prison. No rules
or routines. If she wasn't doing Jared, she would've dragged some other unlucky
bastard down with her."

Bette's blatant disregard for Cassandra was astonishing given her former
occupation. The girl had been mentally ill and no stranger to state agencies.

I won the next three tricks and—feeling superior—launched into a history
lesson during round two. Bette, I felt, needed to know what I already knew.
"Much had been written about Jared after the trial. So much so, I wouldn't be
surprised to learn of a made-for-tv movie based on his life. Someone recently
brought him to my attention, so I ventured a little deeper into his troubled past.

"At the age of five, he tormented a kindergarten mascot, a hamster named
Sunny, by biting off its two front legs. He refused to participate in school
counseling or private therapy and entered ninth grade as an unrepentant bully, a
child most likely to set fire to the school cafeteria. This, according to an
unnamed close family friend. His parents, Josh and Amelia, fought over his care,
behaviors, and future while struggling with reoccurring job loss and the needs

of his three younger siblings. That sad life history could've worked in his favor if handled differently at the trial."

"Well, it wasn't, was it?" Bette said.

"No," I agreed. "White Mountain Vegan Support leaked photos of the backyard burial pits to Canard Daily News. The public sheds few tears when wildlife is killed by those paying for the privilege. Yet when the victims are considered family members the outrage can be explosive."

"Bah. He didn't go to jail for gutting somebody's pooch. He shot up a bunch of cars and road signs. That's what pissed people off." Bette played her last hand, winning round two with seven tricks to my six. She scooped the cards off the table. "That was fun. Let's do it again!"

I begged off another round wishing to end this miserable day and took the conversation to bed with me. Jared's trial five years ago played out during the summer of Mother's cancer treatments. The Atlantic Ocean could've swelled up to swallow Bermuda and I'd have been none the wiser. Ella's momentary involvement proved monumental. To my knowledge, her role was never publicized. So many questions.

A melatonin pill lulled me into three hours of nothingness from which I awoke discontent from the misspent holiday. The mundane menu was predicted. The lodging and company were surprisingly dismal. My nose, ears, and fingertips were cold to the touch from the sixty-five-degree thermostat setting. The carpet, undoubtedly, harbored dust mites. Grace was fully capable of puncturing one or more of my car tires. And Aggie, I believed, was capable of shitting on the driver seat. On and on, my thoughts clouded with consternation.

What had Boynton discovered thus far? What were his avenues of inquiry? My knowledge of the workings of police detectives was limited to television shows Grandpa Bernie and I watched. Most were lucky rather than clever. What would a famous TV detective make of Bette and Ella's detached work relationship? What of Bette's elegantly crafted newspaper pieces? Of Ella's desire to quit Twin Sister and NPK to feed the elderly? Of all the other illogical facts or niggling details I've uncovered? Like the pair of cracked leather ice skates stored in the dining room office. Oh my . . .

The basement stairs snagged my socks on my flight down them. I tore a fingernail spinning off the bottom post. Knowing where to look shortened the search. The skate box sat on a wooden plant stand behind a tall oscillating fan. I pried off the lid to reveal hanging files neatly labeled with WCCS tabs. The cooks were identified on numerous forms. As a bonus, the box held a bound copy of Jared Libby's trial transcript wrapped in a plastic grocery bag. A silent scream of satisfaction echoed between my ears.

Thank you for being a jerk to your mother Arielle. Much appreciated.

I awoke at first light fixated on finding Francis and Vanessa Norelli, head chefs for Worcester County Cares for Seniors. I shelved yesterday's grumblings feeling very much like a child on Christmas morn, full of anticipation of good things to come.

I dined on a meager breakfast of peanut butter toast smeared with leftover cranberry sauce before plugging into my tablet. WCCS boasted a basic, no-frills website. Their mission statement and list of services were interspersed with photos of well-kempt seniors grinning over plated food. Ella's name and image were glaringly absent. Gordon had multiple reasons to be displeased by the prospect of its success. The primary one being Ella intended to give away that which he sought to sell.

A knock rattled the bedroom door. Bette poked her head in. "Coffee?"

"I took the liberty of making a pot."

"Good. We're practically family."

I finished packing before joining Bette at the kitchen table. In a spray of cookie crumbs, she said, "Did you give it some thought? Us partnering up. Us against them."

"Them?"

"You know who I mean. Scared the crap out of me having the cops asking questions. I'm just doing my job here. I like being left alone. Gordon and Loretta might not keep me on with Ella gone. You could use me. One big happy family. All of us pulling together."

A repeat of yesterday's suggestion expressed with a bit more vigor. How to capitalize on her willingness to be a team player occurred almost instantly.

"I must speak with Jared Libby. I need to assure myself he wasn't personally involved in Ella's death. Can you make that happen?"

"Don't waste your breath. He's a loser. A nobody."

I pulled the copied newspaper clippings from my purse.

Bette refused to look. "I thought the kid was being bullied. If it sells, print it. Whatever way the wind blows."

"Clearly, something changed your mind since then."

"They swept the dust out of the closet, didn't they? Nobody could find one good thing to say about him. It's not his fault he turned out so bad. I'll stick to that. The system failed him. He did the rest."

Neither right nor wrong, Bette's morals found a midline.

"I'd appreciate an introduction."

"Why are you looking at me?" she asked.

I tapped the papers. "That was written by Elizabeth Hornick, a retired social worker. It includes information not covered in other local papers."

"Geez."

A young woman in a Bruins jacket wrangled an empty stroller, a beagle puppy, a tyke bike, and a squirming toddler in a failing quest to cross a side street. A black minivan waited on the parade. We did the same unnecessarily as we were on an adjacent street. This, a silly example of Bette's passive-aggressive reluctance to introduce me to Jared Libby. Every nerve ending in my body zinged in anticipation of startling, discoveries within the hour.

"How did you find Jared?"

A too-sharp left turn knocked my head against the window glass.

Bette eased off the gas pedal. "The Libbys gave up trying to sell the house and put it in Tiffany's name. If the kids can keep their heads above water, there's hope for the baby."

Bette went on to describe Jared's girlfriend as "young", "quiet" and "not a whole lot going on". Tiffany worked as a cashier in a dollar store. Within a few months of dating Jared, she became pregnant and gave birth to a daughter,

Hailey, last year. Jared found employment in town at Marsha's Frozen Yo-Yo Gurts. He's been busy since his release from prison.

The car slowed near a stretch of woodland and dropped into the rutted drive of a gray cape house with crooked black shutters. Rows of silver flower whirligigs improved a swath of dirt in the front yard. A graveyard for gnomes courtesy of the dollar store. A darker shade of gray paint, applied by a lazy hand to sections of the siding, poorly disguised a multitude of holes and cracks in the vinyl. The damage most likely occurred before the trial. Whether caused by blows or bullets was difficult to discern. Rocks were free and bullets were plentiful. For some demented folk, the animal remains found in the back yard were a disappointment, undoubtedly the only reason the house still stood.

"Perfect timing," Bette said as red 4x4 truck with an empty gun rack trundled in next to us.

A gaunt woman exited the passenger side cradling a baby to her hip. This would be Tiffany Grajewski, age twenty. A sweater stained with milk puke and jacket cuffs tarnished with grime spoke of priorities. The ill-fitted jeans showing off white tube socks revealed money was tight. Both belonged to Jared. I noted he was shorter and stouter when he trailed behind his family. Bette motioned for me to leave the car and join Jared on the stairs.

"This is Danni Mowrey, the lady I told you about," she said to him.

Jared flexed his nostrils in distaste. A camouflage baseball cap hid dark, greasy hair slicked around his ears. That shininess ran over the angry acne on his cheeks and chin. The rest of him was rumpled in brown twill and in need of a few wash cycles with a strong detergent.

"Do I know you?" he asked.

"We've never met. However, you've heard of my friend, Ella DeMarco. She was murdered recently."

The pitted face swung back to Bette. "Why the fuck you bringing her here?"

"She's paying forty bucks to ask you a couple of questions, numb nuts. Do you want the money or not?"

Jared pocketed his indignation and allowed us inside his home. "Make it quick. I got stuff to do."

When the rest of the Libby family moved on, they left this life behind. The red and brown paisley furnishings were heavily burnished with use. Framed embroidery, odes to hunting and fishing, hung above eye level on two walls. Last year's Christmas photo of Jared, Tiffany, and infant Hailey sat on the fireplace mantel. The baby was wrapped and bowed like a holiday gift in sparkling paper. They all smiled broadly for the mall photographer.

"Why do you think you went to jail?" I began.

Bette brushed crumbs off the couch and sat. Tiffany brought Hailey to the kitchen. Jared picked at a scab on his cheek, thinking.

"Lawyer sold me out." Jared rubbed his fingertips together to indicate money was involved. "We only did it because people were riding our asses."

"What 'people'?"

"The subscribers, dummy. We were gonna get outfitters to put up links to hunting gear. Knives and shit. Scent lures. Diaphragm calls. I never did much hunting. They freaking move too fast. But I can dress a kill. I'm pretty good at it."

I closed my eyes seized by a vision of the senior golden retriever. Jared misjudged the position of its sternum with the first swipe of the blade. The dog thrashed. A second lower cut parted its abdomen and the lustrous blonde chest stopped quivering after Jared plunged fingers inside to unmoor kidneys, spleen, stomach, and other organs, which he laid out on the pavement as he cut them free.

". . . do bad things because I bitched about Degnan's dog barking keeping me up. 'You know what to do.' 'Shut that dog's mouth.' These could be my customers. I figured nobody's gonna pay me to be their front man if I can't do the job. Fuck you and your stupid face! You weren't there."

Bette rocketed off the couch drawing us into the next room. "Got water? I could use some water. I have to watch the time. I got to pick Arielle up."

Tiffany labored in the dining area scrubbing crushed crackers off the highchair tray. A wet circle on her blue sweater marked cleaned-up vomit. My eyes darted over dinged furniture, yellowed doilies, and the black barrel of a rifle resting against a corner cupboard. Behind Tiffany, U-shaped kitchen with doorless cupboards revealed a skimpy inventory of boxed goods and plastic dishware. Family photos of happy events feathered the refrigerator: chubby siblings stuffed into swimsuits, dad posed with a hooked trout, mom blowing out candles on a cake. Front and center, a photo of younger Jared flashing inverted okay symbols while crowding another boy's head out of the picture. Both wore Puke For Petey rock band tee shirts. Good times.

"Why didn't anybody lock up *your* buddies?" Jared asked. "Why didn't nobody go after them?"

A squint seized my left eye. "You believe undercover videos exposing abuse are more offensive than you committing similar atrocities?"

Jared grinned. "Looks like the cops threw the wrong guy in jail."

Tiffany pushed a glass of water into my hand before fleeing again with the baby. Flakes of dried milk floated in the water.

"Cassandra held the camera for you."

"I never said that. You tell me where I said that."

"Cassandra's cat snuff work predates yours. Torturing pets. The mutual hobby that brought you two together. Cassandra told roommates you were her boyfriend. She found the public response to your early videos exciting and wanted a more active role in crafting new ones. Neither of you had a car. How did you secure the dogs?"

"If we're gonna go there you need to pay me."

I fanned the money on the dining table adding two five-dollar bills. Bette sat down with an *oomph*. Jared took the opposite chair and commenced picking at his acne.

"Tell me about the wildlife buried in your yard. How did you kill those animals and transport them here? Without a car. Who helped you?"

"Why did anybody have to help me?"

"No car. No driver's license for that matter."

"Doesn't mean I don't know how to drive. Maybe I took my dad's car. Maybe they came right up to me while I was working on my tan." Jared pointed his chin at a window overlooking the backyard. The ground dipped and swelled under a blanket of weeds. The yard never recovered from the excavations.

A different topic. "What do you know of Marlene Scott?"

"Cassie talked about her. That girl loved her momma."

"Marlene abandoned Cassandra in infancy. Her grandmother raised her. There was neither time for love nor opportunities to create memories to paste to a refrigerator."

"I love meatballs. They don't have to love me back. The feeling's real."

I pounded a fist on the table. The water glasses jumped. Jared jerked upright. Hailey wailed from a bedroom above. Bette yawned nervously.

"What do you know of Marlene's letters to Ella?"

"Never knew she could write."

"You and she and Cassandra and Ella. All acquainted." A guess.

"Marly didn't want money. A job and a place to live when she got out. They cleaned her up in jail. She promised to be there for Cassie."

"Cassandra never saw her mother in prison and was long dead before Marlene was granted parole. You had visitors when you were incarcerated." Another statement I had yet to verify.

"Dad came to shoot the shit. Check up on me. My mom wouldn't. She saw me digging the holes. Even brought me soda when it got hot. What'd she think I was doing? Planting corn?"

The older Libbys were probably delighted Jared played in the yard when off his medication. It kept him away from defenseless, younger siblings.

"Three years incarcerated. None of your fans came to see you? Pity. Marlene was in prison throughout your relationship with Cassandra. When did she first know of you? You communicated, yes?"

"What'd you mean? Like send her a letter or something?"

Bette's glass toppled. Water sluiced over the table. Jared's big hand shot out to claim the money. "I'm done talking. I have to clean my guns." He cast his eyes on the rifle.

Bette bolted from the table slamming the storm door on her flight to the car. Defiant, I walked with steady steps from the house.

On the return trip to Barre, Bette was near tears. "He's mean and stupid. I'm sorry Ella was ever involved with that subhuman thing. I should've said no when she brought it up. I should've told her it wouldn't work. Why couldn't he leave the animals in the woods and save everybody a whole lot of grief?"

"Why did you get involved?"

"I felt sorry for him. Same as Ella. For his whole life that kid couldn't get a break."

"What, exactly, did Ella do for him?"

A cloud passed over Bette's face. "I think she wrote to somebody to get him released early."

Chapter 15

T he Holden address came from a WCCS expense report. The drive easterly
on Route 122 and 122A was an Impressionist's dream in autumn with
long stretches of woodland set ablaze by vibrant orange, apricot, and lemon-
colored leaves flaring against cerulean blue skies. This late in the season the
landscape was clothed in murky grays and greens of a swamp in winter.

The Norelli home was an anomaly in a neighborhood of capes and four
squares. Whether the current owners were pretentious or dedicated rehabbers—
I was soon to find out. The lavender mansion, spectacularly embellished with
red and cream fretwork, boasted stained glass inserts, and fishtail shingles. More
dollhouse than family residence and the children had played rough with it. A
blistered, wrought iron fence encircled a front garden ordered around a sunken
flagstone walkway. I pressed the doorbell half-expecting a petit, parlor maid in
a lace cap to be on the other side. Rather, the caretaker was a dark-skinned
woman with coppery Senegalese braids. Her hand-knit sweater and puffed
trousers were as much an artistic statement as the gilded rose wallpaper and
fluted wood trim behind her. My face registered confusion.

"I don't like the wallpaper either," the woman said, stepping aside.

"I was wondering why you still wore wool."

"Somehow, I thought you'd say that. Welcome, Danni. I'm Vanessa
Norelli."

Vanessa led me to a sparsely furnished sitting room. The gold velour
furniture with hand-carved rosettes and sat low to the floor. The red in the
Persian carpet matched the billowy drapes hanging over turret windows. The
piecrust table between us oriented our gaze toward a scrollwork oak
mantelpiece. I felt tremendously underdressed for this rarified setting.

"Would you like a cup of tea?"

"Thank you, no. I don't wish to take up too much of your time. Just a few questions as I stated in my email."

Vanessa smiled. "Francis and I work from home often. Today is his office day otherwise he'd be here. He'd like to meet you. We're very, very sorry about Ella. She was a remarkable woman. A good and kind person. She could find humor in bad situations. I couldn't have asked for a better friend and mentor." Vanessa squeezed my arm in a warm, strong grip. The contact triggered a ripple of emotion. The air in the sitting room became thick as cotton. Tears collecting on my lashes, and my nose, I feared, would drip.

"I told you something of my interest in projects Ella was involved in. WCCS is intriguing. What can you tell me about the organization?"

"Big question. Where do I begin?"

"Several organizations in the county already feed the elderly. Whose idea was it to create a new one?"

"Mine. I have family in Louisiana. All that good cooking has cut my family in half. Every other time we speak it's an invite to a funeral. When Francis and I moved here four years ago, we borrowed hand tools from our neighbors. We returned the kindness with home-cooked meals. Many of them are grandparents and suffer from the same health problems as my family. They were interested in eating better and liked the food."

"This program feeds your neighbors?"

"Some of them."

"I was under the impression WCCS is a county-wide program."

"Not in the way you're thinking. Let me say, we're not vegan. We don't have all the answers and we haven't started asking *those* questions yet."

"Just to be clear, you rent a commercial kitchen to prepare meals for your neighbors in a barter-type exchange for the use of hand tools?" My left eyelid spasmed. I sat in profile to hide it.

"We turned it into an elder care program available to any senior in Holden."

"A 501 non-profit."

"Yes. We started in August and have eighty-two clients. Mostly low-income residents who struggle to provide for themselves."

"How did you come to know Ella?"

"We met last winter at a cooking demo in Worcester for *Flowering Foods*. Francis and I stayed behind to pitch the idea. No oil, no added sugar, and very little salt. Ella loved it. Before that, Francis and I scoped out every truck stop in the state. Our initial plan was to retail plant-based entrees for eight dollars in their grocery sections. Ella heard us out and had a different idea."

Thoughts rolled in. "Ella personally funded WCCS," I said slowly. "Subsidized it. I'm not wholly ignorant of the program. I reviewed some of its preliminary paperwork this morning. You're connecting more dots for me. What do you think will happen now that Ella's gone?"

Vanessa blew out a shaky breath. "She provided for us in the short term. Coached us on fundraising. She was our backbone, our Chairman of the Board. Ella wanted this to succeed and pay for itself. Eventually."

"You and your husband are employees. Chefs?"

"If we expand, we'll bring in more people."

"Do you know Bette Hornick?"

"Ella's bookkeeper. Bette's our papermill. That's what Francis calls her. She always has something for us to sign. She's a bit different, isn't she?"

"How so?"

"Ella had a way with people. To know her is to want to give her your all. Bette is, hmmm, detached. A separate entity. Ella could be respectful and kind to anyone. You grew into your best self by spending time with her. Bette was unaffected."

I smiled in agreement. "Different topic. Would you happen to know if Ella had a boyfriend? Someone special she met with when out this way?"

Vanessa hiked an eyebrow. "I doubt she had the time. She was always driving from one place to the next. Her manager insisted she hand-deliver things that could've been mailed. Face-to-face meetings instead of emails. He kept her insanely busy. Like he was trying to wear her down. What's the point in that?"

"He was forcing her to choose." I slapped my thighs and stood up signaling the end of our talk. "I'm grateful for your time."

"Uhm, you still haven't said why you're *really* here." Vanessa was more astute than I realized.

Eager to leave, I quickly recast my meeting with Gordon as a job interview for Ella's role at NPK. Eminently believable as it was partly true.

Vanessa nodded in all the right places. "I'll have Francis call you."

"I'd like that."

Out on the flagstone path, I sensed movement in an upper window. I maneuvered my car into an awkward three-point turn to allow for an extended view of the house without craning my neck in an obvious fashion. Vanessa stood in the doorway. A silhouette shifted behind the lace curtain of second floor bedroom window.

The answering machine beeped calling attention to itself. Louis and his family had recorded a holiday greeting yesterday. Nieces and nephews yelled a joyless "Happy Thanksgiving!" in the background. Conversations at Sammons gatherings breached pain thresholds, mine and theirs. Attitudes and opinions were like broken seashells. One walked barefoot over a beach festooned with them to reach waves of open-mindedness. None of us could manage it.

Had Bette not invited me, I would've attended Gray Birch's celebration. Feeding the animals pumpkins and heads of cabbage was always amusing when the goats were involved. Calling it to mind dredged up a dark thought. Do I leave it unexplored and be content in my ignorance or should I act and satisfy my curiosity? Both had consequences. Eddie Peck owned a farm a quarter-mile from Gray Birch. A skilled carpenter, he was Joan's first choice when things required mending beyond Mike's skillset. Eddie answered my call with a gruff hello before I could choose ignorance.

We discussed the cost of shavings, the price of hay tedders, how many acres he leased from Joan Doyle, and whether he received a three-hundred-pound pig named Fanny last winter as partial payment for the tractor shed he had built for her. Eddie was as straightforward with his answers as I was with my questions. The pig was delicious, he said.

Ella found out.

I cleaned up the glass I smashed in the sink, applied a bandage to my cut finger, and got back to my To-Do List. Today's action item was to follow-up with Melinda Ault at Biscuits and Bows shelter.

Melinda was manning the reception desk. "8 Ukridge Road," she said.

"Good afternoon. How was your Thanksgiving?"

"Shut up. 8 Ukridge Road." Melinda hung up.

One blink later I realized it was Piffles' home address and silently thanked her. Unsettling noises followed my gratitude. *Thump. Creak, creak, creak.*

Low grunts permeated the thinly insulated wall between my desk and the upper hall. Either someone was noisily delivering my online holiday shopping or Mr. Peebles' odiferous cooking lured a wild beast in from the cold. I fetched the umbrella from the kitchen and nearly tripped over three file boxes placed on the hall doormat. A man in a tan London Fog coat stooped at the bottom of the stairs to pick up the fourth box.

My "Hey!" boomeranged up to the third floor.

Reese twitched. "I'm cleaning her house. Getting rid of junk."

"You're raiding her home and she's not even buried," I snapped back.

Reese hefted the last box up the stairs and dropped it at my feet. Something delicate tinkled. The volume dropped on Mr. Peebles' television set. I motioned for Reese to haul the boxes inside.

"We have people coming out to assess the property. She owed money. Credit cards. Charge accounts. Loans."

"'We' means Gordon and yourself?"

"She'll be sticking it to everyone. You're not inheriting NPK. It's my headache now."

Money-grubber. I reined in my disgust. "When will she be buried? You haven't placed a notice in the paper. There's been nothing at all in the newspaper. Oh, wait. I did read your interview."

Reese sat at the kitchen table and unfolded a piece of paper. "We'd like to publish this in the Globe. We're doing a private church service on Tuesday. You're invited to the luncheon after at my house. Noontime."

I glanced at the eulogy I posted to Twin Sister's ShowMe page. *How did he obtain it?* "I wrote that for people who cared about her, not her family."

"Walter's coming up from Costa Rica. We're not sure how long he's staying. He doesn't travel well without mom."

"Right. And Mimi never travels. Italy. Croatia. Greece last year? Those pics I didn't see. He hasn't been back since Marc was born. Too late for apologies."

Reese jiggled coins in a pocket. "We're going to televise an appeal for information. The Crime Stoppers tip line is a joke. Whackos keep calling in. Some are saying she faked her death and took an undercover job as a cashier for Whole Foods."

"I'm sure the investigative process is more complex than that." My palms felt damp.

"What process? They don't have any other plan." *Jingle-jingle-jingle* in the pocket.

"You'll turn the appeal into a circus act. Gordon will make it a commercial for NPK. If you're intent on making a spectacle of her murder, why not televise the church service too? Bad publicity is still publicity and may drive traffic to NPK's site. All that morbid curiosity to be satisfied. By now he and the lovely Loretta can cry on cue for the camera. You and Nadine should practice."

Reese started from the chair. It stuttered on the floor. "Always have to go there. Don't you? You need a shrink for your anger issues."

The shiny crescent scar under my third knuckle whitened. I traced a finger over the puckered skin. "You left a tooth mark."

A forced calm reddened his ears. "Let it go. We were both drunk and out of our minds."

"I had just buried my mother. I was grief-stricken. You were drunk and full of yourself. Good to see the crown holding up. A pity there's only one."

"Grow up and get over it. For fuck's sake."

"All I ever wanted was a sincere apology."

Reese clutched the table's edge. "Coming here was Gordon's idea. He said we should be civil. He wants us to stop the hate speech and work together. The past is history. Nobody's perfect when they're a kid."

The kid comment struck a nerve. A dental filling without Lidocaine. Young Reese excelled at malicious creativity. Squashed tent caterpillars fouled Ella's dresser drawers. A beloved guinea pig was found frozen and wrapped in tin foil in the garage. Stovetop cleanser emptied into Ella's shampoo bottle. Had their mother been a tad less jealous herself, she might've quit her denial and defense strategy before the shampoo incident sent Ella to the emergency room. Anger issues? Hardly.

I dialed my anger down to a slow simmer. "Why is the eulogy of interest to Gordon?"

"The police think she was robbed by a drug addict she let into the house. A friend. The eulogy might make people think twice and start talking."

"Why 'drug addict'? Where did that come from?"

"The police found cocaine hidden in the tank of her toilet."

Speechless. I could barely summon my voice. "I want permission to walk through her home one last time."

"The house is locked."

"Lend me the key. I'll lock up when I'm done."

"We cleared out the valuables."

"This is about me being in a place special to her and saying goodbye. I'll meet you there Monday at six. We'll walk around together so you can keep me from thieving. Let me say my goodbyes and you can have the eulogy."

"Monday. All right. Okay." His tone was less than okay.

At the door, I asked, "What did Ella film in the spring? A commercial? A travel segment for her channel? A public service announcement?"

Reese stopped short. "What?"

"Mentioned in passing. I'm curious."

"Uh. The movie. Went belly up in April. They filmed on a farm west of Worcester. That's all I know. No one's ever going to see it. Not all her ideas were good ones. My father's the same way. Thinks he has all the answers when he doesn't know the questions. Ella spent too much time answering questions no one asked."

I watched him leave, giving silent thanks my stepsister didn't intentionally strive to be a malicious bitch. The cocaine discovery shocked me. Unpacking the boxes might stop my hands from shaking.

Ella dotted the I in my name with a smiley face when writing it on the file boxes. I could easily guess their contents. Small businesses seeking endorsements on NPK often sent samples of hand-crafted housewares. Keen to support them, Ella and I would find clever ways to use the finely wrought utensils, loomed linens, and hand-tossed ceramics as props in photoshoots. Gordon had a tantrum. Everyone pays for product placement with no exceptions.

After my departure from NPK, Ella continued the practice. She never quit gaming Gordon.

Each of the four boxes contained office supplies and junk drawer finds. I reached into one liberally peppered with cake crumbs and gum wrappers to pluck out a shoelace and fantasized strangling Reese with it. A knock on the hall door came as I was studying a business card for Raymond Semple, a private investigator, found lying amongst the rubbish. Reese returning? I launched myself at the door faster than I could frame an appropriate expletive.

"Hi sweetheart," Louis said.

Carrie's windblown curls bounced near his shoulder.

"Come inside, please."

I gestured toward the couch studying Louis from the corner of my eye. His once fair hair resembled dirty sidewalk snow. The skin he wore fit like a cheap suit. Mother would be greatly disappointed to see what's become of him in the few years since her death.

"We missed you yesterday," he began. "Everybody asked why you weren't there. Cheryl talked about Ella and all that business. We all understood. You're having a rough time."

"Yes. Thank you. Can I offer you coffee? Tea? I'm afraid I'm shy of snacks to serve with it." One way to shorten their stay.

"Don't bother. Carrie and I are going shopping. Black Friday specials." His cheeks drew back like curtains. "Aunt Lisa's inviting everyone to her house for Christmas. She's going all out. Getting a ham and a turkey. Uncle George'll be on a ladder this afternoon wrapping lights around the pear tree out front."

Ms. Huxley rolled her eyes in a practiced, attractive way. "Good lord. I hope she doesn't tack red bows to it." Carrie wore an off-the-rack charcoal pantsuit nipped and tucked to better fit her slight frame. I had every faith, in time, nips and tucks would dominate her world.

"I'm not sure I can attend. I have a packet of invites to respond to."

"Gotcha," Louis said, a string of spittle dangling from an upper tooth.

"Well, if you'll excuse me," I flexed a finger at the boxes, "Reese DeMarco made a delivery."

"There's another reason why we're here." Louis shifted on the cushion; his lips crimped into a bloodless blue line. "You were seen slugging a guy in a mall parking lot. People talk. It's been circulating Saint Bridget all week. How's that going to look for Carrie? For all of us?"

Carrie batted her eyelashes. "I don't believe a word of it."

An obvious connection occurred to me. I linked the image on Gordon's phone to Loretta and Carrie being on the same volunteer committee at the private school. Loretta had, after all, introduced Carrie to Louis three months after Mother's funeral. How very sad Louis chose to make it permanent by proposing.

"Not the worst of it," Louis went on. "Cheryl wasn't going to say anything because of what happened to Ella."

"What else have I done?"

"Last Saturday a bunch of you caused a ruckus at Andy's restaurant. Scared away a lot of customers. People are canceling reservations. Family doesn't do this to family, Danni."

My eyebrows shot upward. "Anthony is confused. Saturday afternoon I was at his house washing clothes. Saturday evening, I dined in Providence with a friend."

"Your people marched in like Storm Troopers during the dinner rush. Hit customers with signs. Used swear words. Yelled, 'Meat is murder', and danced around with ketchup on their shirts. Why do you hang out with mean people? Why can't we all get along like everybody else? You and I agreed to disagree and it's kept the peace between us. I'm asking you to do the same for Andy and Cheryl. One of the customers recorded the whole thing."

Louis provided the offending video. The camera lens bounced over two tables with six adults and two children facing a short line of protestors wearing Compassion Lives black tee shirts and cartoonish pig masks with bulging eyes and bucktoothed grins. Twilight Zone meets Disney. Salted Stone's mirrored bar shelves, chrome-trimmed counter, and pleather stools identified the establishment. The audio was a mix of static and traffic noises.

"This isn't something we would do," I said, pushing his phone away.

Louis was flush and gasping. His fingernails had a bluish tint. Confronting me was the bravest thing he's done all year.

"Tell Cheryl I'm deeply sorry. My sincere apologies to Anthony too. Assure them I'll look into it and if I find a member of Compassion Lives organized this, I'll take appropriate action."

"Andy lost business this week. He says it'll go through Christmas. Word of mouth is killing gift certificate sales. The staff is mostly part-timers. Can't earn a living if they can't turn tables. Tips feed their families and with Christmas around the corner . . ."

"Yes, of course. I'll take care of them. Tell Anthony not to worry. Christmas is still coming."

"That's great. I'll let your sister know we talked." The color returned to Louis' face.

I walked them downstairs to the hall door and watched both climb into Carrie's Cadillac. And there, dangling from the doorknob, was the key to Ella's house on a curly cord. Monica pocketed the key to the sliders. I only asked Reese to establish I was given permission to enter the home. Just in case.

Chapter 16

M illet Street was three homes closer to completion. Where bulldozers had leveled a forest and all of its native inhabitants stood a behemoth of a house in champagne yellow with six dormers and a four-car garage. Two nearby properties maintained the pace of square footage sufficient for boutique hotels. The Faheys bought in early when the homes were more modest in scale. Five dormers, a three-car garage, and a pool house kept them humble. The Fahey's steel gate opened after I announced myself to an intercom. I parked in their circular driveway under the watchful eye of a camera dangling from the ceiling of the portico. I tacked on a cheerful smile seconds before pushing the doorbell.

"Hello?" Macy stood behind an elaborate door fashioned from glass and scrolled iron. Age eight, and one half of a twin set, she resembled her mother with amber hair and freckles. I knew little about Gordon's three daughters. All were taught to make themselves scarce whenever company arrived.

"Macy! Goodness, you've grown. You may remember me. I'm Danni. I worked with your father and mother."

"I'm Mindy, not Macy!" The girl hissed in imitation of a rabid fox. Her ponytail flew down a wide hall to the back of the house. "Mom. Somebody's here! Some lady for Dad!"

Through a haze of palm prints on the glass, I studied an abstract painting on the second-floor split landing. Swirled rainbow colors on the left funneled into a black ball on the right from which singular rays of color wrap over the frameless edge. Order from chaos. Placed prominently for guests' appreciation, it appealed to the Faheys' egos. *How incredibly pedestrian.*

Loretta stepped into view. "Welcome. Good to see you, Danielle. You look fit." Svelte and stylish in maroon leggings and a cream tunic, Gordon's wife represented the high-achieving mother Cheryl idolized. Yet another reminder Cheryl and I emerged from different wombs. Loretta regarded the monstrous painting. "Fabulous, isn't it? We knew it had to be ours the second I saw it in an avant-garde gallery a friend introduced me to. Trojan Gallery. Have you heard of it?"

"Sorry, no. Ah, I'm somewhat pressed for time. Can you sit in on the meeting? I'd like to discuss a few things with you both." Just like that, the meeting Gordon requested was made mine.

"Me?" Loretta's forehead wrinkled. "I'll do what I can to help. Gordon's in the study. Please, go on through."

White was a bold color choice for a home with three children. Heel marks streaked tiles, gray fingerprints smirched light switches, trails of dirt matted silvery-white carpet. I quelled an urge to spritz everything with bleach including my hosts.

"Knock, knock," I said, opening a French door.

The study impressed guests with carved mahogany furnishings and built-in shelving which required a rolling ladder to access. Gordon's reading was limited to forecasts, contracts, and bank statements. The ladder hadn't moved in years and I was fairly certain the books were purchased at yard sales.

Gordon struck a scholarly pose behind the desk with reading glasses balanced on the tip of his nose. "Good evening. Sorry. Work, work, work. Can't seem to get away from it. Please, take a seat."

"I asked Loretta to join us. I understand she's still handling NPK's accounting. I have questions specifically for her."

Gordon covered his surprise. He wouldn't be leading the meeting. "You've thought about a second run with us. Excellent. The company needs your editorial skills and unique views. You brought a particular humanism to your work. I wish I had said that before and let you know how much we valued your contributions. Things got too heated at the end."

I flashed to a memory of a stapler arcing over the conference table in Wilfred's storeroom when Gordon was displeased with my 'unique views'. It missed my head by inches. A proud moment.

"Can I offer you a beverage? Is it too early for a beer?"

"Thank you, no. Before we begin, I'd like to see the picture you have of the puppy mill protest."

"I deleted it. I would've asked for your input the other day if you hadn't cut me short. I made a mistake in showing it to you. Wrong timing. Poor judgment. Call it—whatever you will. We're all deeply affected by what's happened and I should've known better."

Gordon feeling contrite was a new development. He wanted something.

"We've had trouble at the store we think is related."

"Such as?"

"Vandalism and theft. Someone started a fire in the dumpster. Deliveries went missing. Ugly language written on the building. The first incident happened two months ago. Loretta thinks bored teenagers are to blame. I believe it originated closer to home and took action. Someone new is monitoring *all* posts. Ms. Putnam. You'd like her."

"Karen Putnam monitors Twin Sister *and* NPK?"

"Good to see you're paying attention. There's hope for us yet. We've known Karen for a while. A good fit. She alerted us to the recipe trolling."

I looked over my shoulder. "Loretta, please, come in. No need to lurk out in the hall."

Loretta shuffled in noisily pretending she was newly arrived to the conversation and made a beeline for the chair next to mine. "What did I miss?"

"Danni and I were about to discuss the eulogy."

"Publish it. That's fine. Whose idea was it to keep Ella's service private?"

Loretta swiveled her chair knocking knees with me. "If we welcome in the public, we can't control what happens. We told her family it'd be a peaceful service. They deserve that. They've been through too much." Loretta's hair smelled citrusy. Close up, her eyebrows were too perfectly sculpted to be natural. I felt the stirrings of eyebrow envy.

"Loretta, what can you tell me about WCCS?"

"The food service? Ella's pet project. We're not involved in that."

"Not according to Bette Hornick." I kept my face open. Driving a wedge between Bette and Gordon seemed like the right thing to do.

"WCCS isn't affiliated with NPK," Gordon explained. "Ella volunteered her expertise to a couple interested in starting a meal delivery company. To be honest, I think she did it as a way to get back at me. The third book was dying on the vine. I kept her busy with podcasts and interviews to keep her image fresh. She might've resented it. I never begrudged her time off for charity work. I didn't dictate her friendships. WCCS becoming a nonprofit was her doing."

I heard pinging, possibly from blood vessels bursting in my head. *Ella hired you, not the other way around.*

"My two cents," Loretta said softly, "is that Ella was doing research. Gordon tossed around the idea of a frozen food line last year to ride the wave of popularity of NPK's health coaching services. I, for one, believe it will be a big seller. It's an exciting time to be part of NPK. We'd love to bring you back on board in whatever capacity appeals to you."

"Thank you. I appreciate the vote of confidence." I did not.

Loretta opened the lower drawer of a file credenza to hand me a mock-up for a Salisbury steak meal box. The vital wheat gluten steak bathed in mushroom-onion gravy accompanied by mashed potatoes, peas, and cubed carrots were artfully arranged on a black ceramic plate.

"Impressive."

"We have a pork roast and a stuffed chicken breast meal in the works."

Instead of asking whether the ingredients were organic and sustainably produced, I said, "Reese informed me I won't be inheriting Ella's interest in NPK. Have you spoken to him recently?"

Husband and wife seized up, neither blinking nor breathing, making this the second time I've short-circuited someone with a question.

"A discussion for another day, perhaps. As her manager, Gordon, you were involved in every aspect of her life. Every aspect. What can you tell me about the movie Ella made? Several people mentioned it in passing."

Gordon snapped alert first. "An art-house film. A way to test her acting abilities. From what she said it became too costly to complete on a pauper's budget. The entire cast could fit inside a Smart Car. I read the first few pages of the script. Awful with a capital A."

"Who produced it? Who invested in it? This wasn't something she'd tackle on her own."

"An independent project," Loretta blurted. "The movie didn't concern us or NPK. Ella devoted a month to it and then it was over."

"Which month?"

"Which month?" Loretta repeated.

"Sometime in February," Gordon supplied. "Don't ask the title. I doubt it ever had one. Why are you interested?"

"I'm interested in everything that mattered to her. Perhaps I should mention it in the eulogy as another of her accomplishments."

"God, no. Let it die in obscurity," Loretta said.

I slipped the box graphic into a pocket and patted down the other one for my car keys. "Thank you for meeting with me. I can let myself out."

My exit included a loop of the first floor. A corkboard in a kitchen writing nook served as a lost and found station. Girl Scout badges, soccer medallions, rubber wrist bands, business cards, and coupons protruded from its surface. Wallet-sized photos of the Fahey girls wearing Saint Brigid uniforms were pinned underneath. All were studio portraits using a marbleized yellow background. Amy, the oldest, had an olive complexion and a hawkish face. I had every confidence her parents would rectify her nose if it caused her any distress in high school next year.

Physically exhausted, I crash-landed on my bed. Behind closed eyelids, I boarded a train. All that was good and normal streaked by as greenery seen through open windows. The train was peopled with everyone I'd spoken to since Ella's murder. Some sipped cocktails. Others napped against pillows or read books propped in their laps. All but for the passing landscape were drenched in sepia tones. Monica, dressed in a Roaring Twenties era swim dress, ran barefoot down the aisle. Stuck in a time loop, she repeatedly charged toward me from the front of the car until, finally, her hands slammed into my chest knocking me backward into an empty seat. I hit an armrest and flopped into the aisle bouncing back into my own bed.

A glass of water and the novel on my e-reader failed to provide safe passage off the train. Every time my eyelids drooped shut, someone else wanted a go at me. Arielle Hornick, dressed as Mae West in a satin gown collared with gemstones, tried to stuff me out an open window. Manny Soto in Phantom of the Opera attire wielded a black umbrella as a sword. He jabbed and slashed and nearly succeeded in forcing me to jump from the platform between two cars. All the while, the train went *glug-glug-glug-glug* as it bucked over roots growing over the tracks.

Two trash barrels and a recycling bin blocked the end of Ella's driveway. Reese's cleaning crew missed yesterday morning's trash pick-up. The bins would remain until next Friday. A Subaru wagon blocked Joe Dorvee's driveway. Daughter Stacy continued to struggle with her marriage. Joe would be making breakfast for his grandchildren right about now. No one was out and about to see me shoulder a backpack and slip into Ella's backyard.

The house alarm hadn't been reset. Good. The scrap of plywood covering the busted mullion was missing. Bad. The key on the curly cord didn't fit the lock. I reached in through the rough opening to turn the inside knob. A trail of splinters led to the wood patch. Short screws allowed it to be punched in. I hoped this was the entirety of Reese's mischief.

Ella remodeled the house in fits and starts over the years. Walls came down, windows grew wider, the roof peaked upward. Honey pine cabinets and aqua blue sinks were torn out and replaced with white cabinetry and black granite counters. Ella withstood every inconvenience with an eye toward future happiness: dust, fumes, takeaway food, sponge baths, bunking with friends. This home was her personal sanctuary. And it had been violated, twice.

Reese's handiwork was self-evident. Ella's paintings, sculptures, televisions, and countertop appliances were now gracing his home. Her valuable cameras and lens were now well and truly stolen. Closed boxes and knotted garbage bags stacked on furniture indicated what Reese would keep and what he would dump. In the master bedroom, I dug through several bags retrieving two Joseph Campbell books Ella and I spent countless hours discussing and a black knit hat she favored for long ago, nighttime missions.

Whoever removed the police tape from the basement door had the good grace to mop up the blood ringing the dog hatch. The carpeted stairs had shed their covering. A painter's cloth covered bare plywood on the landing. Ground zero.

I descended the stairs and hopped over it. Unpainted cinder block walls and heather blue outdoor carpeting created an ugly backdrop for Ella's exercise room and the dogs' indoor play area. Bits of rubber and fuzz pried off tennis balls dotted the carpet. I tucked three furry, squeaky toys into my backpack. Rustic twig furniture, nautical decorations, and tribal rugs divided the basement into chapters of Ella's adult life. A life well-lived. Reese would dispose of everything.

At the landing, I lifted the edge of the canvas and lowered my hand onto the stained subfloor. Here was the Ella I could still touch. "I see you. I hear you. I'm so, so sorry. I'm trying."

Fat tears dripped from my chin. Pride and skewered righteousness drove us apart. Gordon's divide and conquer plan succeeded. I never hated him more than at that moment and pressed down on the wood feeling splinters prick my palm. The bloody finger mark on the wall ahead had been washed into a muddy swirl. Investigating officers would've taken a photo of it as first found.

A noise from above shook me from my misery. The echo of heels in the kitchen receded along the corridor to the master bedroom. I tiptoed up the stairs. Cool air seeped in through the open kitchen door. I held my breath, listening. A car swooshed by. Nothing more. Two of the home's three exits were visible. The third was in Ella's bedroom. Quickly locating a rolling pin or frying pan amid all of Reese's packing wasn't possible. Fleeing was safest, but I'd lose an opportunity to discover who and why someone else came here. I crept along the windowed corridor, each step as light as a cat's. The master bedroom door was ajar allowing a slanted view into the room. From the threshold, I saw the edge of the dresser and a lilac sweater carelessly tossed on the carpet. A sleeve pointed toward the slider. I inched forward and slammed into a wall.

Stars exploded behind my closed eyelids and my nose shifted sideways. My fall to the floor was incomprehensible. I woke amid a pile of jeans and tee shirts with a busted garbage bag draped over my thighs. I crawled until my feet were under me and scrambled to the front door. A dark-haired man in a parka stood beside the fire hydrant on the corner. He crossed the road and darted behind a clump of rhododendrons on Jenkins Street. I flung the door open and followed.

Beyond the shrubs, sidewalks and front yards were clear. Not another soul in sight. He was gone. The closest house, a faded turquoise bungalow, sat well back from the road under leafless trees. Under a flag pole, a bathtub grotto sheltered a Virgin Mary statue. A ring of fieldstones protected the upright tub from the ravages of a lawnmower should the mossy yard ever recover and require care. I skirted a white sedan to scale a wheelchair ramp to the door. A thickset woman heavily creased by frown lines regarded me from the safety of her living room. Her ragged crown of gray-brown curls, polyester smock, and discount store slippers spoke of a shrinking life. The smell of burnt toast and diapers confirmed it.

Overwhelmed by her despair and the recent smack to my face, I stammered, "Excuse me, ma'am. Do you know anything about the woman who lived across the street? Ella DeMarco."

"Someone killed her."

"I'm a friend of hers. Was a friend. Her parents are due to arrive from out of town soon. I feel awful not having more information to share with them. Have the police spoken to you?"

"The police walked all over the neighborhood. A day late and a dollar short. Wouldn't of happened if they patrolled the area like they said they would." The woman looked over my shoulder to the green house on the corner. "Me and Evelyn knew her better than the others. I'm Jeanne, by the way. Jeanne Whitman."

"Danni Mowrey. May I come in to speak with you?"

Jeanne found her manners and allowed me inside. "Ella used to make phony boloney for Jerry. He didn't like it much. We knew the family that lived there before she did. The Wallers. Ella would come over and ask us questions about them."

"How very nice. If I could—"

"I cried when she told me she was taking the cabinets out. The Wallers had three boys and two girls so I could see the carpeting going. The toilets. But those cabinets had a lot of life left in them. Guess what?" Jeanne clapped her hands together. "She gave us the kitchen!"

Perverse curiosity and the desire to be polite led me further into the house. An open door beside a China hutch revealed a man's thick arm slung over the side of a chair. The diaper smell came from this room and drifted into the kitchen where Ella's old pine cabinetry was disguised under a coat of gray paint. The battleship color matched the linoleum squares. An unfortunate choice.

"Jeanne, I need to use the john!" The voice came from behind the refrigerator.

Jeanne blushed. "That's Jerry, my husband. He hurt his back and can't make the stairs by himself. I have to help him."

"Can I leave my number? Call me if you think of something?" Given a soiled dinner napkin and a blunt pencil, I jotted down my telephone number. "Quick question. Did anyone else come to your house just before I arrived? A man in a parka?"

Jeanne bumped into a dining chair. "You're the first person."

Something clattered to the floor and shattered in the den. "Jeanne!"

Jeanne shuffled behind me effectively pushing me out the door. I lingered on the ramp to hear her shout, "What have you done now, you goofball? I'll mop it up. Sit still! For the love of Peter, Joseph, and Mary. Don't touch! There's glass."

From the sidewalk, I viewed Evelyn Pallotta's rear yard. Pounded earth circled four molded plastic slides and three green sandboxes. A split rail fence fortified with orange mesh imprisoned the play area. Either Evelyn did indeed entertain a host of grandchildren or she trained circus dogs in her spare time. On the walk to my car, I casually glanced down a marshy embankment. A blur of white showed through an impenetrable snarl of brambles. A closer look brought recognition. I cut the corner of a scruffy yard to push my way into the thickets and quickly realized my mistake. I dug the phone out of my pocket.

"Good morning, Detective. It's Danni Mowrey. I think I found the murder weapon."

Chapter 17

T he two officers who questioned me at the curb insisted I remain with my vehicle while they set up barriers. I had just finished placing several calls and was crunching on a breakfast bar when Boynton arrived in a black and white SUV. A forensic specialist followed to suit up in booties, gloves, and a thin white suit. Boynton confiscated my sneakers and gifted me a pair of paper booties. I sat in the Highlander's cargo hold dangling my cold, stocking feet over the bumper while eavesdropping on a handful of men from various departments. Residents collected on the sidewalks at the intersection. Joe and Donna Dorvee stood by the fire hydrant on the corner of Ella's property. The woman named Jeanne crossed to the side yard of the green ranch. Lavender-haired Evelyn Pallotta sidled up to her. I waved. They waved back.

Boynton was perturbed. I refused to allow an officer to search my backpack or my vehicle without a warrant. I also refused to go to the police station after giving a detailed statement. Boynton's request to take my fingerprints was denied. I hadn't touched the offensive object and questioned his motive. His failure to intimidate me rankled and it showed. Boynton left the edge of the culvert upon seeing me interact with the ladies. Perhaps he thought my mood too light for the gravity of the situation. "One more time, if you please," he said.

"It doesn't please me. How and why I came to this spot won't change simply because you're badgering me. I already told you of Reese's visit, the house key, of me being inside Ella's home. I thought the man who did this," I pointed to my slightly puffy nose, "had gone in that direction."

The chinchilla chin spasmed. "The key didn't work in the lock. You didn't remove the plywood from the door."

"Correct. The patch had been knocked into the kitchen. I reached in through the gap and turned the knob. Somebody should fix that."

"Do you understand why I need your prints?"

"Dust the house again and I'll be happy to provide them. The person who attacked me may have left prints behind."

We watched two officers stomp mud from their booties onto the sidewalk. They had searched the muddy banks and scooped up empty soda bottles and plastic bags, some of which contained dog poop. At least the watercourse was now clean.

"One more time."

"Can I see what you already wrote?"

Boynton flipped pages in his notepad. "Definitive History of Horse and Man. Gift from victim's parents. Last seen in the living room by Monica Jinks. A few days before the murder."

"Correct." I pointed to my phone. "She confirmed it not ten minutes ago. Ask her yourself."

"The supermarket," Boynton interrupted, "Leavitt Brothers. We looked into that."

"And?"

"A bagger reported the damaged cart pen. The manager preserved footage from a security camera. No plates on the car. You're skilled at jumping out of the way. You should've been squashed."

He meant it as a compliment. Yet it didn't cheer me. Attempted murder doesn't make me warm and fuzzy on the inside.

"You're free to go. Stay out of our way. For your own safety." Boynton walked back to the culvert.

I waited until Joe Dorvee wheeled away Ella's trash barrels before leaving.

My list of action items had grown ridiculously long. Something needed to be checked off. Number 17: Review Obscene Messages. To date, none had been transcribed. Nine were left on my machine between May 14th and October 16th.

I began with basic information: date, time, and duration. Each call originated from an untraceable device. The last three calls came in on my most recent nonpublished number. The culprit mimicked the terrified lows, bleats, and squeals of commonly butchered animals. Words uttered were boorish. "You're a cunt." "You suck cow dick." "I'll cut off your titties and deep fry them for supper." One began with, "Here kitty, kitty, kitty, me-OW!" A foretelling of the first cat delivered. Sadness guided my pen over the notebook page. Spanky is a deeply disturbed, young man.

I compared recording dates to events posted on Compassion Lives' ShowMe account. The deep fry message, accompanied by ear-piercing squeals, occurred the day after we gathered to bear witness outside at the gates of a slaughterhouse in Rhode Island. It would seem Spanky alternated personal appearances with phone calls. An outlier of a sort occurred after a disruption at The Fur Vault in mid-September. In that message, he implied he had been present.

"Woof. Woof. What does the fox say? Made the rich bastards choke
on lunch. Feed them Harvard boys. Get you some bump and grind
after the game. Uh-oh. Johnny's got a gun. Bang. Bang. Baby."

Johnny. John. *John?* A common enough name chosen by a delinquent who lacks originality—and scruples. I refused to read anything into it. Discounted like the letter drawn in Ella's blood. At least, until I could confidently assign meaning to them. The mark, most certainly, could've been a G. G for Gordon. One would assume.

Alicia Breault video recorded The Fur Vault event and sent participants copies. Mine was saved to a flash drive that had settled to the bottom of the rattan basket. Watching it again with new eyes might offer clues to Spanky's identity. I plugged it into the computer and steadied my pen.

Boston's Newbury Street bustled that sunny afternoon. Clerks primped mannequins in bowed windows decked with flower boxes dripping vinca. Diners in college sweatshirts hunched over bistro tables. Servers recited daily specials. Shoppers in cashmere sweaters and tall boots flitted like sparrows from one tony establishment to the next. All were too preoccupied with spending money to notice our group strolling along the sidewalk.

Fourteen of us gathered before the shop's tall windows. Inside, crystal chandeliers scattered prisms of light on racks of skins and the people caressing them. Monica remained outside claiming the sidewalk. The rest of us entered The Fur Vault to form a loose circle around a group of tufted benches. We removed black hoodies to expose the red-drenched collars of white tee shirts.

"Your coat had a face. A heartbeat. A life," I began. "Dozens of animals are killed to make a single jacket. Some live up to ten minutes after being anally electrocuted, defleshed, and flung into a waste pile. They die of shock, exposure, and blood loss. There's nothing prestigious in wearing the skins of tortured souls. Creatures born and killed to suit your vanity."

Eight would-be customers fled the store.

The lanky store manager unbuttoned his suit jacket and assumed a defensive posture with fists raised. "Stacy, call 911."

That set the tone for what followed. A withered patroness in a coyote-trimmed jacket struck Cindy in the chest with a leather carryall. Coyote's companion, a mustached woman in brown spandex, spit on Adrian. When he remained unflappable, she declared his mother was ashamed of him. A snowy-haired man in business khakis reached under his jacket. A woman in a matching gray windbreaker stayed his hand. "Ben, no, not here." He responded, "They're domestic terrorists. This shouldn't happen in America." A blonde teen in a maroon Harvard sweatshirt panned the showroom floor with his phone camera. His raised middle finger was locked into the frame. While this played out, two clerks in gaily patterned wrap dresses conferred in nervous giggles. The police weren't summoned.

Nothing usable here. Alicia focused the camera on us. Store patrons were captured with heads turned and features blurred. Outside, slim blocks of color indicated moving bystanders. I went back to puzzling together separate thoughts. Monica called at the midpoint of an epiphany.

"Are you on drugs?" she asked.

"Please answer your phone so I don't have to text you."

"Is Boynton going to call me?"

"Maybe."

"There's your answer. No." Monica blew cigarette smoke into the receiver. "You found the book in a ditch?"

"Across the street from Ella's home. It's the murder weapon. Per my eavesdropping, the book weighed more than five pounds and was dented. An officer said, offhandedly, the blood spatter suggests the killer used one hand to heft it. Meaning, a strong person. Probably male."

We took a long, quiet moment to process the information.

"Now what?" Monica asked.

"We keep at it. What frustrated me from the very beginning was Boynton's lack of curiosity in our work. Too few questions. Ours is a complex history of counterculture activities. We're bound to have enemies galore. Why would he *not* be intrigued and ask more questions?"

"The answers don't matter?" Monica suggested.

"Correct. Ella wasn't the victim of a robbery and she wasn't killed because of her activism. Something else is at play. An entanglement."

"Is this going to turn into a physics lesson? Do I need to break out a calculator?"

"Spanky's crimes were initially opportunistic. A broken bottle used to cut electrical cords. Props stolen from unlocked cars. Something changed. Stink bombs and deer urine ordered off the internet. Bolt cutters, paint, and sawhorses hidden in allies. He knew what to bring, what to steal, and when to attack. That requires advanced planning. How did he evade our sentries?"

"Is this a real question? Or a fake one where you give me the answer."

"Since May, our group events have either been interrupted by vandalism or referred to in a hate-filled phone message. Sometimes both. I'm inclined to believe the caller and the vandal are two separate individuals working in sync. Spanky and Stinky. The goal is to stop us from gathering, not to object to any particular activity. Furthermore, they do so with the help of a mole. Someone who acts as a lookout.

"We have to be extremely careful in what we say to group members. I'll continue to trust Adrian. The voice on the machine isn't a match for his and he lacks a mode of transportation. Anyone who remains at college for nine years because he can't decide on a career path lacks the ability to plan."

Monica responded with a gurgling sound, her inner gears shifting. "My brain is starving. This is all gobbledygook. Food and a movie. Ella's movie. Adrian found it. Pay-per-view."

The world tilted sideways. "It exists! I knew it! Gordon and Reese are horrible liars."

"Ya think?" Monica laughed.

"We'll watch it together. I'll make supper. First, you need to do something for me."

"Am I going to like it?"

"Probably not."

Monica grumbled her way up the deck stairs dragging three bags of trash and a face full of curiosity. I handed her a beer at the door and set the bags in the front hall. I didn't have the heart to tell her I decided against shifting through it.

"Mixed bean chili coming up," I said.

"You had me at beer." She clinked her bottle against mine. "What's the deal with the crapola?"

"Reese swept through Ella's home tossing out much of her life. He could've discarded something with hidden value. It's worth a look." Probably not.

We ate chili and corn biscuits at the coffee table. I loathed the idea of discussing the Salted Stone restaurant disruption. Monica is an obvious choice as a suspect. As my second-in-command, she also places the order for our tee shirts. She'd deny involvement. I'd lean toward disbelief. Already I was beginning to hate myself for doubting her answer to a question not asked.

I lowered my spoon. "I saw a vial of amphetamine salts in your bathroom. When did you start taking them?" The ADHD medication explained her dilated pupils, which I previously attributed to other drugs.

Monica gargled beer to clear a chunk of biscuit from her throat. "Started when I was thirteen. My parents told the pediatrician I was acting crazy. What teenager isn't?"

Of the thirty pills prescribed, nearly half were gone four days after refill. A tiny plastic sleeve in one of Reese's junk boxes contained seven, little blue pills. I stowed additional questions. Keeping the peace tonight.

The television's browser found Ella's movie, *How We Remember,* a psychological thriller with an R rating. "Anything I should know before we take the plunge?"

"We'll need something stronger than beer."

"Help yourself."

Monica selected bottles from the closet bar and fired up the blender in the kitchen. She returned with something orange and frothy in a water goblet. "Adrian said it came out three weeks ago. Film critics didn't 'get' the movie. Perverts gave it five stars. Manny Soto and Gordon Fahey produced it. EnablingU Films. Manny wrote it, supposedly. They raised $376,000 through crowdfunding."

The spoon slid from my fingers and cartwheeled off the coffee table.

"Reese DeMarco ponied up $15,000 on FlowMoney. He got a tee-shirt, a signed movie poster, a beer coaster, and an invite to a fancy dinner to meet the cast."

I hit my head on the edge of the coffee table searching for the spoon under the couch.

"Ella's the leading lady, Michelle Travors. Only—get this—the actor credited is Simone de Beauvoir. The Twisters have a Simone de Beauvoir. Adrian looked her up. Profile pic is a piglet eating a strawberry. Simone hasn't been active in a couple of weeks."

The lump on my head throbbed. "They all lied to me." I aimed an angry finger at Monica's glass. "Can you make me one of those, please? A big one. Very big." Monica crafted another cocktail, her version of an orange Creamsicle. The vodka fumes were ignitable. I held it aloft. "It's showtime!"

The movie's opening scene presented as a false start, a flashback. A girl ran through a black and white forest of autumn leaves. A voice-over giggled and panted in sync with her exertions for a full minute. I tensed waiting for something awful to happen. Monica grinned wide in anticipation. The next scene picked up the true timeline of the movie beginning with a cliched rained-upon cemetery. Ella's character, Michelle Travors, dressed as a vamp in black lace. Her parents and older brother had been killed in an accident of some undisclosed nature. A series of night scenes and rainy days emphasized her inner turmoil as she attempted to assuage her grief with an excess of sex, drugs, and rock and roll. Endless battles with her boyfriend, Roderick, and sudden job loss at a nameless company furthered her depression. Family photos and handwritten letters filled voids in the dialog. Memories of childhood mishaps, filmed in grainy black and white, surfaced repeatedly in Michelle's dreams increasing a sense of dread the audience was supposed to share. Orchestral music ebbed and flowed throughout to sway viewers' emotions in ways the mediocre script couldn't.

At the forty-five-minute mark, we paused the film for refreshments. Monica worked the blender. I switched to expresso and my e-cigarette hoping to fire up my intellect and uncover Ella's motive for starring in such a ghastly production. To her credit, Ella made a fair actor. The same couldn't be said of others. Missed cues, rushed lines, and melodrama were constant distractions. The movie wasn't crafted to be a blockbuster and it served no purpose from an activist standpoint. I tapped the Play button to resume.

Drone footage of snow-glazed pastures and a quiet town center foretold a major shift in Michelle's lifestyle. She accepted an invitation for an extended stay with an estranged, widowed aunt and her son, who ran a dairy farm. Bad acting accompanied torrential rain. Multiple black and white scenes of lowing Holstein cows caked in mud. Three cousins with questionable hygiene were introduced during an evening mass scene. What began as a revival ended as an exorcism in the church basement. Michelle's unwillingness to intervene during the torture of a delinquent teen marked her fall from grace. More disturbing were cringe-worthy scenes of incest amongst the relatives inserted randomly. Michelle's dream sequences soon parallel the grotesque deaths of the farm's animals. Eventually, local authorities were called in to investigate. Eight main characters became caricatures enmeshed in the depravity of their unraveling lives with displays of promiscuity, sadism, and egregious violence.

I paused the movie to scribble furiously. Monica rubbed her eyes as if to unsee the past thirty minutes. "So, Michelle humped her cousin on the stairs? Were those Ella's tits? Drowning the aunt in a bucket of milk, well, she was asking for it. What's up with the creepy cousins? I was totally okay with the guy having his nutsack ripped off by the milking machine. The girl? Over-kill beating her with her own severed leg. She would've bled out anyway. Killing a bunch of chickens in the yard with a pitchfork was totally uncalled for. The only thing worse was when they set the snakes on fire. Was that supposed to be a voodoo church scene?" Monica stopped only because she ran out of breath.

"In the scrotum-wrenching scene, Michelle was symbolically killing her brother, who was already deceased before the start of the story," I explained. "The midnight rendezvous with the cousin on the farmhouse staircase refers back to an incestuous relationship from her youth. All of that was foreshadowed in black and white mid-way through. Which, of course, makes you wonder how and why her family died at the start of the movie."

"Who were they chasing in the woods? An escaped pig or a man?"

"I think it's a police officer. The short pot-bellied man, who first came to investigate. Let's finish this."

With head bowed, I wrote through human screams, cow coughs, and sheep bleats until a final crash of music forced me to look at the screen. Michelle, blood-splattered and staring wildly, sat on the back seat of a police cruiser. A law officer circled the car failing to notice she had a long, thin rod in her hands. I recognized the device as a Cassou pipette used for artificially inseminating dairy cows. The music crescendoed when the officer slid behind the wheel. Michelle somehow drove the plastic rod through the seat to impale him. For fifteen excruciating seconds, he flailed about vomiting blood onto the dashboard and windshield. Bile burned the back of my throat. No closure in the movie's finale. Ella's character escaped, unpunished, after murdering six people.

Monica slapped her thigh. "Damn. Not a cop. The cow gored the preacher's son, who came to set the barn on fire."

"Ridiculous. He's barely a character. We saw him once when he winked at her during the snake service."

"No one watches slasher pics because they're logical." Monica laughed at my naiveté. "If they were, it'd ruin them forever. The best ones have a dozen people getting offed in rivers of battery acid. The think-pieces have nice people tortured for two hours in totally gross, messed-up ways. Oh, yeah. And a bunch of sex scenes. You know what? This movie is pretty good. A little bit of everything. Two thumbs up."

I slow blinked, owl-like—Monica was beginning to scare me—and paused the credits to jot down names. "These are the individuals Manny spoke of. They attended a party at a restaurant the night Ella allegedly attempted suicide. I understand why Karen Putnam mentioned the movie. She's a credited actor! I saw her in multiple roles. Karen Putnam as a woman. Kevan Blaine as a man. How stunningly odd."

"After seeing this I'm thinking Ella didn't have a reason to whack herself. This would've made a mint in the theater."

"Fiction pinned together with facts. I recognized inside jokes and family tragedies. Manny wrote this with Ella in mind. The vile, miscreant brother. Absent parents. Bumbling officers. The death of the aunt. The same background music for tender, animal care scenes *and* stunningly brutal, slaughter scenes. Upbeat and romantic. That's the activism. The wall she was attempting to tear down. Cognitive dissonance."

"Quite a stretch for a logical person like you. Did we watch the same movie?"

"We're back to entanglements."

One of Monica's eyelids comically spasmed, her version of twirling a finger beside her head in imitation of my idiosyncratic habit.

"I think an effort to derail the production occurred later. That would explain the lies. One or more of them was unsatisfied with the end result. A war waged between pivotal players? I know who was involved. They're all named in the credits. I can speculate their motives."

"Which are?"

I slouched into the couch cushions. "Money. Revenge. Hate. Control." I pulled the stolen library video off the bottom shelf of the coffee table.

Monica squinted at the minuscule print on DVD's jacket. "Looks stupid."

"A gift from Manny. His inspiration for the snake scenes?"

"Looks stupid." Monica tossed it back on the shelf.

Chapter 18

S o much for a day of rest. I achieved it if that meant being tired and sweaty while slogging around in shit covered boots with condensed breath soaking my muffler and icing my neck. Last weekend I scratched my name off Gray Birch's leader roster. I sensed the rapid advance of Olive's decline and didn't want to spend my limited time here shepherding volunteers from task to task. After learning Olive had been sequestered in a box stall midweek, I declared the little red barn my turf and shooed the others away.

Olive wasn't old for a pig and far too young in my mind to have developed cancer. Her new pen didn't open to the corral which protected her from rambunctious goats. The great sow grunted appreciatively when I laid beside her on a fresh mound of hay and treated her to two homemade granola bars while crooning one of Nana Tilly's favorite Gershwin songs.

. . . No dates that can't be broken/No words that can't be spoken/Especially when/I am feeling romance/Like a robin upon a tree . . .

Though Olive was today's main attraction, something else required attention. I kissed her on the snout in parting and walked to Jonathan's burnt repair shop to sit on the exposed concrete pad. All around, soot and cinders and molten globs of plastic Mike had yet to pry off the shop floor. Mike fancied himself a "fixer" like his father. We all joked whatever went in the garage shop was unlikely to come out. No one cared about the decrepit tractor or the truck with a blown head gasket anyway. None of us questioned why Joan asked for bales of hay to be stored there either. The scrape of shoes on grit didn't turn my head. I knew she'd find me. Eddie Peck would've told her of our conversation.

"I admit I've wished for this place to burn down a hundred times over," Joan said. "Usually when my arthritis flares up and I can't roll out of bed at five-thirty in the morning. When the water buckets ice over and shit's frozen to the barn floor. When the coops flood and feed gets moldy. When it gets sticky in July and August and the flies bite anything that moves." Joan sucked in a ragged breath. "I didn't set this fire."

"Of course not." I rubbed a little warmth into my chilled thighs. "Mike did. At your request." I pointed a boot at a charred mass that once was a push lawnmower. "Ella saw what I didn't. She wrote two checks in the spring and cut ties. The Twisters don't sign up to volunteer here anymore." I rose to my feet and dug into a coat pocket to hand her a check, the last of my hopes.

Joan rubbed a thumb over the paper. Her tone turned icy. "I convinced Jonathan to buy the farm when he sold his company. Raising four boys was thankless work. Jonathan had real accomplishments. Friends. Travel. I was four somebodies' mother. A woman without a last name, who volunteered at school and drove kids to baseball games. This farm was supposed to be my accomplishment. A bed and breakfast. A petting zoo. A mini golf course. Guests would help with chores and ride the horses.

"We didn't know how to raise animals or bring in the hay. We muddled through and fell in love with the life. Fresh eggs in the morning and goat's milk for sauces. Apples and corn and squash picked right here. The sun rose over the big barn and set in the meadow. The boys and their friends would go sledding in the pastures. Every winter we dragged pallets out there for bonfires."

Talk of fire propelled Joan away from the ruins of the shop. I followed knowing it would be the last time we walked together.

"I don't remember a day when we weren't short-handed. Hired hands expect to get paid," she said. "Jonathan spent too much on equipment when our investments weren't doing so well and we had three boys in college the one year. The boiler in the farmhouse went bust and took out four radiators. Then Jonathan got sick. A big basket of awfulness. When you and Ella came with those two sickly calves, I knew fate brought you. Wanted us to be friends. Partners in this venture."

"Lily and Lilac," I said quietly. Twin sisters. They also died suddenly, quietly, and went away. Eddie Peck tersely reminded me of the expense of caring for sickly animals: a luxury cash-strapped farmers could rarely afford.

Joan's eyes glistened like pond ice. "We both got what we wanted when we needed it."

My stomach dropped leaving my chest hollow. I hid my disappointment by looking to the farmhouse where Janet lay sleeping.

"Mike's taking on the farm," Joan said, her voice firm and resolute. "Mom and I are moving to Vermont. I already put a down payment on a place. Crystal Lake. We'll shop at a country store. Get to know our neighbors."

"Sounds delightful. You do that," I said without rancor.

Manny's movie overwhelmed one's senses with scenes of graphic violence and debauchery grounded in sophomoric desires. The scene in which Michelle drowns her aunt in a bucket of milk was written by Ella.

String lights sagged off bamboo poles bringing starlight to the gravel patio behind Monica's carriage house. The six of us gathered with drinks in hand around a fire blazing in a giant steel bowl. It was all very pleasant despite Nosferatu lurking in a woodsy corner of the yard. Monica warned us her landlord, Billy 'Nosferatu' Dudka, would contrive a reason to linger nearby. He wheezed with the effort of stomping on fallen tree branches for a pile he felt compelled to create. His frightfully pink scalp and slender hands seemed disembodied in the gloom under the pine trees. We all reluctantly agreed if the man didn't quit soon, we'd go inside.

Monica poked a crackling log with a golf club and blindly groped behind her folding chair finding only the slim stack of newspaper used for kindling. She eyed Billy's woodpile.

"Don't encourage him," I whispered.

"Who's ready for a refill?" she asked.

Lee Anne and Rachel offered to help concoct the next batch of spiced rum. John followed for a bathroom break. Adrian watched them turn the corner of the house before saying, "You watched the movie?"

"I'm still processing its outrageous vulgarity. The movie was Ella's most notable, personal accomplishment this year. In a bizarre twist, the very people who profit from promoting her works have erased any reference to it. Why on earth is that the case?"

Billy gathered up an armload of sappy pine sticks, dropped them at Adrian's feet, and strolled to the side of the carriage house.

"He's lonely. We should invite him to join us," Adrian said.

I held up one hand. "Monica attempted to befriend him when she first moved here. Billy's been peeping in her windows ever since. Wait for it. One, two, three—"

Three women shrieked inside the house.

John returned to his chair slapping a palm to his forehead, holding back a laugh. He tossed sticks from the pile into the fire. A few twigs with green needles popped and hissed perfuming the air like a Yankee Candle.

"Danni, you get my message about Curtis?" John asked. "He's a no-go. Doesn't want to be seen with us and have anyone think he supports gun control. Some bullshit about his boss being into hunting goats."

"No worries. We all do what we can, John. That job, I'm sure, means a lot to him."

The ladies returned presenting the carafe with a flourish of hands and ungraceful bows. John white-knuckled his water bottle. More for the rest of us.

"Anyone? Good news?" I asked, getting straight to work.

John jabbed a finger at Lee Anne and Rachel. "Thanks to Xena of the Jungle and her sidekick, Unicorn Avenger, word got out of what you wanted. My email's swamped with photos. I'll forward whatever stands out."

Lee Anne plucked the cinnamon stick from her mug and tossed it into the fire bowl. Another festive candle fragrance. "After helping Wonder Boy get started, me and Rach asked questions. We all sort of agree the trouble started in January at Whole Foods and stopped in June with the race track bang-up. Other than that, nobody's got much to say. Ella wasn't buddy-buddy with any of us lately."

"I was at the race track fiasco. Tell me what happened at the supermarket."

Lee Anne set her mug down. "Some creep tossed milk jugs into customers' carts. Exploding milk bombs. Made a huge frigging mess. The manager banned us from the store because we set up shop near the dairy aisle when it happened."

"What was Ella's reaction?"

"She wasn't there," Rachel said. "Every time we got hit, Ella wasn't there. She protected us the other times. Our lucky charm."

More than one way to read that. "Was it a Twin Sister event?"

Lee Anne shrugged an eyebrow. "Nutjob only went after Twisters. East Coast and White Mountain don't have problems until we're around. They would've kissed our sorry asses goodbye if I hadn't gone after the car. Everybody's giving us the stink eye saying the asshole's only got it in for Twisters. Me slamming him at the racetrack put an end to it. Finito. Sayonara."

"Lee Anne, you ran an occupied car into a guard booth. Dangerous and unnecessary. Criminal. Don't expect commendations."

The group faced me as one with expressions of amusement, indulgence. A human response to a tantrumming puppy.

I continued, "Lee Anne, what color was the car that rushed us?"

"You saw it too. What'd you think? Gray or silver? A four-door sedan."

"Close enough."

John fed the fire bundles of newspaper as Monica patted her pockets to produce a joint. Ever the gracious host, she allowed John to light it with a flaming twig and take the first hit. I fetched my laptop and a tray table from the cottage. Bobbing heads tipped with interest to watch me wrangle an extension cord and power up the computer.

Before plugging the thumb drive into a port, I recapped Jared Libby's crimes. Rachel shivered in sudden discomfort and Lee Anne burnished the scarred knuckles of one hand with the palm of the other. I said my piece and read their expressions. All were willing to continue to indulge me.

"Previously, I thought Jared Libby played a role in Ella's death. More than enough was reported about his significant mental health issues. The role he played in the videos was never in dispute. Having said that, the totality of producing them required knowledge and resources he clearly lacks. I also examined the crime scene. Ella's house alarm has a panel in the kitchen and another in the bedroom. Both have panic buttons. Ella didn't fear her killer. Jared is admittedly crazy; hence, he didn't kill her. I believe the unknown person who helped him create the videos *might* be involved in Ella's death and is quite likely our stalker."

Everyone's mouths began moving at once. A murmur of starlings. The other half of my theory remained unspoken, still a tangle of shifting images and unassigned motives.

I held up both hands for quiet. "A working theory. I should have said 'one of our stalkers' as I believe two people are involved. In my mind, this level of coordination suggests someone is paying them."

Monica thrust the nub of the joint at me. "Here. You need this me more than me."

The burnt oregano smell bit into my nasal passages. I sneezed. "No, thank you. But please, everyone, indulge. Perhaps it'll make what you are about to see surreal and, thus, less horrifying."

I started the videos.

A quiet calm descended on Dolly Road every evening. Through traffic followed a different route after six o'clock and houses went dark after prime-time shows ended. As I ran, I could hear my breath and every connection made to a solid surface. I rounded the corner onto Wenton Street and pounded out nervous energy on the mailbox, retaining wall, tree, and chained link fence. I let my body do all the reacting. Hands and feet propelling me skyward and cushioning my return to earth. The clench and release of core muscles. The jolt of impact absorbed by loose knees and hips. Great gusts of cold night air chilled my lungs and seared my ears. Sadly, it did little to remove the horrible video images from my brain. I doubled over to lock hands around ankles in a standing stretch and took in an upside down view of a passing gray car. The *glug-glug-glug-glug* from its tailpipe drove an icicle of fear between my ribs.

I ran back to the green house at top speed. Once there, surrounded by all that was familiar, I felt braver. The safety of the front door was within reach and so was a package on the stoop. The small cardboard box leaked a shiny red liquid onto the wood decking. Even with its odor muted by the cold, the substance was unmistakable. Blood. My new-found braveness ignited a blaze of anger. An inferno.

I cut through the backyard scooping up the gargoyle memorial and headed in the direction the car had traveled. Two streets away, a man kneeled under a street lamp to refasten a license plate on a gray Nissan car. Plainly dressed in jeans and a navy jacket, he looked quite ordinary except for the ridiculousness of oversized sunglasses at this late hour. My first thought was, *I could take him.* Hormones kicked in before sanity prevailed. I dashed across the street.

My foot met his ass, repeatedly. The man grunted in pain and made a pitiful grab at my sneaker. I unleashed long strings of vitriolic words that included "fuck" with every thrust of my foot. Frustration flowed from my body into his. He retrieved the dropped screwdriver and attempted to bury it in my thigh. I kicked at his hand, arm, thigh—whatever was closest—until he dragged his body, whimpering, over the curb. With anger plentiful, I vented on his vehicle. The gargoyle clanked on the hood until it broke and I was left holding the edge of a concrete wing. I retrieved the body from the road and smashed it against the windshield. The glass fractured into a giant spider's web. This was payback for the cats, the messages, the damage to my friends' cars. All of the anxiety and terror he and his cohort had unleashed upon us for months had come full circle.

I limped home feeling as light as a snowflake while he wept in the gutter. The enormous grin making my bruised toes bearable slid off my face when I emptied the gargoyle pieces from my pockets.

I never looked at the license plate!

Chapter 19

L ydia summoned me to her office shortly after nine. The sharpness of her voice confirmed she had already worked herself into a snit. I doubt she was upset over my choice of shoes, the slippers that were gentle on my ravaged toes.

"Take a seat, Danni."

Misaligned shirt buttons under her black bolero jacket had me cocking my head at Peter Bradt in the guest chair. The ankle balanced on his knee showed off checked blue socks that didn't match his blue striped tie. The smirk on his lips explained why he hadn't responded to my email. The trace of lipstick on his front tooth confirmed the direction of this meeting.

"I think you know why you're here," Lydia began.

Her three-minute tirade ended with, "You never showed an ounce of respect for the company."

In between, she touched upon my many failings to which I added perspective. Arriving late, leaving early—*with permission*. Personal phone calls made from my desk—*doesn't everyone?* Insubordination—*not according to Human Resources*. Disparaging remarks made to co-workers—*unpleasant truths*. Threatening violence in the cafeteria—*to a plate?* Shocking that she hadn't accused me of breaking the revolving files. Had I put up a fuss she might've.

In my defense, I said, "I'd like a box for my cacti."

Lydia said, "Consider this your exit interview," which I did.

Peter Bradt uncrossed his legs and attempted a solemn face. "Sorry, it came to this."

"Everything is a choice, Peter." I rubbed a finger over my front teeth until he understood and did the same.

Claire was given the onerous task of overseeing the removal of personal effects from my workspace. Lydia hadn't sent a security guard because she wished to be seen as a reasonable supervisor. Claire eyed with interest the dusty job training manuals on the file cabinet. Calling upon our friendship, I sent her to the cafeteria with gossip-hungry Bryana to purchase coffee and donuts for the accounting department. A parting gift. In the meantime, I tidied up my computer deleting search history and email files. Screw them.

Aiming to lift my spirits, I drove into the countryside to Aimees Market. Situated between a plowed under sorghum field and a cemetery occupied by 1918 pandemic victims, the family-owned business was a gem hidden in plain sight. The white clapboard house with a central fireplace and additions that telescoped in three directions confused passersby, who missed seeing the brown sign at the edge of the driveway. Aimees carried a sizable variety of goods in small quantities. Staple items sold out quickly. Broccoli, oranges, lettuce, tomatoes—forget it. Jicama, blue Hubbard squash, and loin's mane mushrooms—bins 13, 21, and 28.

The store was populated by clerks related to the owners for all their Roman noses and dimpled chins. I knew several by first name and said my hellos while pacing creaky wood floors between bins of celeriac, artichoke, cherimoya, rambutan, and cellophaned jack fruit. Their fine selection of mushrooms had me placing several packages in my basket with thoughts of sauteing my way to happiness this evening. The scent of cinnamon, nutmeg, and vanilla welcomed me into the bakery section. Slanted pine tables displayed flaky pastries and cider donuts. A quick study of ingredient labels and I left the lot behind. In the tiny natural foods aisle, I picked up a bag of vital wheat gluten for my next seitan project. This was not the week to test my flour washing skills. Bright lighting and glossy white cases pulled me to a remodeled section in the rear. The tang of blood permeated the air in what was clearly an autopsy suite for the depraved. Each shiny package of red dyed flesh and sawed bone received a captioned sticker from my pocket. The true meaning of Truth in Labeling applied to the eviscerated animals on display. I turned to the freezer case with the same intention and was stopped short by a row of square packages that, in fact, surprised me.

"Wait—what?"

I stowed the costly groceries in my car feeling a tad more upbeat. When reaching for the e-cigarette in the cup holder my sleeve drew back revealing a thick smear of blood transferred from the meat case. It painted the underside of my wrist like a gash of desperation.

How We Remember didn't improve with repeat viewings. The characters and storyline remained reliably inconsistent. Even several prominently featured farm animals came and went without express cause. In the closing scene, Ella's Michelle flopped out of the police car and got away. The girlish voice-over of the first scene resumed as a low snicker, then abruptly stopped. A statement on the decline of morality in modern-day society? Prelude to a sequel?

Ella wrote a lengthy college paper on the French existentialist, Simone de Beauvoir. It defined her college activism before I convinced her a humanistic approach better served our goals. In my mind that provided another compelling reason why she starred in the movie. Or did it? Frittering away the afternoon second-guessing her motives was tempting but not necessary. Despite our later differences, I trusted her dedication.

Generating different concerns were acquaintances cast as multiple characters in nonspeaking roles. The Dorvees and Loretta Fahey accompanied by her three daughters were made mourners in the cemetery and shoppers in street scenes. Karen Putnam and Arielle Hornick were identifiable as office workers and worshippers. I presumed Karen transitioned into whatever role, male or female, was needed for retakes. Her characters smoothed rough gaps in the timeline left by more notable actors. Sloppy editing: abrupt scene transitions; unfinished segments of dialog; and gaffs in wardrobe made the assumption highly plausible. Given the number of salacious scenes, significant changes to the film must've occurred post-Ella's involvement. Ella's uncredited stunt double in the shadowy sex and slaughter scenes could be Svetlana Ustinova. The women shared many physical characteristics other than facial features. Monica was correct in noting Michelle's hands. Those same hands measured flour in the latest NPK cooking video, one not filmed in Ella's kitchen.

Knowing who played what role earned me extra trivia points without deepening my understanding of Ella's death. The masochist imp on my shoulder prodded me into skimming online, public reviews of *How We Remember*. I discovered the film was well on its way to becoming a cult classic for testosterone-laden, teenage boys. Judging from their sophomoric writings most had slept through English Language Arts classes and probably made their parents weep. One such reviewer, PieHOL269, snagged my attention. Monica enjoyed saying "shut your pie hole" and 269 was the tag number of a rescued calf who galvanized an Israeli animal rights movement in 2013. He wrote:

Cum on, dudes. Me and woody give it a rock hard 12 out a 10.
Eff-able Michelle goes on a dick humping, blood pumping rampage.
I give you carpet A-hole burns on the stairs, twerking the Jesus snake dudes (soooo mnay dicks in one room. YOWZA). Ponyplay? Got it!
Hang onto your nutsack when you get to the chopping block. Doesn't show how Goldilocks leg came off. Beating her titties with it—priceless.
A must see for hard core, hard on fans.

PieHOL269 shared his witticisms on three other movie review sites. Verbose and unabashed, he did offer something of value: a brief mention of EnablingU Films' ongoing fund-raising campaign shifting to a different platform. *Were they planning a sequel?*

Of sudden interest in the murder folder were notes taken on Ella's ShowMe rants. Another fan stood out. IMhere. The writer defended Ella's indefensible challenges as nonsensically as she had presented them. A show of support. A reflection of devotion? John's suggestion that a sexually deviant fan murdered Ella was plausible. And though possible, it wasn't probable. Such things were rarer than syndicated crime shows would have you believe.

At least, I hoped they were.

No Need to Apologize

At four-forty I stood outside Framingham State University's media center. The zeal I usually bring to these events evaporated this morning in Lydia's office. Canceling with forty-plus students registered to attend wasn't a conscientious option. I sent a note to Adrian. Should he be loitering on campus he had sufficient time to walk here for the start of my five o'clock lecture. Inviting him to dinner afterward appealed to my immediate need not to be alone this evening. A home-cooked meal in exchange for gossip about his brother. I lugged my laptop bag to a bench under a tree and eagle-eyed pedestrians before drawing the e-cigarette from a jacket pocket. Behind me, a stalwart nineteenth-century brick building adorned with gracious turrets, arches, and chimneys roused my affinity for history and architecture. The State Normal School relocated here to Bare Hill in 1853. Back then a flowered meadow and packed dirt roads surrounded May Hall. The school's motto: Live to Truth. Today, bands of asphalt cut through the hilly campus connecting it to the busy highway below. Somewhere within its fringe of tall, block-style dormitories, Adrian might be lurking, though I doubted it by four-fifty-five.

The divine Ms. Huxley called in a favor to arrange this event assuming her magnanimity would indebt me to her. Had she inquired rather than commanded, she would've learned of my two prior lectures here. Today's topic repeated one given at Quinsigamond Community College in the spring: Ethical Living in a Modern World. The information presented was neither new nor incredible. In the media center, bored student leader, Renata, handed me a security badge and led the way to the meeting room. A white screen and a lectern had been provided. She dug a lighter from the pocket of her knee-less jeans, excused her lack of interest poorly, and wandered off.

Students trickled in while I shuffled cue cards. I gauged the crowd removing certain slides to avoid hecklers, clipped the mic to my collar, and introduced myself as Danielle Mowrey, cofounder of NPK and life-long activist. Half of the audience shut off their cell phones. The rest continued to peruse social media accounts.

Ethical Living focused on three Rs: Reduce, Reuse, and Recycle. Unfortunately, that 1970s catchphrase only appealed to Girl Scouts nowadays. To meet the intellectual demands of young adults with short personal histories and even shorter attention spans, I riddled the presentation with catastrophic images of rampant consumerism. I discussed our global waste crisis and our failure as a society to embrace recycling in a meaningful way. I separated marketable plastics from contaminated ones, briefly touched upon hazardous metals in electronics, and exposed the plethora of microplastics in our food chain. The EPA got three slides to clarify the meanings of "landfill", "pollution" and "clean up".

The students were solemn when viewing pictures of the Great Pacific Garbage Patch estimated to be twice the size of Texas. Especially so, when told an unaccountable amount had already sunk out of view to the ocean floor. A few cringed seeing pictures of rotting sharks, impaled turtles, and garroted seals entangled in plastic muck. Their eyes widened on a mountain of refuse in New Deli and lit up when viewing a trash fire in Mumbai as photographed from space. I stayed clear of politics and special interest money with only one slide on the purpose of the Basel Convention. Once overwhelmed with the complexity of the problem, the students were ushered back to the three Rs.

Only this time there were four: Refuse, Reduce, Reuse, and Recycle. Reduction wasn't helpful given our ever-growing human population. Reuse only delayed the inevitable. Recycling was laughable. Refusing to purchase plastic-laden products was the path forward. The presentation ended with handouts and a list of websites for independent study.

Lukewarm applause and a half dozen questions about NPK's glamour column followed. Back row students bolted to noisily bother each other in the hall. Front row students rose hesitantly leaving plastic takeaway cups under their chairs. From a center seat, a dark-haired teen in a white sweatshirt made eye contact.

"Yes? You have a question."

Students closest to the young man sat down. Several aimed phones at him.

The boy cleared his throat. "Your generation screwed the planet. You denied climate change and didn't do anything about it. Why do we have to clean it up? Why blame us? We weren't born then."

I sounded just as absurd a decade ago at his age. "If you're a human being living on this planet, you're part of the problem. Past. Present. Future. Makes no difference. It's up to each of us to be part of the solution. What did you eat for lunch?"

He waved it off. The question deemed irrelevant.

"Methane is a greenhouse gas. In many ways, far more potent than carbon dioxide. Animal agriculture is the main contributor to global—"

"That's a bullshit answer from a Fascist Liberal."

Had I been given a handheld microphone I would've thrown it at his head. "You've no idea what either of those words mean. Your parents pay your tuition, yet didn't see fit to buy you a dictionary."

The young man reddened, threw out his chest, and rambled nonsensically. His might-makes-right soliloquy ended with two upright middle fingers. The teen turned full circle posing for classmates. My ah-ha moment arrived. These students came to see his show, not mine. Only, not all of them were in on the gag. A brunette girl in a red parka threw her leg into the aisle to trip him in passing. The hard landing on his belly drew a round of guffaws and a smattering of claps. That behavior wasn't appropriate either. Oddly enough, it diffused the tension and he joined in the laughter.

"Jesus Christ. Shut up, Joe. You stupid libertarian," the girl said with a grin.

I gave her a scout salute and packed my things. That went exceedingly well. Someday, the kids may actually listen and learn.

Still no response from Adrian on the walk to my car. Drawing near I saw someone had pressed a very different message onto the windshield of the Highlander. A severed cow's tongue oozed bloody water onto the wiper blades. The color of rouge and spotted black, the muscular organ licked the glass. I've seen worse. By those standards, this was a love note rating a one on a ten scale of horribleness. Many butchers sold inexpensive offal on tidy Styrofoam trays. The culprit wasn't the badass he thought himself to be.

A voice gasped, "Good golly. That is nah-stay."

I nearly jumped out of my boots. "Karen?"

"Scooting by and what do I see? Your car, here. I thought you were smart already."

Karen Putnam had shrink-wrapped her masculine frame in a blue Lycra jogging suit. Denim platform sneakers elevated her to six-two forcing an upward glance to meet brown eyes hedged with globs of black mascara that clashed with her teased wig, this one a brassy blonde. One of her C-sized breasts had migrated to her sternum producing an off-center mono-boob.

"Darlin', what'd you do now to get the haters riled up?"

"I gave a talk on trash," I said, securing the laptop in the back seat and a cloth rag from the cargo hold. "Did you happen to see anyone loitering by my vehicle?"

"Waltzing over, I passed some boys in ass-saggy jeans and high tops chuckling up a storm. Mmm, mmm, mmm. Makes me wish I was a young starlet again." Karen winked, noticed her misalignment, and gave it a sideways tug creating cleavage. "Speaking of trashy talk, how'd you get on with the juicy tips I gave you? Did you find out who wrote the letters? I am so sorry I went a little Will Smith on you. I can be a bit much. Have I said that?"

I pried the tongue off the glass, folded the rag neatly around it, and carted it to a trash barrel. Karen was teasing apart stuck eyelashes when I returned. "Your nudge motivated me to take a closer look at Ella's affairs over the past year. I've spoken to people I wouldn't have otherwise. For that, I thank you."

Karen bowed with an awkward flourish, then stared at the rubbish receptacle. "What'd that feel like in your hands? Come on. Be honest. I saw you hesitating over there. What'd that remind you of?" Karen's face lit up with amusement.

The weight of the cow's tongue was imprinted on my hands. A tongue that licked newborn calves. A tongue that shaped cries of desolation when her babies were stolen. A tongue that licked the farmer's hand too when he loaded her onto the truck that would take her to be chopped up into bloody pieces to fill white foam trays.

"It felt like despair, fear, and death. Thanks for asking."

Karen attempted mock umbrage with a *well-excuse-me* expression.

I wasn't amused. "Since you mentioned 'starlet', explain your role in the movie *How We Remember*."

Surprised, the big woman batted her eyelashes and had to unstick them again. "Somehow, I knew we'd get there. What'd you think?"

Karen's roles were negligible. Mourner in the cemetery. Person on the street. Office worker. Congregant. Wholly unremarkable. A few random lines of male and female dialog netted her credits. I smiled warmly, "Brava."

She curtsied with a grand sweep of one arm. "Thank you. Thank you. I'll do anything for a hundred bucks. Aw, don't be a dirty girl. I'm a big supporter of artistic expression. How else am I going to leave my mark on this world? I'll be dead and this stuff will still be circling the internet. People may not know me, but they will know I was here."

"Did you enjoy working with Ella and the crew?" And, more to my interest, "Any problems on the set? Manny can be difficult to work with."

"Nah. He's as sweet as caramel corn. A real charmer. Got the best out of us. If he wasn't so short and skinny, I'd use him as a bed warmer. Can you imagine? Tee-hee."

"Did Ella find him charming? Did she enjoy filming the movie?"

"Who knows? Everyone complained about something and she was right there with them. Rainy days. No electricity. Mice in the kitchen. 'Manny, we ran out of gin.' Whoops. That was me."

"Is that where you met Ella? On the set?"

"Ella and I go way back."

"Really? How far?"

Karen groped for the wallet dangling off her wrist, peeked inside, and said, "Listen, sweetie. I got to see a man about his horse. Can't have him starting without me." Wink. "Let's do this again super soon. Yay for trash talk."

"Of course. I'd like that."

Karen wobbled toward the other side of the lot adjusting her cleavage along the way. I hurriedly drove to an upper street and parked facing the highway. My brain slogged through what I knew of the woman, which was decidedly deficient in details. Eighteen cars zipped by. None were driven by a bombshell with a bouffant.

Chapter 20

M edia crew vans were granted access to lower Clapper Street to set up for Reese DeMarco's broadcast. Residents limited parking with homemade barriers. Since private citizens can't restrict the use of a public road, I helped them stay within the law by flattening an obstacle course of plastic water jugs and ramming a recycling barrel to upend it on a sidewalk. Monica arrived ten minutes later driving over a canvas director's chair and tossing a girl's pink bicycle into a hedge to claim her spot at the curb.

"Tissues?" she asked. Her black lace dress adorned with twenty silver crucifixes seemed more or less appropriate. Ella as Michelle wore something similar in the movie's cemetery scene.

I pulled a wad of tissues from my purse. The corded key slid under my wallet. "I doubt this will be a moving tribute to Ella. Gordon will use it an opportunity for free publicity."

Nadine met us at the door and blocked entry into the house. Tending to her husband and children left her scant time to prepare. The dusty shoulders of her black dress and smeared eyeshadow aroused my sympathy. My chignon and black tuxedo dress provoked her ire. Monica took a wide-legged stance twirling a long-chained crucifix lasso-style. Nadine retreated to the dining room, which allowed us to waltz through to the kitchen and secret a bottle of wine to the den. We each drained a goblet of an unremarkable chardonnay before being summoned to the press conference unfolding on the front lawn.

Reese's family joined hands and looked down from the porch onto a crowd of fifty. Manny Soto, Leslie Meisner, and the Fahey clan conversed quietly behind a row of reporters jockeying for elbow room at the bottom of the porch steps. Leslie's perfectly styled auburn hair and carefully constructed face advertised her skillset as a cosmetician. Loretta and Gordon stood resolute and regal in navy wool jackets trimmed with silver buttons. Give them a bottle of champagne and they could be christening a ship. The Faheys' young daughters, coifed and maturely dressed, grinned at their phone screens. My eyes slid easily from Amy Fahey to Manny Soto, whose deeply tan face was an anomaly in the crowd.

Reese recited a handful of impassioned lines from an index card, then entertained questions from the newscasters. Every blubbering response detailed his loss, rather than Ella's murder. Gordon stiffened, agitated. He climbed the stairs to insert himself between Reese and the microphones and read aloud the opinion piece he had authored. Monica grasped the longest crucifix she wore and mimed stabbing herself in the eye with it. To avoid laughing, I moved off the lawn toward a trio huddling beside the Tasteful Affairs catering van. Unfashionable haircuts, padded jackets, and heavily scuffed shoes indicated they didn't live in the neighborhood.

"Good afternoon," I said.

The taller woman shook my hand. "We came by to say our condolences. Ella was a nice lady. We live in a horrible world and people do terrible things. You see that on the news all the time."

"Thank you. Have we met before?"

"Kristi Dutcher."

The man stomped out a cigarette. "Dale Nichols."

The shorter woman did the same. "Erin Sutkas."

Their names sounded familiar in a forgotten way like a car salesman you spent an hour kicking tires with.

"Ella hung out with us. Talked about what she did after high school," Erin said. "She told us stories about where food comes from. Stuff about the environment and water and underpaid workers. I should've known she was famous. She had the hair for it."

The mention of high school tugged on my senses. Close up, they looked about my age. Ella and I had few trusted friends in high school and these kind folk certainly weren't them. "How did you reunite with Ella?"

"My brother, Will, sent her our way," Kristi said. "I don't know who called who. Maybe they had a thing in high school and found each other on ShowMe.

My brother's married, by the way, so that wasn't going to fly. Dale's my boyfriend. Ella didn't care about him."

"Ella cared about everyone," I said automatically.

"He didn't play field hockey. Me and Erin were on the varsity team. Ella was writing a story about girls' sports. Do you know when it's supposed to come out? I want to show it to Will. He thinks he's a big man because he got a gift certificate. No workplace accidents in ninety days."

"Ella interviewed you?"

The women nodded.

"Sadly, whatever she was working on at the time of her death may not be published."

All three visibly deflated, their disappointment palpable. Someone considered noteworthy showed interest in their lives and now that person was gone.

"You shouldn't be out here in the cold. There's food and drink inside."

I escorted them into the house, my thoughts careening on divergent tracks. Ella, the consummate interviewee, rarely interviewed others. Offhand, I could think of a dozen angles for a story about high school sports but strained to imagine Ella capable of the same.

In my absence, Monica had interrogated the waitstaff. She identified hors d'oeuvres safe for consumption. We filled two plates and returned to the den. Monica unabashedly made elbow farts to clear Reese's neighbors from the room. I stayed her elbow when Leslie Meisner poked her head through the doorway.

"There you are."

"Here I am."

Leslie received credit as the lead makeup artist for *How We Remember*. Monica knew this too and didn't squawk when I shoved her off the love seat. "Monica, be a dear. Please fetch Leslie another drink."

We shared a perfumed hug and Leslie briefed me on the service at Saint Anne Church. The reverend admitted to not knowing Ella. Her thirteen years of activism were summed up as, "Ella DeMarco was known to be an animal lover." Reese wept, delivering a short eulogy portraying himself as Ella's financial adviser. When Walter DeMarco was summoned to the pulpit to read a letter received from Ella, he complained of chest pains, and left the nave to smoke a cigar on a bench out front. Gordon Fahey made a lengthy announcement detailing NPK's health coaching program which would continue in honor of Ella's "wishes".

"You know I'm broken up by her death," Leslie said. "I was her stylist for two years. We were like sisters. Don't take this the wrong way. I have to be practical. I'm out of a job. Three days a week at Macy's selling eyeshadow and skin scrubs doesn't send my kids to sleepover camp. I'll lose my mind if the kids don't go to summer camp. Gordon said he's making you the new face of NPK. I could do amazing things to your skin."

"I'll keep that in mind, Leslie."

Leslie wasn't satisfied she'd made an adequate impression and refamiliarized me with her cosmetology credentials, which began at Nashoba Valley Technical High School. An unplanned pregnancy and early marriage kept her close to home and delivered her to Macy's counter at the Natick Mall. A chance meeting with Loretta Fahey during the sale of an eyebrow pencil brought her to NPK.

I made a T of my hands for a time-out. "You can help me this instant. I am perversely fascinated by the making of *How We Remember*. What was that like?"

"Six weeks of full-time work. The hours sucked. The commute sucked too. The farmhouse was filthy gross and super cold. Brrrrr. Manny's a cheapskate. He wouldn't turn up the heat. I worked in fingerless gloves."

"Six weeks of filming? Unbelievable. Have you seen the finished movie?"

"Me? Nah. I got the gist of it mixing up buckets of fake blood. All that stabbing and hacking. We used it to camouflage cheap, rubber props. Wash it in blood and no one cares."

I've made small batches of Kensington Gore for protests and was familiar with the process. Nothing in the movie could accurately compare with the messy smears in Ella's basement.

"A tight schedule creates enormous pressure. Filming day and night. Exhausted actors. A small annoyance can take on a life of its own. Tempers must've flared. Did anyone fight on the set?"

"Every day." Leslie gave a wry smile. "Manny hired college grads for the production crew. Most didn't know their ass from their elbow. Dumb, dumb,

dumb mistakes. I did hair and makeup for the majorettes for two Independence Day parades. We had a lot less bitching and fewer catfights."

"Do you remember any specific arguments? For example, did Manny and Gordon squabble over money? Had Ella expressed reservations about the script?"

Leslie rolled her eyes in thought. "Money, yes. Script, I don't know. Manny was okay with getting Ella's feedback and ignoring it. Low water pressure in the bathroom really bugged her. The farmhouse was old and she had to wash up a lot. Ella was kooky-weird when it came to the animals and helped the farmer up the road feed them every day. I don't think he was thrilled with the arrangement. I heard she kept asking him if he was happy about what he did, you know? Between the cow shit and fake blood, Ella spent most of her time in the shower or in my chair."

"Were people present during the filming that you didn't recognize? I'm not sure how to phrase this. People not part of the cast or the technical crew."

"Friends of Manny, yeah. They usually showed up when everyone was leaving late in the day. Manny didn't introduce them and I wasn't all that big on talking to him if I really didn't have to."

"Karen Putnam was credited as an actor. Is that where she first met Ella? On the set."

Leslie's face contorted in unattractive ways. "Oh, Jesus, don't get me started. You know she's working for NPK now." Leslie drained her wine glass. "All lies. See? All. Lies. We were shorthanded and she was looking to cash in. She told Manny she was a certified professional. He stuck her in the movie *and* made her my assistant. Jeepers. I wanted to stick her in the chair and give *her* a complete makeover. Why the cheap, nylon wig? Own the look and get yourself something better. And her shoes? I've seen basketball players with smaller feet. I can't tell you how often she rolled her ankles stomping around the farmhouse in heels. Pantyhose and she doesn't shave her legs? Kidding? How can anyone do 'girl' so bad? Great makeup tutorials online she's never seen. I sat in my car and laughed until I cried when he told me she wanted to be my assistant."

"Did you just say all that out loud?" Monica raised an eyebrow.

Leslie's laughter faded. She searched our faces. "Wait. You don't understand. I'm not homophobic. Gender phobic. Whatever you're thinking. It was stupid, funny. Like, ha-ha stuff."

The back of my neck steamed. "If you found Karen's visage so offensive, perhaps you should've offered a few makeup tips. Befriended her. Got to know her. Her life, I'm sure, is difficult enough. Small-minded people like you are ruining this planet."

Leslie stammered something. I didn't hear it. I stomped into the kitchen and pretended to watch the servers reload platters. Monica followed, pulled a cigarette from her bag, and jerked her head toward the back door. Leslie left the den, saw us, and hurried into the bathroom.

My hands shook with disappointment. I mishandled the conversation. I should've asked about Ella's state of mind. I should've asked about so many other things.

Guests wandered freely between food and wine stations. Sterno cans flickered blue under aromatic chaffing dishes and corks squeaked out of bottles to the clink of glasses. Uniformed servers eased around splayed legs and arms flailing in and out of jackets. I suspected the catering staff merely served to impress the Faheys. With all eyes and stomachs distracted I tested a theory and tried the corded key in the garage door, the back door, and the front door. No joy. Where had it come from?

I presented the key and the question to Reese, who was melting into a porch rocker and sharing a pocket flask with a paunchy, red-nosed man. The Costa Rican sun had freckled Wayne DeMarco. The extra thirty pounds he did himself. I never cared for Ella's father and didn't offer my condolences. He didn't need them.

"Where did you get this key?"

Reese hiccupped. "Gordon gave it to me. Ella gave it to him."

"This key doesn't fit her doors."

"What do you want me to say? That's all I got."

"How did you get inside her house to clean?"

Reese made a fist showing off a long red scratch back of his right hand. *The wood patch.*

"Didn't you find it odd Gordon gave you the wrong key?"

Reese stared unblinking at a birch tree. The frat boy was drunk. That would explain his tears at the church. With Ella gone he had no one to blame and no one to brag about.

Heels pounded the porch boards. Loretta grabbed my arm and swung me around to face her.

"Whoa. Nice grip," I said of the hand pinching my biceps.

"Years of Zumba. I've been looking for you. Can we talk privately? In the garage." Loretta pulled me through the house and closed the garage door behind us sealing off all warmth. "I know Gordon mentioned renewing a role in—"

I held up a palm. "Don't ask. This conversation is a bit premature."

"The real question should be: Do you honestly believe you have the chops for celebrity status?"

"Excuse me?" I didn't care for her tone, a tad too bitter for a friendly conversation. "The other day you were very supportive."

Loretta gathered steam pacing the length of an empty bay. "Ella had oodles of personality. She could charm paint off a house and talk people out of lifelong, bad habits. She was honest about her shortcomings and never shied from those discussions. People loved her for it. Ella could sell menstrual cups *and* beard oil. Successfully! You were a fact-checker, a cookbook proofreader."

"Disposable?" For the umpteenth time I was grateful Loretta and Gordon considered me unmarketable. My presence was barely acknowledged. I was little more to them than Ella's footstool.

The hard lines of Loretta's face softened. "You left us to pursue a career as an office clerk. Do you have any idea how awkward you'll feel being quoted constantly, tweeting your daily activities, emceeing promotional events, opening up your home to strangers? What sort of kitchen do you have? Good God, I've never seen your apartment. Gordon had no business extending that offer. We all want what's best for the company. Continuity for customers following our nutrition plans. A built-in fan base for the frozen entrée line. I'm against NPK getting an unnecessary facelift. Gloria Vanderbilt, Mary Kay Ash, Kate Spade. No one is replacing them." The flush in Loretta's cheeks ebbed. She blotted her palms on dress pockets. Perspiration had already wrinkled the armpits of her long dark sleeves.

If there was more to come it was shunted aside when a woman screamed and furniture crashed. Loretta flung open the door to the sound of Gordon shouting. We squeezed between bodies fleeing the living room. Someone's fork raked my arm. A buckle snagged my dress. I held my breath until I reached open space in the dining room.

Manny, bleeding from a split lip and a cut below one eye, sat on the floor between two overturned chairs and a shattered plate of breaded cheese cubes. Gordon, with glasses askew and golden hair tousled, towered above the mess.

"You had no right. I will sue you from kingdom come and back. You're a leper. You disease everything you lay your hands on."

Manny scooted backward to lean against a table leg. His foot shot out to spin the fallen chair. The collar of his shirt was twisted as if hands had wrung the fabric. "A cheater like you talking smack about me? She's gone. It's over. You did that. You killed her with your big plans. Lying sack of shit. If I'm a leper, you're a bloodsucker."

Reese lurked at the other end of the table clutching the photo of Ella that had been propped next to her urn on the credenza. His untucked shirt and bloody knuckles told of who punched Manny. Nadine stepped out of the walk-through pantry. Her eyes latched onto the skewered table cloth, the chaffing dishes and flaming cans dragged close to the edge. She dropped several cloth napkins onto someone's spilled drink and blotted the mess with her foot.

All at once, everyone began screeching. Loretta to Gordon. Gordon to Manny. Manny to Reese. Reese to anyone present. The air filled with profanity-laced accusations of who took advantage of Ella more and who would undeservingly benefit from her death.

The snake was eating its tail.

Someone jostled my elbow. "Hey, cookie. Let's get the flock out of here." Monica held my purse and coat. "Some old biddy in the kitchen is calling the cops."

Gaze averted, I missed seeing Nadine pick up Ella's marble urn. I did see her hand it to Reese, who stepped toward Manny.

"Think fast!" I frisbeed my clutch at Reese's head.

Round Two of chaos. The purse clipped Reese's temple. The urn hit the floor. Both he and Nadine yelled, albeit for different reasons. Manny scrambled outside. The Faheys gave chase. While Nadine mourned a dent in the wood floor, Reese trudged after them, slapping at hands that sought to console him. Out on the front lawn a loose circle of guests collected around the arguing foursome. No one intervened to end it. Who was the aggrieved and who was the aggressor was debatable.

Monica and I left. She snugged a bottle of wine under her elbow. I took Ella.

In the quiet of my car stray thoughts coalesced. Leslie's critique of Karen's femininity was deplorable, hence, it pained me to agree with her after reviewing my encounter with Karen yesterday. What was I to make of Claire and John's unclear connections to the hopeful starlet? Why did she become friends with Claire, a woman difficult to like? Curtis taunted John about his flirtation with Karen. When did that occur? Was there more to it?

The drive home happened in a fog of question marks.

Ella's marble urn brightened the fireplace mantle. A dirt-scented soy candle flickered to its left. Her favorite snacks, a clementine and a handful of salted almonds, were set at its base. Fresh tears ran unchecked wetting my collar.

No need to apologize. I think I understand.

Unfortunately, my understanding didn't bring release. It didn't make things right. There was still much work to do. I retrieved the murder folder and called Boynton. The call went straight to voice mail.

"Good afternoon. It's Danni Mowrey. I attended Ella's memorial luncheon. The Faheys, Manny Soto, and Reese DeMarco got into fisticuffs. Also, I spoke with Leslie Meisner, Ella's stylist. You should take a closer look at the movie. I think it might be the root of the mystery."

My call to Raymond Semple at Midline Private Inquiry Service was routed to a menu board with nine options: Unexplained Death, Divorce, Probate, Missing Person, Workplace Accident, Fraud, Theft, Background Check, and Other. I pressed the One button.

"Midline Private Inquiry Service. How may I assist you?" a man said.

"I'd like to speak with Mr. Raymond Semple."

"This is regarding?"

In my most professional office voice, I said, "Investigative work completed for Ms. Ella DeMarco. My name is Danni Mowrey. I'm calling on behalf of her estate."

Scratchy, unpopular 90s music entertained me while on hold. I silently rehearsed my pitch.

"Ray Semple. How may I be of service, Ms. Mowrey?" said the same voice now echoing on speakerphone. I imagined a one-man office and said man had his feet propped up on the corner of a desk, the edge of a business card poking lunch out from between his teeth.

"As you may be aware, Ms. DeMarco was murdered two weeks ago. The circumstances surrounding her death preclude the settlement of her estate."

"Sorry to hear that. My condolences."

"We have reason to believe her death is connected with the work your company did for her. Should that be the case, the police will be most interested in your report, perhaps, taking a broader interest in your business practices. I'd be happy to come to your office to discuss it in private. When's a convenient time for you?"

"Well, Ms. Mowrey, I doubt anything I do is of interest to the police. Ms. DeMarco asked me to look into a very specific matter. My work was satisfactory. I charged her the going rate. It didn't yield the results she hoped for. There's nothing I can do about that. Facts are reported as I find them. If you're handling her estate, you must have access to her computer. I advise you to go there before you come here. Have a good day." Semple hung up.

"Dang."

The stillness within my flat threatened to suffocate. Alone with the murder folder, self-reproach, second-guessing, and Ella's urn—I could easily drown in a deep well of regret. I had to exit my head and enter my body. Sex with Russell wasn't currently an option, so I changed into a jogging suit. The phone rang as I was plucking my keys from the table. A familiar voice full of apology whimpered drunkenly into the answering machine.

New plan. I swapped stretchy exercise clothes for black night gear and stuffed the necessary tools into my backpack.

Chapter 21

Reese's third call came in as I was signaling a turn onto the driveway of Mockernut Farm, which didn't exist. Manny's movie renamed Pleasant Hill Farm. Clues to its true identity were found in drone footage of rural routes and long shots of a town center Manny used to describe Michelle's transition to the countryside. An examination of satellite photos directed me to the town of Spencer, twenty minutes south of Gray Birch. Hardwood trees on the defunct dairy farm included hickory, also known as mockernut. I could've verified this research by asking Leslie Meisner, but I was too preoccupied with being an ass.

A dirt drive connected the property's assorted buildings, which had been in prime condition a generation ago. Little paint now clung to dried-out wood surfaces. The farmhouse had speckled beige and brown like a clutch of killdeer's eggs. Fresh holiday wreaths hung from rotted windows sills and two dwarf spruce in black urns guarded a front door flaking orange paint. The lockbox on the doorknob explained the superficial efforts to gussy the place up.

With sunset an hour away, the clock tick-tick-ticked on my mission. A wooden bulkhead jutted from a snarl of privet on the left side of the house. A firm tug wrenched the door open on cranky hinges. The smell of wet stone and musk wafted out. Mattress wire springs, scraps of cardboard, and shards of broken mason jars melded with the earthen floor. The unused root cellar wasn't connected to the upper floor; something I should've considered well before passing the flashlight over quivering bundles of black and white fur. They uncurled and blinked at the light. The skunky smell had been a warning. I flew up the bulkhead stairs laughing at my fear.

A trip to the car for more tools yielded a mason's chisel and a twelve-inch screwdriver. Both had come in handy in the past and didn't disappoint on the fourth window, which still possessed functioning sash weights. I heaved myself over the sill and flopped onto a musty tan carpet. Water-stained wallpaper and tilted door frames were dominant features. On the staircase, five raw pine spindles marked the spot where Manny cut away obstructions to film the infamous sex scene. The very thought of it created a fantasy of me soaking my eyeballs in hand sanitizer.

That Ella repeatedly showered in the upstairs bathroom astounded. Copper in the tap water streaked the porcelain tub turquoise. Black mold had infested grout lines on walls and floor. Mouse poop peppered every corner. With Manny refusing to pay for adequate heat, wintertime showers would've been unpleasant.

The realtor left specification sheets in the kitchen. Pleasant Hill Farm boasted a price tag of one point five million dollars. To substantiate the value, a framed movie poster for *How We Remember* hung on a wall. Ella was unrecognizable as a stringy-haired, wild-eyed Michelle Travors wielding a pitchfork. The farmhouse, with lights blazing against a stormy evening, loomed in a bluish haze over her left shoulder. Clichéd graphic art for a low-budget film.

I existed out the window to follow the drive to the iconic red and white English barn that I guessed had drawn Manny to this property. Inside, metal stanchions for thirty cows were divided by a wide concrete aisle channeled with manure gutters. One-third of the interior had been whitewashed and sections of plywood partly covered the gutters. Dusty cobwebs as thick as barn swallow nests bridged corners to the ceiling. My flashlight picked out an attempt to clean a wall, wide gray swirls. All around, drips and splotches, red turning black.

The drive branched toward other buildings. A shed with wire mesh windows sheltered tractor parts and stacks of rough lumber. Behind it, the stump of a tree served as the movie's butchering block. Black stains, mildew attracted to the corn syrup in the fake blood, had seeped into its ringed surface. The most exciting finds were a roll of cinnamon lip balm and a bag of lime in a sinking outhouse recently updated with a green plastic toilet seat. Back in my car, I scribbled my thoughts in a notebook.

The garden center two minutes south on a bend in the road was my next stop. When searching for the farm's address, I saw an advertisement for Berry Hill Market. The film's cast and crew needed to dine somewhere close. This could be it. A crooked fieldstone wall bordered an apple orchard on the right. Just beyond it, the rustic market building and its attached hoop house hugged the sweeping curve. A carport sheltered two 1950s-era Ford pickup trucks, one pastel blue, and the other army green. The blue car trundled along the street at the start of Manny's venomous church scene. A glossy red car beside the green one would better fit the market's wintry decor. Fragrant fir wreaths bowed in gingham, pilgrim plywood cutouts, and signs promoting blueberry wine screamed quaint New England.

A chalkboard on the service counter offered locally raised emu butchered into a stew and double scoops of pumpkin spice ice cream. Fortunately, nothing simmered in the crockpots behind the register.

"Good afternoon. Do you know anything about the farm down the road? The one listed for sale?"

The husky lad at the counter closed a People magazine and pushed up a knit cap to scratch a pimple embedded in a dark, bushy eyebrow. "The Riley's farm? Yeah, I know it. His kids are selling it. You a farmer?"

"A film buff. A movie was filmed there earlier in the year. One of your cars was used in a scene, yes?" I said.

The young man tensed. "Why'd you want to know?"

"Idle curiosity. I worked with the production company at one time. Just curious to know how they got on." Somewhat truthful.

He looked to the tattered cover of the magazine. "They weren't there for very long. Regular people. Nobody famous like the Avengers. We were in the movie. Saw them guys every day."

I encouraged him with a smile giving subtle permission to gossip and he rambled on for ten minutes, the boredom of a quiet Tuesday afternoon now alleviated. The cast and crew ate at the market for six weeks, he said. Most were nice. Some were jerks who complained about the toilet and the service. They ate in the greenhouse and were noisy and messy. His father, Derek, struck a deal with the film's executive producer. In exchange for bit roles for three Berry Hill family members and the use of the blue Ford F-1, EnablingU Films promised to promote the market. The family sought bragging rights. They had land for sale, too.

The boy, Martin Legget, beckoned me over to a doorway draped in heavy plastic sheeting. The giant plastic bag that was their hoop house stank of drowned earthworms in the gravel under a row of picnic tables. A wall heater blew out tepid air and rippled the plastic overhead. Martin pointed to a movie poster screwed into the store's wood sheathing. Same cheap frame as used in the farmhouse but with a different picture. Ella, deranged and saturated, leered large with a diminutive Berry Hill Market set in a rolling pasture in the background. Cast signatures defaced the bottom of the poster. Karen Putnam's scribble read, 'XOXO Love my hillbilly boys! Giddy-up darlins!' Which seemed appropriately eccentric for her.

"My dad's still pissed off because of the damage. They told us they didn't have the right kind of insurance. We never heard anything back." Before Martin could provide details, the door rattled, and he rushed to assist three elderly customers struggling with canes and collapsible rolling carts. "Welcome to Berry Hill Market."

I slid behind the wheel of my car knowing the market hadn't received the longed-for credit in the movie. An argument over property damage would've made the omission intentional. I recognized Martin in the role of the pastor's son who attempted to set fire to the Mockernut barn. I should've asked how it felt to get kicked to death by a mad cow. His death scene was especially melodramatic.

Halfway home I called into my answering machine to replay Reese's messages. The brother of the deceased wasn't the least bit contrite. He claimed self-defense when Manny antagonized Gordon. Because of my association with NPK, he thought I might partner with him for the good of the company in memory of Ella. In other words, after eavesdropping on a sordid conversation between Gordon and Manny, Reese threw the first punch to align himself with Gordon. He just as quickly realized he couldn't trust Gordon to protect his interests and now regretted taking such an open stance.

I nearly pulled a gut muscle laughing. It ended abruptly when I heard Monica's voice message.

"Claire's been attacked. Get your ass to the Framingham hospital."

The elevator doors pinged open letting in the screechy voice of a distressed woman. I followed the echo to a nurses' station at the intersection of four corridors. A stout woman in a garish red and black checkered sweater gripped the counter. A lanky nurse in pink scrubs seated on the other side leaned back precipitously checking her watch. She was timing the rant.

"I don't care diddly squat what she said," Claire's mother bellowed. "I'm telling you she won't eat. Stick a needle in her damn arm and pump her up with sugar water. Isn't that how you do it? How's she going to get better if you starve her? How's that helping?"

I scurried into Claire's room before her mother could marshal reinforcements. The space was made cheerful with a rose floral arrangement, several pink and blue foil Get Well balloons tied to the bed rail, and a pink and white heart patterned blanket on the bed. Claire was anything but happy. Neon pink tape formed a cast on her right arm and a square of gauze pushed up her dark, kinky bangs. The bruises under her eyes came from sleep loss. In the next bed, a grossly obese woman honked as she snored. I drew the curtain around Claire's bed.

"Goodness. What happened to you?"

Claire struggled to sit upright which was awkward with the busted arm. "Who told you I was here?"

"Monica called and said you'd been mugged. Were the police notified?"

"Why do you care? What business is it of yours?"

Claire basked in drama because her parents rewarded it. That much I knew. I pulled a lidded tub from my backpack. Chocolate avocado pudding. The expresso granules might keep her up tonight, then again, so might her roommate. Claire pounced on it like a cheetah on a warthog.

"Monica said you quit the group. It's not for everyone. I understand. You did good and important work. Thank you."

"Humane slaughter is yuppie bullshit. Hip-hip hurray." Claire snorted a sarcastic laugh into the pudding aspirating some of it. I thumped her back knowing I'd be leaving soon.

"Did you see the face of your attacker? Can you identify him?"

"How could I see his stupid face? It was dark. I was in Natick center. He snuck up behind me and slugged me and tried to rip off my purse. He could've been following me all over town waiting to get me alone. I defended myself pretty well. No thanks to you. You should've canceled the Thanksgiving party."

"Finish the pudding. You'll feel better."

A bird's eye view of Natick's picturesque common took shape in my head. Like many, it was a manicured green space with a gazebo presided over by a spired church. The post office, library, fire department, and police station were within view and well lit. Claire knew better than to loiter alone in dark spaces. How many times had I lectured the group? The empty tub rattled on the tray table. All that remained was a brown smear on Claire's ample chin. Maybe I'd tell her before I left.

"Why weren't you transported to the Natick hospital? It's closer."

The balloons bobbed. Claire played with the strings.

"You didn't report it last night," I said slowly. "You drove back to Framingham."

Claire spoke to the balloons. "I felt okay. Only started hurting this morning. My mom made me come to the hospital. A nurse in the ER called the police. Public safety. Blub, blub, blub. I was okay not calling them. What can they do? The guy's gone."

I arched an eyebrow. Something felt very wrong. Claire seemed disdainful of my help. I'd leave this for others. I shouldered my backpack.

"Wait." A tremor of panic in her voice. "You have to do something for me. My mom's going to my apartment to pick up clean clothes. I gave her the key and was like, oh no, she'll look in all my drawers. She looks everywhere. Promise you won't freak out?"

I dropped into a chair. "Tell me first."

"I have Ella's gun."

My head spun 360 degrees or so it seemed.

"I can't ask Megan or Alicia." Claire's voice rose in pitch. "You can put it back in Ella's house."

Questions flooded my face.

Claire picked up on it. "I live by myself. The jerk bothering us could follow me home one night. Ella let me borrow hers to see what it was like having a gun around. Whether it scared me. I never did anything with it."

I found my voice. "Ella would never keep a gun."

"Someone broke into her car and sent her hate mail. That's what she told me. If it happened to me, I'd get a gun."

"And yet, here you are." I tapped a finger on her pink cast. "When did you take possession of the gun?"

"Four, five weeks ago. I hid it in a bag under my bed. You have to get rid of it for me."

A rush of anger curled my fingers into fists. "Why do I have to do anything?"

"The gun's in Ella's name. People will think she's a criminal. A crazy animal person. Maybe that's what the killer wanted. The gun."

I allowed myself a delightful little fantasy of beating Claire with her cast. "Was taking the gun your boyfriend's idea?" Boyfriend. Girlfriend. Neither had been proven to exist—yet.

"He's not my boyfriend anymore."

Yup. "This isn't something I want to involve myself with."

"What am I supposed to do?" Claire's eyes welled up. "What if the police find it? I don't have a permit. I could go to jail. I don't want to go to jail."

We were back at B.C. Wethers with me holding Claire's hand in the ladies restroom, talking her through some minor calamity she was convinced would end either her mundane career or her love life forever. On a cosmic level, Claire and I were even. No outstanding debts. Though, she wasn't altogether wrong about the presence of a gun muddying the investigation.

Mr. and Mrs. Steele's home on Loney Drive evoked the label of a floor cleanser. Lemon-yellow siding outlined in pine-green trim. Claire's roost in the detached garage sat slightly behind the house. A full dormer expanded the loft above two bays. Claire assured me her parents would be dining out and their house was, indeed, unlit. I left my car carrying a box wrapped in brown paper. A delivery or so the neighbors would think.

The spare key lay under the black rubber welcome mat. Inside the loft, Claire's pubescent stylings assaulted my senses. Wall posters featuring baby animals and an English garden of floral upholstery competed for dominance in an unobstructed view of the kitchen, living room, and bedroom areas. Half walls to delineate space and preserve corneas would be welcome additions. Poor Claire. The thumbtacked posters came from Scholastics catalogs and the white bed frame was mottled with ghost images of cartoon stickers. Monica would pee her pants laughing were she to see this.

I squirmed under the bed. The faux ostrich skin bag was designed to hold a bowling ball. A black 9mm handgun and a box of bullets rattled inside it.

"Holy friggin' Hell."

The smart move would be to call Boynton. Yet, I didn't know the full extent of Claire's involvement. She previously implied she and Ella were strangers. That proved to be a lie. Who was her mysterious boyfriend? Could he have amplified Claire's paranoia to get the gun out of Ella's house? Could he be Ella's killer? I disliked uncertainty.

I peeked inside cupboards and drawers and searched the refrigerator and the bathroom medicine chest. I rifled through the waste bin with a discarded bread wrapper covering my arm. A smashed bouquet of daisies had me plucking out the shredded message card it arrived with. Disturbing finds included a package of frozen chicken thighs, a vibrator, and a black cell phone in a black case. Claire's smartphone had a rhinestone case. Who owned this one? Four tacky smudges aligned with numbers on the passcode screen. I might get lucky and open it to find out.

A car coughed in the driveway and doors clapped shut. The senior Steeles argued in a chatty way before climbing the stairs to the loft. The conversation slowed their progress allowing me to squeeze myself under the bed before a key scraped the lock.

"Oh, for crying out loud," Mr. Steele said. "She left the door open."

"Don't yell, knucklehead. I thought I locked it," Mrs. Steele responded. "I was in a hurry to get her there. What the heck did she want me to bring?"

"You're asking me?"

"Of course not. Shush. It'll come to me. Ah, yes. She wanted a change of clothes and her other phone. A black one."

"Why do kids need so many doohickeys nowadays?"

"Shush. She needs it for work."

The Steeles clomped over the floor to wrench open dresser drawers and whisk back the closet curtain. Hmm's and oh's punctuating their endeavors. I slowed my breathing and tried to meld into the linty rug beneath me. If either lifted the dust ruffle to search under the bed, one of us would scream.

"She's got it her coat pocket. It's at the hospital. Can we go now?" Mr. Steele said. "We got a six-thirty reservation. These things don't grow on trees."

"What's this box? Did you bring it in?"

"Leave it! We have a reservation. I swear to God—if they run out of shrimp. I don't know why you had to do this tonight, Emmy. We're going to be late."

"Keep your shirt on. Get the bag, will you?"

The Steeles exited as noisily as they entered. I waited for the stomping on the stairs to subside before sliding out to tinker with Claire's new gadget. The ninth numerical combination I tried lit up the screen with a picture of the B.C. Wethers building. The device had been wiped clean of all recent activity. The only number stored in the contact list was that of the phone itself. I slipped it into my pocket and inspected Claire's tiny pink bathroom. A closer look at the vinyl floor and shower drain revealed strands of silvery hair sprinkled about.

Claire, what have you been up to?

Chapter 22

I rolled out of bed at eight o'clock taking the quilt and one pillow to the floor with me. Neither cushioned the landing. I curled in a ball and laid there for ten minutes letting my brain warm to the fact I had no place to be. My unemployment would remain secret until after New Year's Day. The misappropriated pity would cause my soul to burst into flames and Christmas would already be difficult enough. I dragged myself to the kitchen table and sent a text to Monica.

> *Danni: Hi Monica. Has Boynton contacted you about the message you received from Ella?*
> *Monica: I told him to piss off.*
> *Danni: Why not be helpful? It might move the investigation forward.*
> *Monica: I don't like the way he looks at me. All judgy. If he wants it, he can go Big Brother and pull phone records. They're going to do that anyway.*

"Arghghggggg."

A fully charged espresso and several pulls on the e-cigarette sharpened my senses and steadied my nerves. I skimmed the newspaper online sailing over a multitude of gut-wrenching stories to drop anchor in the Metro section.

Stolen Car Found Ablaze in Woods

Framingham — A passenger vehicle was found burning in a wooded area off Route 30 in Framingham yesterday. Firefighters responded to a call from a passing motorist, who reported the blaze around 9:30 p.m. The fire engulfed the vehicle and ignited the surrounding brush. Framingham Fire Department quickly subdued the fire, which did not threaten nearby homes, according to fire department spokesperson, Kelly Anders. The 2015 Toyota Corolla had been reported missing Tuesday from the Kingston Street area in Sudbury by its owner, according to Sudbury police. The theft and the fire are under investigation. Anyone with information is asked to contact the Sudbury Police Department.

Everyone has troubles these days. I really should stop reading the newspaper altogether. Compassion Lives members post enough doom and gloom on our social media page to replace two daily papers and the eleven o'clock news. Why wallow in misery?

Breakfast perked me up somewhat as did another espresso. I toyed with a secondary list of suspects. The Doyles scammed an insurance company. One NPK or Twister fan had been deeply infatuated with Ella. Francis and Vanessa Norelli's fledgling business took an unforeseen turn because of Ella's involvement. The status of Ella's latest book project and the selling of Pleasant Hill Farm generated questions I wasn't willing to entertain presently.

Last night John emailed photos submitted by fellow Twisters. Slightly grainy, they were taken during rainy weather early in the year. A set of photos focused on two clean-shaven men. One gent was in early middle age with side-parted, platinum hair, and wraparound sunglasses. He could be the driver I thrashed in the street based on body type alone. The other man carried the rough leanness of youth. The bushy, brown hair under the Bruins cap sat proud of his scalp suggesting an artificial layer, a wig. I'd know the obscene caller by voice. Misplaced r's and o's pronounced as ah's identified him as Massachusetts or Rhode Island raised. I could be mistaken.

Another set of photos of two women raised the hair on my nape. One woman appeared twice in the same clothing: high cuffed jeans; a brown jacket trimmed in white fur; a striped knit hat; and oversized sunglasses. Activists pictured in the background wore jeans and long sleeve tee shirts. Far too warm for a heavy jacket. The other woman, taller and trimmer, wore baggy khakis and a white baseball cap over braided blonde hair. In three photos, her skin glowed an unnatural, citrusy tan behind Ray-Ban shades. Most disturbing was the scout salute she offered to someone off-camera.

Manny returned my phone call when I was elbow-deep in sudsy dishwater.

"Ha! Word gets around. All of a sudden, I'm a big somebody. Your pal. Pretty good for a no-talent weasel like me."

Ludicrous how sad him saying that made me feel. "I admit the movie surprised me in many ways. From you I expected an arthouse film. A tawdry affair between a MOCA artist and a heroin addict. Everyone writhing in dope and angst. A slutty slasher flick? Major wow."

"Ella had faith in me. She believed in the script."

"The one you presented to her. Yes. She even collaborated on changes. I caught the references. The aunt drowning in a pail of milk. The evil brother. Clueless police. Bungled butchery."

"I know what sells and I finished inside my budget. Aye, give credit, would ya?" Voices laughed and music blared somewhere in the background.

"Financed by crowd-sourced donations in exchange for a promise of me-time with Ella."

"Worked, didn't it? I'd been sitting on that script for years. Took more than you'll ever know to get it produced. I busted my balls bringing it all together."

"I think, in the end, Ella wasn't happy at how you reworked the movie in her absence. How on Earth did you explain the new sequences filmed with your mystery actors? Is that why Gordon punched you?"

Manny snorted and spit out something disgusting. I hoped he was still out on a sidewalk. "Gordon's a stupid piece of shit."

"You chose him as a trusted partner."

"The things you don't know. Here's one. Me and Ella came up with an idea for a cable cooking show. Gordon nixed it. He knows squat about that business and didn't want to turn over control. He went gorilla on her. So much so she wanted out. Bye-bye. Cash-out. Cha-ching."

"I'm aware she was planning her exit. She had more than enough reasons to do so. Am I wrong to think her involvement in the film was a contractual pit of Gordon's making that she fell into?"

"Jesus. Are you not hearing me? Cash-out. She got paid for the movie. She wouldn't do it otherwise." Manny was panting. Street sounds, mostly the passing of vehicles, rumbled around him.

"The movie wasn't an achievement Ella could've been proud of."

"We didn't hurt no animals. Movie magic. Nobody listens. You only know half what you think you do."

"Fine. Explain it to me."

Keys tinkled. A door creaked. "Tomorrow night. I got tickets to a drag show at Firehouse Theater. Eight o'clock. My plus one bagged. Pay me for the ticket and buy your own drinks. I'll drown you in my genius."

"I can hardly wait." I had more to say, but he hung up.

The meeting at Wilfred Draperies to continue our discussion of my career opportunity at NPK was slated for two o'clock. I would arrive at one. Gordon committed himself to the dictates of his desk calendar. A rearrangement of appointments would throw him off-kilter. I wove a French braid, powdered my nose, and practiced expressions of innocence and curiosity in the bathroom mirror.

A short drive northwest brought me to Marlborough. Wilfred Draperies was conveniently located in a small industrial park ten minutes from the Faheys' elegantly filthy home. Its maroon awning jutted from the middle of a blue, aluminum-sheathed building. Sandwiched between Bro Dogs Funhouse and Ripleys Leatherworks, Wilfred was treated to their residual stink during the summer months, and Loretta and Gordon's odiferous personalities the rest of the year.

Arlene stood up excitedly from the reception desk when I sauntered into the showroom. She'd gained a few pounds since last we met and reverse highlighted her silver hair with strands of ash blonde. Her wide smile remained infectious.

"Danni! Hello. Look at you. It's been too long. How are you?"

"Very well, Arlene, thank you for asking. How's your family?"

"The same. Jon-Jon's a senior in college. Susan's a year behind him. Poor Al is tired of his new job already. I knew that was going to happen." Arlene looked past my shoulder at a young couple dressed in business casual who were circling the showroom.

The woman paused to caress a display of wood blinds while her partner opened a manufacturer's brochure. The tapestry swags, padded cornice boards, and honeycombed blinds that jutted from the walls hadn't been updated in some time. The couple would soon leave.

Arlene dropped into her chair and consulted her computer. "You're early. Gordon's in with someone. I have you scheduled for two o'clock."

"Darn. I must've written the wrong time. Is it okay if I wait? We can catch up. I'd love to hear your thoughts on Gordon's movie."

Arlene rolled her eyes. "I haven't seen it. I've heard them argue about it plenty. Horror. Ick. Why'd they do it? Gordon has a million pots in the fire. Loretta too. Always working on something other than curtains." Arlene chuckled thinking that funny. "She's in and out with volunteering at the school. Hasn't been around in a few weeks. That woman's amazing. The queen of community service. If one of her daughters doesn't grow up to a be doctor—" Arlene shook her head considering that impossible. "As long as one of them shows up to let me in I'm happy. Want to see my latest?" She dragged a canvas sack out from under the desk and opened it to show a crocheted blanket under balls of yarn. "I sell them on Etsy."

"Lovely." I cooed over the blanket's tight stitches, watched the couple make a quiet exit, and said, "I'm going to scoot to the toilet. I'll be right back."

A wide corridor off the showroom led to business offices, a staff kitchen, the toilet, and the delivery and storage room beyond. Overhead, a failing light flickered, resetting shadows under the brass-plated plaques that framed the conference room door. The commendations were for work completed by Clean Green Earth Project. To my right, Gordon's office door muffled terse male voices. Around the corner, the door to Loretta's office opened at the push of my hand. The dull white office was as impersonal as her husband's. A hurried search of desk drawers revealed her affinity for paperclip chains and a passion for Sudoku puzzles. In the hidey-hole beneath the desk, she kept a gym bag with sneakers, latex gloves, and a spray bottle of disinfectant. Two tall bookcases held decorative items borrowed from the Fahey home. A horizontal cabinet was equally divided between hanging files and a mishmash of personal items I felt obliged to paw through. A box of worn rubber stamps rested under a stack of New England travel magazines. One still held moist ink. I stamped my forearm for a ghostly imprint: M_A_d_es Pap_r Su_p_y, 368 E_st Str__t, Elg_n, IL. Tucked behind the file rack—a laptop with two sticky circles on its lid. The marks were undoubtedly left by googly eyes recently removed. Blood whooshed between my ears.

Ella sat opposite me at the conference table. She looked up from behind her laptop, laughing. "Get it? The eyes? Now, you can't say I'm not looking at you when you talk to me."

I should report the find to Boynton. Instead, I headed to the storage room and inspected the rear entrance. The shipping and receiving area was a maze of metal shelves stacked with curtain cartons and a computerized workstation dotted with scraps of mailing labels. The delivery door wasn't monitored by an alarm system. I could set the laptop outside the door, meet with Gordon, and circle the building in my car to retrieve it. Easy.

Raised voices echoed in the corridor. I dashed toward the restroom and collided with a big man leaving Gordon's office. The crash resulted in a frame knocked off its hanger. The man never looked back. His buzz-cut and navy attire hinted at his profession. The L-shaped scar behind his left ear confirmed it. I rehung the commendation letter giving it a cursory glance. The Faheys had raised funds for an ill school girl. Carrie Huxley, the school district's superintendent at that time, had authored and signed the letter. Gordon saw me through the doorway and stood up from his desk.

"Two o'clock already?"

"I was in the area. I hope now is a good time for us to meet."

He checked his watch, face flushing. "Yesterday was a disaster. You'll want an explanation."

I planted myself in the guest chair which was still warm from the police officer who had vacated it.

"Manny was fired in September. The memorial gave him an audience."

I feigned surprise. "Oh, my. Who's been filming the cooking videos?"

Gordon patted his head searching for the eyeglasses on the edge of the desk. "We found a photographer to fill in. A nobody. Who cares? What's important is in here." He tapped a polished fingernail on a yellow folder. "Loretta has misgivings about renewing our business relationship. I take—"

"Have you seen *How We Remember?*" I interrupted. "Your name and reputation are attached to it. Ella's too. How does that make you feel? How do you think her fans will react?"

Gordon stretched his neck awkwardly. The ligaments holding his bones together snapped back and he shrank by inches. The silence between us stretched on uncomfortably until he said, "I won't bore you with the complexities of filmmaking. Even the actors don't know what the finished piece will be. How it'll hold together. *If* it'll hold together."

"You're credited as the executive producer. How could you not know?"

"I didn't. Manny lied. He reshot scenes. Claimed there was a problem with the soundtrack. Technical or copyright. I don't remember. Later he blamed the delay on an issue with the distributor. He stalled in order to produce a film I wouldn't have approved of."

My sympathetic face calmed him. That he and Loretta lied to me was apparently irrelevant. "So, what will you do about it?"

"We'll sue. He had no right to release it. That's all I can say."

"Where were you the night Ella was murdered?"

Gordon cupped his eyes with his hands. "I've spoken with the police. Have I been arrested? I'm not a suspect."

"Is that why the officer was here? I recognized him from the original broadcast." I flexed a finger behind my ear to indicate the scar.

Gordon waved his hands, flustered. "Giving an update on the investigation."

"Of course. So, humor me. Your alibi? We're building trust."

"I worked late fine-tuning Ella's speech. I drove the sitter home at eleven when Loretta returned. A neighbor's daughter, Bonnie. We pay her to engage the girls and help them with their homework. It allows me to enjoy a gin and tonic in peace."

"Where was dear Loretta?"

"She and Amy went into Boston for a Celtics' game." He fumbled with his phone to flash a picture of Loretta and Amy hugging cheek to cheek in Boston's TD Garden arena. "Please open the folder."

"What do you think happened at Ella's house?"

"A burglary. The police made that clear."

"Why did you need Joe Dorvee to enter Ella's home when you already had the key?"

"Out of politeness. He called me, distressed."

"Why did you break door glass?"

"Why would I? I had the key." A vein flared in Gordon's neck. His fingers drummed on the folder. Tiny beads of sweat glittered across his forehead.

"I think Ella wanted to leave NPK as early as last year to dabble in the frozen food market," I said. "Starring in the movie was a ready means of seed money for her new adventure. But you weren't ready to give up *your* cash cow. You knew exactly what Manny was doing. *How We Remember* was designed by you and him to defame her. To force her out of it entirely. Only, Manny had a few other ideas."

Gordon launched a pen at my head. I ducked, expecting it.

"I take it this meeting is over," I said, grinning.

The Dunkin' Donuts restaurant provided a comfortable place to loiter and was empty of customers due to their smashing drive-thru business. Aided by memory and free wi-fi, I easily found Donna Dorvee's work address. I ordered a French vanilla coffee with almond milk and drove to the business park dominated by Syper Industry's tawny, monolithic building.

The cavernous first floor gleamed with a polished concrete floor and several groupings of modern furniture for impromptu conferencing. Practical and pleasing. I slid onto a yellow, vinyl sofa and waited. Donna Dorvee held a position similar to mine at Wethers. She'd become a fixture that would happily retire to no acclaim. Taking in the sleek furnishings and the aesthetics of architecture balanced by steel girders, I wondered if I would've fought to keep the job had Syper been my employer. Doubtful.

The elevator chimed and out stepped the first wave of departing employees. Donna wasn't amongst them, but she fit the culture. Nearly every woman wore short combed hair, baggy eyes, and a quilted jacket over a coordinated pants suit. The elevator opened and closed again before I spied her and waved hello.

Donna's hug and condolences felt stilted. Polite talk in polite surroundings. "Did Joe mention my visit?"

Several women with ugly leather bookbags passed us. Donna joined in on a loud round of "Have a good night" and "See you tomorrow" until the ladies stepped out the door. She followed them with her eyes, almost wistfully, saying, "Joe spoke to the police and the reporter. He's all talked out."

"I understand. By the way, Stacy and your grandsons were excellent in *How We Remember*. You all were. I watched it for the first time the other night. Pay-per-view. They were extras in three scenes."

"Four." Donna's grim face brightened. "Stacy had the worse time keeping them quiet during filming. Especially when they brought the snakes out. You know how excitable children are."

"You're pleased with the finished film?"

Donna set her pocketbook on the coffee table and we sat down together on the sofa. "We don't watch scary movies. The whole thing was a favor for Ella. I mean, we did get paid. But that really wasn't the point."

"Satisfactorily? Paid, I mean."

"I suppose so. Ella asked a lawyer friend to review the contract."

"Excellent move." I snugged in closer creating a more intimate space between us. "About this current awfulness. How did Joe seem afterward? After finding Ella."

Two furrows marred Donna's forehead. Something undecipherable moved behind her eyes. "Are you asking if he's depressed? We loved her like a daughter. Treated her that way. How could you even ask?"

Given what I suspected, a snarky response felt deserved; though, saying it wouldn't serve my purpose. "Ella loved you both, dearly. Her own parents weren't particularly supportive and it hurt her deeply. You and Joe represented 'home' to her. She could've left the neighborhood at any time. She had the resources. I believe you were her reason for staying. You and Joe. I also believe she trusted people she shouldn't have. Do you know what I mean?"

Donna tugged on a gold button earring. Her eyes filled with tears and darted over the striped rug coming to rest on her low heels. "We tried to be good neighbors. Helped her when we could. There were instances when she had misgivings about people she let inside her house. Little things went missing. Face cream. Earbuds. We laughed at first. Everyone gets forgetful. Lose things and find them later."

"Some things were never found?"

Donna nodded. "The Polish girl was let go. Then the dogs' Reiki therapist. Jeffrey was an odd bean. The thefts had nothing to do with him getting ousted. She found someone better, I think. The dog sitter was another one."

"Monica."

"She failed a test of some kind. We took it to mean she stole something Ella left out on purpose. Honestly, I don't know. Ella brought them both back later."

My stomach twisted in on itself. "When did this happen?"

Donna shifted her weight. The vinyl couch farted. We giggled breaking the tension. "Before Joe's birthday. Middle of August."

For several minutes, Donna explained Ella's struggle to find replacements and her increasing reliance on their goodwill, which ended with Joe refusing to watch Clyde and Reno on that fateful weekend when they knew they'd be well-occupied with grandchildren.

"Friday evening after dinner she came over and pleaded with us. Clyde was missing a vaccine and couldn't be kenneled. She found a sitter who could take one dog, not both. The dogs have a reputation for being hyper, you know. The thought of shutting them up in a hotel room all day was inconceivable. What could we do? We had a right to be annoyed, but this seemed cruel. Ella had commitments. A career. Joe told her, fine, we'll do it."

"When were you to go over and fetch the dogs?"

"Ella was to call us on her way out. She didn't. We thought she might be waiting on her cleaner. Ella rehired the same girl." Donna frowned at her left shoe. The heel was cracked but holding.

"Gordon Fahey called you on Saturday because he couldn't reach Ella." An educated guess based on his call to Bette.

Donna slumped against the couch and stuffed her fisted hands into her lap. "Is Joe in trouble? Are we?"

"Not at all." I practiced my nonchalant face. "When did he contact you?"

"Sometime after two. Two-fifteen, I think."

The next question had to be unstuck from my tongue. "Were you still at home when the delivery man knocked on your door?"

A tear tumbled from Donna's eye. "There wasn't any delivery man." She re-crossed her legs. The damaged heel hit the carpet and cracked in half.

If I had more energy, I'd go to one of a handful of breweries in the area and pick up a treat for later. Rather, I keyed Piffle's address into the navigator and soon cruised by a Dutch colonial two streets away from a middle school. The averageness of the street told me nothing. The kidnapper could've picked up the cat when driving by.

On the way home, I voice-activated my phone. "Race track redemption."

Lee Anne's voice boomed inside the cabin. "For fuck's sake. An accident."

"Oh please. I spent an hour at the police station denying your existence. I was threatened with obstruction of justice, unlawful assembly, and groped by an officer, who had the nerve to issue me a parking ticket after preventing me from moving my car in a timely fashion."

"Dougy should've worn his glasses."

"I doubt very much the police would've followed up a description of that vehicle. Thank goodness the guardhouse was unoccupied and only slightly damaged."

"Somebody had to go for it. Nobody threatens us and gets away with it."

"He tapped Doug with the bumper. That was the accident."

"Asshole revved his engine. A threat. Plain as day."

"Not until everyone started shouting."

"Oh, bite me, Danni."

"See, this is why you made the naughty list."

Lee Anne burst into staccato laughter. A kookaburra in my car. "You're killing me. Okay. Okay. I'm in. What'd you need, Toots?"

Chapter 23

P ost-Thanksgiving Day sales at Shoppers World attracted a legion of shoppers determined to get in and out of the outdoor mall quickly. They clogged all major routes in, blared horns, and yelled through their windshields. Traffic slowed significantly and drained away residual holiday joy any may have felt. When Boynton requested my presence here, I was immediately agreeable. Twenty minutes stuck in traffic on Route 9 and I was less so.

I sat on a bench under the overhang of Designer Shoe Warehouse and scanned scores of parked vehicles for any sign of his big black coat. A middle-aged woman and a young man in a red Boston University jacket crossed the window glare of an electronics store. Boynton strode three steps behind them, paused to share words, and quickened his pace along the sidewalk upon spotting me. He dropped onto the bench with one quick flick of his eyes to the store his family had entered.

"Good evening, Detective," I said.

"Still investigating?"

"How should I answer that?"

Boynton flattened the scarf tucked under his chinchilla chin. "I'll start. The movie was funded with private donations. Possibly nontaxable. How the company reports the income next year might be a different story. Detective Sollecito watched the movie and gave me the highlights. Not my cup of tea. Yours?"

"Hardly."

"Mr. Fahey provided information on permits and hiring practices. We're a bit short-handed and verifying all of that isn't a priority for us. So far, nobody who worked on the film filed any complaints. That's where we're at."

"Did you receive a call from the Shrewsbury police department yesterday? An awful fight at Reese DeMarco's home after the service."

Boynton puckered his lips. "Grief does strange things to people."

"Which is to say Ella's murder is far more complicated than you realize. I have several letters threatening violence against her. I'd be happy—"

"Hold up. Muriel Nadler sent copies alerting me. I can't promise different results. The lady's dead. Car crash. An investigation into the accident showed her to be at fault. The guy in the car with her was picked up at a bar. If she had friends, they scattered. It's a dead-end is what I'm saying."

"Why did you call me here, Detective?"

"You know Evelyn Pallotta? You triggered her doorbell camera the other day. I saw you waving at her and Jeanne Whitman when we recovered the book."

I flexed my wrist casually in imitation of the wave. "I met her once. She gave the impression she wanted to invest in NPK. Why?"

"She's dead. Mrs. Pallotta went out to grab a newspaper this morning and was struck by a car. Never saw the vehicle coming. Goes without saying she never heard it—her being deaf. The perp took out the mailbox too."

Evelyn read lips. "That's horrifying." A ghastly scenario played out in my head causing me to shiver in revulsion.

"Pallotta triggered the camera when leaving the house. The vehicle that struck her doesn't fit the make and model of the vehicle at Leavitt Brothers. This one's been identified as a Corolla."

"A tragic accident and the driver panicked?" I offered, knowing it wasn't true.

"The paper was stolen from a neighbor's front step. Pallotta's habit to pick up junk blowing out of recycling bins. A good bet she'd go for it."

Whoever killed Evelyn knew her routine and also that she was deaf. Evelyn hid her disability in plain sight for those who were less preoccupied.

"Are you linking her death to Ella's? Could she have seen the killer?"

Boynton scratched his chin releasing flakes of dandruff. "Let's make a deal. We swap info and you let me get on with doing what the fine taxpayers of Massachusetts are paying me to do. You stay out of it. Keep yourself safe."

I pretended to consider his advice. "Please continue."

"Did Ms. DeMarco do recreational drugs?"

"Not to my knowledge. Why? What did you find?"

"Coke stashed in the toilet tank. Main bathroom."

Reese gets a bonus point for not lying. "Manny Soto, her photographer, uses cocaine and other drugs. Until recently, he was in and out of her house on a somewhat regular basis. How often do you look inside *your* toilet tank? My turn. I'd like to see the photos taken of her home. I don't want to see her. Just the condition of the home."

Boynton airdropped several pictures onto my device. The speed with which he did it assured me I'd find nothing extraordinary. "What did the book in the culvert tell you?" I asked.

"Blood and hair matched the deceased. We recovered a crushed cell phone with the Sim card removed. Do you know where her laptop is?"

That he asked meant the Faheys kept that secret. Game face and a head shake. "How did Ella die? The cause of death."

"A fall down the basement stairs."

If I hadn't examined the staircase, I would've satisfied myself with blissful ignorance. "Often, I get the feeling people are lying to me. Some to deceive. Some unintentionally pass on misinformation. A few lie to spare my feelings."

The detective averted his eyes. "Broken neck. C2. C3. Multiple strikes when down. Very few defensive wounds."

A second horrific scene played out in my head followed by a third, even more vulgar. Ella was barely hanging onto life at the bottom of the basement stairs. She wouldn't have had the wherewithal to mark the wall. The killer tried to implicate Gordon. If a kind and just God did exist, Ella would've been unconscious when she was bludgeoned to death.

Boynton reached over to pat the chilled hands in my lap. In doing so, he opened a release valve on my heart. The slow escape of heavy emotion curled me into a self-hug. I was grateful he chose that moment to leave.

"Don't forget what I said. Stay out of it. Your friend? Monica Jinks. She didn't get a text from Ms. DeMarco on the night of the murder. Be careful who your friends are."

The warning repeated itself a few moments later when I viewed the photos. Ella's home hadn't been ransacked, per se. Open drawers, doors, and cupboards suggested a controlled search of some kind took place. The kitchen escaped such messiness according to the photos. In one, a heavily zippered black pocketbook slumped on Ella's kitchen island. The same one that dangled off Monica's arm at the potluck.

We met at eleven-thirty behind the headquarters of a portable toilet supplier. Both of us dressed head to toe in black, the color of night. A herd of fenced-in beige latrines separated us from Wilfred Draperies at the next address. Lee Anne slid into my car and attempted uninspired potty humor.

"Talk about a shitty location for a meet-up. When you told me to meet you here, I nearly shit my pants laughing. That's a shit-ton of crappers."

I failed to see the humor. The plastic structures were reminiscent of something other than receptacles for human waste, a birth and death cycle of human design. Newborn cow calves are separated from their mothers after birth. The males are often killed. The females are stored in uninsulated, plastic sheds and fed powdered milk formulas. Every year, thousands of those gentle souls freeze to death in winter. Lee Anne's hoarse cough shattered the distasteful images but removed little of the vile aftertaste.

"We're going to run over there and jimmy the lock?" she asked, squinting at the blue building through a ragged net of trees. "I do my job and I can take off? We'll be even."

"Correct."

Lee Anne pulled a slim pouch from her hoodie pocket and unzipped it. Dashboard lights shone on an assortment of bent and wavy metal rods. "Best investment ever. Smartass Dickie thought he could screw with me by locking me out of the house and the pizzeria. I got another set for the car. Both our cars. Ha."

"I hope that's resolved by now. You divorced, what, six years ago?"

"Something like that. We'll always be going at it. Kind of fun. Everybody needs a hobby." Lee Anne smiled to herself. That she still harbored deep feelings for her ex-husband was evident.

I grabbed my backpack from the back seat. "Let's roll."

The undeveloped land between the buildings was overgrown with burdock that snagged our pants and gloves. A sliver of moon guided us down an embankment to a shallow drainage ditch. Lee Anne stumbled into the water releasing a torrent of whispered curses. Mud suctioned off one of my sneakers. We charged up the opposite bank cutting a path through the trees to come out next to a dumpster.

"Why didn't we walk on the road, Einstein? The place is deserted," Lee Anne hissed.

I didn't have a clever answer. I had worn the wrong shoes.

Behind the building, ambient glow from a light pole cast our shadows over Wilfred's delivery door. Lee Anne attacked the lock with two picks. I studied the graffitied wall. Four or five colors swirled and exploded outward as high as a human could reach and as wide as the Faheys' leased space. The perpetrator hadn't initialed the work or left a verbal message.

"This ain't happening." Lee Anne stowed the picks in the pouch.

I retrieved the corded key from my backpack and inserted it into the lock. The knob turned. "I wasn't certain. I needed a plan A and a plan B."

Lee Anne glowered and stomped to the tree line—done for the evening.

Fluorescent tubes lit up the storage area casting shadows upon shadows. I removed my muddy shoes and sped to Loretta's office. The laptop slid easily into my backpack. Something seen and half-remembered this afternoon prompted me to examine the back of Loretta's computer monitor. A white sticker gave the 800 number for Whole Solutions Small Networks. The company's logo was prominently featured on the WCCS site too. I snapped a picture and exited the building.

A bear-sized form lumbered out from behind the dumpster. "Danni. I dropped my car keys."

We returned to the murky ditch zigzagging with penlights to cover more ground. Greenbrier, nature's green barbed wire, pierced our gloves with thorns as sharp as sewing needles. My socks and sneakers soaked up all the icy funkiness of the environment. Worse, a police cruiser out on patrol circled the portable toilet lot pausing near our cars before returning to the street. Lee Anne and I scampered like raccoons out of the ditch to press ourselves against trees.

The cruiser turned onto Wilfred's drive. Its headlights winked out on the other side of the building.

"Found the keys." Lee Anne pointed to a clump of metal glittering beside the dumpster.

I ran from cover and threw myself flat against the bin. Despite the cold, the giant metal box reeked of dog excrement. The circling cruiser highlighted several squashed bags dotting the pavement before driving out of the lot. A bag dangling from the lip of the bin felt wet against my forehead. Lee Anne kindly joined me on this mission, so it would be incredibly rude to throw the car keys, let alone a poop bag, at her head.

This morning Cheryl offered the use of Louis' washer and dryer. The invitation stated they bore me no ill will despite recent events. A peace offering, a chocolate tart, would help secure their forgiveness. The dessert took little wits to put together. Grinding almonds and Medjool dates in the blender for the crust created the usual rock-tumbling racket. Joan Doyle left a message on the answering machine during the chaos.

"I brought the vet in this morning," she said. "All things have their time and place on this earth. Olive had a long life. Most do not. Find solace in that. Mike will treat her right. See she's laid to rest in the oak grove."

I stared dry-eyed at the ceiling feeling emotionally wrung out. An entire storyline in my life had ended. Full circle reached on a singular act of compassion for a sickly piglet destined for a PAC ending. Only, not so simple when you're fresh out of college, living in a tiny flat in Springfield, and your new roommate could grow to five hundred pounds. Joan, despite her betrayals, made Olive's continued existence possible. Maybe someday I'll speak to her again.

Belgian dark chocolate was melting in a pan of coconut milk when the machine ticked on again to capture a smooth voice. The recording confirmed a long-held suspicion about Louis' desire to circumnavigate Mother's will.

"Good morning, Danielle. It's Leo Everson. I trust you're doing well this holiday season and wish you the merriest Christmas. We have business to conclude before year-end. Louis Sammons contacted our office on several occasions requesting we divest funds from—"

The Skip button silenced Leo. I couldn't predict the future. Leo believed he could, which is why Mother hired him and trusted his instincts. I valued his performance as the ever-vigilant watchdog but really disliked speaking with him even on an exceptional day.

At loose ends. Flat cleaned. Laundry sorted. Tart made. Laptop breached. *Ugh.* I'd allow myself a smidge more time to crack Ella's passcode before surrendering the laptop to Boynton. If Raymond Semple emailed his investigative report as he claimed and Boynton were to find it, he could be relied upon not to share its contents with me.

A few hours to fill before I could wash laundry and then leave for the theater with Manny. Much of what I planned to ask him pertained to the movie. Which made me think of the fight on Reese's lawn. Which led to me ponder the trio standing by the caterer's van. Which in turn provoked a question of a different sort, one worthy of exploration.

Ella convinced me to decline the invitation to our tenth-year high school reunion. Our classmates were largely assholes, she said. Reminding was unnecessary. Rejection in high school leaves scars. By October of our junior year, a certain clique of classmates had taken to openly intimidating us, the girls who didn't eat hamburgers. I ignored them. Ella traded barbs. The week before senior year Christmas vacation, Ella's locker was jimmied open and everything inside smeared with menstrual blood. The number of tampons used indicated a concerted effort. Up until then, school administrators dismissed smaller infractions: tripping on crowded stairwells; theft of textbooks; and vandalized art projects. For this, they made us pariahs by chastising the entire student body over the PA system the following morning. Over the holiday break, Ella dyed her hair black, and grew suspicious of all authoritative bodies.

What was so intriguing about writing an article on high school sports that Ella set aside her loathing and contacted the very people who caused her such adolescent pain?

My high school yearbook sat under the rattan basket on the closet shelf. Another set of memories rife with ambiguous emotions. In the team sports section, Erin Sutkas and Kristi Dutcher posed for a photo on the pitch wearing field hockey gear. Teeth gripped mouth guards, fingers clutched candy cane sticks. Their goggles reminded me of chemistry lab. Fifty pages on, my and Ella's senior portraits made my cheeks hurt with grinning. Ella, braces off and fabulous, before the severity of her black hair. Me with lighter brown highlights and a zig-zag part. Both of us coquettish for the camera as only teenage girls can be. Little in the year book dredged up ideas worthy of an article of reminisces.

I logged onto my account at the Crispus Attucks Library. From there I searched digitalized yearbook photos of other graduating classes. Older and younger siblings of my classmates were recognizable by eyebrows and noses. The slow crawl through hundreds of photos was agonizingly dull. Twice I threatened to quit only to click on the next page and the next until one image made it all worthwhile.

Tall, broad-shouldered, small-breasted: Karen Putnam was androgynous in her basketball kit. She had been photographed dunking a basketball in a tournament. The he as a she began life as Kerry Evan Blaine and graduated with Monica.

A bittersweet experience coming home to roost especially when home was ever less recognizable. Louis razed the pink rambling roses Mother and Nana Tilly pinned to the fieldstone wall at the driveway's entrance. For a fleeting moment, I could conjure them up in floppy straw hats and leather gauntlets laboring under a blue August sky. All that was unnecessary snipped away. A metaphor for living a good life in a messy world, Mother would say. Carrie replaced them with boxwood. They reeked of cat urine during warmer months. Another metaphor.

Entering the manor-style house was akin to sliding into an ice bath face first. The shock of it gave way to a promise of numbness. In a rush to please Carrie shortly after she moved in, Louis unwisely tore out the pocket doors and layered moldings on the first floor. The walls were then glazed the deep purple of eggplant. The chandelier picked out patched nail holes where paintings once hung. Original furnishings were placed in storage rather than listed by Sotheby as a begrudged favor to me. With heavy draperies and thick rugs removed, nothing absorbed sound or provided warmth. The dull echo of my boots rose up the central staircase. Such sterility is rarely found outside a hospital ward.

Louis shuffled into the foyer. Where he ended and the faded chambray shirt began was difficult to discern. He glanced at the laundry basket and the frozen tart balanced on top. "Hello sweetheart," was all he could think to say.

I spared him the awkwardness of extending a dinner invite. "Good afternoon, Louis. I'll just pop these in the washing machine. The dessert is for you all, after dinner. A thank you."

The clamor of children's feet sent Louis shuffling toward the kitchen. I moved to the laundry room and set a load of clothes to wash. The distant squeals of my nieces and nephew in the kitchen sped up the task. They had discovered the tart.

"Wait until after dinner so as not to ruin your appetite," I told them.

Michelle glared, saying nothing. Christmas was too near. Brody returned the pie dish to the freezer and curtsied like a ballerina. Cora pouted in imitation of her older sister's chagrin. I flicked my fingers, '*Poof! You're gone*', and the children skipped out of the room to parts unknown.

Cheryl exited Louis' study. Her unwashed hair and picked nails were familiar signs of internal conflict. "Anthony isn't here," she said in greeting.

"Dodged that bullet. Where's Carrie, our bride-to-be?"

"She's attending a meeting at Saint Brigid. She's generous with her time giving back to the community. People ask for *her* advice."

"Carrie seems to be in demand weekly for these after-school meetings. A sad retirement for a former superintendent—yes? The Faheys send their girls there. I've been told Loretta's a dedicated volunteer."

Cheryl shoved a finger in her mouth and commenced gnawing on the side of it with enough gusto to draw blood.

"Louis recently told me a disturbing story. Whatever happened at Anthony's restaurant know it wasn't my doing. He explained the difficult situation it placed you both in. I mailed a check."

"Did Leo Everson call you?"

"He left a message."

"And you did what? Told him to go to Hell? Do your friends know how mean you are?"

"I'm trying to be fair to everyone." Because I was mildly peeved, I couldn't resist adding, "Have I mentioned how fabulous your basement renovation is? The custom cabinetry is truly stellar."

Cheryl ignored the bait. "We'll go into Boston together. You can pick the restaurant for dinner. No raw shit. Dad won't eat it."

"I understand."

"I'm not so sure you do understand. You're selfish."

"All of this," I twirled a hand over her mismatched activewear smudged with food, "is because I haven't given Leo an answer?"

Cheryl rolled her eyes. Apparently, I was a comedian.

Louis and Anthony defined Cheryl's place in this world. Because of it, I could forgive almost anything. Though lately, I'd grown tired of being made into an ogre, her personal tormenter. I swallowed back a bit of snark to change the topic. "I assume you'll be celebrating Christmas day here. I brought gifts for the children. Where is Carrie stashing them in the meantime?"

"In the playroom. The kids never go in there."

Gathering the bag of toys required a quick trip to my car. Lugging them to the second-floor playroom allowed pauses for nostalgia. I conjured up familiar sounds: the hum of Nana's sewing machine, the murmur of Father's television, the gush of water into Mother's tub, the slap of a book on Grandpa Bernie's desk. Their everyday noises washed over me warming the ice bath.

The act of trespassing unexpectedly took me to Grandpa's study, the only remaining time capsule from my youth. Louis had yet to dismantle it, perhaps hoping someday to find extraordinary value in the books, homemade gadgets, and fantastical scribblings of the long-retired electrical engineer. Ever frugal, Grandpa Bernie documented his many ideas on scraps of brown butcher's paper that he stored inside an apothecary-style desk. Its drawers of tiny fasteners and electric components never ceased to fascinate me as a child. I peeked through its compartments not expecting the same delights and found cards exchanged between Louis and Mother during their brief courtship and other mementos of their marriage. A deep blue folder edged with silver foil reminded me of the luxurious Alaskan cruise they enjoyed after Mother was first diagnosed. A small metal box, never seen before, piqued my curiosity. It felt heavy in my hands and a hard object slid inside when I shook it. I returned it to its place and closed the study door, gently.

The playroom instilled a twinge of sadness. Only a rose velvet settee remained of the toys and furnishings brought over from England. Cheryl had taken the rest in preparation for Michelle's birth and discarded it all as too feminine shortly after Brody arrived. My earliest childhood memories were moldering in a dump somewhere.

Christmas presents were stacked hip-high in the narrow playroom closet. Satin bows and glossy wrapping papers covered packages of every size. Patterned bags spouting snow-glitter tissue lined the top shelf. The child in me impulsively sought out nametags. I found two bearing my name taped to what felt like paperback books. A curious find on the top shelf, a half-full bottle of vodka swaddled in glitter paper. A gag gift for Louis, surely. Good to know Carrie expanded her sense of humor. Mine shrank daily.

I returned to the kitchen where Cheryl brooded over the farmhouse table. White papers covered its broad surface end to end. Graphs and labeled columns identified their singular topic. This was the real reason she extended the invite. If I wouldn't go to Leo Everson, Cheryl would bring a meeting with Leo to me.

"Where's Louis?" I asked.

"Outside. Skating."

"You should clean that up before dinner unless you plan to use them as placemats."

I snugged on my coat, skirted the broad patio and pool fencing, and made for the ice rink. The snow of two weeks ago emboldened Louis to assemble the skating rink a month early. Lacking weather to sustain thick ice, the rink was inches deep in gray slush. The children flopped on plastic saucers while he smoked in a director's chair. The cold calmed me and my mind went utterly blank. A black blankness. So much said and done and duly noted between all of us that the whiteboard blackened with script leaving no voids to aid comprehension. Louis shouted instructions to Brody breaking my trance. The boy face-planted and little Cora, splattered with icy wetness, began to cry. Michelle forewent spinning circles on a snow saucer in favor of paddling on a pool tube. She quickly lost her enthusiasm for slogging along in a turtle crawl and angrily commanded her grandfather to fix the snow. He laughed a little too loud seeing me and stepped over a wood sidewall to take up a push broom to groom a path for her. Witnessing him kowtow to Michelle didn't bring pleasure. Louis made Cheryl and Cheryl made Michelle.

Cora's distress grew more raucous. I called her over to the boards and attempted to blot her ruddy cheeks dry with my scarf while resetting the earflap hat over her pale curls. She tolerated my cooing, stopped fussing, and with an unmittened hand jammed three little fingers into my mouth. The fish-hook yank on my cheek was surprisingly painful. Her other tiny hand raking my cheek was dumbfounding.

"You shut up! You don't touch me!"

It was all I could do not to cry. Spending an evening out with Manny gained immense appeal.

Chapter 24

W e met at Manny's place in Providence. I brought enough cash to cover the cost of my ticket and several drinks. Their food offerings were an easy no. Firehouse Theater served frozen appetizers, deep-fried into hard lumps. I checked my teeth in the rearview mirror for stray bits of fresh spinach before knocking on Manny's door.

"Ho-ho. Looked what the cat dragged in. Couldn't find something nicer to wear?"

"That's you. Always a gentleman."

Manny wore a fresh application of aftershave and his dark hair had curled from a shower. I dearly hoped his pressed trousers and crisp tan shirt weren't for my benefit. I dressed for comfort against the cold in ankle boots, corduroy pants, and a thick sweater under a black puffy coat. I hadn't bothered with my hair assuming wind damage would occur. We would walk to the theater.

Manny's flat was cleaner than on my first visit. The shredded posters and stacked frames were gone, vacuum tracks streaked the pewter carpet, glass tabletops gleamed nearly invisible. Even the plump couch pillows slumped with decorative V wedges.

Manny opened the refrigerator. "I got beer. Vodka in the freezer. Won't cost you twelve bucks here. How 'bout I drink some and make you look prettier. Ha. It's a joke. You look okay."

"Point taken. Pour me three fingers of vodka. Maybe I can pretend I'm with someone else."

He poured into shot glasses. A disappointment. The cheap vodka tasted like every other, which is to say, fine.

"Can I show you something?" I asked..

Manny squinted at the Salted Stone protest video Louis reluctantly shared to my phone. "So what? It's crap."

"Why is it 'crap'?"

"I thought you went for the gut punch. How're you going to do that when nobody hears anything and you can't see a face? What are they saying? Is anybody crying?"

"It was filmed by an amateur."

"I get that, genius. I got a nine-year-old nephew who takes better pics on his flip phone. These people aren't worried about freaks in masks. Where's the angry waiters wanting to drag them outside? Even the kid keeps drawing on the table with crayons. I would've filmed from the table. Right in their faces. Up close. The thing you got to watch out for is the lights. They can screw things up."

I pictured the arrangement of wall sconces and pendant lighting inside the Salted Stone restaurant. Everything else came into view filling out the putty-toned interior. The hostess podium to the right of the door, a perimeter of black tables, a row of chrome-rimmed stools against the wood bar to the left, the kitchen and restrooms in the rear.

"If filmed from the table, rather than the lower street level as it was, the mirror behind the bar forms part of the backdrop. The camera would catch the reflection of the videographer."

"That ain't good."

"You're right, it isn't," I agreed. Another mystery solved. "Tell me about the fight with Gordon. Be honest. You have nothing to hide from me."

Manny slopped vodka refilling the glasses. "I sat on that script for six years. When I saw Ella, I found my redeemer. Gordo didn't like giving up creative control of her."

"How could you know she'd agree to it?"

"I didn't until she asked me to make a play for you. Bug the shit outta you. She wanted you out. I do that . . . Yeah, that's how I got my Michelle."

"You said Ella was paid for the movie."

"That too."

I drained the glass. The flame racing down my throat felt deserved. That Ella would prostitute her values as part of a misguided effort to protect me from Gordon was something she would do.

"Tell me about the snake scenes. A tad heavy on the symbolism."

"Glad you're a fan of my work."

"Not at all."

"The first shots I lifted from *Equus*. Gordo and Ella freaked. Most people still like horses in this country. The whole pony sequence got cut. Ha-ha. I made a joke." Manny widened his eyes for emphasis. "Lost six minutes and some great visuals. Ha! Did it again. We made up for it elsewhere."

"You cut dialog for violence. Cut violence for sex. Used snakes instead of ponies for fear factor?"

"We had great material to work with. Did you like *Vipers*?"

A crossword puzzle of thoughts lined up, down, left, and right. "Ella agreed to star in a very different movie. You deceived her. Is this why she attempted suicide?"

"That never happened. She got drunk at the party. That's it."

"Why would anyone jump to that conclusion then?"

"Doesn't take a brain scientist to see Gordo was making her miserable. He had an opinion for everything and only his was worth listening to."

"Gordon tried to kill the film." Plausible.

"Everyone made mistakes. Gordo made them bigger. Payback's coming."

"A lawsuit? You're going sue Gordon?"

"Yep, there's gonna be a lot of lawyers involved. Not the ones you're thinking. You want more you got to buy me drinks with umbrellas in them." Manny shrugged into a leather jacket. "Vamos."

The route to Firehouse Theater led us away from Manny's dope connections and through a cluster of historic properties. Founded in 1636, much of Providence was historic. I identified three, nineteenth-century architectural styles during our double-time march. We crossed a corner onto a main street. The rehabilitated brick firehouse rubbed shoulders with businesses clad in stucco and weathered concrete. People bustled about its arched, wood doors. Uplighting flaunted carved corbels and a slate roof. A tall, muscular gal worked her way through the crowd handing out flyers. She shimmered in a blue, fish-scale gown. Spotting Manny, she moved our way.

"My darling, Manuel. We missed you at Celia's. Is this the little bird keeping you away from us?"

Manny rushed in to peck a heavily rouged cheek. "Cinderfella. Looking good, babe."

Cinderfella extended a lace-covered hand and we introduced ourselves as Manny turned aside to answer a call on his phone.

"You look spectacular," I said, gushing.

Cinderfella struck a flamenco pose with raised arms, arched back, and bent knee. She pouted at Manny. "She's divine. You're a beast. We're on in twenty. I have to finish this. Here." A stack of flyers was shoved into my hands. "Done." And off she scurried as fast as three-inch heels would allow.

Manny pocketed his phone and glanced down the street. "I got to go back for something. Tickets are at the window. Get us a table."

I stood in the ticket line people-watching then moved to the concession stand to buy a rum and coke and inquire about the ingredients of a cellophaned blondie. A curved staircase led upstairs to the unmanned doors of the theater. Rows of folding chairs faced a curtained stage. Trays served as tables inserted into the rows. I set my heavy coat on a chair reserving it for Manny. Spotlights hit the curtains to the applause of a hundred people and the magic began. Cinderfella emceed. We'd be treated to eight, song and dance acts themed after Disney stories. I finished the rum and coke and ordered another from a hairy guy in a cigarette girl dress.

The quality of the queens' costumes and performances varied. Some personas were the full-on glitz of sky-high wigs, fishnet stockings, and circus makeup. Others dressed more suggestively of movie characters and bounced smaller cleavages with flowers or tiny animals glued to their wigs. I couldn't identify any of the laboring peasant princesses as being Disney-related, though the fault could be mine. Television never figured prominently in my upbringing other than the detective shows watched with Grandpa Bernie. The audience laughed and clapped and sang along as performers left the stage to interact with them. Tips were gingerly stuffed into corsets. One patron was allowed to caress a performer's stiletto-heeled foot but not the leg attached.

The cigarette girl crisscrossed aisles on either side of me. A bit of a nuisance really, her bid for an order, and a welcomed tip. I waited until intermission to refresh my beverage and wonder about Manny's absence. Patrons dashed outside to smoke cigarettes or to claim spots in toilet lines. I stood up to bolster my circulation. In doing so I spied a blonde woman rising from her seat, heading toward an exit. Her tall, curvy frame reminded me of Ella. Though Ella would never have paired a drab brown cardigan with a sparkling silver catsuit. Svetlana Ustinova might.

The cigarette girl returned as the lights were dimming. All the better not to see her stubbly cheeks. "Sweetness. Are you Dannielle Mowrey?"

"I am."

Square knuckles unfolded a slip of paper. "A note from Manuel. Please forgive. He's tied up with business. Will return ASAP. Enjoy the show." She crumpled the paper and pushed it into her mouth, chewing, and swallowing. "Five-dollar tip if I ate it. Who can't use an extra five bucks?"

I settled in with a fresh rum and coke, my mood growing darker than the room. I could do without Manny's grab bag of accusatory chit-chat and boasting, but he might have answers to pressing questions. Denying me the opportunity to extract them rankled. Midway through the sixth act, I left.

The achingly cold hike back to Lindenberry Street cleared some of the alcohol vapors from my head. I boldly sang the lyrics of *Fishy-Wishy Girl* as performed by Fistof Love and reimagined her lion mane locks. Studded with sea stars, the riotous wig remained motionless as she pantomimed swimming behind a fan-blown sheet of blue fabric. A sight to behold.

"I'm a fishy-wishy-swishy-bitchy girrrrrrrl . . ."

The lights were off in Manny's flat. I paused beside my car to give the entire street a one-finger salute motivated by the rum coursing through my veins. That's when I noticed Manny's front door was ajar. That wasn't safe. An invitation to trouble.

"Manny? Hello! You left your door open."

The stillness of the interior relieved my sense of responsibility. Or it would've if I hadn't heard the faint rustle of footfall. I groped for the lamp switch. Manny's shoes were next to the couch. His wallet lay on the coffee table. The tidy living room smelled strongly of glass cleaner.

"Manny. You missed an excellent show."

Nothing.

I closed the door sharply and stood perfectly still thinking I could trick him into showing himself and we'd have a proper conversation. Another door clicked open followed by what could only be a glass storm door easing shut. Manny was sneaking out the back. I marched to the kitchen archway and nearly tripped over a large shape on the floor. A flick of the wall switch yanked a scream from my gut.

Manny stared at the ceiling. Blood seeped from a hole in his tan shirt and stained the white charging cable knotted around his throat. Flecks of white powder dusted the underside of his nose and peppered the rest of his face. I pinched his wrist, which was warm and tacky with blood. There was no pulse. Manny might've survived the shooting if he hadn't been strangled. Which, I guess, was the point. I gasped; suddenly aware I too had stopped breathing. Whoever did this might still be here.

Broad strokes of blood traveled over the threshold and into the next room. The leather jacket used to smear his blood lay in a heap on the carpet. I stepped around tripods, rolls of white fabric, and boxed lights to reach a door that let out onto a tiny fenced yard. A sliver of moon outlined a footpath that arced to a shed. Muffled scraping sounds came from within.

I ran to the shed and threw out my arm intending to lock the beast inside. It's doors flew open with an explosive growl knocking me to the ground. In a daze, I watched a motorcycle break sharp in the alley and reverse. The thrum of its engine vibrated my teeth. Bike and driver, encased in black and glinting chrome, loomed over me. I was in the presence of my own death. The silhouette of an arm descended toward my head. Adrenaline kicked in. I gripped the ground and lashed upwards with a bicycle kick. An object cartwheeled off into the night. A volcanic boom, a spray of grit, and I was alone.

They kept me waiting, first in an ambulance for an evaluation, now inside a police cruiser. The evening could've unraveled further. An hour before I arrived here, a neighbor reported hearing shots fired. Police officers patrolling the area found no signs of gang activity. The gent who confiscated my boots and searched my car was kind enough to relay this information. Had he requested my fingerprints and been denied, he might not have been so chatty.

Sleep overcame me despite the seizure-inducing emergency lights, the road jam of vehicles, and the burble of responding officers. Soon, another joined me there in the backseat. Ella stationed herself behind the driver's seat. We consoled ourselves sharing niceties of Manny.

"Manny took fabulous photos."

"He really got me. You know what I'm saying? He got me."

"Manny wore that silly pork pie hat to every meeting like a comic book character. What was his name?"

"He dazzled me with his genius."

"The movie was a courageous endeavor. Manny deserves credit for following his vision and finishing the project."

"I think we were soulmates on some things. Do you think I'm crazy?"

"Manny's loyalties changed daily. A mishmash of self-serving activities. He tried to convince me, you—"

"He let me explore ideas outside my head. He didn't set limits. I grew as an artist."

"Why did you have to die! Why?"

"Aww. Sweet pea."

"I saw the movie. They lied to you. They lied to me."

Ella's hands bounced in her lap. The whites of her eyes glowed like twin moons.

"I do understand, Ella. Most of it, I think. No need to apologize. Not to anyone. I miss you so much it hurts."

My anguish was twofold. A flash of movement. An intake of breath. And then—a shiny metal rod protruding from my belly. Blood oozed out of the puncture to be wicked up by my sweater. I tapped the metal for solidity and transferred glossy streaks of red onto my fingers. The color became unnaturally brilliant in the sharp shadows of the car.

Ella clutched the trigger handle of the pipette. Her face serene, a half-smile below wide, friendly eyes. "We all die, Danni. That's the burden of living."

Hard knuckles hit the passenger window. An officer in a knit cap and black jacket leaned in to poke my bent leg. "Ma'am. You can go. We found the gun."

Locating the murder weapon wasn't a condition of my release. My presence here was entirely voluntary. Exhaustion trumped sarcasm. "Thank you."

Detective Monroe, the lead investigating officer, watched me exit the vehicle from Manny's living room window. The female officer who checked on me before the nap gave a slight nod from her post at a sidewalk barricade. A black SUV with tinted glass parked in the spot previously occupied by an ambulance. Manny was still in the kitchen. I wanted to say goodbye, to hold his hand, to apologize for being a shitty coworker, and an even shittier friend. Had I been with him, I could've protected him. He'd be alive. I would've chased the bad guy away.

Chapter 25

A day without blistering analysis and mayhem was but a dream. Dreams too were becoming increasingly bizarre, fraught with severed body parts, menacing sounds, and sticky blackness on the nights I forwent taking an antihistamine tablet. I woke a few minutes after five a.m. convinced my left thumb had never been. Four fingers and a rounded palm. The thumb on my right hand perplexed me. An unexplained drive in my car to no place familiar ended with me finding a left thumb on the passenger seat. Smooth, unblemished, pliable skin. I had no idea how to attach it or whether I should and woke astounded that I somehow did. On a scale of sheer awfulness, my dreams rated a solid nine out of ten. Plenty in my social circle would find that hilarious, rate them no greater than a three, and call their therapists to have a good laugh at my expense.

Until the murders.

The mutilated dream hand attached to my wrist had swollen. I had the presence of mind to remove two friendship rings while in the ambulance last night. The fingers would've been lost by morning had I not. Ice packs, pain relievers, tea, and toast soothed somewhat. An unprompted call from Russell was the medicine I craved and that was not forthcoming.

I sat at my desk for a good, long think with the murder folder in hand. People close to me presented as problems. Impetuous and impatient, Dill had help carrying out the open rescue. Which members were bold enough to assist him and smart enough to text in code? What of the thirty-five-second video clip recorded at Salted Stone? Carrie provided the video to Louis without explaining how she came by it--supposedly. A shame I suspected Monica of orchestrating the disruption. Worse, I accompanied her when she stole Ella's black pocketbook on the night of our escapade. The awkwardness of asking why she did it gave me cramps. Perhaps if I asked her to discover the origin of the cartoon animal masks, the task might ping her conscience, and elicit an explanation.

Research previously assigned to the Glories populated my email inbox. Lee Anne, Rachel, and John sent multiple messages summarizing information uncovered about the principal players. Lee Anne forwarded Yelp reviews lambasting Reese's insurance services. I already guessed him to be in a downward spiral. He ceased advertising in the Yellow Pages and the golf clubs seen in his garage were of fair to middling quality. Aging family vehicles hadn't been traded up. A public school bumper sticker papered over a private school sticker on Nadine's car. The wine served at Ella's memorial luncheon retailed for eight dollars a bottle. Amazing what is right before one's eyes.

Less was offered on Bette than Manny. Per Rachel, Bette married and divorced. The retired social worker wasn't socially active online keeping her secrets to herself. Manny moved to Providence from a small town in Nevada to study filmmaking and exhibited photography in four galleries before finding employment with NPK. Manny's bragged-about cable commercials for two auto dealerships appeared to be resumé embellishments.

Loretta and Gordon bought their first home in Amherst according to John. Gordon sold telecom services after college and advanced to Selectman for a cluster of villages in western Massachusetts before marrying Loretta. Wilfred Draperies, headquartered in Nashua, New Hampshire, was owned by Loretta's father, Wilfred Kent. She joined the family firm as a teenager. Notable siblings who achieved a measure of business success included a philanthropist brother who had once been arrested for drunk driving.

On impulse, I called John at the car dealership. I worked on a theory while waiting for him to pick up the transferred call, then interrupted his sales greeting with, "Did Ella accompany you to your meetings at the Worcester rehab center?"

John made a strangled noise. "Why is that your business?"

"I was uncertain, until now, though it was plain to see. You blushed when around her. Contrived reasons to linger in her presence. Brought her little gifts from the car dealership."

"Air fresheners. I detailed her car. So what? Doesn't mean I had the hots for her."

"Under the pseudonyms JoYz654 and IMhere, you posted love notes on her social media accounts." I paused, waiting for an objection that didn't come. "Ella was kind but not encouraging. The uncertainty spurred your drinking. She felt guilty and offered to help."

John breathed quietly into the phone. A PA system squawked in the background. At last, he said, "She loved me. In a different way. It was love."

"It was love," I agreed, and let that sink in. "Who did she interact with at the rehab center?"

"Nobody. I went in by myself. Ella stayed outside in a corner park. There was a bench and a flag pole. A big stack of cannon balls. She'd sit and read a book and wait for me."

"Did she speak to anyone?"

"Sometimes there'd be a lady on the bench with her. The two of them laughing and getting on. Ella liked talking to people. She could talk to anyone."

"What was the woman's name?"

"Ella wouldn't say, which made me think she was a patient. I never asked after the first time."

"Would you recognize that woman if you saw her?"

"From what? The back of her head at twenty paces."

"Were your meetings on Thursday evenings?"

"Sometimes on Tuesdays."

"I'll send pictures. Look carefully at them and get back to me."

John readily agreed. I doubted he would.

A chubby family of three in New England Patriot tee shirts bowed heads over a platter of foiled wrapped breakfast burritos. All averted their eyes from Dill, who sat alone mumbling loudly to himself. The rapid, upward roll of his eyes indicated he'd developed a tic. The seat opposite bore the brunt of his furry—splattered red and reeking of chili powder. An anxious female clerk fetched Toby for me. He pulled on a hoodie, shoved a cigarette in his mouth, and motioned for me to follow him outside. We stood between the dumpster and Toby's white Subaru in a light freckling of rain. Brooding clouds promised a heavy encore. The young man lit up with shaky hands. The smell of fryer grease formed a haze around him.

"Why is he here, Toby? It's ten o'clock on a school day."

Toby reset the name badge on his visor and stared at a car idling at the drive-through window. "Dill slept on my couch last night after pounding back a beer. He said he couldn't go home because his mom would be all over him."

"What is wrong with you? He has the mental acuity of a twelve-year-old. You gave him beer? Of course, he wouldn't want to go home."

"I didn't give him anything. He took it from my frig. I drove him home this morning and he showed up here an hour ago. My boss won't call the cops because he thinks he's a buddy of mine. Dill isn't a friend. He's too needy. Acts like a fuckwit. Talking to him didn't do any good. He's all jacked up and scaring the shit out of people."

Technically, this wasn't my problem. I could walk away and let Toby deal with it. He could very well lose his job and then I'd feel responsible. It really wasn't Toby's problem either. The burden for Dill's behavior fell on Dill. Or more likely Paula. Only she'd blame someone else. Most likely me. I leaned on Toby's car feeling a divot against my spine. "What on Earth happened to your car?" The white hood was riddled with fresh dings, deeper dents, and long scratches.

"I hit a deer on the highway. Sucker nearly killed me. I wasn't going to say anything because you know how they are."

Indeed. I knew several members who actually drove into ditches to avoid striking and killing animals. They expected others to do the same. I surveyed the damage. "A deer can easily ride up the hood and sit in the front seat with you. You could've been killed. How fast were you driving?"

"Too fast." Toby stomped out the cigarette. "You going to help me out here?"

"I will, if you'll reciprocate with a favor for me."

Toby's hands stopped shaking. "Go. Name it."

"I need a window into Dill's world to figure out what's going on inside his head. Talk to the high schoolers that dine in. Ask who his friends are. I want first *and* last names. I trust you marginally more than I trust him, which shouldn't be construed as a compliment. Deal?"

"Yeah, sure. No problem." Toby sparked up a second cigarette.

I left him chain-smoking in the drizzle. Dill saw me coming and locked arms over the tabletop spreading more hot sauce.

"We should talk." I sat at an adjacent table and folded my hands in a prayer pose to keep from dope slapping him. "This behavior isn't appropriate. You could get Toby fired. This isn't how friends care for each other."

"Why are you talking like that? Do you even hear yourself?" Dill pressed hands to ears. His eyes spasmed upward.

My desire to protect Dill from his worse instincts made me his nanny. He wanted the privileges of adulthood without doing the adulting part. Nearby, the family binging on breakfast burritos ceased smacking their lips to better hear our conversation. A military badge glinted on the father's cap reminding me boys had an affinity for war games and rebellion.

"Okay. Forget them," I said in a hoarse whisper. "Do you think you can handle a big assignment? Can you man-up for some truly serious shit?" I made a show of looking around and not liking what I saw. "Not here. I don't want Toby to overhear us. I don't trust him. He talks too much. They all do." Hooked, Dill followed me to my car despite knowing I was driving him home.

"You're right to think I baby you. You have everything else wrong. I've been protecting your potential. The dedication is good. You being a minor is better. The police won't arrest a minor. That's priceless to the movement."

I spoke fast and drove slowly delivering him to his doorstep. He hopped out of the car thoroughly confused but convinced if he "acted normal" I'd include him in a high-level, rescue operation. I ran verbal laps around the location of the attack, the species of animals to be rescued, and which Big Ag concern was doomed to unflattering, splashy publicity. I estimated two antic-less weeks until he grew overly suspicious and openly questioned "the plan" or someone else doped slapped him for being gullible.

The last square of leftover lasagna would be my lunch. A chicken pot pie box tumbled to the floor when I opened the freezer. It had been an impulse purchase from Aimees Market for reasons I couldn't articulate at the time. The frozen box resembled the package mock-up taken from Loretta. Placed side by side on the table, they were a near-perfect match in color scheme, font, and graphic sizing.

Frienderland Foods produced and distributed the meat pies. The Fahey's Salisbury steak package was mysteriously blank below the Nutrition Facts panel. I knew in an instant what was destined to appear there.

I reopened emails to read previously skimmed-over details of Loretta's family—maiden name Kent. Stray facts lined up. Marvin Kent served as CFO of Frienderland Foods in Maine. The same name was printed on the jacket of the stolen DVD Manny gifted to me. I did what I should've done previously. I popped the documentary into the player and thumbed the remote.

Folksy fiddle music provided atmosphere and signaled what was to come. A female narrator led the audience on a scenic journey through scrubby hills in West Virginia. Viewers observed a small group of men collecting copperhead snakes from rocky crevices, bagging them in burlap, and transporting them to a plexiglass box inside a bland white building situated in the middle of nowhere. Every person encountered along the way spoke with a distinctive twang and wore clothing from another time. The documentary was produced seventeen years ago according to its jacket. The rural church served charismatic congregants. Theirs was a simplistic understanding of God's mercy and punishment. All of it giving rise to much soft-shoe tap dancing, guttural screaming, and the laying on of hands during services. The pastor of the church, Elwood, explained the King James bible passage that formed the bedrock of the venomous snake handling ritual. Elwood's bible training came from the former pastor, his uncle. "If it's my time to go, it's my time to go," he said with conviction, undoubtedly repeating what he had been taught.

The journey continued with a trip to a Pentecostal-type church in Kentucky. Five congregants passionately explained why they sipped micro-doses of strychnine and singed the hairs off their arms with candles. This, in addition to, speaking in tongues and dancing with live snakes draped over their shoulders. Deaths from such practices were recorded as shots of headstones, local news broadcasts, and screaming rants outside of courthouses. None spent a moment contemplating why their version of God would ask them to place their lives in grave jeopardy every week when other believers had no such burden of proof or heavy penance for living. Believers in other faiths went out into the world to alleviate human suffering. These went home to eat pig sausage. The only subjects of the documentary exhibiting any compassion or common sense were the snakes. Relatively few attacked their tormenters despite being wrenched from their homes, imprisoned in dank boxes, and terrorized by screaming humans on a regular basis.

The surname Kent featured large in this ghastly production. Matilda Kent produced and narrated it. Marvin Kent wielded the camera. Loretta's mother and younger brother, respectively. Certain aspects of the film and its dearth of crew members indicated this was a low-budget, labor of love.

As the credits rolled, I gyrated in a protracted happy dance that nearly tore out a rotator cuff. A connection. *Entanglement!*

Back at my computer, I scrounged up more information on the Kent family. When not in their New Hampshire showroom selling cornice boards, Matilda Kent drove around the country looking for God. *Vipers of Redemption* was her third endeavor and the only one mentioned by title. Son Marvin lived in a stone mansion in Maine overlooking the Atlantic Ocean. He married into the Frienderland clan. His wife Judy was fifteen years older and an avid collector of Civil War wax death masks. As Lee Anne would say, "The lady's a few sandwiches short of a picnic."

Ironic then to read the subject line of one of Rachel's emails: Lee Anne's Stalker Boyfriend. I called Rachel for clarification of the meandering missive. "I can't make head nor tail of your message. Walk me through it quickly as if your hair was on fire."

"Hahaha. Okay. Uhm, so, I got inside the squirt's headspace like you asked. Kids hate school, parents, and shirts with buttons. They love gaming and jerking off. Who doesn't? Dill's keeping secrets but can't be a tough-ass without somebody to brag to. Ta-da! I looked for people he might've bragged to. Peter O. from White Mountain VSN said Dill was racking up hates talking guns and anarchy. Before that, he was super friendly with a guy, Robert the Bruce. Peter said their conversations were hinky and he knew Dill was a minor. After he blocked them, they showed up as Twisters on some of the dumber posts. Then the kid went away to join *your* group." Rachel laughed without mirth.

"Whatever became of Robert the Bruce?" *RTB.*

"Someone like him popped up on two dating sites Lee Anne and I use. Boston and Worcester. Dangerous Don. Hetero and horny, he said. That scary dude was giving Lee Anne some loving. She told me they never hooked up. I don't know if I believe her. Whenever she gets a little too happy, I get suspicious. I'll send you his pic."

A screengrab of an avatar popped up next in my email. The cartoon man wore aviator sunglasses, a pewter forelock, and a smarmy smile.

Dang.

Chapter 26

The blue Civic coupe pulling into the driveway didn't register as meaningful. Mr. Peebles occasionally entertains the odd guest. I continued with my task and nestled a replacement gargoyle, this one made of resin, into the dirt over the first cat's grave, then sprinted up the deck stairs. At my door, I heard a voice call out.

"Hey, gorgeous. Come here often?" Russell leaned against the coupe.

I shrieked with delight. "When did you get in?"

"Why do you shut your phone off?" he asked.

"Keeps the bogeymen at bay. And those who wish to criticize. Long story."

Russell moved too slow retrieving a duffle bag from the car. I paced the deck full of excitement until he stood beside me. We kissed unabashedly at the door and waltzed into the kitchen wrapped in an embrace. Shoes and coats fell to the floor. He hoisted me up onto his hips. My knees bounced off two doorways on the trek to the bedroom. Amid the tickling and giggling, clothing was tugged off and flung away. Small objects knocked from the dresser hit the floor with dull thuds. Fingers glided softly over smooth skin. Tongues followed, blazing new trails over sensitive hollows at throats, hips, and knees until we were nearly brought to tears with longing. Our patience was hardly virtuous, but the reward for delayed gratification was great. An arduous round of shudders and moans crescendoed when, together, we rode the magnificent wave of an orgasm muffled by screaming into each other's mouths.

Eventually, my eyelids fluttered open. My entire body steamed with perspiration. I'd arched and moaned through a cosmic sauna and emerged detoxed of negative energy. Even my banged-up hand didn't hurt. Russell's thumb and forefinger massaged a nipple and my nether regions pulsed faster than a hummingbird's wings. I squelched the budding desire. It could easily lead to an afternoon in the bedroom and I had marginally more important things to do.

"I missed you," he said.

"I could tell," I said with a sly smile. In truth, I couldn't. Seven texts in twelve days doesn't exactly scream passionate longing.

"Question—I don't judge, everyone can raise their freak flag—but I have to ask, why do you have so many bruises?"

"Parkour. I'm a traceur. I'll explain some other time." My stomach rudely gurgled. I'd forgotten to defrost the last slab of lasagna earlier.

Russell chuckled. "Should we feed that thing?"

"Yes. Later. Right now, we should eat lunch. I'm famished."

We rolled out of bed like two saddle-weary cowboys. Russell pulled on my fuzzy lilac robe, which showed off his firm thighs. I slipped into his white tee shirt and striped boxer shorts and brushed tangles from my dark locks. Someday I'd craft a five-course meal for him just to show off. Today was not that day. A late lunch for two would be seitan patties with pickled red onions on seeded rye bread and chickpea hummus with assorted fruits. I expected him to like it or at least pretend to and said as much while I browned the burgers in a pan.

Russell pointed his cider bottle at the lidded tub on the counter. "Why are you saving the water from the can of chickpeas?"

"Aquafaba. I use it for other things. Mayonnaise. Meringue. As a binder."

"Meringue?"

"Bean water is starchy with some of the same properties as egg white. Whipped, sweetened, and stabilized with cream of tartar, it turns glossy white and expands with trapped air. Viola, meringue for a pie. Food wizardry. Can you serve up the seitan, please? Help yourself to the marinated mushrooms and tomato."

We ate sloppily and with gusto. After-sex food, whatever it may be, was a favorite. Second only to triple-layer carrot cake packed with walnuts and cashew cream filling. Fortunately, my family hadn't ruined that guilty pleasure.

"What are your plans for the rest of the day?" I said, scooping up hummus on a zucchini spear.

Russell made a silly face as I ate it. "Eat, wash your back in the shower, nap."

"As tempting as that sounds . . ."

A pink flush crept up his neck. "Sorry. I shouldn't assume you don't have other commitments."

I played my fingertips along the back of his hand. "Tomorrow I'm off to see Ella's aunt, Muriel Nadler. Come with me. It'll be an adventure. I've said little about my investigation in my texts. You should know what I've been up to. There've been two more deaths."

Russell opened and closed his mouth. The questions remained in his head.

After clearing lunch dishes, I led him into the parlor. We sat on opposite ends of the couch with legs entwined and a bowl of oatmeal raisin cookies cradled between our knees. Russell placed his surprisingly flexible toes between my legs and it was a test of willpower to stay focused. Having to discuss the events of the past three weeks with a non-Monica human filled me with a mix of happiness and dread. It forced me to streamline my conclusions into comprehensible sentences. I set a timer on my watch and stuck to it. Try as I might, my retelling wasn't chronological in the strictest sense. At the five-minute mark, I stopped adding asides for clarification and just let the information flow. Easy when I omitted certain details related to my bodily harm, gun possession, and breaking and entering.

Russell studied copies of the photos John sent and said nothing. He hadn't known Ella, Manny, Evelyn Pallotta. My quest for justice didn't involve him. I was sure at any moment he'd ask for the return of his underwear. Instead, he wandered into the kitchen and brought back the demitasse cup holding paper fragments. We pieced together the message card from Claire's bouquet.

You light up my world. Never forget how special you are. Always a classy lady.   Rob B

"Robert B. RTB," I said. "It's one of Dill's codes. His mother said he made friends at work. New friends."

Russell, a quick study, made the same connection. "Let's go to Bottoms Up and see if we can make positive IDs. Claire could've been their lookout. The reason why you never caught the guys."

I jumped to my feet. "Wow. You *do* know how to romance a girl."

Talk in the car explored two theories I had developed regarding the making of the movie. Russell cautioned me to build upon facts rather than speculation lest I drive myself insane. This triggered a bout of laughter that carried us into Bottoms Up's parking lot. I deposited Russell at its door with a thumbs up and a good-luck kiss. Sharing my investigation with him made it an adventure.

The setting sun dimmed the car's interior making the glow of my e-reader inviting. Romantic comedies tend to sustain my interest for roughly one hundred pages before the protagonist's lack of common sense forced me to abandon their mission to maintain my own dignity. This novel originally appealed because the lead character was named Tanya like my mother and she chased after a lost love in Italy and in parts of Britain. The settings were nostalgic and, lately, helped dispel some tremendously dark thoughts. I had just been transported to Edinburgh Castle when the car rocked with Russell's return.

"They're both in there. What do you want to do?" Before I could respond, Russell pointed to a red-capped figure moving through the lot. "He's leaving."

"He followed you out?"

Russell frowned. "I wasn't looking behind me."

"Should we follow? We don't have anything better to do, do we?"

"I could think of a few things." Russell slipped his hand between my thighs.

I found his libido endearing and started the car. Our target drove an azure blue Ford Fiesta. I nearly lost sight of it leaving the lot—distracted by the brown and green sign for Turner's Coffee Depot.

"Elevate your mind from my lady parts and tell me what happened."

"I asked the girl at the desk for a tour."

I stopped for a traffic light three cars behind the Fiesta. Russell placed the printed photo of the curly haired young man on the steering wheel.

"His name is Colin. The girl's new and couldn't remember his last name. She said he's been there for about a year and a half. Colin can get to work in a few minutes. He must live in the area."

"How did you get her to tell you that?"

"I asked about a job for my younger brother. Lisa couldn't wait to complain about the jerks she works with."

"Lisa? Were you flirting?"

Russell grinned and straighten an invisible tie at his throat.

"Anything on RTB?"

"He's a shift manager. The girl referred to him as Mr. Bush. Rick, not Rob."

"Huh. Rick Bush."

We cruised into Westborough. I knew the roads. I didn't know our destination. We rolled through multiple stop signs and darted under red lights to keep up with the Fiesta.

"So, what do we know? Rick, the gang leader. Colin, his helper? Claire, a possible girlfriend. Dill, a hapless convert. The open rescue being part of a grooming process. A way to sustain his trust?" This made sense to me.

"I'm beginning to understand why you said entanglements. Two friends acquainted with the guys tormenting your group. Doesn't look good."

"Rather awful, isn't it? Only, there's more." I summoned up the courage to accept his concern and told of the disgusting messages, the frozen cats, and the attempted hit and run at Leavitt Brothers.

"Someone tried to kill you? Great. Not how I wanted that night to be remembered."

I pinched his thigh. "The high point of that particular evening came later. Hmm, twice."

That brought a smile.

The blue car signaled a turn onto Quintin Road. The navigator's map showed the street bisecting a large oval, Redbud Drive. When Rick veered right, I turned left and parked at a curb near a whiskey barrel spilling out moldy pumpkins and frost-nipped mums.

"Let's go for a walk."

The 1990s subdivision looked as fresh as the day the bulldozers left. Homes painted varying shades of desert sand sat proudly on neat, square lawns. American flags flapped from yard poles. Anytown, USA. Residents decorated for the holiday season with door wreaths and icicle lights clipped to gutters. Russell and I traded hats and scarves in a feeble disguise should anyone glance out a window. The sound of voices urged us onward to a white split-level with a basketball net hanging over its short driveway. The man with the red cap was coaxing a little girl out of a booster seat. A laughing boy in an orange jacket bounced a soccer ball off the car's fender. The children must've darted ahead of Rick at the trampoline park to be hidden from view between parked cars. I absorbed certain details such as the house number, the car's license plate, the little girl's pink sneakers, and paper snowflakes taped to their home's picture window. The children bounded up the house stairs seeking warmth inside. Rick lingered the sweep the stoop. He cast a long look in our direction. Russell threw an arm over my shoulders and I leaned into him tugging aside the bunched scarf, the same bold scarlet and white striped scarf Russell wore inside Bottoms Up.

The echo of a voice halted my step. "What was that?" I whispered.

Russell drew me closer. "He said, 'Have a good night, Mowrey.'"

The incident on Redbud Drive propelled Russell from bed well before sunup to study the murder folder. I greeted the cold, clear Saturday a few hours later with enthusiasm not felt in weeks. Applying a name and a face to our bogeyman gave me power over him. Glimpsing his home life was bonus material. Before bed last night, Russell burrowed into RTB's past to discover his online resume. Rick claimed he volunteered as a U10 soccer coach in his spare time. I couldn't avoid attaching significance to it.

My best thinking occurred when moving. A one-handed workout in the attic with free weights, elastic bands, and the stability ball got blood pumping to my muscles and didn't impinge upon bruised tissue. My left forearm was in storm cloud phase with deepening shades of purple emerging. The injury assured me that I'd remain on top for the duration of Russell's stay. A delicious outcome.

"Danni! Breakfast is ready!"

"Coming!" I yelled down to the second floor.

The scent of raspberry jam and flaky pastry greeted me on the landing. Russell's culinary skills extended to brewing a pot of coffee and baking frozen turnovers. A side of vanilla soy milk yogurt added a touch of nourishment.

"Do you work out every day?" Russell asked, brushing crumbs from his lips.

"No. I have too many excuses."

We ate in companionable silence, Russell reading the newspaper from his tablet and I reading the Providence Police Department's web page from mine. Their published activity log recorded an incoming call at 9:06 pm reporting shots fired on Manny's street. The investigating patrolmen couldn't substantiate it. Manny wasn't dead at that time. I was sure of it. The neighbor, I believed, had heard the motorcycle arrive.

Russell glanced at my tablet and poked a finger at the murder folder on the table. "What's up with the cigarettes you found behind the shed?"

"I'm fairly certain the man named Colin left them. RTB is too short."

"I played the messages saved on the answering machine. He needs to be stopped before someone gets seriously hurt."

To my credit, I'd didn't make crazy eyes and shout hysterically that three dead people are as serious as it gets. "Agreed. Normal, healthy people rarely wake up one day and suddenly choose to terrorize. They tend to build up to it starting with lesser acts. We know nothing of Colin's past. More upsetting, he's working with Rick, and the pair of them are influencing Dill. I can't force the boy to quit his job and I can't bring conjecture to Detective Boynton."

Russell disagreed citing the obscene messages and the Salted Stone video, which he credited to them for this or that reason after watching it twice. I poured more coffee and explained, briefly, why not all evidence is of equal value in a court of law. Furthermore, the conspiring between Rick, Colin, Dill, and possibly Claire, appears to be unrelated to the murders, at least superficially.

"My plan is largely unchanged. We'll continue to postpone events. Dill and Claire will be expelled from the group later. I may need them."

"For what?"

"Don't know. I haven't gotten that far yet."

Chapter 27

R omance be damned. The ninety-minute westward drive to Northampton was to include shopping at an antiques mall in Sturbridge because I enjoy romanticizing old stuff and a stop at Cutting Board in Palmer for lunch and a pinch of interrogation. Five miles outside of Framingham a stuttering snore filled the cabin. Sleep-deprived Russell finally succumbed. I couldn't see waking him to ask that he gawk with me at dusty Shaker baskets or botanical prints cut from textbooks. Hence, I drove directly to the deli entertaining myself by tracing a light fingertip over his nose and watching him twitch.

Online photographs of the New York-style deli screened out adjoining businesses: a newsstand in disrepair; and a sex toy shop. In fairness, the deli's sleek black metal and umber wood façade made all else look exceptionally shabby. The door sounded with a guitar strum opening into a white and brown tiled restaurant dazzling under globe lights. Six, benched customers awaited takeaway orders ahead of me.

A girl in a striped apron chirped, "What can I get for you?"

"Hello. I'd like to speak with a manager."

"Is there a problem?"

"Not at all. I have a question about event planning."

"Sure. Please take a seat."

I perused the menu at a red enameled table. Seitan pastrami, smoked carrot lox, and truffle walnut pate would delight any plant-based gourmand lucky enough to stumble upon this place.

A stocky, ginger-haired young man approached. He pulled out a chair and extended a hand. Smudges under his eyes told of hectic days. "Gilroy Loucks. How can I help you?"

"It's a pleasure to meet you, Gilroy. I'm Danni Mowrey, here seeking information about the grand opening ceremony with Ella DeMarco."

"Is this about a story?"

"Just a dear friend looking for answers."

From what I read, Gilroy and his partner-chef Dave scrambled to fill the opening day agenda without their featured attraction. A disappointed food writer from a local weekly, The Crier, published two anemic paragraphs and a tiny photo of a Reuben sandwich.

"Business good?" I asked.

"Could be better. Listen, I'm sorry about your friend. We met her once. Fantastic repartee. She was someone special." He splayed his fingers. "I hate sounding like a dick. I don't know what to say. Er, orders are backing up."

"Then don't sound like a dick. Talk to me."

A tired smile pushed his lips up. "Okay."

"Why did you choose Ella?"

"Easy. She draws a decent crowd. Wrote two cookbooks. Gorgeous. Dave suggested her. I wasn't happy with the hit to our budget, but I could see dishing free samples and passing out coupons wouldn't be enough. Bringing in her fans would go a long way to paying the rent."

"Did anything unusual occur around the time of her scheduled appearance? Threats. Vandalism."

"Nothing like that. The community's very supportive. They see what we're trying to do here."

"What did you think happened when she didn't show up?"

"The police phrased the question differently. They said what they wanted us to agree to."

"Which was?"

Gilroy sized me up and took a deep breath. "They said your friend was involved with drug dealers. Dave and I refused to give them anything to work with. Like I said. We met her once, here, when we were setting up. She was very cool. Into healthy living. We couldn't make that connection."

"Did you speak with Detective Charles Boynton?"

Gilroy shook his head no.

"What did you think of her manager, Gordon Fahey?"

Gilroy's face darkened. "Plenty. None of it is good. He's subtracting an advertising fee from our refund. The poor woman didn't show up because she's been . . . you know, and we're getting hit with a fee for publicizing she would be here. That's cold." Gilroy fidgeted in his seat and eyed a customer at the counter. I thanked him for his time and sent him back to the kitchen with my order.

Russell ambled into the shop. "I woke up and you weren't there. Almost went to the toy shop looking for you."

"Deviant."

"It's what attracted you to me," he said playfully. "Are we stopping for lunch? I'm hungry."

"Already placed the order. We'll feed Muriel too."

While we waited, I extolled the virtues of the antiques mall we bypassed. Russell listened patiently and gave me permission to stop there should he be asleep on the return trip. The brunette version of Gilroy—same longish hair, tightly trimmed beard, and black jeans—approached our table carrying takeaway boxes bounded in twine. I guessed he was Dave, the partner.

"I haven't paid for the order."

"On the house," he said. "I included chocolate babka and blondies. Let us know what you think. Gil's not sold on the babka." Dave slid a pristine copy of *Flowering Foods* in front of me. "I was going to ask Ella to sign it."

Russell's sleepy eyes fluttered when I opened the book and inscribed the flyleaf. He craned his neck to view the photo on the dust jacket of Ella and me mugging for the camera.

I handed the book to Dave. "Gilroy said you recommended Ella."

"Well, the idea came from a sous chef I worked with at Thad's Café. It's embarrassing. Gil and I only recently heard of NPK. I'm not long from Virginia. Gil wasn't on social media much."

"Your friend's name—if you don't mind me asking?"

"Vanessa Norelli."

I covered my astonishment. "We met recently. How well do you know her?"

"We worked together not quite a year. She left before I did to pursue 'other opportunities.'" Dave made air quotes.

"Which were?"

"Could've been anything. She dumped half of her inheritance from a dead aunt into her husband's business. All Solutions for Networks. Big or small? Something like that. Didn't go well. That mistake left her strapped for cash for her big dream. She wanted to be another Linda McCartney." Dave laughed. "I could sit here and talk about it forever, but Gil would have a hemorrhage in the kitchen."

"How awful. I certainly hope he doesn't. Please. This is incredibly important. Something Ella was involved in could've gone wrong and led to her death. That something might very well be someone. Anything you care to share could prove eminently helpful."

Dave retrieved a paper menu from the counter and dragged another chair over. "I can't have this coming back on me. We're a small community." He handed me the menu. "Write something nice on it."

"Understood." I mimed locking my lips, tossing away the key, and contemplated what heartfelt thoughts I should scribble.

"For starters, Vanessa's in it for *her* health. Always was. She thought it'd give her an edge, make her sound reasonable to the head honcho of NPK. The guy shut her down. A condescending prick, she called him. Vanessa can be a pit bull with a rubber squeaky if she thinks she's being dissed. She dug in and wouldn't give up. Vanessa and her husband. Derrick?"

"Francis."

"Yeah, him. They stalked Ella DeMarco's social calendar. Worked their weekends around it. Groupies. Creepy. Did that until they could pitch their ideas and get Ella to agree to work with them on a line of frozen entrees. The whole thing went bust because of a noncompete clause in the contract Ella signed with the owner, George Falhey."

"Gordon Fahey. Manager. Not owner."

"Really? Are you sure?" Dave regrouped. "Any hoot, that guy. Vanessa was rip-roaring pissed. She and hubby were fighting. Are they still married?"

"When was this?"

"January. I think. Last I heard, Vanessa was working part-time in a soup kitchen for old folks in Worcester. Vanessa dreamed of being the head honcho of her own company. Giving it away for free seems like admitting failure."

So much to untangle.

Russell laid his head on his arms on the table.

Please don't snore.

"When was the last time you spoke with Vanessa?"

"Before or after she asked to use our kitchen?"

"Dave! You're needed at the counter!" Gilroy sent us dagger eyes while ringing up a customer order.

We parted company, each happy with the exchanges made. Russell shook himself awake on the sidewalk. "Did you get what you wanted?"

"Maybe. Right now, I'm incredibly confused."

Russell avoided direct eye contact focusing instead on his smartphone. I guessed he was Googling me. My critics were many and the photos unflattering. Which brought to mind the action photo of me on Gordon's phone. RTB, the assailant who threw the first punch. I was certain of it. Colin, no doubt, worked the camera in a car in the intersection. Which meant Gordon was in contact with them. Revenge fantasies filled my head before we reached the interchange of I-91 and Route 5 in Northampton.

Red brick churches, municipal buildings, family-run shops, and eateries stood shoulder to shoulder funneling traffic down Main Street. Russell perked up. We passed four churches. Tomorrow was Sunday. Best not to mention it and create an awkward obligation should Russell be the church-going type. I gave in to nostalgia and steered away from Smith College to cruise treed streets populated with old houses. I walked and biked this neighborhood for four years. While I'll never regret moving to Springfield after graduation, I often questioned remaining in Framingham to be close to Louis and Cheryl after Mother's death. Picturesque Northampton has been calling me home since I left a decade ago.

The scenery grew woodsy again as Muriel's Greek Revival house came into view. It impressed at a distance. Drawing closer, one noted loose siding and blistered paint the color of Dijon mustard. With my back braced against a fluted column under the roof overhang, I saw streaks of green film and felt the sag of soft boards underfoot. Every year the house settled into the ground another half-inch unlike Muriel, who aged backwards. She answered the door barefoot in a tie-dye tee shirt and a layered scarf skirt. A crown of fabric daisies on her silver head made her a flower child.

"Sophie and I are the same size," she explained, twirling to make the skirt float. Addressing Russell's stare, she said, "Please, I was a baby in the sixties." She swung a gray au naturel braid off her shoulder. "Is it the hair?"

I nudged Russell aside to claim a hug. "Auntie M's a seamstress. She creates costumes for a theater in town. She's also an herbalist. Don't drink the tea."

Russell extended a hand. Muriel ignored it going in for a hug.

"How exciting. I haven't had overnight guests in ages. At least a month. What's wrong with a little boost of tea?"

We ate in the kitchen at the wood-topped island under a pot rack swagged with dusty herbs. Potato salad, pastrami, sauerkraut, tabbouleh, noodle soup, pickles, and challah bread served with hard cider discovered in a crisper drawer. Muriel claimed to have forgotten the cider after we refused herbal infusions. She wasn't fooling anyone. Russell didn't suffer from constipation and my mind was as sharp as ever.

Russell quickly became the topic of discussion. Muriel wrung out loose details of his work as an investment analyst and his everyday life in Camden, New Jersey. She glibly asked questions about his political views, moral leanings, income and investments, and lastly, what he found attractive in me.

My attempts to curb her intrusiveness were weak. "Is that really necessary?" I was just as curious as she was.

Russell, still in job interview mode, asserted his boundaries. "I'd prefer not to discuss my tax returns." He ignored a haphazard guess about his nationality to blurt awkwardly, "Did you know she wrote a book?"

"She wrote two books," Muriel said to him and, "Where'd you find this guy?", to me.

"He'd have no reason to read either." My meaning clear. Before Muriel could assassinate Russell's character or rate his hypocrisy, I shooed him away from the table by saying, "We'll clean up in here. Please go upstairs and select a room for us."

Russell comically blotted his forehead with a napkin on leaving the room.

"Couldn't a man be interested in me for my winning personality? Why must they be enamored with my meager accomplishments?"

"I never said that."

"Not out loud."

"What happened to your vow of aversion? He's not your type."

I laughed, spitting up the crumbs of a blondie. "They outnumber us substantially. After the ridiculousness of Henry, I made allowances so as to have sex again."

Muriel snuffled and began clearing plates without my help.

"Manny Soto was murdered." No preamble. Bare, brutal fact. My throat tightened.

Muriel softly closed a cupboard door. "I have faith you'll do what you can." Her hug braced me up and steadied my knees. We stayed like that for a long moment soaking up each other's energy.

"Why didn't you attend Ella's service?" I asked.

We both reached for our e-cigarettes and I explained what transpired at Reese's house. My odorless vapor swirled into the sweet, nutmeg scent of hers.

"I planned to go," she said. "Nadine called the day before to uninvite me. The divorce fourteen years ago is still fresh in everyone's minds, she said. They invited Avery. Naturally. Wouldn't miss a chance to do that. Pat said his dad didn't show up. Too busy opening another Suzuki dealership. Avery never gave two figs about his niece."

"I'm sorry."

"Don't be. I never liked that side of the family. Two-faced assholes. I spent time with Ella when it counted. I'm sure it was boring as hell right up the fight."

Russell was slow to return. When he did, I sent him to the living room to collect my backpack. I unzipped it carefully on the island. The framed photo of Ella, Muriel, and I dressed as pirates and hoisting beer bottles wasn't what made Muriel clap her hands or Russell's face lose all color.

"Mine to keep?" Muriel asked.

I nodded. "Reese was going to use her in the commission of a crime with Nadine's help. They're unworthy."

Muriel caressed the marble urn with her fingertips. "You're home, dearest."

When Muriel suggested a woodland walk around Fitzgerald Lake to view the largesse of the Clean Green Earth Project, I assumed we'd all experience it with the same reverence. The forest pulsed with life and movement. Chattering squirrels raced up scaly bark to drop nuts onto our path. Brittle leaves crackled underfoot startling a scarlet, northern cardinal from a sassafras tree. The hollow rapping of a pileated woodpecker echoed over the water. Being here invigorated me. I marveled at the tenacity of muscular tree roots growing through rock fissures. I pointed out ornate splotches of blue-green lichen on boulders and shelves of wavy conks protruding from stumps. Russell showed little interest. He faltered over knots of roots and loose stones easily avoided. I toyed with the idea of fetching him a walking stick from the undergrowth, but his manhood would've suffered. Muriel's withering gaze, fixed during the car ride here, showed little signs of abating. Leaning against her car back at our starting point, she was fully consumed by a scowl.

Russell sought to lighten the mood by amicably patting his flat belly. "Thanks. I needed a good stretch to walk off the big lunch."

"I didn't bring you here for exercise, doofus," Muriel snapped. "Danni needs protecting. Ella talked up Gordon Fahey doing great things with Clean Green Earth Project because he collected all kinds of awards saying so. The man's a turd. Why would he do anything good for anybody else?"

I couldn't picture Gordon dusted with dirt and clutching a shovel in his hands either. "Ego? Publicity? Volunteers did the work and he took credit."

"Credit wasn't the only thing he took. Him and that wife of his were very good at opening peoples' wallets and making friends on town councils. The price tag on improvements here was close to ninety grand."

Russell issued a thumbs up. "Impressive. The guy can't be all bad."

Muriel balled her hands against her jeans. "The Broad Brook Coalition did it. Not him! Clean Green raised a bunch of money and dumped two loads of gravel." She stomped a foot to indicate we were standing on it. "Everything you saw in there was paid for and done by others. Where's the rest of the money? What was that spent on?"

"What money?" I snapped. "What are you talking about, Muriel?" A lovely walk ruined by her complaints and dislike of Russell. Telling her of my previous fling with him while washing the lunch dishes was a grave error on my part. She undoubtedly blamed him for my perceived loneliness since Henry.

"BBC has been buying up land for decades to protect it from development. The name Gordon Fahey didn't ring any bells over there. He never raised funds for them. Same story out of Montgomery with a Boy Scout troop. A garden club in Goshen got scammed on a street beautification project when the Faheys came on board. Where'd the money go? Embarrassed communities don't want to publicize their mistakes and these were small potatoes, money coming from twenty-dollar donations." Muriel sucked in a lungful of air. "That, my dear, is why he moved his family away from here. People started asking questions and demanding better answers. Who knows how many years he bilked retirees out of cash? How many projects he collected for that never got done."

Russell was done humoring us. "No hurry," he said, sliding into the back seat of Muriel's car.

"What did Ella say when you yelled at her?" I asked. "Because—I imagine you did."

The angry creases in Muriel's face softened, "She believed the money was sitting in escrow or spent on a different project. I couldn't get her to see reason."

"Which is?"

"The Faheys were in cahoots with the planning boards. Members on each project protected them from prosecution."

"A conspiracy theory?" Disbelief sharpened my voice. "Well, it would be several conspiracies. Wouldn't it? Multiple town boards and pertinent citizen groups. State officials too. Cross agency collaboration."

"Gordon's a pro at making friends where it counts. Rob Peter to pay Paul with Mary's money. A real schmoozer. He's coming for you to fill the hole Ella left behind. Don't give him a chance. That man is evil."

Ella's horrific death damaged Muriel in ways I hadn't foreseen. Gordon was egotistical and excessively compensated. A petty dictator to those dependent on his good graces. All true. Yet annual, independent audits of NPK's financial dealings had never uncovered criminal wrongdoing. Muriel wouldn't want to hear it.

"Let me think on this and do some homework. I don't believe it to be directly related to her death, though I do appreciate knowing your concerns."

Muriel slid into the car and started the engine. "Don't think too long. There's a guy you have to meet."

I sat in the back seat to keep Russell company. He reached for my hand. This morning I said Muriel was my honorary aunt and raved about her positive influence on my life. When he meets her, she's delusional and hateful. None of this was conducive to the romantic getaway I promised him. When Muriel began to hum and eased up on the gas pedal, I commenced fact-finding.

"Did Ella sell her interest in NPK to Gordon?"

"Ask Gordon, not me. Ask Reese. Isn't it all his now?"

"Why did Ella hire the private investigator, Raymond Semple?"

"My suggestion. She had eight thousand worries. Whatever he found out didn't fix them. You should sweet talk some answers out of him."

"I have Ella's gun and laptop."

Russell dropped my hand.

"Good. Keep them safe."

We headed north away from the lake. The colors of rural suburbia dimmed with the sinking sun. The car bucked over a series of potholes and passed cultivated fields. A flutter of house sparrows, frightened by the car's leaky muffler, quit scrounging in furrows and took flight. Ahead on the right, a raggedy stretch of lawn and a brown cottage peeked out from behind two mountainous arborvitaes. A gate separated the shrubs. The rest of the perimeter fencing was long gone. Two antiquated cars and a storm-damaged party tent sheltering an empty rabbit hutch didn't require securing against theft.

Russell scrolled on his phone. He was probably searching for a nearby hotel.

"We're here, Danni. Pay attention to what Mr. Flansburger says."

Muriel rang the rusty cowbell hanging off the closed gate. A thin, elderly man in droopy slacks and a turtle neck sweater exited the house clomping along behind a walker outfitted with tennis ball feet.

"Evening, Carl," Muriel said, raising her voice a few decibels. "This is my niece, Danielle. She's interested in the goings-on of the Clean Green Earth Project."

"Evening." Carl's raspy voice traveled three feet.

"Carl's grandkids volunteered to bushwhack the lake trails. Kids have big ears and ask pesky questions." Muriel turned to her friend. "Tell them the boys' story."

"Hello." Carl tapped a finger to one ear.

Muriel repeated her request.

Carl tapped his ear.

"Does he wear a hearing aid?" I asked.

"Only one. Deaf in the other ear." Muriel palmed her forehead. "Shit."

Carl lacked Evelyn Pallotta's skills. He gave the ear a final tap and shrugged apologetically. Dead battery. Knobby fingers dipped into a pants pocket for a rumpled mass of folded newspaper clippings. "For you." The old gent patted Muriel's cheek.

The front door screeched open. A sinewy, young man with a sizable top knot hung spread-eagle between the aluminum storm door and its jamb. Bare fingers and toes poked out of his sweater and jeans to grip the frame. "Grandpa! Mashed potatoes or fries!"

Carl acknowledged him with a gummy grin. "That's Trey."

Our smiles evaporated. A plump rottweiller darted through Trey's wide stance.

"Don't move!" I warned Russell.

The dog knew the fence wasn't there. It darted around an arborvitae, growling and snapping, to bump Russell's thigh. I considered kneeing the dog in the snout but fancied I'd lose a patella to two rows of diamond-hard teeth. Muriel chose my moment of hesitancy to shriek. The dog sank into a crouch and began a slow crawl toward her. Fear fueled anger which prompted action. I snatched Carl's walker from his grip and pinned the dog to the ground with it. The dog, half my weight and in a frenzy, barked and thrashed against the lower bars. Claws scraped my ankles. I hopscotched to avoid them. A shrill whistle pierced the air and the canine lay still. I think it smiled at me.

The grandson circled the shrub. "Hey! What are you doing to Lucy?"

"Trying not to get savaged," I said.

"Get off her, asshole."

I jerked the walker off the dog. Lucy pranced around his legs until he produced a treat from his pocket and patted her head.

"Did you release her to intimidate us?"

"An accident. She got by me."

"I don't believe you. You should apologize. Your dog could've injured someone."

"That's her job, shit-for-brains."

I've encountered people like him before. Terrorizing others made him feel strong. Maybe he was another Spanky in the making. Sweat wetted my brow. A raptor's talon pinched my shoulder blade. The imp was highly disturbed and so was I. Any hearsay of Gordon's wrong-doings coming from a young man who clearly lacked scruples himself was of little value to me or the police. My rising temper formed a fist. My brain launched it into Trey's gut. He issued a squirrel-like bark and crumpled to the ground.

Lucy dropped to her belly to lick his face. She might've smiled at me then too.

Tablets out, Russell and I sat comfortably leg-entwined on the pillowy couch awaiting Muriel's grand entrance. Frequent guffaws had him watching humorous videos. His need for light entertainment was self-evident. I delved into the workings of CGEP to keep my momentum going. The website had been removed. To access it, I consulted the Wayback Machine.

CGEP posted its last financial filing five years ago. The nonprofit claimed income and assets in the one-hundred-thousand-dollar range. Operating expenses were a trim ten percent according to a charity monitor. CGEP funded clean-up and beautification initiatives in western Massachusetts by awarding grants to small, community-based programs. Per its defunct website, one grant installed a rain garden at an elementary school. Another gifted a baseball dugout to a middle school. Another built nesting boxes for a bird sanctuary. The BBC lake project wasn't listed. The clippings Carl gifted us were advertisements snipped from a local penny saver and coupons from a Sunday newspaper dated from October, possibly the last time he last wore those pants. Fire logs, deli meats, grapes, a roof rake, and a twenty-four-inch television had caught his fancy. What Muriel sought might've been tucked into his other pocket. Only Carl knew for sure.

A sharp, "Uh-hum," drew our eyes to the staircase. Muriel's headscarf, blousy white shirt, and tall boots—I had seen before on many occasions. The vintage sailor pants with the oddly buttoned front flap was a recent addition. She modeled the outfit posing with a plastic dagger clenched between her teeth.

"A musical?" Russell asked. "Pirates of Penzance?"

"Church of the Flying Spaghetti Monster. A different sort of theater," I explained. "Auntie M is a Pastafarian. The local chapter gathers for spaghetti and meatball dinners and everyone talks like pirates. So, that's why you wanted me to come this weekend."

Both she and I looked at Russell. He wisely said nothing.

Muriel sheathed the knife. "I told everyone you were coming. Bummer. I bought extra beer."

Russell shook his head. "You eat pasta dressed like a pirate?"

Muriel crossed her eyes. "Brain food for when we discuss the failure of this country to separate church and state. Thoughts and prayers for the victims of gun violence? Religious exemptions for public health initiatives? Oh, and sea shanties. We sing them in praise of his noodley appendages."

"Arghhh!" I agreed. "A fine idea, lassie."

"You two are on your own for dinner. I won't be home till late. I know, cry me a river, matey." Muriel shoved her arms into a wide-cuffed doublet and hoisted a canvas duffle bag onto one shoulder. When she left, Russell exhaled loudly to ensure I would notice.

"I know," I said. "An undisclosed cache of beer. The nerve of that woman."

Russell shook his fist in the air to express indignation to the powers-that-be and made an angry face until I laughed.

"Okay. How about a romantic a dinner to make amends for an awful day. Auntie M's rudeness is inexplicable. Normally, that's not the person she is."

"She wants the best for you and doesn't think I'm it."

I answered by scrambling to the other side of the couch and wrapping myself around him. Kissing led to groping and the shedding of clothing. I tugged off his chinos teasing him with how formally I arranged them on the floor. Russell wore a silly grin. His boxers strained to contain his excitement. I performed my own striptease with each item carefully folded and added to the pile. A red welt on his thigh sparked my immediate concern. Lucy had indeed bitten him. I leaned in to examine the wound and was pulled into his hunger.

All was sweaty, breathless, tingling good fun until Russell decided he should be on top and we could flip positions without missing a beat. My gimpy, bruised arm gave out at a quarter turn and we toppled sideways falling onto the coffee table. Two of its legs broke. The splitting crack of wood prompted me to yell, "Timber!"

Once our laughter faded and we had thoroughly rubbed all the sore spots, I set him to work repairing the damage to the coffee table while I crafted our dinner. A decade of living in condominiums had dulled any handyman skills Russell may have previously acquired. That or he simply enjoyed rooting around Muriel's cellar for supplies. We finished our respective projects at the same time.

A striped bedsheet, a cluster of candle stubs in brandy snifters, and yellow and green shrub clippings spilling out of a beer stein transformed the kitchen island into something special.

"Takes me back to my college days," I said, pointing an asparagus spear at the beer stein.

"I never ate this good in college." Russell spooned creamy polenta into his mouth. "How did you make fried eggs and hollandaise sauce out of tofu and cashews?"

"Read my first book. The magic is in there."

"I will. After dinner."

"I have better activity in mind. Did you see the clawfoot tub upstairs in the connecting bathroom? Muriel makes bitter teas, but her bath bombs and soaps are incredible."

"Are you saying I'm a dirty boy?" He crooked the corner of his mouth. I nearly swooned.

"You're a very dirty boy. One thing I wouldn't change about you."

"What are the things you would change?"

I stared at his plate. Tuesday, when he's gone, I'd think on it, maybe even obsess over our differences. For now, we'd enjoy each other's company.

After dinner, Russell was tasked with tidying the kitchen. I raced upstairs to ready our bath. A mourning dove cooed from my phone on the nightstand. I ignored it until the tub faucet churned up fragrant water speckled with flower petals and softened with Epsom salt.

Claire Steele had called in a panic. "My work phone is missing. If you have it, bring it back. I'm out of the hospital. I'm freaking out. I really need it. For work. Thanks for the other thing. Bye."

My yellow-eyed imp screeched with glee.

Chapter 28

Our leave-taking after breakfast was bitter for me and sweet for Russell. The original plan required a two-night sojourn to allow ample time to discover whatever Ella may have left here and to arrange a meeting with Peter Ortell, founder of White Mountain Vegan Support Network. In fairness to Russell, who demanded we leave early, Muriel's behavior was less than hospitable. She called him "doofus" three times, crossed her eyes at him twice, and stated I could easily take him down in an arm-wrestling contest.

Last night, we feigned sleep when she returned from the spaghetti dinner. Giddy on beer and sugared up on pasta, she wished to engage. We did not. Thus, her *tap-tap-tap-tap-tap* on the door and loudly whispered, "Danni, you awake? Danni. Dan-ni." went unanswered.

Our fragrant, fizzy bath had been a prelude to watching *9 ½ Weeks,* eating Snickerdoodle mug cakes, and racing back upstairs to bounce under the sheets. The sexual euphoria generated exhausted us beyond the ability to politely deal with her sniping. I reminded myself repeatedly I was responsible for Muriel's disdain for Russel. Twenty minutes after her return, I rose to use the connecting bathroom. Muriel's voice, directed at another, slid under the door.

"Can you believe it? Poor Anna. The not-knowing. I knew Dominic from way back. Ah. Enough to say hi at the bagel shop and ask about his family. Everyone is saying he wouldn't leave his kids and run off with another woman. I hope it's nothing. A big misunderstanding." Pause. "The dumbest thing I ever heard. Not you. Sadie. Drama momma. Nobody is saying he's dead. I can't handle another one. Too soon."

Muriel's anxiety spurred me to open my tablet and search local newspapers after snuggling back under the quilt with my butt comfortably pressed against Russell's. Sleep came as I puzzled over a recent story, another mystery.

Who is Dominic Waitely and why did he go away?

Because of it, I woke late with two pink-tinged eyeballs and a promise from Russell he'd drive. Keys in hand, he could dictate our departure time, and did so immediately after breakfast. Bleary-eyed, I fasten my seatbelt and settled in to sift through a small box of odd bits Muriel bequeathed to me.

When visiting, Ella typically bed down in the room overlooking the herb garden. I searched that room while waiting on the tub to fill and amassed a pile of papers that Muriel did her best to explain over breakfast. Ella frequently bought items for the house. A new sprinkler for the herb garden. Linens for the bed Russell and I shared. A set of tires for Muriel's car. Ella also paid the plumber's bill. Ella charged the purchases and kept the accompanying paperwork in the nightstand. Muriel couldn't explain the magazine picture cut-outs of trees, the green paint swatches, the baggie of embossed metal medallions or the flattened food wrappers. None of it meant anything to either of us.

Peter Ortell left a voice message for me sometime after midnight. "Sorry I missed your calls. I'm cruising around Nova Scotia. Fucking fantastic here. We'll talk when I get back. I already talked to Rachel Opalka. Get in touch with her."

Not to be defeated by disappointment, I convinced Russell to stop in Hatfield on the drive home. A short detour. "Half an hour, tops," I said. Russell allowed me to key the business card address into the navigator. Its close proximately surprised us.

A two-story, gray cube of striated concrete blocks housed Raymond Semple's office. Russell and I stiffened in our seats. Brutalist architecture living up to its name. Signage at the curb listed six businesses within. My car was the fifth in the lot. A lackluster Sunday morning.

"I don't have an appointment," I admitted. "He may not be in the office today. Looks lively across the street." A café and a sandwich shop were notable attractions in a bustling strip mall fronted by storm-damaged pear trees and gutters quivering with paper napkins. "You do a walkabout. I'll find you."

Midline Private Inquiry Service rented a suite on the first floor of the cube. I stated my name and the reason for my visit into an intercom. A gentleman in a sweat shirt with gelled black hair examined me from a sidelight before unlocking the door. He escorted me to a couch by an unoccupied reception desk and continued down a short hallway to the right. Ultrafine dust cloaked the desk. I took care not to disturb it when opening drawers. Little of interest in the office supplies and promotional folders stored within. To my left, a conference table filled the center of a meeting room. The mini refrigerator wasn't plugged in and the coffee pot on it had never been used. Semple, ostensibly, conducted all of his business over the internet.

The same man returned wearing a trim silver blazer over a starched white shirt. He joined me on the couch. The resemblance to Leo Everson was uncanny.

"Ms. DeMarco was a past client. I can't say much more. Guarding client privacy is our number one priority."

"I understand. Mr. Semple emailed a report to her. The police don't have access to her laptop. Would it be possible for him to send a hard copy to her next of kin?"

The man squinted as though confused.

"What was the nature of the work? Nonspecific. What button did she push on your phone menu?"

"Ms. DeMarco presented ideas and Mr. Semple tested them."

"How did that work out?"

A crinkly smile said he was too clever to divulge information. "Mr. Semple may still be of service. One of the areas he specializes in is untimely deaths. I believe Ms. DeMarco falls into that category. I'd be happy to arrange a consultation to discuss his services."

I held his gaze a moment longer than necessary. "Is there a form her next of kin can sign to obtain the original report?"

"Mr. Semple could recreate it using field notes. Organizing data will take two weeks and remove him from current surveillance work. The delay in his schedule could be costly. He's a man of integrity. Reputation is everything."

My left eye twitched. I gently patted it. "What prevents him from resending the email he sent to her? A few taps on the keyboard."

"Time is money and you're asking for his time."

There it is. "You won't give a copy of a report that you can sell."

A jaunty tilt of the man's head.

"How much will his time cost?"

The man opened a reception desk drawer and placed a midnight blue folder in my hands. The name of the agency was stamped in silver foil on the cover. Glossy, four-color print flyers inside advertised the agency with pictures of cityscapes and bulleted lines of text.

"Our fee schedule is on the website."

I dropped the folder on the desk, thanked him for his time, and went in search of Russell. He was exiting the coffee shop with a cup, which I snatched from his hand. "Lovely. How did you know?" I took a long swallow. Fat in the cow's cream created an oil slick on my tongue. We grimaced together. "Ew. Shouldn't have done that."

Russell shrugged without apology. "Come see something."

We walked leisurely along storefronts passing an appliance repair shop featuring vacuum cleaners in its window and an ophthalmologist's sign of blue neon lights curled into eyeglasses. Russell stopped before a set of windows papered with glamour shots of young girls and boys dressed for theatric roles as sprinting chimney sweeps.

"Yes?" I snapped, still stung by his condiment choice.

"A talent lawyer. The investigator she hired is over there. You said she was always short on time. Maybe, when the opportunity presented itself?"

Gold lettering on the glass read, Myers & Cardi Talents. A sign beneath indicated the office was closed on Sundays. I muttered, "Next time."

Russell and I stood on the sidewalk watching stop-and-go traffic in the intersection. I told him of my unproductive meeting at Midline.

Russell aimed a finger across the road. "Is that him?"

The man in the silver blazer thumbed a key fob at a red Chevy sedan.

"Yep."

Russell dodged traffic to a symphony of horns. Both men hopped into the sedan simultaneously. I followed at a safer pace watching the car bounce on its suspension. Arms were flailing in the front seat.

"Don't speak in the third person!" Russell yelled. "People are going to think you're crazy, man. What is wrong with you? Trying to shakedown a lady!"

Raymond Semple's face flattened against the driver's side window. One eye, a sideways nose, and a squashed cheek smeared the glass with perspiration. A flounder impersonation.

I stepped back from the car, repulsed. "Don't hurt him!"

The private investigator was smaller than Russell and soft in places where Russell was firm. That meant little if the man carried a gun.

"Answer the lady's questions! Your client won't complain. I'm pretty sure she'd approve."

Semple's cheek peeled away from the glass. Dark hair hung in greasy strands over his forehead. "Not too bright, fuckhead. I'm a businessman with connections. I got friends on the force. I snap my fingers and you're dead meat." All pretense of sophistication gone.

Thwap! Thwap! Thwap! The car swayed. Semple's face pancaked repeatedly. This time his nose got in the way. The smears were red and runny.

"Lady present. Watch your language."

Russell's aggression stunned me. I surmised the fear that paralyzed him during the dog attack had become an embarrassment. That or he had his own angry imp to satisfy.

"Russell, be careful. Please." The possibility of a struggle over a gun inside the car worried me. And yet, I didn't open Semple's door to release him. He couldn't do it himself while gripping the hands bunched up under his chin.

I slid into the back seat and felt something small and hard under my butt. I swept it to the floorboard before glancing down to recognize it as a zipper pull tab, a stray piece of junk. Meanwhile, Semple was swiping fingers under his nose to keep blood off his blazer.

"I didn't find anything. Okay? DeMarco paid me three grand to run checks on a couple of people."

"Go on." Russell and I said in unison.

"Somebody messed with her vehicle and it went to her head. Made her paranoid people were following her, watching her house, calling her."

"Who called her house? Did they leave messages?" I asked.

"She hung up. Had nothing show me."

Russell uncrimped his fingers from the blazer. "Who'd you follow?"

"Garden variety nut jobs. I couldn't connect them to her fantasies. She dropped it. So should you." Semple's eyes flashed. "Unless you're willing to pay me to finish the job. Get the guy who got to her. Five grand and I'll throw in a copy of the report I did for her. Can't do better than that. I'm the best in the business."

I tugged the cell phone from my bag. "Good day. I'd like to speak to Detective Charles Boynton. This is his niece, Danni. Uh-huh. I'll hold."

"Hang up." Semple's snarky tone assured me he believed none of it. He merely wanted to get on with his day. Also, one of the men farted and everyone's eyes were tearing up. "I give you four names and you get out of my car. Next time I see you, I'll find a reason to shoot. Elizabeth Hornick. Lee Anne Germain. Loretta Fahey. Manuel Soto. Get out of my car."

My uber-manly lover became jittery after bullying Semple. I took the wheel. Traveling eastward as a crow flies would've cut the distance significantly if only the Quabbin Reservoir wasn't in the way. Twelve billion gallons of water has a sizable shoreline. I decided not to rush the time left with Russell and drove leisurely through towns bordering the lake hoping to entertain him with idyllic scenery and tidbits of memorized history.

"Quabbin is one of the largest man-made reservoirs in the world."

"Four towns were flooded in 1938 to build it. Dana, Greenwich, Prescott. I forget the other."

"They exhumed bodies from cemeteries and relocated them. Thousands of bodies."

"Some roads here lead directly *into* the lake."

"Higher ground that wasn't flooded was absorbed into other towns. Sort of."

"There's a lovely overlook in New Salem. We could stop."

"Oh, look, a zebra."

Russell interrupted his quietude every so often by cracking a toe or a finger knuckle. The snap of his joints echoed in the car yesterday afternoon after leaving Carl's home too. Muriel started a conversation on menopause baiting me into a tirade over the manufacture of Premarin from pregnant mare urine and the unpardonable slaughter of their birthed foals. Talk of her recent shingles vaccine segued into a discussion on why collecting the blue blood of wild horseshoe crabs was endangering the survival of several species. When she brought up the bear bile industry, I wisely kept my mouth shut and let the topic wither. In hindsight, her goal wasn't to elicit a laundry list of moral convictions. She wished to undermine Russell's interest in me by testing his patience and politeness.

Crack . . . crack . . . crack.

Maybe his limit had already been reached. Maybe he wasn't actually beating on Semple back there.

After a perfunctory goodbye kiss beside his car, Russell exited my world again. His return was not guaranteed. Brooding over my loss ended at my kitchen door. Someone had been inside my flat. I was sure of it.

My home is tidy, though, not obsessively so. My father was a compulsive straightener, a picker-upper, a duster, an alphabetizer. I inherited that neatness trait but refuse to allow it to rule over my environment. Toothpaste speckles on the bathroom mirror; hair in my brush; crumbs on the table; the weird pink drips in the tub: all are ignored until truly noticeable. Clean, not obsessive.

The culprit noted the overall tidiness of the flat and returned things to a fitting state after rifling through my possessions. They squared up the magazines on the coffee table shelf that I had nudged with my foot the day before. They shut the desk drawer without leaving it crooked by a half inch as I am wont to do. They squarely reset the sticky note hanging from the edge of the computer monitor. They aligned the telephone with the edge of the coffee table rather than angling it toward the couch. They searched between the mattress and box springs tucking under the bedsheet and smoothing a kink from the dust ruffle. Everywhere, signs of violation in neatness.

The mattress.

The yellow bowling ball bag snagged on an exposed box spring coil. I shimmied belly up under the bed frame to bend the loop handles to pull it free.

Empty. No gun. No bullets. And, most likely, not a single fingerprint other than mine and Claire's.

"Oh, no, no, no."

A rash of ugly ideas crept in. I took possession of the gun on Tuesday. Manny was murdered on Thursday. Detective Monroe recovered the murder weapon from a neighboring yard. Was it a 9mm pistol? Had anyone said? How common were these things? Had a stranger broken in on Wednesday too? Could this be a different person with different intentions? I hyperventilated into a pillow.

Reason cut short my escalating emotions. If Manny's killer had stolen the weapon from me and the police have it in their custody, why come back? My flat wasn't ransacked. What few tchotchkes I own are all accounted for. If the killer stole it on either Wednesday or Thursday, why hadn't I noticed that intrusion?

Boynton should be notified. What would I say? I had Ella's gun? I transported and stored a weapon and ammunition without a permit. Lovely. I'm cast as the villain. Deep breath. Deep breath. The previous door incident sprang to mind and pushed me downstairs to Mr. Peebles' flat.

He answered my knock by yelling "Come in already!" from the comfort of his reclining chair.

"Mr. Peebles. It happened again. Someone has been inside my flat."

The old gent batted his eyelids, the earnest expression on my face dismissed. "See if you can make the clicker work."

I scrolled the TV guide, selected a game show, and hit the mute button. An opened fruit cup, a half glass of milk, and toast crusts marinating in runny egg whites scented the air with spoiled milk and sulfur. Mr. Peebles and the flat looked unusually clean and orderly. This was not his doing.

"Did Bethany come for a visit?"

Mr. Peebles cast a dismissive glance at the China hutch, which moved me to open a cupboard door, and seek out the little spiral pad. Missing.

"Bethany thinks I got Alzheimer's and wants me to go live in a home for the walking dead. I'm not going. I made other plans." A string of mucus glistened under his prominent nose. His watery eyes were alert and centered on mine. "Jason said it'd be more convincing if somebody else agreed with her. Pretty good, huh?" He gave himself a thumb's up.

The first time I met Mr. Peebles' son, Jason, he was rummaging through my boxes in the attic. On our second meeting, he surprised me in my own kitchen attempting to borrow the stand mixer to make cupcakes for his father, or so he claimed. Our last encounter involved my Cannondale bicycle, which was chained to a deck post. Jason hurriedly hid a hacksaw behind his back upon seeing my car pull into the driveway. The bike remained locked inside my flat until he left.

"Prove your memory isn't impaired. Who came to the house this weekend while I was away?"

"Same guy as last time."

"A UPS driver?"

His features curved into a Stan Laurel smile. "Your boyfriend."

"How do you know it was my boyfriend?"

"He parked in the same spot the night your buddies were over."

"It was fully dark when you arrived home that evening. We were already here. How do you know where my boyfriend parked?"

"Only one car on the corner. Seen it there after that. Your boyfriend."

My stalker. "Can you describe the car and the man?"

"You forget what he looks like? Ha. Hand me the clicker. Close the door hard on the way out. Sometimes they spring open."

I waved the television remote out of his reach. "First, let's test your memory. Describe the car and the man."

Mr. Peebles harrumphed. "Gray. Or white. Could be blue. On the tall side. Dark hair. Could've been wearing a hat. He walks funny in boots like he's got a load in his pants. Like he got off a horse. I watched him out the window. Who's that country singer that wears a cowboy hat? Heh. They all do." Mr. Peebles guffawed. "You can pick them."

A better description couldn't be had from him in his current state. "You say you're staying put. How do you know this?"

"I gave Jason power of attorney. He's going to fix up the house after I sign it over. Jason's got big plans. New handrails. A wheelchair ramp for when my knees go. I can live here free and easy."

I nearly rubbed my eyes out of their sockets. All that nonsense with his car and his dishes. Stealing my mail. Bumbled speech and filthy clothes. Two years of trickery? A seasoned actor—maybe. Mr. Peebles had no such talent. Whether he truly suffered from Alzheimer's was a matter for his doctors to decide. But he was indeed slipping and falling and scrambling back up again mentally.

Multiple scenarios presented themselves. Each involved me initiating extended conversations with Bethany and interviews with elder care advocates. Inserting myself into a complex situation uninvited.

I said, "That won't end well."

Chapter 29

Mail repossessed today from Mr. Peebles included an envelope from Donna Dorvee. The contracts she and Joe signed to appear in *How We Remember* was an apology of sorts. A handwritten note from Joe to his wife scrawled at the bottom of one referenced a positive review conducted by Teddie Myers of Myers & Cardi Talents. Russell got it right. I read them once before calling Boynton.

"You've reached the voice mailbox of Detective Charles Boynton. Leave a message at the beep." *Beeeep.*

"Hello, Detective Boynton. It's Danni Mowrey. You're undoubtedly tired of my texts, so I'm going a different route. Please, hear me out. Joe and Donna Dorvee were actors in *How We Remember*. Per their contract, EnablingU Films promised additional compensation if certain monetary goals were met." *Click.*

". . . Charles Boynton. Leave a message at the beep." *Beeeep.*

"The film never reached theaters but is doing well in pay-per-view. That's how Gordon Fahey convinced Joe Dorvee to lie about a burglary after he stole Ella DeMarco's laptop. The promise of a later payout. Joe did it for his daughter, who is most likely filing for divorce." *Click.*

". . . a message at the beep." *Beeeep.*

"By the way, I have Ella's laptop. Long story. Call for details."

A hand-crafted meat and cheese plate thawed during my jaunt to Northampton. The pistachio and cranberry encrusted cashew cheese remained firm. The glazed, seitan ham had the right amount of beet powder for color; hickory smoke, and maple syrup for flavor. Paired with a pale ale, the food energized me for an evening of desktop sleuthing and the tedious task of examining her bank records yet again. I'd missed something obvious.

The murder folder had become an ungodly mess of scribbled pages. Dozens of arrows to connect this up here with that down there. I'd become Ella in that regard. The scrawl in her check registers was barely legible. A number of line items had been blotted out altogether with a black marker. Without access to her personal bank statements, I couldn't reconcile them. I assume the police have those. Twin Sister's monthly statements showed activity between the accounts. Every private transfer Ella made to the nonprofit was quickly gobbled up by a host of small invoices issued by vendors I didn't recognize by name other than McArdles Paper Supply. Organizations as insignificant as Twin Sister can get by with an inexpensive, year-end compilation report prepared by a certified public accountant. Bette saw to that. It might explain the seemingly perfect bookkeeping with so few adjustments.

Jared's trial transcript had slipped off the desk to wedge itself between the wall and a mass of computer cables. I've resisted extracting it not wanting to increase my workload. No better time than now to set the pages on the scanner and convert them into a PDF file. Keyword searches were faster than a tedious read.

Miscellaneous items sifted from the boxes Reese delivered still awaited disposal. They filled two paper bags I couldn't quite bring myself to part with. My eagerness to dive into an anthill of dead ends was disturbing. I hung another sticky note off the monitor, this one instructing me to search for a therapist for myself, then made a call.

"A-oh, Danni. You have job for me?" Svetlana Ustinova said.

"Not exactly."

I detailed the odd finds that Reese gifted to me.

"Pah. Who is perfect?" she asked. "You, me, no one. Everyone has dust under bed and crumbs in drawer."

"None of this means anything to you? All rubbish? One of Reese's jokes."

"Could be." Svetlana blew into the receiver a second after the snick of a lighter. "Lock and key. Ah, locker! Ella swim at gym. Mmm. Pretty stones? Baubles. Big salt stone for armpit. No more stink. Seeds? Ella grow food. Now you grow food. Pink paper?"

"A receipt." I plucked it from a bag. "Numbered zero-one-nine-seven-six-eight. A customer copy. Someone wrote the number three and circled it. Dated two days before Ella's death. The other date written on the bottom is ten days later. There are words. A language I'm unfamiliar with. Not Chinese or Arabic."

Two more puffs on the cigarette. "Korean cleaner for dresses. Very pretty things, her dresses."

Svetlana gave me the name of the dry cleaner, Superstars Wash and Fold, located a mile from Ives Street. A new action item. I thanked her profusely, squelched the desire to ask a plethora of movie-related questions, and hung up.

Superstars Wash and Fold was tucked between a paint store and a liquor store in a low beige building. I've never been inside P. Leon's paint store despite the arty lion made of hundreds of color swatches glued to its window. Ella, I knew, purchased house paint there. Wagmon's Liquor World had shelves constructed of wine barrel slats and inexpensive wine spritzers perfect for lazy sangrias. I knew because I purchased them here. The dry cleaner recently replaced a dog grooming salon, Dip N Clip, that defleaed rescued dogs and cats for us in years past. The waiting area had always stank of expressed anal glands. Today, the scent was sandalwood. A major improvement. A young woman with bobbed black hair in a hanbok jacket grinned at me from the counter.

"Good afternoon. I'm here to pick up an order." I held out the pink slip.

She raised a finger signaling me to wait. I studied the shiny white counter and the revolving racks of plastic-draped clothing seeing little of Dip N Clip in the new store set-up. The ceiling tile, perhaps. A short man with lead gray hair and an angry expression came to the counter.

"You're late. We charge for storage," he said with a heavy accent.

"That's fine." I unzipped my handbag.

His heavy eyebrows scrunched. "One hundred ninety-five dollars."

"Excuse me?"

The man produced a white slip with a breakdown of the charges. Two dresses dry cleaned. One full-length fur coat cleaned, mended, and stored.

"I think you've made a mistake. This order belongs to a friend of mine. She doesn't wear fur."

"That lady made a mistake when she said she would sue me. I told her, 'no money, no coat.' I tell you the same unless you pay me."

"That's ridiculous. My friend would never sue you."

The man raised his arms, helpless.

"Can I see the order? This is the only slip I have and I really do think you've made a mistake."

The man called out in Korean to the young woman who was steaming pants on a press at a workstation. The conveyor hummed and plastic swished. She carried the slippery bundle in her arms like a deflated body and hooked it on a tall metal rack. The brown coat was mouton, sheep pelts sheered to mimic mink. Far too small for Ella, who stood at five-nine. The pleated, low-cut rayon dresses with delicate beading were definitely hers.

"A woman recently stopped by to pick them up?"

"From next door." He tapped his shirt pocket and spoke in Korean to the young woman.

In accented English, she said, "Jeanne. On her apron. Her name is Jeanne."

Jeanne Whitman's face matched her wrinkled, pink cotton shirt. Flattened brown curls and a wide yawn confirmed she'd risen from a pre-dinner nap.

"I hope you don't mind me showing up unannounced. Your supervisor at the paint store said you didn't work on Sundays."

Jeanne's eyes latched onto the mutton coat dangling from my arm. "My mother's. I never thought I'd see it again." She grabbed the coat and would've slammed the door shut had my foot not prevented it. Jeanne laid the coat on the dining table; a passionate viewing of a dead thing. Canned laugh tracks boomed from the den. Jerry's plump, hairy arm hung over the side of the upholstered chair. His high-rounded belly rose above it. The chair's fabric was worn and sagging. Jerry ate all his meals in that room. Such a small world.

A different observation. "The green paint on your dining room walls matches the color of a smear I noted on Ella's kitchen doorknob. How did that happen?" I was lying about the smear but it tied into one of my theories.

Jeanne tipped her head. "My son knew Ella."

"Son?"

"Craig. He comes around to give us a hand. He keeps up with the leaves and snow shoveling." Jeanne's fingers probed buttons reattached to the coat with shiny new thread.

"Craig's been inside Ella's house?"

Jeanne's palms smoothed creases from the new satin lining expertly stitched in place.

I whisked the plastic wrap off the floor and set it on the table with the receipt face up. "Why did Ella dry clean your coat?"

Jeanne gripped the hanger. I pinned a furry sleeve under my knuckles. Her face crimped with desperation. "I can't pay you. Jerry's on disability. I'm part-time at the store."

"Answer a few questions and we're even. How well did your son know Ella DeMarco?"

"They're friendly. They met when Ella brought over the phony bologna."

"Were they romantic friends?"

"They had things in common as young people do. Ella was Craig's date for Allen's wedding. Allen's my oldest. Craig got into a fight with his girlfriend a week before the wedding. Ella took her place. I was stupid. Stupid, stupid. Showing off the coat when they were serving cake. I bumped into a waiter. Everything went all over. The blue in the frosting. Oh, how I cried."

"An expensive favor," I said.

"A peace offering," Jeanne corrected sharply. "Ella and Craig talked about Jerry's disability during dinner and a bridesmaid overheard. Ella embarrassed us terribly. This was her way of saying sorry." Jeanne resumed stroking the coat in ghoulish adoration.

Ella's largesse often mystified me. I lifted my fist from the coat. "I know of Mrs. Pallotta's accident. My sincere condolences."

Jeanne pulled a crumpled napkin from her pocket. "Evelyn and I raised our children together. My grandchildren played with hers. I thought she'd always be there. The police are useless. Every one of them."

"Had her husband already left for work?"

"Husband? No. They divorced." Jeanne dabbed her nose. "How she doted on her grandkids. They ran rings around her. They loved my brownies." The memory made her smile. "Evelyn fenced the yard to keep them safe and called it her 'petting zoo'. Course Eric couldn't see the love and had to raise a stink. Telling everyone they were in danger." The smile turned churlish. "He made Evelyn agree to Jackie Knapp's daughter coming over whenever the kids were dropped off. Some people live to be mean-spirited. We all knew before Evelyn did that her marriage was over."

"Sorry to interrupt." Not even a little sorry. "What do you know of Evelyn's accident? By now, everyone has had time to think it over."

"Donna Dorvee heard the crash. Sounded like a tree falling on a shed, she said. Poor Evelyn lay there on the lawn. Nobody to hold her. Nobody to tell her she was loved. That's not right. The Lord knows that isn't right."

"Jeannie, when's dinner? I'm starving." The volume on the television dropped for her response.

"In a minute. Turkey and rice soup. I'll open a big can." Jeanne mopped her face with the used napkin. "Dale Knapp found her on his way to work. The car kept going. Right over the mailbox. That monster's going to burn in Hell."

I examined Evelyn's driveway after securing the coat and saw the ragged stump of a four-by-four post. The stolen Corolla would've sustained noticeable damage on impact. That it was abandoned and set on fire a mile away from here made perfect sense. The audacity of the killer's attack did not. Hatred? Poor planning? Or something else?

Jeanne carried the coat upstairs, her slippers shushing on the treads. Jerry sneezed presenting an opportunity to inquire about his health and show sympathy. Through the doorway, I caught him leaning forward, ogling my profile with a leer and a cocked eyebrow. I scowled back. I've apparently done my part to entertain already.

A gold-framed portrait above the fireplace lured me over. Diffused lighting and a marbleized ochre yellow backdrop indicated a studio-made photograph of three young children dressed as fairies in togas, tulle wings, and wreath circlets. The trio posed around a tall concrete urn filled with spring blossoms and unfurling ferns. A bumblebee floated above the oldest child's head. A striped caterpillar inched along the lip of the urn. A goldfinch spread its wings to balance on the stem of a gladiolus bending under its weight. A moment passed before I realized my mouth was hanging open.

"Those are my David's children," Jeanne said from the staircase. "Craig's a photographer."

"Of course. It should've been obvious."

Bands of sunlight shot through the blinds. A ray warmed my cheek. Two prior days of togetherness with Russell had me longing for the dip in the mattress and the scent of woodsy cologne on the sheets. I rolled out of bed and sent him a text saying so. Expressing vulnerability was new to me. I hoped he would respond in kind.

After downing a cup of peaberry decaf, I stuffed myself into stretch knits. My parkour practice has suffered lately. Today I would be clear-headed, strong, and spot-on. More curb, less fence, higher on the tree trunk. The altered sequence took shape in my head. I envisioned myself running up the tree and flipping feet over head. I crashed the landing when my latest phone ring-tone, a Blue Jay, jeered at me.

"Hello, Monica. What can I do to improve your day?"

"Save the make-believe. I know you got canned from your job," she said in a rush. "Guess who I had dinner with on Saturday? Claire and Alicia at Retro Grande. Claire joined the Twisters last winter. I'll bet you another box of donuts—double or nothing—that's where she met the boyfriend. She took a mighty dump on you over a black bean burger and fries. Guess who's keeping your old seat warm at Wethers? Yep. She set you up. You're an idiot for not telling me. For the love of Pete, I'm your best friend."

"Wait a moment. Are you saying you owed me a box of donuts?"

"Who can say? We may never know," she remarked sagely.

"I kept the news of my firing private because I needed time to digest the humiliation of losing my livelihood."

"Call coming in." Monica hit the hold button. Uncle Ned never updated the recording. Crackly pop music annoyed my eardrum. When Monica rejoined the conversation, I blurted, "Why did you insist on going to Ella's home?"

"We were talking about Claire."

"Tell me about the black pocketbook you took from Ella's house."

Monica, to her credit, didn't hang up. Instead, she made a weird animal sound, then, "Busted. It's a limited edition Miochi. Ella won it in an auction. We bartered. I've been watching her dogs without collecting a paycheck to pay it off. Jeez, Danni. Do you think Reese's just going to hand it to me? The six hundred bucks hit *her* credit card."

"I never saw the text of Ella canceling your dog sitting gig."

Monica sniffed into the receiver.

The little blue pills found amongst Ella's disposables were eroding my calm. I lost the will to beg for disclosure. "You gave Ella your Adderall."

"What? Are you going to slap my hands for it? A cure for fuzzy brain. Ella juggled a shit ton. Gordon kept throwing more balls in the air. I did her a favor. Cripes. They give this stuff to five-year-olds. Aspirin kills more people."

Another argument I'd never win. "Tell me about the message you *didn't* receive from her."

"Fuuuck," Monica muttered. "I lied. All right? Payback. Ella accused me of stealing. Holy hell. Do you have any idea how hurtful that is? She accused Svetlana of stealing too. I was going to take her pups for the weekend. The Miochi was mine after that. First, she had to sweat over it. I'd show up Saturday morning and say, hey girl, here I am. Ha. Ha. Gotcha ya."

"You drove to her home Saturday morning."

"Wrong. King Kong hangover from Friday night. You were there, remember? I ran late and called to explain everything, but she never picked up. I figured she was mad at me and made other plans. When I saw the news, I lost my frigging marbles. People knew I was watching the dogs that weekend. No way do I want cops crawling all over me. If Ella canceled it herself, I'm in the clear."

I did see her logic. One last unsavory topic. "The disruption at Salted Stone."

"Right. The video you sent. Haven't seen it. I'll get to it."

"Why did you do it?"

"Can I buy a vowel?"

"Several weekends ago, you and fellow Compats attacked customers inside Anthony's restaurant and hit them with signs."

"No way. I was dumpster diving in the junk bin at the transfer station. That's where I got the fire bowl. I bought a shit ton of bagged gravel for the patio. Nearly blew the shocks on my car hauling it home. Pick on somebody else."

A detour down memory lane for that evening placed me on the party porch in Providence. Manny. Did she know?

"Manny Soto was murd—"

Monica shrieked. A long chain of stunningly creative curse words included my name. A definitive *click* on her end silenced it.

I hoped the plumbers' shop was empty of customers.

Chapter 30

S vetlana Ustinova and Craig Whitman were officially removed from my suspect list. Svetlana was given a second chance at stardom in Ella's cooking videos as a hand model. She stirred cake batter left-handed, smoked cigarettes left-handed, and stroked another actor's groin left-handed. Ella was right-hand dominant. She forgave her housecleaner's sordid role in the movie. I suppose I would too once her name appeared in the credits as Ella's body double. Craig Whitman, a latecomer, never actually made the list. Ella recommended him as Manny's replacement at NPK and, most likely, for the role of school photographer at Saint Brigid. Craig assumed Reese recovered the mutton coat and sacked me with the bag of clothes when making a desperate attempt to find it to appease his mother. I wouldn't fault him for it.

Gordon, while devious, was not Ella's killer either. Because he excelled at micromanaging her schedule, he believed she had already left when he arrived to steal the laptop. Something stored in a file was incredibly valuable to him; possibly, Raymond Semple's report which contained information about Loretta's weird family. Gordon parked on Jenkins to enter Ella's home through the patio door unaware her car was stationed in the driveway facing Ives. He could've taken the computer and ignored the dogs bloodied, presumably, by the broken vase. He did, after all, punch in the door glass to gain access and set the stage for a burglary. Instead, he found Ella and wanted others to find her too as quickly as possible. He unlocked the front door from the inside, returned to his car, and called Joe to stage their entry. Within an hour of touring the house and its ghastly contents, the two men had come to an agreement. The movie contract played a large role, no doubt.

I scrubbed my face with my hands and briefly contemplated flinging myself from the attic studio window. My failure to identify Ella's killer had proven to be an incredibly taxing experience. The best I could hope for was a breakthrough made by Boynton. Exposing Rick Bush and Colin remained my responsibility as I hadn't been able to connect them to Ella's death. I set to work creating a package of Ella's laptop, the thumb drive of Jared's videos, copies of my notes, and pertinent newspaper clippings. A holiday gift Boynton was sure to appreciate.

The short drive to the Framingham Police Department elevated my spirits. This was it. The end of my involvement was in sight. Boynton's team would unlock Ella's computer files and the killer's name accompanied by incriminating evidence would magically appear in a file, in boldly printed capital letters, ready to be copied into a search warrant. The visual sparked new questions. Why had the killer left the laptop behind? Oversight? Ignorance? Bravado?

Ridiculous, circular thoughts followed me to the door of the Framingham police station. I pushed instead of pulled and crashed into its glass panel leaving behind a face print and a fair bit of dignity. The female civilian desk clerk heard the collision and scrutinized me severely through a veil of uneven bangs. The smell of fruited chewing gum and tobacco lingered along the glassed-in counter. I stuffed receipts for my confiscated shoes into the slot. The laptop wouldn't fit and the clerk was obliged to open the side door for a hand-off. I stated my business watching her expression sour. After a twenty-second phone conversation with the powers-that-be, she said, "He'll be down shortly."

I used the time to sort voice messages and texts. Certain group members harbored an endless desire to complain or suggest. Others believed my name ended with Ph.D. A voice message from Violet at Biscuits and Bows Shelter stilled my finger-swiping deletes.

"Clyde and Reno passed doggie boot camp and were adopted by a couple who knew your friend. Melinda handled the placement. They live in a big purple house and have a nice yard for the dogs. You don't have to worry."

At last, good news. The backpack of woes strapped to my back got a smidge less cumbersome. The next voice message had come from Cheryl after eleven last night.

"Dad was taken by ambulance to Framingham Union. Carrie's hysterical. We think he had a heart attack. The kids have a half-day at school tomorrow. We'll go over later."

I bolted out the station door and sprinted for three blocks. Vehicles, homes, the public library, and other sidewalk pedestrians passed me in waves of blurry color that threatened to trickle in tears down my cheeks. My sneakers hammered the pavement to the beat of the voice in my head. *Don't, die, don't, die, don't, die, don't, die, don't, die . . .*

I reached the hospital's main entrance as dazed as the other lost souls gathering here. An elderly man with a leg cast clawed his way between a wheelchair and the back seat of a sedan while a bored orderly looked on. A ragged, teenaged couple smoked cigarettes in a handicapped parking spot. A prowling security guard yelled at them causing the girl to wail. A tear-streaked man in a raincoat banged his fists on the automatic door when it failed to open quickly enough. I slipped by him going the other way.

Inside the lobby, a flash of realization moved the walls inward and compressed the air into a solid state making it unbreathable. I spun in a dizzying arc studying the familiar space with unseeing eyes. How many days had I spent roaming this hospital's halls while waiting on treatment for Mother? On how many occasions had I done that alone?

Every family crisis strained the weak bonds between me and *them*. This would be more of the same. Cheryl will attack me to disarm her fear that she was not the real mistress of her universe. Carrie will patronize in the manner of a high-born matriarch. Louis will play the besieged pauper done in by life. Anthony will sulk at his perceived loss of whatever. And when the children disrupt the solemnity of this place with wild laughter and squeaking sneakers, I will press hands to face and scream inside my head. Through their eyes, my many inadequacies were obvious, irreversible, and an unfair burden they bore. Laughable, as none had earned their place in this world. All that they have, they stole from my family. I will not have my sympathy ridiculed. Not this time.

The walk back to my car happened at a leisurely pace. I had other concerns to attend to.

Toby Berrigan rented a first-floor flat in a two-decker. The front porch shed paint chips onto the sidewalk and one slim side yard glittered with broken beer bottles. I had come here once before for a Halloween party. The rubber hands, fake entrails, smashed pumpkins, and fog machine gussied the place up. This neighborhood was best described as down-market. My maintenance-deferred flat was half the size for slightly more money. Quality of life is incredibly subjective.

The doorbell dangled off wires below a crumpled mailbox. Fearing an electric shock, I rapped on the door. Toby glared at me from the other side.

"Is this what emergency means to you!"

I remained impassive. Everyone on my contact list emphasized urgency with cartoon emoji faces exploding, vomiting, or screaming. Sometimes all three appeared in the same message.

"How can I improve your life today, Toby?"

"Claire Steele. She's got mental problems."

"Most of us do."

Toby's living room was as ugly as he was pretty. Secondhand upholstery in shades of blue and walnut laminate tables from different decades suggested an attempt toward cohesiveness. Weather-spotted walls and drippy window sills excreted a damp suitable for fungi spores. Toby was underdressed for the chilliness of the place in a tee shirt and droopy jeans. His bare toes snagged on the matted brown carpeting.

"Tell me about Claire," I said. A few gyrations of his lower jaw and an away glance told me more than I wanted to know. "You slept with her?"

"Not often."

"You asshole! What is wrong with you?"

"She tried to kill me."

The quiver in his voice reminded me he was a man-child and should be treated as such. I moved to the couch and patted a cushion. "Sit. Tell the doctor everything."

"Friday night she showed up half-cocked, crying her head off about her cast. Nothing is ever her fault. I told her to go home. I was nice."

"Was that the first time Claire came round uninvited?"

"The last time. First time I was with my mom and dad in Natick for my mom's birthday. We went to that fish restaurant. Claire was hanging all over my car when we got out. I told her to go away. Nicely. The next week she started calling me at work getting the manager to pull me off the grill for fake emergencies. She's trying to get me fired. I got Dill for that."

Inwardly, I cringed. "Were you leading her on? Insinuating the affair was a real relationship? She isn't pregnant—is she?"

"Forget it. You can't hang a Me Too sign on my back. Claire knew we were having fun. Grab and poke. I never lied about it."

"Claire's sensitive. Hmm, delicate. Don't you ever think?" *With anything other than your penis.*

"Delicate? She's got a few miles on her. The other guy is older. Waaaay older. Like forty. She tried making me jealous. I don't give a rat's ass who's banging her. I want my belt back. Mushroom leather. Cost me a paycheck. I asked her to drop it off. Didn't work for her. I had to go to her place. She lets me in and I see a guy making for the bathroom. Old guy. I thought it was her dad. Why is his ass hanging out? Okay. Not her dad. I got this thing I have to show you." He stood up, unzipped his jeans, and let them fall to the floor.

I nearly backflipped over the arm of the couch. "What the fuck, Toby! Are you mad? Absolutely mad." If Toby had been a stranger, he'd be on the floor writhing from a punch to his solar plexus.

"Look!"

Toby's hairy thighs were dappled with bruises. Yellow, green, purple. The produce section of a supermarket. The scratches on his hands, then, were not work-related. Toby refastened his pants and pulled up his tee-shirt to expose a ragged cut centered inside a long, hideous bruise on his rib cage. His face nearly broke apart watching mine.

"Did Claire's boyfriend attack you?"

"I'm sure she wanted him to. I didn't get my belt and he didn't do this. She did."

Stunned, I hurried into the kitchen to hide my disbelief and groped in the cupboards for two water glasses. Lentils, mung beans, and chickpeas sprouted in mason jars near the sink. I peeked inside the refrigerator. Cucumbers and lemon slices floated in a jug of filtered water on the top shelf. The shelves overflowed with leafy greens, root vegetables, and plastic tubs of berries. The boy continued to amaze me. My mind returned to Taco Bell and a past conversation with him.

"Claire was the deer," I said, handing him a glass of filtered water.

"Her old man dumped her. I felt bad, right, but where's my belt? That's inconsiderate."

"Sure."

"Cost two bucks to mail it. I said I'd give her the money back." He shook his head and glossy curls bounced. A shampoo commercial. "I didn't let her in the night she did this. Saved my life. You could kind of see where it was going and she knew where my knife drawer was. I told her to leave. Nicely."

"Claire attacked you?"

"Ripped the mailbox off the house and started whaling on me. Hurt like a son of a bitch. I pushed her off the porch. Not hard! A hip check. She wouldn't stop screaming. My neighbor opened his window and threatened to call the cops. Then she has a go at my car with the mailbox." Toby braced his face in his hands and spoke to the coffee table. "I said screw it. I'll call it into the insurance company. If shithead wants to call the cops, let him."

"Claire left when she finished with your car?"

"Yes. Right after she hit her arm on the hood and started screaming for real."

"Any other witnesses?"

"The whole neighborhood! Go ask them."

Truth be told, I saw his message on Friday but thought it Dill-related and ignored it. Whether the rest of the story mattered was debatable. Claire would be the victim in her version. My sympathies lay with Toby, the boy who didn't retaliate in kind. Claire, I was certain, assisted Rick Bush in tormenting members of Twin Sister and Compassion Lives. Another witness could help prove it.

"Can you identify the boyfriend from a picture?"

When shown the photos sent by John Rockler, Toby aimed a finger at Rick Bush. "I'll never forget his flabby white ass running to the bathroom. Colin's another creepy dude. Lives in Marlboro. Colin, hmm, something. I gave him a ride home from Bottoms Up. He paid me eight bucks."

"And you just happened to be there."

Toby's pretty face went cherub smooth.

"I really don't care, Toby. Why they go to you instead of a pot dispensary is beyond me."

"That dude isn't vegan."

"You are and you work at Taco Bell. How is that relevant?"

"He smelled funky. Kind of like the dumpster when the wind's blowing. Roadkill rotten."

This observation of personal hygiene fit neatly into my developing picture of Spanky. I knew the cause of the smell. I needed to uncover where he did it.

"The guy's a dick too giving me lousy directions. I drove around the same streets three times. I think he was pissed I charged him for the ride."

After coaching him, I voice-recorded Toby's recollection of the instructions given. The route taken from Bottoms Up involved more markers than street signs. I'd transcribe it later when in front of a map. Colin left the car to continue walking on his own. Toby hadn't found that odd. Piffles' home was bound to be close by.

"Help get Claire off my back?"

"Whatever became of you checking up on Dill for me?"

"Nobody from the high school hangs out with him. He gets in trouble doing stupid stuff like writing love notes to teachers on homework. Pissing in the girls' bathroom. One time he pulled the emergency door on a bus to jump out. Told everyone he forgot his dad was picking him up."

"Did his father pick him up?"

"I asked that too. The guy sounded like Flabby White Ass to me. I dunno. Claire? Come on. I'm dying here."

"Okay. Get rid of your stash. The next time she morphs into a psycho on your porch ring the police yourself. Failing that, keep up the deer story."

Chapter 31

Barging into an establishment packed with frolicking children and watchful parents to demand the purpose of Rick and Colin's actions could easily lead to my arrest. An impromptu visit to Rick's home could get me shot. It's been known to happen. A better option would be to apprehend them in the act. Once captured, either might strike a bargain and divulge the identity of their boss. Claire's relationship with Rick put her in the middle of it. The tattered flowers suggest they parted acrimoniously. Toby's account confirmed it. Would she offer incriminating information to avenge her shattered sense of self?

I left my car on Loney Drive in a dark stretch between house lights and crept up the stairs to her loft. "Claire. It's Danni. Let me in."

Heavy feet stomped one way, then the other. Claire answered in a flannel nightgown the sort Mrs. Santa Clause would favor. "Did you bring the phone? You shouldn't have taken it. That's stealing. Give it back." A puffy palm shot over the threshold.

Presenting myself as a compassionate friend grew increasingly difficult. Residue anger bubbled in my blood. I swatted her hand aside and shut out the cold night air. The flat again strangled my senses with its garish meadow of upholstery and the ark of baby animals peering down from the walls ready to eat it. Rick Bush chose Claire wisely.

"Do you have the gun?" she asked.

I shook my head.

"Is this about work? Lydia offered me the job after you left. I didn't say anything bad about you. It wasn't like that." A tall glass of soda, an open package of coconut snack cakes, and a manicure set were spread out on the wicker ottoman. My surprise arrival interrupted Claire's self-love session.

"How does your broken arm feel?"

Claire stared at the neon pink cast. Her parents had drawn hearts around their well-wishing with Sharpie markers. "Itchy. My fingers get cold. It makes it really hard to sleep."

"Glad to hear it." I moved to the curtained closet and parted shirts on hangers. There, on a hook on the back wall, was a brown coat with faux fur trim. I returned to the couch and patted a cushion. "Come sit with me."

My ex-friend chose the armchair. Her stubby toes, sparkling with emerald nail polish, pressed hard into the rug.

"Tell me about your boyfriend and his sidekick, Colin. I know you and Dill acted as lookouts to ensure they were never caught."

Claire rolled her wide eyes over the floor as though tracking a crazed chipmunk. When her gaze returned to her glorified toes she said, "Stop being a jerk. Go get my stuff. I could have you arrested for that."

Something stretched and screeched inside my chest. The imp forced its way through my ribs and flew into a poster of a rabbit. I hurled the open bottle of nail polish after it creating a green spirograph below the poster. Claire sprang up from her seat. I lashed out planting my sneakered foot in her gut. The chair rocked when she fell back into it.

"Sorry. I jumped ahead. Explain why Rick wanted you to have Ella's gun."

In a rush of rising hysteria, Claire babbled, "I live alone. I could get robbed! Raped in my bed. Murdered! Why do you act like I'm stupid? Nobody ever listens to me. I heard what Monica says about me. She's the freak. Look at her. I only stayed with the group because he asked me to. He believes in giving everyone a second chance."

"Second chance? You went to Twin Sister searching for another home."

"They're honest about what they do. The stories you told weren't. You and Ella made-up stuff to sell your crappy books. Everybody says so."

"That's what *everyone* says?" I squelched an urge to throw a fist at her face in defense of my vanity. "Is that how your boyfriend explained it? A second chance at happiness for him with you. I'm sure he used the same excuse when he dumped you for his wife, whom he never left. So many lies. He even lied about his name. Richard. Not Robert. Doesn't that bother you? A little, perhaps? Rick suggested punishing Compassion Lives members for slighting you. An opportunity to return some of the humiliation. I presume he sold a similar idea to Dill. Don't get mad. Get even. Had you never questioned why he would isolate a vulnerable member and use them against the group? Or were you simply thrilled you found a champion at long last?"

"He still loves me. He'd divorce his wife if he didn't have kids."

"Will you harass them next? Morals so corrupted you'd target young children to get what you want, what you feel you deserve?"

"We love each other."

"Just like you loved Toby? You covered him with your love. I saw the marks."

Claire made talons of the fingers in the cast.

"You, specifically, are of little consequence to Mr. Bush. He tried to court Lee Anne Germaine before you said yes. Possibly others. Who does he work for, Claire? Who pays him to attack us?"

Claire flashed a middle finger. "Most people can't stand you. They stay in the group because they feel sorry for you. Everybody knows you're nothing without Ella."

"Fine. Let's talk about something else. Rape and robbery aside, why take Ella's gun?"

"Why did she want it? Two-faced and full of it. Living in peace and harmony. Yeah, because she has a gun by her bed. *I* made her honest."

"Hmm. Ella purchased a firearm to protect herself from the person stalking Twin Sister members. On advice from your boyfriend, you took the gun away. Weeks later, Ella is beaten to death inside her home. Defenseless. You did a bad thing, Claire. Very bad. Heck, your boyfriend Rick might even be her killer. How does that make you feel?"

Claire's face blanched as it had on that dark day at Wethers when she was inconsolable. The reason being the same. Guilt.

"What of Colin? The man who left vile threats on my answering machine for months? How on earth did Rick explain that friendship?"

"I don't know who that is. I don't know a Colin."

"Bullshit!" I leaned over the ottoman to growl in her face. "Whose idea was it to bash in Ella's skull? To make her unrecognizable to her own brother. To crush her face and leave her to bleed out. Do you think she recognized her attacker as your boyfriend and damned your soul? Tell me what you think, Claire! I'm listening. Talk to me, Claire!"

Her response erupted as a hot stream of vomit. I vaulted over the back of the couch to avoid splatter. Foul-smelling goo washed over her shiny toes, the rug, and filled the nooks and crannies of the wicker ottoman. I saturated a dish towel with icy water at the sink. My pitch hit her high on a cheek snapping her head back. *Thwap!*

"Clean yourself up. You're disgusting."

Claire's face cracked open with tears and cat-like mewing.

"Tell your boyfriend we're coming for him. Oh, and go fuck yourself."

Applying pressure wins games, staunches bleeding, and forces votes. It can also compel otherwise crafty people to do stupid things. I stacked supper dishes in the sink, opened a beer, and contacted Lisa at Bottoms Up. Whatever Rick Bush had done as the manager to piss her off worked in my favor. She volunteered his schedule for the week and transferred me to his extension where I left a curt message, "The last cat was a mistake. Too close to home."

Closer to Rick's home, I would not tread. Mrs. Bush might have a raging fit if she were to receive anonymous information detailing her husband's infidelity. The well-being of their children concerned me.

Comparing Toby's dictation to a satellite map of Marlboro gave me a general idea of the neighborhood Colin lived in. Should Rick fail to react to the bait, I'd push hard on Colin. Manny's death seemed coincidental and unrelated to these other happenings, yet, it was possible Colin was my attacker on the night of his murder.

Paula Schaffer would tighten the umbilical cord around Dill's neck if she knew of his special friends. I'd implore her to confiscate his phone to cut off Rick and Colin's easy access to him. Dill's temper tantrum would be epic. She might even force him to quit his job. Epic meltdown, indeed.

"Mrs. Schaffer?"

"Yes. Hello? Who is this?"

"Sorry to disturb you at this late hour. I have frightening news. There's something you should know about the company Dill keeps."

Manny Soto's obituary in the morning paper was all of twelve sentences. One hundred and seven words that inadequately summed up a life. Described as a thirty-six-year-old professional photographer, Manny spent years working off-stage for local theater companies handling lighting, sound, stage sets, and videotaping. His work for NPK was stated perfunctorily with little in the way of details. Professional credentials or associations weren't listed. Manny called Rhode Island home for thirteen years. He left behind a mother and four grown siblings in Nevada. None were given names. Per the obituary, donations were being accepted by Righteous Roy's Tattoos to offset the cost of burial back in Nevada.

What does one wear for a tattoo, I wondered. Slouchy comfort with a loose neckline seemed appropriate as did a splash of Amaretto in my morning coffee for courage.

Within the hour I stood on Righteous Roy's front stoop reading a CLOSED sign. A figure moved in front of a light at the back of the shop, the size and shape of a stocky man with a full beard. The tattoo parlor's entry alcove provided a comfortable spot to wait. At ten-thirty, locks scraped back and the door jangled open.

"Morning, Roy."

"Miss Mowrey." Roy doffed an invisible cap. We sat on the bench turning to view the sidewalk and the slow push of traffic. "I know who you are. Manny never shut up about NPK. That place burned a hole in his heart."

"Sorry to hear that."

"Wasn't all bad. He tried like hell to make it work. Might have had some fun too. I sure hope he did."

I smiled. "I think so."

"I'll say this too, Manny wasn't the best of men, but he was a good friend to me. Here when it mattered, when my dad was sick. But I think you'd rather talk about Ella. She was something else. We were moths to a flame. You hear me?"

"I do."

A Trojan Gallery flyer lay on the window sill. I glimpsed it on my first visit here and examined it now. The featured image was a seated woman thrusting a straw hat at the camera. Long, blonde hair streaked pink shrouded the face and shoulders above the hat. Shapely, bare legs and heeled feet formed an inverted V below it. A tiny tattoo graced each ankle.

"Tell me about Ella."

"Seeing is believing." Roy handed me a key. "I promised I wouldn't hang any out here."

Intrigued, I took the key. The longest eleven steps of my life ended at a locked door at the back of the shop. Inside, a battered desk and a wheeled chair wrapped in promotional stickers for dog food, wheat crackers, motor oil, and other products were first attempts to personalize the utilitarian space. Framed photographs on the walls transformed the room into a temple. Each image elbowed the next leaving slim spaces of white wall. Breathtaking.

Every photograph told a short story. Ella, in a translucent gown, walked a dappled horse along a stormy beach. Ella, in a business suit, looked wide-eyed at a barn owl on a briefcase. Ella in an orange tutu astride Olive in an orange tutu, both wearing pointed party hats. An oversized masterpiece hung above the desk. Ella and a rabbit posed on a silver motorcycle. The white rabbit balanced on the handlebars sniffing the air. Ella was naked except for a wide red ribbon circling her throat and diamond-studded heels. Wind blew streamers of pink hair over her arched back. Not a garage pin-up. A museum piece. Manny proved himself a brilliant photographer.

"How did you come by these?" I asked.

Roy stopped setting up a tray of tools. "Manny cut me sweet deals when he wanted extra cash for living. There was talk of a calendar and a book. I don't think he got too far with either. Ella was giving him a hard time."

"How so?"

Roy cast his eyes on the flyer, then fired up a large boxy e-cigarette. I did the same and strolled about the shop studying drawings pinned to the walls. Most were cartoonish, two-dimensional. A few were extraordinary requiring many hours in the chair to achieve.

"Ella liked being special, but it had to be done her way. With style. You know what I'm talking about?"

"I do."

"The guy managing her company ran her life. The nudie shots were a thumb in his eye."

"Gordon Fahey knew about the photos?"

"Oh yeah."

A book of client tattoos lay open on a pedestal. Roy released a dragon cloud of vapor. It reached me as a memory of cotton candy. "You said 'hard time'?"

"Manny tried to control her too. Artistically, speaking."

Ella couldn't fake the joy exhibited in the photos. *How We Remember* was a protest piece gone terribly wrong. Manny was responsible for that too.

"He didn't mean to cuck up so badly. I believe that down to my bones. Since the first time we met—did he tell you? He wanted me to fix his knuckle tattoos. I told him, man, keep it. A little reminder we all make mistakes. This, after he's bragging about the movie he's going to make. He wouldn't have without her. She brought friends in to work on it. And personality. Big, big personality." Another storm cloud of sweet-smelling vapor transported me to a county fair.

"Ella never agreed to star in what the movie eventually became."

"I don't suppose she did. She wasn't trying to make a name for herself that way. Manny found another woman who would." Roy's mouth twitched. "A couple of times, she did."

"You still haven't said what hard time Ella gave him."

Roy squinted one eye. "I see where you're taking this and that don't jive with the Manny I knew. He's not a killer. Not for real. Those other scenes had to go. He refused. Told me it couldn't be done. He'd have to reshoot and didn't want too anyhow. That's when she made up her mind to leave the company and Manny lost his day job."

Artistic freedom. Revenge. Control.

I looked down at the section I'd reached in the book. Tattooed eyeliner and eyebrows. The second picture on the right was a pair of artfully crafted, tawny-brown eyebrows below a lightly freckled forehead. The owner's whole face wasn't pictured. It didn't have to be.

"Manny and Loretta were lovers. They met up when she brought her daughters to Bottoms Up trampoline park and passed the time at a donut shop across the street from it. Murray's Bakery." Random observations puzzled together.

Roy glanced at the book's open page. "Revenge comes in all sizes. Manny said Loretta made promises she couldn't keep. Business, I'm thinking."

A weird shiver raised the hairs on my arms. I had people to call but, first, "I'd like a tattoo." I pointed to a green V on the illustration board.

"You ever get inked before?"

"I'm a virgin."

"It'll sting."

"I know pain." I got comfortable in his chair and swept hair off the side of my neck. "Put it right here."

Chapter 32

S elf-guilted into being a more responsive leader, I determined I would answer calls and messages in a timelier manner. Rachel was the first to call. I set aside a delectable lunch to focus on her chittering shrilly into my ear.

"Those dickheads wound her up last night saying Jared Libby was inside Ella's house and he killed her. When I talked to her today, she said she was okay. Horse pucky. I know she's going to do something awful. Ohmygod-ohmygod-ohmygod. She's not answering her phone. You have to stop her."

"Where is Lee Anne now?"

"Working at the pizzeria till five."

I glanced longingly at the remoulade dappled artichoke-leek fritters sitting atop a mixed green salad. "Are you certain she'll be there until five?"

Silence, except for Rachel's panicked breathing.

"Damn it. I have to go. I'll call you later."

A series of frantic telephone calls went unanswered. Lee Anne. Bette. John. Harried counter help at Roadside Pizzeria placed me on hold twice before disconnecting. Jared deserved the shit mess he made of his life. His girlfriend didn't and neither did their baby.

I headed to Canard nibbling on a fritter wrapped in foil. Deep blue storm clouds rolled in from the west ushering in an early twilight and a greater sense of urgency. I slipped under yellow traffic lights and darted through intersections. I swerved around slower-moving highway traffic grateful for dry roads. The time saved by reckless driving was not enough. A row of five vehicles marked a break in the trees and the lip of Jared's driveway. Lee Anne's Outback was amongst them. A man and a woman scrambled to the road's shoulder walking briskly toward me. I recognized each by face as a Twister.

"What's happening?"

The woman stopped. "Lee Anne broke a couple of windows. She's been arguing with that asshole for a while. Someone should call the police."

The man paused by his car. "You crazy? Not until I'm out of here."

"Don't call the police. I'll handle it."

More Twisters, two men and a woman, stood beside a double-trunked oak just off the gravel drive. They quit talking on my approach. My stomach flipped. How many others knew Lee Anne would come here? The woman pointed at the body sprawled belly up on the lawn with a pile of freshly dug rocks at one elbow and the ax used to hack them out of the driveway at the other. The silver whirligigs had been trampled into confetti. Diamond-like chunks of glass framed a smashed window on Jared's truck. Somewhere within the freshly bombarded gray cape house, Hailey wailed and Jared raged.

"Hey, Lee Anne. Sweetie. It's Danni." I crept up slowly, scanning the darkening yard for hunks of granite that had bounced off the house to become trip hazards.

Lee Anne sat up. "He has to tell everyone what he did."

"Sure. Sure. Why the stones? You can't throw for shit."

Her quick smile dissolved into tears. They cut muddy tracks through dust settled on her cheeks from her labors.

I stepped on the ax handle pinning it to the ground. "This isn't you. This isn't the person I know you to be. Let's, you and I, talk it over away from here."

"Look what he's taken from us? We can't go back and make things the way they were. Everything's changed. It can't ever be like that again. All of us together. We had fun. Didn't we? I miss that. Don't you?" Lee Anne was speaking of the loss of Ella and, probably, her ex-husband. Grief made her tremble.

"Jared didn't kill Ella. The men who provoked you have been stalking both of our groups. I've gathered enough evidence to get the police involved. They can be stopped."

"Why you and not the cops? They're in on this. Must be. All this time and nothing to show for it. That asshole should've been in jail from day one. How come that never happened?"

I slid the ax toward me, backed up five paces, and flung it into a strip of woodland. My blood pressure dropped when the ax buried itself in fallen leaves. That sigh of relief lasted all of five seconds. Lee Anne sprang to her feet, her face a mask of anger.

"Fuck it. Let him shoot me. This is happening, Sunshine. I'm taking him down with me. I should've done this weeks ago."

Lee Anne lobbed a rock at the living room's bay window. A crystalline explosion of glass was accented by a shriek from Tiffany. The storm door burst open. Jared's anger, palpable at twenty feet, rolled down the barrel of a rifle aimed at Lee Anne's chest. The spectators gasped and ducked behind the oak tree.

Lee Anne yelled, "Coward!"

Jared charged forward yelling, "Fucktard!", and mercifully, dropped the gun to dive at the big woman's thighs. The tackle slammed her to the ground. They growled and snorted and tore at each other's heads. Two grizzlies in a death match.

"Someone help me!" I begged the watchful Twisters.

None broke cover.

I danced around the combatants' flailing limbs, tugging here and there in a futile attempt to separate them. Both were cussing and drooling and deaf to my entreaties. A steel-toed boot slammed into my shin bone. I tumbled to the earth howling in pain. Lee Anne punched Jared's face tearing loose a flap of nostril with her friendship ring. He cried out and gave up the fight crawling awkwardly toward the house. Rivulets of blood crisscrossed the lower half of his face. Lee Anne scuttled crab-like to the rock pile and unleashed a hailstorm of missiles. Jared veered toward the dropped rifle. I scrambled after him taking direct hits. The stones were as large as turkey eggs. Two struck my back, the third drew a line of blood across my cheek. A giant blur passed between us shielding me from another attack. The tall, square-shouldered man hooked Jared under one armpit dragging him and the gun inside the house. Just like that—it was over.

Lee Anne dropped to her butt and gingerly probed plump welts rising on her face. Nervous laughter infected the bystanders. They moved hesitantly from the safety of the tree intending to help her now that the danger had passed. She shook them off, staggered to her feet, and cut a zigzag path to the road. Someone honked a car horn and Lee Anne yelled, "Fuck you!"

A hulking shape loomed over me. I blinked upward at a familiar face made dark by encroaching dusk. Without the garish icing of cosmetics and the brassy blonde wig, Karen presented as a striking, thirty-ish man.

"Giddy up, girlfriend. Time to go. Nothing to see here."

"How did you—"

"Peacekeeper extraordinaire. I take my monitoring duties seriously and my calming demeanor has worked miracles again. Thank you! Scratch that. *You* can thank me later with a sky-high gin and tonic. I'll be in touch. Come on. Upsy-daisy." Karen jerked me up by my coat collar and gave my back a forceful shove.

Protesting the rough handling and hitting her with a barrage of questions was beyond my present capabilities. The blow to my cheek stung and bruises were expanding across my back. I did as ordered, scooping up a baseball-sized rock on the walk to my car. The lightning crash of shattering glass played on a loop inside my head. My senses returned a quarter-mile down the road. I drove on until the white sign for a Fast Mart lit the sky. A sign for an ATM lured me inside. This was me offering a bear honey before poking it.

A short while later, Tiffany's silhouette bobbed behind a bedsheet in the living room. She struggled to move across an arrangement of chairs to fasten the fabric over the gaping hole in the bay window. She answered my knock with a roll of duct tape dangling off one wrist and two band-aids wrinkling the side of her neck.

"You told them where we were! Look what it got us. How are we going to deal with this? We don't have money for diapers half the time."

Glass sparkled on the carpet. "You should vacuum. For Hailey's sake."

"Oh." Tiffany darted into the dining room. Her daughter was strapped into the high chair at the table. A gassy hot dog smell wafted off a stove. Past meals were imprinted everywhere, from crumbs on the sink counter to sauce splatters on the backsplash. The blue vinyl floor crackled with dried cereal. Some of it was stuck to Hailey's forehead. A semi-orderly household upended by contact with me.

"Where's Jared?"

Tiffany filled the baby's chair tray with corn chips. "He went looking for his gun. That big dude pitched it in the woods."

"What did you think of the 'big dude'?"

Tiffany blew a raspberry and Hailey giggled. "He talks like a cop. A big, faggety-ass cop. Why'd you set him on us?"

"Not my doing. What did the big dude say to you?"

Tiffany ate a chip and scrubbed salty fingers on her jeans. "He told Jared to go wash up and patched up my neck. Said it was all Jared's fault because he isn't supposed to have guns. Bull-shit-ski. A man has a right to defend his home. He didn't start anything until Godzilla broke the truck window. We were going to turn up the TV and tell them all to go to Hell. Who was that lady? Jared had never seen her before."

The back door rattled and Jared tromped into the kitchen cradling the rifle like a newborn. "Queer broke my gun." The stock was split. Jared fingered the crooked seam in despair before noticing me. "What d'you want?"

A close inspection of his injuries revealed a gouged eye socket, a split lip, and the string of a bloody tampon hanging from a nostril covered in white tape. His whole head was red and swelling.

"Let's sit and talk." I sat at the dining table, arms in my lap. The table was sticky with juice.

"You need to get the hell out."

"Not until you answer my questions, truthfully. You owe me."

"How'd you figure?"

"The woman pitching stones at you has access to weapons. Killing you wasn't her goal. Getting you to shoot her was. You'd go back to prison until Hailey graduated high school."

Tiffany pulled the baby from the chair and backed out of the room.

"What do you know about the threats against Ella DeMarco?"

"Ah, Jesus, not this again."

I dug into a jacket pocket and laid three, crisp twenty-dollar bills on the table. Jared scooped up the money.

"Whose idea was it to record the videos?"

Jared's mouth slid sideways into a smirk.

"I could phone the police. You'll pay a lawyer much more than that to speak for you."

Jared pushed back from the table and ran upstairs after Tiffany. Alone with the broken rifle, I placed it on the rear deck and locked the door.

Jared returned, saying, "I'm going to need more money. Two grand."

"Five hundred. I'll mail it."

"Bullshit you will."

I left, allowing the storm door to slam shut behind me. Nearing the road, I groped a pocket for the car key fob. The crunch of gravel reached me before Jared did.

"I'm okay with a check. Eight hundred would go further."

We sat in my car with the heater blasting. More for him than me as he was shivering. The pain in his head must be excruciating.

"Money's dried up," he began. "The only place that'll hire me is the yogurt shop. You know how many hours I get in the winter months? Fifteen last week. I'm the working poor. It ain't easy with the baby and the house. Tiffany don't make much at the dollar store. I shouldn't've gone to jail. Cassie was already posting some pretty sick shit trying to figure out how to make drug money. Sixteen and out of school, she couldn't get working papers. Couldn't pass for eighteen either."

"Cassandra is dead! Leave her be," I snapped. "Tell me who helped you make the videos or get out of my car and forget about the money."

Jared plucked off his ballcap to scratch a greasy hairline. "Colin had the idea."

"Colin who?"

"Empey."

Suspicion confirmed. "How do you know this, Colin Empey?"

"Our dads drank at the same rod and gun club. Fishing buddies." Jared toyed with the tampon string tickling his upper lip. "It all went down the shitter fast. Colin got bored because Cassie stopped putting out for him. I only got—"

"Stop! I don't want to hear about her unless it's connected to Marlene's extortion attempt." A nervy feeling uncoiled in my gut. In truth, I didn't want to know the awful details of Cassandra's life because then I could never unknow them.

"No one was going give Marly money," he said. "She would've asked for a real job. Like picking shoes in a shoe store. Something that didn't have her blowing guys for lunch money."

"How do you know that?"

"Cassie's grandma talked about Marly when she got drunk. Or high. Cassy learned all about her momma that way. Marly was on a high school baseball team. Called the Hornets. Maybe, Wasps. Something that stung."

This could be another rabbit hole. Best to avoid tumbling into it. "Where does Colin Empey live?"

"Don't know, don't care."

"None of this is worth the money I already gave you. Maybe you should get out of my car."

Jared gripped the dashboard. "Jeesh. Hold on. Let me think." He picked at the nails broken against Lee Anne's face, then poked at the tampon in his nose. Rock bottom was always within his reach. "A guy came to see me last year. Said he could fix me up good moneywise if I gave him a hand. Wanted to set DeMarco straight."

"For what purpose?"

"Never said. I didn't ask. Not my business."

My hands curled into fists. "You'll have to do better than that." Fumigating the car with air freshener wasn't going to remove his stink from the upholstery. I made a show of shoving the keys into the ignition.

"All right. All right. The guy said she was asking about him. Too many questions and wouldn't let it go. He didn't want anybody to her hurt. Maybe set her grass on fire. Take out her mailbox. Follow her around and let her see me do it. I dunno. Give her something else to think about it."

My eyes nearly rolled back inside my skull and it hurt. "You were to frighten her as a distraction? To keep her from uncovering information about . . . his business?"

"You deaf? Ain't that what I said?"

"Does this man have a name?"

"Stan."

"Can you describe Stan?"

302

Jared described Gordon in a cashmere sweater and Ugg boots. "Next time he came around, I told him to keep the money. Swear to God, hope to die. I was on probation. I'm not that stupid."

I highly doubted Jared refused because of his probationary status. Gordon was notoriously stingy with money. "You told Stan to make the same offer to Colin Empey."

The young man made a gun of his hand and dropped his thumb, the hammer. "Stan was going to get somebody to do it no matter who. I knew Colin wouldn't hurt her and get us in trouble. We had to make sure she kept on being rich and famous."

"Tell me about Colin and the money."

"Same difference. Who's the retard now?"

I'd missed something crucial. "Okay. Enlighten me."

"After what you did?" Jared flung a sideways glance at the house. "What goes around comes around." He hoisted himself out of the car. "If I don't see that check next week maybe I'll come to your place and bring some rocks to help you remember."

Once he moved beyond the range of the rearview mirror, I retrieved the phone at my feet. I sent the recorded conversation to Boynton and dropped the big, round rock out the window.

Chapter 33

G o time. Bottoms Up went dim and Rick Bush exited the building with two employees. Both were too short to fit the description of Colin. The threesome spoke for a moment beside Rick's Ford Fiesta before parting ways. I latched onto the Ford's tail lights as it merged with traffic and followed at a discreet distance keeping two vehicles between us. The dashboard navigator displayed the same roads Toby supplied me with. I could reasonably predict Rick's turns before he signaled them. The dead-end street, his destination, did not come as a surprise.

Lingering cloud cover from the evening rainstorm cloaked the landscape in gloom. I shut off my headlights, rolled up to a fenced yard, and left the Highlander as though it had a right to be there. The only telltale of my sneaky trespass across lawns and through border shrubs was the faint clicking of tools in my backpack. I thought of leaving it behind but wasn't quite sure what opportunities the stalking would present. "Better to have it and not need it, than need it and not have it", Mother often said. An oddly placed light drew me to the Fiesta which was open and unattended in a derelict area between two homes. A square, pale house perched above a steep rise of weeds on the left. On the right, a dark cottage poked out of a nest of overgrown privet. The tiny stucco building behind the car could belong to either. I watched as Rick emerged from the building twice with overstuffed garbage bags. When he dallied to puzzle fit them into the back seat of his car, I left the shelter of a wood fence in a mad dash to the backside of the little building.

A window festooned in insect cocoons provided a view into a crude taxidermy workshop. This was Colin's little shop of horrors. A mangy collection of squirrels, rabbits, ravens, cats, and small dogs fixed to wood bases threw

304

fantastical shadows onto the walls. Elsewhere, foam mounts sat on gore-stained benchtops littered with cutting tools. This was the stuff of childhood nightmares.

Rick reentered in a huff, grabbed two kittens posed wrestling over a golf ball, and shoved them into a fresh bag. Sleep-posed puppies were piled on top. Wilder creatures with marble eyes watched from wall shelves as their companions were removed one by one. Rick returned from his car with a box of newspapers and a red gasoline jug. I thought of confronting him and just as easily imagined him locking me inside the structure after setting it ablaze. He flung sheets of newspaper and the contents of the jug. Lit matches arced over the concrete floor like mini comets. His work was done.

When the Fiesta and its macabre load cleared the curb, I stormed into the workshop. For what seemed like a thousand heartbeats, my boots tap-danced on flaming newspaper. Orange embers sloughed off. I had no way to fully extinguish them. The two buckets of noxious liquid by the door could be anything. I suspected one was urine. A search for incriminating evidence began in earnest. I found a yellow foam pet tag mired in dirt under a table and a tuna can brimming with cigarette stubs. A *whoosh!* spun me around. Smoldering newspaper had given rise to new flames that split into flickering trails of blue. They multiplied and climbed walls to eat up white foam bodies. Coils of acrid smoke stung my eyes and clawed at my throat. Flakes of silvery ash drifted down from the ceiling. Under a card table, a forgotten cat with misaligned eyes and a snaggle tooth grimace. I flung the cat out the door and ran up the weedy hill.

Great gulps of cold night air calmed me enough to realize an anonymous tip from my phone was impossible. I pushed onward and upward to the porch of the square house and pummeled the door.

Bang, bang, bang, bang, bang. "Fire! Fire! Call the fire department!" *Bang, bang, bang, bang, bang.* The side of my palm ached and rising hysteria squeezed air from my lungs. "Fire—"

The door swung open on an elderly man in a loose green shawl. Tufts of white hair feathered his balding scalp and outlined thick lips that said, "Hey-hey-hey. Why you beaten on my house?"

I babbled. Fire. Garage. Burning up. Call now. Emergency. Phone. Where is it? Where is it? I stumbled into the house. All around me threadbare furniture, cast-off clothing, and bookcases holding everything except books. "Where's your phone? Excuse me. Sir!"

The old man had stepped back into a dark doorway. "You tried to burn me up. Sonomabitch. You're no good. They sent you, didn't they?"

"I'm here to help."

"Help? You brought the fire!"

At first glance, it would seem so. My boots and jeans were blackened. The backpack had melted in spots exposing the tools within. Smudged with gray ash and reeking of smoke, I resembled a human fire log.

The old man raised his right arm and charged forward. In his hand—a wood rasp. Time slowed. His lips drew back and a hoarse scream pushed hot, fetid breath into the air between us. The rasp plunged downward punching a hole in my jacket sleeve. A searing burst of pain sped up the clock.

I dodged the next strike and grabbed his forearm. The tool dropped into his free hand. I caught the movement and blocked another thrust. The rasp sailed away to punch a hole in a wall. The old man slammed me with a chest bump. We fell in a heap upon the coffee table and slid off onto the floor. He clawed his way up my body. Frail and utterly crazy, he probably broke a few ribs, and yet, he persisted. A knee jammed into his gonads forced him to uncurl his fingers from my throat. I heaved him aside and made my escape.

At the bottom of the grassy slope, the workshop's metal roof had split apart from intense heat. Flames roared skyward and smoke drifted over the land like a heavy fog. In the driveway of the square house ghastly flickers danced upon the pitted hood and fractured windshield of a silver sedan.

A fully charged tablet and a steaming mug of chamomile tea balanced on the bath tray. The bath, enriched with one of Muriel's salt bombs, removed all traces of last evening's fire from my hair. I determined to lie submerged under a cover of rose petals, lavender, and Epsom salts until either my skin pruned or I discovered all there was to know about the deranged old man, whichever came later.

According to today's newspaper, Roger Niznik was eighty-two years of age and a widower. Roger was also not above lying to officials. When fire and ambulance crews arrived at the blaze, they administered medical care, and reported his injuries were the result of a fall on his front steps. Colin wasn't listed as a resident of the house, which didn't matter as the silver car tied his partner, Rick Bush, to the household. Roger was represented on social media by others. Family and friends tagged him on ShowMe in photos taken at his eightieth birthday celebration. Those people led me down myriad paths until one relative shared a post of a drawing contest submission, an underwater tank resembling a spider that could shoot missiles guided by satellite technology. Fuzzy photos of the artist were included. The young man self-identified as a consummate gamer, who appreciated combat vehicles designed for future universes. The water had grown cold and my toes were shriveled like currants by the time I definitively linked Roger Niznik and Colin Empey to Bette Hornick's ex-husband, Wendell Empey, as uncle and son, respectively. Arielle had a twin brother. And I had slept in his bed.

I delayed joyful happy dancing until my tattooed neck and abraded arm had been freshly anointed and rebandaged. Then, I let loose with abandon nearly concussing myself on a door jamb.

The scanned transcript from Jared's trial promised revelations of a different sort. I opened the computer file and skimmed over boring parts, the posturing of lawyers, and the generic opinions of neighbors. I searched for traces of Colin's involvement, which I believed to be money, transportation, and know-how. As expected, criminal charges related to excessive cruelty were abandoned. Defense lawyers had successfully argued the videos were works of fiction despite the discovery of a dead dog in the bakery's rubbish bin and the bodies uncovered on Libby property. The videos had indeed been edited but for clarity, not deception. A keyword search for the name 'Colin Empey' produced zero results. I scrolled to the end and, in doing so, noted the PDF file was short twelve pages according to the page numbers on the transcript. They were physically absent from the hard copy taken from Bette. I examined the paper and envelopes used for Marlene Scott's extortion letters, which were recycled transcript pages from her trial. An ah-ha moment triggered a cascade of Dominos sounding off *tink-tink-tink-tink-tink* inside my head.

Raymond Semple, the paid professional, was lousy at his job. I wasn't much of a detective myself. All along I had wrestled with the notion that Marlene cared about Cassandra. In reality, Marlene was too sick to care about anyone but herself, and she certainly didn't think anything at all about Jared, a boy I was certain she had never met.

I knew of one person who wouldn't have missed such easy clues in this dust storm of distractions and his voice boomed from the answering machine as if on command.

". . . whereabouts of Dill Schaffer? His mother reported him missing and mentioned you, specifically."

"Good morning, Detective Boynton!" I said, once I caught my breath from leaping over the coffee table. "What has that young man done to earn your ire?"

"He didn't show up to school this morning."

"Are all truant children reported to homicide detectives?"

"The kid threatened his mother yesterday with a pot of boiling macaroni water. She says he's hanging out with the wrong crowd and fears for his well-being."

"Dill's a member of our loathsome foursome. He's gone to ground—I suspect."

"You see him, call me. Do not attempt to engage or apprehend."

Dill wasn't my present concern. "There is something larger you should know about." I relayed an appropriately edited story of the workshop fire and my utmost disappointment it received so little attention in today's newspaper. "Search for the cat I threw clear of the fire. Evidence of a kind."

Boynton, to my utter astonishment, didn't scold me for my involvement or risk taking. "I'll inform the fire chief."

"Does this mean you're taking me seriously now?"

"I never said I wasn't."

"Glad to hear it because there's more. You may remember dismissing Marlene Scott as irrelevant. Turns out, the letters we credited to her were forgeries. Marlene crafted envelopes and letters from pages of *her* trial transcript and mailed them to Bette Hornick as directed. Bette kept the original envelopes for the postmarks and prison stamps and substituted extortion letters she authored on a transcript she had easy access to, Jared Libby's. Her interest in his trial was wholly motivated by her son's involvement. Colin Empey had been Jared's unnamed partner. On this, I feel a bit foolish. All I had to do was turn the pages over and study the transcript."

"You're losing me. How does Hornick's son fit into *my* investigation?"

"Detective, please, keep up. He's a central player. Didn't you read the letter I taped to Ella's computer? Colin tried to teach Jared to shoot moving animals by first teaching him to shoot moving vehicles with a predictable trajectory. That bit of vandalism placed a bounty on Jared's head. When he was apprehended, Bette offered to pay for his silence to keep Colin out of it. A hefty financial burden for a recent retiree on a pension. Only, she had the means. Bette was the social worker involved in the Fahey's adoption of daughter Amy. Loretta can't possibly be her birth mother. While conducting interviews and assembling information for their home study, Bette undoubtedly dredged up inconsistencies and, clearly, didn't report them. I'm being presumptive—this is all theoretical-- but it does fit with all that I know.

"When Colin landed hip-deep in trouble, Bette reacquainted herself with the Faheys. They neutralized her as a threat to their scheming by making her Twin Sister's bookkeeper after I quit. A fortuitous thing, that. With their knowledge— if not their blessing and guidance—Bette created dummy invoices to embezzle from Twin Sister. Later, she convinced Ella to open a line of communication with Marlene Scott to set in motion an opportunity for a big pay-off. Bette intended to retire on her stealings."

Boynton whistled. "One heck of a story you got going there."

"Ella would've questioned the discrepancies given a chance; hence, Gordon kept her extraordinarily busy and did his best to create distractions. He hired a man named Richard Bush to intimidate Twin Sister members and attempted to bring in Jared Libby as the fall guy should things go awry. Jared refused and suggested Colin Empey in his stead. A full circle. An incestuous plot. Double-dealings. Entanglements."

"Dumb question. Do you have proof or are you going by gut feeling?" The detective's sarcasm seemed forced.

"Speculation grounded on facts. Have you made any headway accessing Ella's laptop?"

"About that. I got a guy working on the computer. Any ideas on what we might find?"

"Look for information regarding a new NPK venture, a frozen entrée line. Loretta partnered with her brother, Marvin Kent, of Frienderland Foods. Marvin's a member of a snake-handling cult. Manny Soto grotesquely incorporated that into the film to expose him and humiliate Loretta. Manny was unhappily employed at NPK and intended to burn bridges when he left. The unauthorized script changes in his slasher film would've struck a major blow to Ella's career and, by extension, robbed the Faheys of future money. Or so he believed."

"Huh. Interesting." Boynton's tone indicated a connection made. I dearly wished I could see what expression he wore.

"Please, detective. We're like family at this point. Families share. I'm practically a junior colleague."

The big man let out a deep belly laugh. Rather pleasant. I wished I had given him reason to do that sooner.

"Seeing as how we're practically family," Boynton began, "what would you say if I told you Loretta Fahey checked into a walk-in clinic two days after Soto's murder claiming she accidentally shut a car door on her hand. Two bones fractured."

The phone toppled to the floor when I did a swirly-handed happy dance. The soft-shoe shuffle was an unnecessary embellishment I felt entitled to and abruptly ended when Boynton yelled, "You still there?"

"Sorry. Sorry. I'd say it was her right hand, two metacarpal bones on the outside of the palm. She and Manny were lovers. Roy Torres, the proprietor of Righteous Roy's Tattoos, was a witness to the affair."

"You didn't include that in the envelope you dropped off."

"I only learned of it yesterday. Oh, and do check the bottom of Loretta's shoes for Manny's blood. She spent extra time in his flat cleaning up after herself and I'd love for her to have failed that. What did Detective Monroe tell you of the gun recovered at the scene?" On this, I held my breath.

"Registered to Mrs. Fahey. She claims the gun was stolen from her place of business a few months back and her husband reported it stolen. He claims he thought she reported it. Mr. and Mrs. could get Oscars for their performance.

When asked how it got to a crime scene, both agreed Soto stole it from them for protection and inadvertently supplied the killer with a weapon."

I had to lift my jaw from my chest to speak. "Ella never owned a gun?"

"Who said she had?"

My face flushed a steamy red. So much for feeling clever. I accepted Claire's word without hesitation. *I'm an idiot!* Loretta gave the gun to Rick. He stashed it in Claire's apartment. I took it from Claire. Loretta broke into my apartment to retrieve it. Full circle again. In theory. I'm an awful detective.

"Did they offer a motive for the murder too?"

"They were full of helpful ideas. The missus claimed a pizza chef owed Soto a grand for drugs. Cocaine. He was paying it back in pizzas. One of them wanted to change the arrangement."

"Of course, you don't believe that. Loretta had multiple reasons to kill Manny."

"Early days. Anything's possible. You couldn't ID her in Soto's yard."

True. As much as I wanted to.

Boynton lowered his voice. "There's a killer on the loose. You learn anything useful call the tip line or call me directly. Don't act on it. Dead heroes are boring conversationalists."

"Ha. That's something I would say."

"I know."

Chapter 34

W hen presented with the yellow foam tag and a plausible story, Violet hugged herself. She would've hugged me if I hadn't exaggerated my recent bodily injuries to emphasize the importance of my mission. The bandage on my forearm was sized up twofold and covered a good deal more than the abrasion.

I sat in my car for a half-hour reading a hardback book devoted to explaining a revised account of evolutionary processes. It was a refreshing departure from romance novels. I intended to read it until Russell shows more interest in my tattoo. The photo sent earlier of my neck received a one-word comment: SEXY.

After a family of four bounded out of the building with an excited terrier dragging the youngest member behind him, I reentered daring to hope.

Violet pointed to a contract on the counter. "I found it."

"Brava. You amaze me."

"He adopted a senior cat in June. I processed the application. That's my handwriting," Violet said. Her dark finger traced words on the page. The thumbnail portrait of the cat showed the snaggled-tooth kitty I rescued from the fire. "What bad thing did he do?"

"He should never be allowed to adopt any animals, that's all." Violet deserved that kindness. We live in a very sick world.

"Melinda got weird vibes too and made him go through extra steps to verify his address and employment. She said if he ever came back, we were to refuse him. He never did."

Per the contract, Colin used Rick Bush at Bottoms Up as an employment reference and an address in Westboro as his place of residence. Loretta Fahey was listed as a personal reference. I'm inclined to think Colin tore a page from his mother's extortion handbook. If each coconspirator in this criminal enterprise had indeed implicated others for personal protection purposes or blackmail prospects, Boynton's job would be made easier. Right now, I'd provide the dear detective with a little guidance in getting proof.

"Do you have a fax machine?" I asked.

The wait for positive news on any front was unbearable. Three days since Violet sent the fax and Boynton remained silent despite my calls. The long-awaited response from Russell came last night and it wasn't what I expected.

"I'm exhausted," Russell sighed. "My lease expires at the end of January and I can't see myself renewing it. Rent's going up and they still haven't fixed the elevator. I'm on the god damn fourth floor. A neighbor across the hall said we're losing on-street parking in March to a Tex-Mex restaurant opening up in the next building."

"Do you have a place to go to if you don't renew?"

"Housing isn't a problem. My buddy Paul has a spare bedroom and a spare parking spot. It's the job search. I'm a senior analyst getting offered junior positions here and in Boston. A five-year setback. I could ride it out. See what the merger brings. I'm the only guy in my group actively looking to jump ship."

We spoke for three-quarters of an hour. I managed plenty of sympathy but little in the way of applicable, anecdotal wisdom. I had worked for my father's company, created NPK with Ella, and stumbled upon the accounting position at B.C. Wethers. Being forced out of each job wasn't the same as departing voluntarily on your own terms. Russell reviewed his aggressive job-hunting strategies and bemoaned a lonely Christmas in New Jersey. He expressed no interest in discussing us or my sexy tattoo or advancements in my investigation. His disappointment felt very much like the muddy socks I wore the night I broke into Wilfred Draperies. I found myself almost eager to disconnect.

Louis wasn't particularly chatty when I called to inquire about his recent health scare and brief hospitalization. He summed it up simply, "The doc said angina. I'm okay. Missed seeing you at the hospital, sweetheart."

Rather than confess what was truly on my mind, I lied. "Sadly, I think I'm developing a horrific head cold. I wouldn't want to infect you in your fragile state. We're too close to Christmas. I'll check in again soon."

Monica's budding head cold, which had given me the idea, was such that a rant by me after hanging up on Louis would most certainly be unwelcome. I was at loose ends in the longest spell of inactivity since beginning my inquiries into Ella's murder. A breakthrough of some sort would discharge the tension. What was there left for me to do?

The answer seemed ridiculously obvious and pushed me out of the flat and behind the steering wheel of my car for nearly an hour. I intended to elicit a confession from Bette. I rehearsed questions and forecasted answers. In some scenarios, Bette cried and begged for understanding and forgiveness. In others, she grew angry and spiteful in the face of my accusations. Very few had her reaching for the knife drawer.

I arrived at the little white house determined to 'borrow' several items from Colin's closet that would also be of interest to Boynton. Bette answered my knock with circles of sweat staining her tee shirt despite the home being expectedly chilly.

"Uh, Danni. We were just talking." Bette said this to Arielle sitting on the couch. A news broadcast flickered on the television, which Arielle promptly shut off. "Come in. We'll, ah, have coffee. How nice you coming out to see us."

I followed Bette into the kitchen. "Have you spoken with Detective Boynton?"

Bette fussed with the coffee carafe at the sink. "That one? Nuh-huh. He called. I didn't pick up. A townie cop came by yesterday asking questions. I have nothing to say to them. I don't know why they bothered."

I lacked the necessary patience to waste time on niceties and plunged right in. "I'm aware Jared Libby was blackmailing you. You stole from Ella to pay him. When that wasn't enough, you forged Marlene Scott's letters demanding a large sum of money from Ella."

The half-smile slipped from Bette's face. She worked mechanically to set up a fresh pot of coffee, her hands trembling slightly.

I dragged out a kitchen chair and sat, hissing at her hunched shoulders. "Colin has serious mental issues. As his caretaker, you were well aware of that. He stalked Ella and now he's stalking me. His behavior is frightening a lot of people. Colin is committing awful crimes."

Bette pulled out of her stoop to stand taller, more self-assured. Confidence replaced confusion in the eyes that turned upon me. Frumpy, uncultivated Bette Hornick had reverted to Elizabeth Hornick, the seasoned social worker who wrote eloquently about deficiencies in the state's mental health programs.

"You have no idea what it's like to mother a child who has cognitive difficulties. Year after year filled with frustration dealing with a system unwilling to meet the special needs of your child. School. Counselors. His pediatrician. All crowing the same party line. Everyone pushing medication as the answer when he only wants to be heard. The system is set up to punish kids that are different. Kids who can't follow rules or score on tests within expected ranges." Bette shook her head blinking back tears. "I did the best I could when Colin's father left us. He wasn't committed to the process. In the end, I was all that he had. I took early retirement to be there. A proper mother."

"You wrote the articles for Colin, not Jared."

"Colin wants to do the right thing. Deep down, he's a good kid at heart. I can see it. Why can't others?"

My stern face exploded. "Your son is a thief! A vandal. Someone who derives pleasure from abject cruelty and heinous threats. He fired guns at moving vehicles. He could've killed someone! How could you overlook that? A proper mother would've alerted the authorities herself. Gordon made Colin his pawn and, you, his puppet. Both of you will face serious charges."

Bette clasped her hands and closed her eyes. "The truth will come out. Jared had an extraordinary hold on my son. Colin was always a daredevil. Ready to take on any challenge. The damn internet turned their heads around. It corrupted their thinking. They would've gotten bored with their little movies and moved on if Ella hadn't involved herself. She shares the blame for what happened. Three families were destroyed. She could afford to pay."

People with heavy burdens of guilt, still in deep denial, never fail to flabbergast me.

Bette barked out a nasty little laugh. "The thing about the money? Amelia Libby's idea. Her son was going to prison no matter what. Jared shot up thirty cars and signs. Insurance companies are horrible to deal with and slow to pay.

The whole damn community shunned them. Josh lost his job. There wasn't a hairdresser in town who'd cut Amelia's hair. The Libbys were forced to move out and they didn't want Jared showing up on their new doorstep. I promised to help him and Amelia promised to forget the name Colin Empey. Ella didn't miss a few hundred dollars a month."

Mentally, I was palming my forehead. "On that point, you're wrong. Ella knew you were embezzling from Twin Sister just as she knew the Faheys were probably stealing from NPK. Court battles to prove it would've destroyed both organizations in the ugliest possible terms. Ella wouldn't risk having her life's work ridiculed in the aftermath. She planned her exit and was preparing for something new."

A different thought formed, hammered into my head with each bang of a cupboard door as Bette searched for mugs and gathered condiments. "This is Gordon's handiwork. You. Me. Ella. I'm beginning to wonder if she asked for a buyout and, instead, he had her murdered."

That's when it truly hit me. An instant of slow motion falling off the dining chair and into darkness.

I woke feeling crumpled and pressed upon with the smell of mildew tickling my nose. My fingers were slow to wake, flexing one by one. They crept out to explore the smooth, cool walls hemming me into a tight space. The dimensions triggered a memory and an awful realization. Bette and Arielle had stuffed me into the busted freezer chest in the basement. A tremor of panic shook my body. Blood roared between my ears. A suffocating sense of isolation made me feel woozy. My inner voice shouted for calm.

Deep breath. Remain calm. Think. Think.

I transported myself to the first time I saw the freezer. A vinyl tablecloth festooned with daisies covered its top. A pattern of holes on the lid indicated a missing handle. An old hasp, corroded and bent from use, replaced it. The situation wasn't as dire as first thought.

Kicking the underside of the lid would generate noise and alert them I had awakened. I made myself small, flipped over, and pushed my spine upward. The lid rose half an inch letting in light and familiar sounds. Both the washer and dryer were chugging and whirling, processing loads of clothing. That either Bette or Arielle would tend to such a routine chore with my body thus encased chilled the pit of my stomach. That hurt more than the lump growing on the back of my head. *Fuck it.* I flipped over and attacked the lid with both feet. A steady beat of kicks jiggled apart the makeshift latch and pin. On the floor lay a splintered wood ladle, the same one Bette used to stir the Thanksgiving mashed potatoes.

I crept upstairs on sore feet to the dark kitchen. The window above the sink framed the moon. Day had faded to night while I lay unconscious. Moonlight outlined the shadowy contours of a purse on the counter. Car keys, phone, and ready cash were missing. Indignation kept me from bolting out the back door. My hair was a tangled, gritty mess and every part of me ached, provoking dreadful thoughts on the exact manner in which the pair dragged my body down to the basement. Admittedly, I'd lost the will to confront either mother or daughter with fists raised. I wanted to go home. Boynton could deal with them. Which meant I must locate my car keys.

The sound of running water in the second-floor bathroom steered me in that direction. Arielle gargled a nonsensical tune under the showerhead. I veered left into a tidy bedroom. This was Bette's room. A suitcase lay open on the bed packed with summer clothing and three pairs of scuffed sandals. A passport, issued seven weeks ago, was tucked into a zippered pocket alongside a flight itinerary. Bette and Arielle were headed to Georgia, then Florida. In the other bedroom, I waded through mounds of balled-up clothing and musky bedsheets to reach a dresser. My keys and cell phone were nestled in a pile of costume jewelry. Arielle was a slob and a procrastinator. She hadn't begun to pack for their getaway.

I exited quietly through the front door leaving the exterior lights off. The Highlander wasn't at the curb where I left it. I circled the house trailing my fingers against the siding to avoid stumbling through an obstacle course of garden ornaments and loose stone edging. A steamy bathroom window shined above the blackness of the rear yard. The outline of something large and slightly paler than the night air had me tripping over my feet to reach it. I whooped for joy when my car's engine started.

Light flared from the kitchen windows and—an instant later—a white-robed figure wobbled over the frozen lawn. Arielle stood squarely between the beams of my headlights; one hand clutched a cast-iron skillet, the other shaded her eyes. My hands trembled with nervous energy. I couldn't deliberately drive over another living thing no matter how threatening. Arielle let loose a guttural scream and swung the pan at a headlight. *CRACK!* I revved the engine as a warning. Arielle laughed, raised a middle finger, and smashed the pan into the other headlight. *CRACK!* She thought she knew me better than I knew myself. My hawk imp puffed out its breast feathers on the passenger seat and screeched.

Not quite. I shifted into reverse and cranked the wheel swerving blindly into the side yard. The tires tore up clumps of lawn massacring fairy figurines and squashing their acorn houses. A *TADUNK!* echoed in the cabin when the rear bumper flattened a bird feeder on a pole. More clatter rained upon me when two rails of vinyl fencing cartwheeled off the car's roof. I jerked the wheel struggling to control a hasty three-point turn on the street. Arielle had raced to the asphalt too planting herself in the middle of the road. The iron pan swayed in the headlights, back and forth like a pendulum. Her robe parted to reveal plump nakedness beneath. How utterly ridiculous and supremely terrifying. She raised the pan and yelled, "Die you motherfucker!"

I stomped on the gas pedal. The much-abused passenger mirror clipped Arielle's elbow in passing. Her howl of pain, I'm ashamed to say, brought happy tears.

The first stop sign flashed as a smear of red and white. I slammed on the brakes to roll through the second one. My body hummed with adrenaline like strings plucked on a guitar. Or maybe the buzz came from my cell. I veered to a curb at the next corner to answer it.

"You okay? Where are you? Tell me where you are!"

"I'm here, detective." My voice sounded far away. I strained to hear it.

"Are you safe? Do you require medical assistance?"

"I'm okay. I'm fine." *No, I'm not.*

Swirling blue lights and screaming sirens commandeered the road. Louder and louder until two cruisers, breaking sound barriers, rocketed past my car.

"I'm in my car. Police went by."

"On their way to pick up Elizabeth Hornick and her daughter. We've been monitoring their movements. The daughter was seen driving your vehicle and tried to make purchases on one of your credit cards this evening. Hornick's been making the rounds of ATMs trying to clean out accounts."

"Good. You do that." My brain had gone very quiet.

"I need you to come in. I'm going to send a car for you."

"Not now. I'm fine in my car."

Boynton prattled something about sending an ambulance because I "didn't sound fine to him".

I shifted into gear and drove on, savoring the sensation of a lazy smile.

After a moment, he said, "Do you have a safe place to stay for the night? Somewhere other than your apartment."

"Sure. I can do that. Tomorrow, Detective. We'll talk tomorrow."

A low whistle slipped into my dream as a steaming kettle on a stovetop. Under Mother's watchful eye, Grandma Tilly spooned tea leaves into the Brown Betty and poured hot water in. Mother set a strainer over her cup as I pushed the milk and sugar in front of her. She mouthed 'thank you, love' and my eyes snapped open to the blankness of a white ceiling and the cloying herbal scent of marijuana. After a tick, I realized I lay bundled up on Monica's couch. My brain rushed to make sense of it all determining that either Monica whistled when she snored or an American robin was in her bedroom smoking a joint.

I dragged my achy body into the kitchen, made a cup of tea, and scrounged in the freezer for a stale English muffin. The refrigerator was woefully shy of whole food nutrients. Monica's diet would never suffer a shortage of Oreos. I mentally added her to my holiday fruit basket list, finished breakfast, and dressed for a walk.

Countless visits to this street enabled me to see details beyond the range of street lamps. This was a neighborhood of cottages with mossy carports, aging sedans, and disintegrating street hockey nets. Few folks here invested more than the minimum in their properties. Most struggled to hang onto jobs and health care. Despite constant complaints about her landlord, Monica enjoyed the distinction of living in the carriage house of the largest home on the street.

On my return, the living room lights were on.

"Honey, I'm home," I sang from the door.

Monica sat cross-legged on the couch in blue penguin pajamas clutching a mug of hot chocolate. Her sleep-swollen face, chapped lips, and drippy red nose indicated she wasn't happy to be out of bed this early on a Sunday morning.

"Feel any better?" she asked.

"Not until all the bad guys are incarcerated. And you?"

"Meh. I'll survive."

"Glad to hear it."

"Nice tat. How come I wasn't invited?"

Monica had a tiny red heart imprinted above her left breast. She'd yank her collar aside to show anyone willing to look. She was small-breasted, so few did. To me, it resembled a cherry angioma.

"Next time," I said with a wink, and huddled at the opposite end of the couch hoping she wouldn't breathe on me.

Monica poked the TV remote finding a twenty-four-hour news channel. She lowered the volume, then turned to me. "Ready to talk?"

My mood last night wasn't conducive to intelligent conversation. Today hadn't brought impending good cheer, but I'd give it a go. "How much would you like to know?"

Monica blew her runny nose into a wad of tissue sounding very much like an elephant issuing a mating call. "I've no plans for the day other than dying in bed. Whatcha been up to?"

"Quite a bit, actually. Lee Anne was fed false information implicating Jared Libby as Ella's murderer. Enraged, she went to his home and broke a slew of windows. Karen Putnam arrived as Kevan Blaine and stopped Jared from shooting her."

"Whoa."

"More bizarre, he as a she is truly a she. Karen Putnam AKA Kevan Blaine is Kerry Evan Blaine. She graduated high school two years behind Ella and me. You might've had classes with her." A quick search on my smartphone brought up the yearbook picture of Kerry dunking in the state championship game. "Ella wasn't writing an article on school sports. To learn more about Karen without alerting her, Ella contacted people from her past, from high school. Ella did this after breaking ties with a private investigator she once used, Ray Semple."

Monica grabbed my phone. "Give it here. Let me see." She worked the screen with both thumbs, the most flexible joints in her body.

"This isn't about living her truth or making a statement. The only gender conflict happening is what Kerry encourages others to believe."

"Not transgendered?"

"Not even a little. Everything is a ruse like the assorted names she goes by. Leslie Meisner complained, 'How can she do girl so bad?' The question should've been: *Why* would she do girl so bad? The awful makeup, unshaven legs, ill-fitted clothing."

"So, we'd think she was a poor slob of a man."

"Exactly. We'd immediately accept her without cause. Another disenfranchised soul like the rest of us. A relatable person. Accepting her without question extends blind trust. Something she never had to work for."

"How's that bad? We all want friends to hang out with."

I flapped a tufted pillow gently against Monica's red nose. "Kerry isn't interested in making new friends. She snookered us. We should figure out why."

Monica made her own observation. "Did you look at her yearbook portrait? The quote." She waggled my phone. "Karen wanted to study law enforcement after graduation. I bet she's a cop! Oh shit. Did I smoke pot in front of her?"

I batted her hand away. "Let me finish. There's a bit more. I followed one of our stalkers, Rick Bush. He set fire to his partner's shop of horrors. Colin Empey. Where the kitties came from. I sought help and was instead attacked by Colin's great uncle Roger." I pulled up my sleeve. A bumpy, red crust covered the abrasion.

"Shi-it. You've been super busy—in a bad way. Want a beer?"

"It's seven in the morning."

"So?"

"Good point. Though, I'd prefer a hot chocolate. If you're making." I dropped the shoulder of my sweater to examine an angry red welt.

"Yikes."

"Last night Bette Hornick and her daughter tried to kill me. Arielle clocked me with an iron frying pan and they stuffed me inside a freezer chest. Thank goodness it wasn't plugged in." I patted the lump on my crown and winced.

Monica's jaw unhinged and her eyebrows danced. I've been keeping my own counsel for the past week. Dumping a basket full of woes in her lap overwhelmed her.

"I'm unworthy," she said with a heavy sigh and kowtowed theatrically.

"Then add extra marshmallows to my hot chocolate," I advised.

The chocolatey oat milk drink was creamy, nutty, and sweetened with a giant cube of marshmallow. It fulfilled my sugar quota for the week. In between sips, I answered a host of ludicrous questions. Monica wanted entertainment, not information.

What kind of mileage does a Fiesta get? A pail of piss—are you shitting me? Was it stinky gross like a butcher's shop? Do you think Roger was a World War Two veteran? Think he and Nosferatu have a lot in common? Did Arielle have any tattoos? Arielle, Claire, and Karen are like twins, in a weird way—am I right? A personality disorder.

After a while, Monica lost interest in asking questions and quieted, transfixed by the television screen. I finished my lukewarm cocoa in peace watching a house finch cling to a window screen backlit by the rising sun.

"Too much news will rot your brain," I offered jokingly when the bird flew off.

"Shhhhhh! It's an update," she said, raising the television's volume. "You'll like this. It started yesterday afternoon. Sit back and enjoy. I wish I had popcorn."

The news broadcast began with three studio-based news anchors expressing shock at a surprising twist in an alleged kidnapping. Dill Schaffer's high school portrait flashed on the screen. Then it became a jumble of roughly edited video clips. A moving camera zoomed in on a podium where a bald officer decorated in brass buttons announced arrests made in an ongoing investigation. The scene shifted to a helicopter view of a reddish pink, split-level home in Westborough. Three police cruisers were parked in the front yard. If not for an expansive bog captured in the aerial view, one would think it a low-brow auto dealership. Law officers sprang up like mushrooms outside the pink home with the arrival of a

Dutch Shephard named Bullet. Back in the sky, the helicopter's rotor blade flattened yellowed grass to reveal rotted tree stumps and a lone man wading in and out of mud surrounding black pockets of open water.

My eyes widened. "Is that, who I think it is?"

The helicopter herded Colin, barefoot in a sweatshirt and loose jeans, toward drier ground. Undeterred by the sight and sound of the hovering helicopter, Bullet gave chase loping through a field of red and brown weeds. Colin stumbled, fell, and curled into a ball as the dog set upon him. The animal's handler lagged behind, winded. A very bloody Colin screamed and wriggled for five seconds before the news anchors cut back to the home and a close-up shot of a police cruiser. Dill Schaffer peered defiantly out the rear windshield.

"Kismet?" Monica asked.

I grinned. "I do believe the universe has spoken."

Chapter 35

M aple Hill Cemetery is where I sought the approval of my elders. Mother, Father, Grandma Tilly, and Grandpa Bernie rested here. They inhabited my dreams and, on occasion, I strengthened that connection by coming here. Sadly, while they bring me joy and insight, I offer only grief and indecision. Three years ago, I asked for advice on dealing with Henry. He proposed marriage a week earlier in an ill-timed bid to salvage our relationship. Unbeknownst to Henry, Russell and I had been together for several glorious weeks. Had I known Russell accepted the job in New Jersey, the conversation would've been different. Their response, as I imagined it, wouldn't have changed. *Follow your heart.*

The cemetery lost some of its charm in the intervening time. The fieldstone chapel at its gates stood unprotected. The giant silver maple that rained apricot leaves on its slate roof every autumn recently split apart after a lightning strike. By a quirk of fate, its massive limbs fell away from the early twentieth-century structure. Branches as thick as coffins radiated over the ground awaiting a chainsaw. I clambered over the lost limbs to touch raw wood; inhaling the sweet fragrance of shredded bark. My assessment of the fatal event produced not a single, novel metaphor. This was, after all, a place for death.

My feet took me to a grouping of rose granite headstones, the Mowrey family plot. The polished gray obelisk and surrounding concrete berm topped with wrought iron edging separated my ancestors from the farmers and mill workers, who had come to rest here too. I leaned against the base of the obelisk hoping for a quieter mind. The cemetery's living inhabitants moved slowly around me in accordance with their day. A chipmunk stole a carnation from a vase of wilted stems on a grave marker. A tufted titmouse whistled a three-note song from a rhododendron. A gray squirrel scampered over to perch on the curlicue edging. It spat an acorn from a cheek pouch and ate its breakfast. Four ravens swaggering and hopping along the access road. They flapped to the top of a gray headstone and lined up, shuffling position. I guessed them to be mated pairs. With keen eyes and ruffled feathers, they studied me. This one or that one turned its head or stretched its neck for a better view. I noted the name on their granite perch: Janus. A smile of knowing curved my lips. I gave the birds a scout salute.

I love you too.

Boynton quieted when a sulky teenager entered Crispus Attucks' sunlit reading lounge. The boy chose a chair by a window overlooking the sidewalk. The detective wasn't inclined to give up our plush seats overlooking the globe fountain in the library's memorial garden to keep our conversation private. My family's name was on the plaque and Boynton was trying to make a point of some sort.

"Figured it all out, did you?" he asked.

"Most of it. Why didn't you tell me sooner?"

"What is it about me being a cop and you not being a cop that you don't get?"

I suppressed a wry chuckle. "Over-inflated ego. I let it get the better of me. I never questioned how I could stumble upon so-called clues while you, an experienced detective, could not. The man in the brown coat leading me to Jeanne Whitman's home was not Craig Whitman. That was a bit of misdirection. The book in the ditch, the laptop, the address stamps, the Easter card—maybe even the letter hung on Gordon's wall. Real or fake. Confusion and doubt. Suspicion cast into the wind like oh so many grains of pollen. All in all, a very successful campaign of misinformation."

The detective pressed his elbows into the arms of the chair and looked at the boy who had removed a Chromebook and a sheaf of papers from his backpack. Boynton scratched his chin for a good, long while and arrived at a decision.

"According to the feds, the Faheys have been at it sixteen years. Mr. and Mrs. get cozy with local officials and take up volunteerism like the good citizens they are. They worked hard to get people positioned as mayors, councilmen, superintendents, city planners, police, and expected leeway in return. Money turns up missing with everything they touch. Discrepancies. Allegedly. A little league baseball diamond. Paved lot for a trailhead. Little Mindy Loo's cancer fund."

"Why hasn't anyone stopped them?"

Boynton splayed his hands. "They get the work done. Usually. They're there when nobody else is and put in the hours. That's worth a little extra. Or so I'm told. Financing the movie through crowd-sourcing is a whole separate deal. Also, out of my hands. I have to build up the case with my name on it. Everyone named in Ella DeMarco's case is lawyering up and shutting up. I got nothing concrete to tie Rick Bush or Colin Empey to the disturbances at your gatherings. Each is giving the other an alibi for the night of the fire. Bush bagged the mounts and disposed of them. Allegedly. Not much we can do about the crooked kitty. Animals aren't people."

"People are animals."

"I don't disagree with that."

"What of Bette Hornick?"

"Our star witness. She claims—alleges—her scheming was sanctioned by Loretta Fahey in exchange for access to Colin Empey. Mom finally making him pay his own way, I guess. Bush and Empey were hired—allegedly—to scare off you and your friends. The end goal was to discredit both groups by making you all look crazy. You and Ms. DeMarco in particular. The Faheys worried you might testify against them someday. The pranks and property damage were supposed to go public in a big way. Never happened. Nobody called the cops or filed complaints. Nobody demanded interviews with reporters. You kept it under wraps. Didn't give them much to work with."

"But why attack Compassion Lives? Ella wasn't a part of it."

"I don't think Mr. and Mrs. saw you being all that different. Two halves of the same avocado."

"Hmm. Quite a few Twisters did switch to my group. Several of those angry souls suspected the Faheys of wrongdoing and retaliated with graffiti and deliveries stolen from their store. And please stop saying allegedly. We'll prove everything in court. We have enough. This brings us to Loretta killing Manny."

Boynton rubbed his beard. "Soto reshot scenes after they were out of the picture. Heh-heh. Good one. He put the Faheys in charge of fundraising knowing they'd pull something making blackmail a retirement option. He set up Ms. DeMarco as a hypocrite to seal a no-deal on the frozen food venture. I'm thinking Loretta Fahey blabbed family secrets during pillow talk. Thanks for the tip. The Kent documentary. They are something all right."

I mulled over a niggling assumption. "In retrospect, I doubt brother Marvin would've been troubled by negative publicity. The rich and crazy find ways to take advantage of every situation, good or bad. Something more valuable was at stake—Loretta's public personae. Benevolent soccer mom, dutiful wife, brilliant businesswoman. She, not Ella, protected Manny's job to protect herself. They were clandestine lovers. The timing of his risqué art exhibit at the Trojan Gallery and the movie's unauthorized release up-ended carefully laid plans and were a significant blow to her ego. Ella suspected wrongdoing on several fronts and hired Raymond Semple to piece it together. He knows far more than he'll admit to."

"He's on my list."

"Now what?"

"We shake the rotten apples out of the tree and make applesauce. Don't worry. You won't be around to bear witness."

North Chatham was forlorn on the eve of winter. Clouds and rain forecasted for the duration of my stay. Agitated by recent storms, the Atlantic spit up clumps of Irish moss, bladderwrack, and fishing gear. I've suited up in a slicker and wellies for the past four mornings to collect trash on lonely shoreline walks. The task filled hours of otherwise unproductive time. The battery in my cell phone hadn't been charged in two days. Passive protection. Boynton's campaign of intimidation was designed to force suspects to communicate with their coconspirators. In doing so, he hoped to inspire mistakes. Summons to the police station for lengthy chats and the arrival of a police cruiser at one's business or residence had a notable effect on the human psyche. I was glad of his no communication rule with friends and family. There was enough chatter inside my head. Silencing it this morning was somewhat hampered by herring gulls, who loudly objected to my presence on their stretch of sandy turf. I redoubled my efforts to meditate by absorbing the muted shades of purple, gray, and gold that blanketed the beach. Everywhere else, silver shingles and white trim sparked memories from my youth.

Many homes here adopted that particular style as though agreeing a uniform look would meet tourist expectations of quaint New England. It did. Loads of charm to be found in renting someone's million-dollar summer home with its broad deck and beach view while noshing on deep-fried clam bellies. I was staying at a cedar-shingled inn for the week at a slightly more affordable rate. The proprietors were kind enough to lend me trash buckets. Today's catch: a length of yellow rope; crumpled wire from a lobster trap; half of a foam net buoy; four plastic water bottles; a foil balloon; a floss stick; and glass shards from several beer bottles. I stowed the bucket in my car and drove back to the inn. Grasses by the ocean had paled to blend with the sand, but well-tended properties were still green and sprouting miniature Christmas trees decked with seashells and stars made of braided marsh grass. Adirondack chairs and cabanas facing the Atlantic had dwindled to small groupings on more luxurious properties where vacationers clung to romantic notions of being at the seaside in any season. My refuge placed its outdoor furniture under the cover of a wraparound porch. I've been vaping there with a glass of wine after dinner each night. Pleasant but not romantic for I was alone.

My oneness was made all the more palpable when thinking of Mother's friend Freda, who lived further inland in a gracious Georgian colonial. Its weathered gray dock stretching over marshy ground to touch the waters of Oyster Pond readily came to mind. Adolescent me would run to the end and eagerly await a ride in Freda's skiff. Freda was passionate about the natural world and volunteered for the National Audubon Society. She could speak eloquently of the parasitism of red dodder and with her next breath discuss the plight of the endangered New England cottontail rabbit. My fascination with birds was a direct result of our friendship. A shame I hadn't called upon her recently and was prohibited from doing so now. Boynton insisted I be completely unavailable, invisible. I was instructed not to roam in the unlikely event I was recognized and my whereabouts broadcast far and wide by a well-meaning group member. Had I fully comprehended Boynton's plan, I would've suggested the Grand Canyon or Hawaii. The department was paying.

Today's agenda included returning to several shops along the main drag where I spied delightful textiles and a center for inter-spirituality that operated a gift shop. Boynton was quite clear that I not go to extraordinary lengths in search of food. Skirting the directive pushed me in the direction of breweries. Several growlers were chilling in the Highlander for the trip home. This vacation from my life costs only my time. For now.

The emptied waste bucket went back to the inn's kitchen before I climbed the stairs to my room. I changed into a dry sweater and corduroys, washed sea spray from my face, and screamed into the mirror.

Never had my flat on Dolly Road seemed so dear as when I returned to it after a seven-day absence. A sense of comfort and continuity restored. A lost friend joyously found, however disagreeable the relationship or widespread the leak in the bedroom closet. My holiday shopping deliveries had piled up in the hall. Mr. Peebles was slow to quit the pretense of incompetence and allowed the packages to get rain-soaked before bringing them inside. I notified him of my return, dutifully changed the channel on his television to a game show, and removed the note taped to my door.

With a grapefruit ale in hand, I busied myself posting vacation pictures. Photos of the inn, the shops, a beach clean-up, and a brewery populated my social media accounts. I included pictures of the spirituality center and lamented missing the chance to be guided toward a fully-centered self, which was the purported reason for my impromptu trip.

Monica: Next time, invite me! We'll get centered around a bottle of vodka. Hee-haw!
Amanda: What did YOU eat? Any gluten-free pastries?
Megan: LOVE the seashell ornaments. Cute! The sea star dish towels would look great in my kitchen. Can I order them online? Store name?
Doug: You drank beer without me? Fer shame, fer shame.

Kind remarks and obligatory questions were answered with links to Cape Cod businesses and articles on coastal wildlife. A new friend, PerfecChuck, inquired what my immediate plans were. How would I wind down from the obvious excitement of my vacation?

Parkour in the park, I responded, and detailed my exercise plan. Twice.

F. Gilbert Hills State Forest is a testament to the forces of nature. An Ice Age glacier scoured the landscape peppering the thousand-acre preserve with massive granite boulders. Free climbing is an unfulfilled objective on my personal To-Do List. I clung to parkour because it kept me closer to the ground, reasoning—gravity's a bitch—and I'm currently too spontaneous to travel with a crash pad and a partner.

I circled the woods close to the park headquarters building where an assortment of paths hemmed in wetland and a forest road allowed for easier crossing between trails. Here and there I encountered other hikers: a woman running with her dog; two mothers pushing infants in fat-tired strollers; a trio of boys playing tag within the trees; an elderly couple foraging for late-season edibles. I moved on to examine CCC water holes. The forest map in my coat pocket pinpointed their locations with numbers. These rustic, little stone-lined pits were beautiful. Moss and fern grew around them. Dug into the earth nearly ninety years ago to be used for fire suppression, they served as water sources for wildlife and offered sanctuaries for frogs and newts. Approaching the second hole, I heard the distinct snap of twigs breaking. A large animal hurried in my direction.

The blow to my lower back hurled me to the ground face-first. A gasp to reinflate my lungs introduced bits of dirt and rain-blackened leaves. My assailant sat on my hips pinning me down with her extra girth.

"Why you running, Danni? You a scaredy-cat, darlin'?"

"Karen."

"Karen's outlived her usefulness. Like you." Kerry leaned sideways allowing me to see her slicked brown hair and shaved-off eyebrows—a sinister Mona

Lisa. She leered over the barrel of a small black gun. "Let's walk and talk, girlfriend."

I was yanked upright by my collar. The gun's muzzle jammed into my shoulder gave direction. We moved away from the water hole and into the furrow of a dirt bike trail. Anyone traveling on it would pass us quickly. The scenery was too serene for the gravity of my situation. Birds flitted from bare, sunlit branches dotted with lichen and the air tasted crisp like melted snow. I wasn't sure where we were headed but knew the odds of me leaving the forest alive were dismal.

"You knew we'd accept you without question," I said.

"Like that, did you?" Kerry's southern drawl disappeared. It no longer served a purpose.

"Why did Ella have to die? Brag a little. I doubt I'll be telling anyone."

Kerry considered the gun in her hand before answering. "We met up to discuss the film. I was going to let her in on everything Manny had done."

"Why did that matter to you?"

"It didn't. That's what made riling everyone up so much fun. I threw out a welcome mat and hosted pity parties. Feed their insecurities and they'll talk forever. Her Highness worried about what the movie would do to others. Who gives a holy flying fuck? You're all weak in the head."

"Why did she have to die?" I stopped moving. Kerry's boot scraped my heel. I braced for a crack on the head. Nothing happened. Voices drifted over amber fern and tangles of wild blueberry. Others were on a walking trail nearby.

Kerry lowered her voice. "I went to remove a few things from her office. She wasn't being helpful. My emotions got the better of me. Oopsie."

Every nerve ending in my body rapidly fired. If not for the hunk of metal aimed at my spine, I'd knock Kerry down and search for a rock to introduce to her forehead. "Hurting Ella wasn't part of the Faheys' plan. Can't milk a dead cow. But you aren't working for them, are you?"

"You're the one with the fancy education. Figure it out, Nancy Drew."

My beleaguered brain refused to make new connections in Ella's death. I was preoccupied with envisioning escape routes across every rise and dip in the terrain. Kerry randomly varied the distance between us anticipating any kicks or trips I'd attempt to slow her down. We veered off the path picking our way through spindly trees and slogging over brittle brush and humps of matted leaves. The rolling view widened and I recognized our location. Up ahead, mammoth slabs of granite lay in a jumble. Behind them, a cliff band rose up fifteen feet. I recognized it from online photos. Free climbers had bestowed names on the vertical rock faces worth climbing. The Emergency Room. The Operating Room. The Morgue. Kerry's plan unveiled itself in a length of rope dangling from a slender tree. My stomach shriveled and my mouth began to work in hyperdrive.

"Carrie Huxley? The closet alcoholic. You met her at a Worcester AA meeting site."

Kerry snorted out a laugh. "God, you are thick. I'd shoot you in the head, but the bullet would ricochet."

"Louis Sammons?"

"Your sad sack stepfather? He's got his own thing going on."

"The movie."

"Getting warmer."

"Someone involved in the film is paying you. Marvin Kent?"

"A perfectly good education wasted. The college should get a refund."

"Something horrible happened on the set." I spun around. "That's why people assumed Ella attempted suicide. Someone got hurt."

"She wrote the checks to the wrong person. Happy? Get moving."

I wove a path through the tumbled-down stones to the base of the most challenging rock face. Finding finger and toe holds in vertical crevices was easier for me than a hulking figure clutching a loaded gun in one hand. Kerry fumbled and growled in frustration below me but managed to keep up. I hadn't anticipated her clenching the gun between her teeth to free up both hands. On top of the plateau, she had laid out a simple machine, a length of rope threaded through the crotch of a tree. One end was fashioned into a loop. The other had been knotted around a large rock that would serve as a counterweight. Once the noose encircled my neck, Kerry would push me off or dislodge the stone. Either way, I'd be dancing a jig until my neck snapped.

"This is completely unbelievable. I'm not the suicidal type."

"Sure, you are. Ella's death was devastating and your crappy search for justice threw you over the edge. Rumors are already circulating. I know because

I started a few. Put the right word in the right ear." Kerry flashed a delirious grin.

"Why is any of this necessary? Manny is dead. The Faheys will be indicted. Twin Sister and NPK will cease to exist. How is that not enough revenge?"

"Pick up the rope."

"What did *I* do wrong?"

"You failed to follow directions. I drew you a map. That was supposed to be the fun part. My reward. You're useless too." Kerry aimed the gun at the noose. "Pick it up or I'll shoot. I got a pocket full of bullets. May take a while for you to stop screaming."

A pull tab was missing from her jacket's breast pocket. Such a small detail.

"Earn your paycheck." I snapped the rope attached to the rock. The hemp cord rippled like a sidewinder bumping against Kerry's ankles. "Why do you hate me?"

"Love. Hate. Why get emotional? I only play for winning teams. I'm an overachiever."

I filled my lungs with a grounding breath and gripped the noose with both hands. My imp dove off a branch of a tall pine tree. Tawny wings flapped wide to slow its descent. Pearly breast feathers and sunny yellow claws passed through Kerry's head as it braked hard to land on my shoulder.

"Well, isn't that a hoot coming from a shitty basketball player like you."

"Are you testing me? What a brave, brave girl."

"Big. Dumb. Skanky. Ugly. Not exactly prom queen material. Am I right?"

"I'm tired of this assignment. You are not amusing."

"And you're not a convincing woman despite being one. How does that make you feel?"

A gun blast cleaved the air. Weightless, I tipped my face skyward. Wispy clouds were caught in a net of gray tree branches. In that wondrous instant, I felt connected to every living thing that ever was or ever will be. Then the rope jerked me sideways.

Kerry cried out from the plateau. My plunge had tightened loops of rope around her feet whisking her off the cliff. I hung on to the midpoint of a return swing before releasing my grip. The earth rushed up to steal my breath in a musty embrace. When my eyes cracked open, the forest exploded with life. Large animals moved in my direction.

A bent leg marked the spot where Kerry landed. Being wedged in a gap between massive slabs of granite wasn't pretty. Less so when the counterweight stone followed to bang her in deeper. Kerry's hips were twisted in an unnatural position with one arm angled above her head and the other somewhere beneath her. Her nose had migrated closer to one ear. A Picasso face. She moaned softly pushing bloody bubbles through toothless gaps in her shattered jaw. I crawled over the rocks that cradled her body to gently comb back hair mired in oozing blood. In her ear, I whispered, "Oopsie."

Boynton pried apart the straps of the Kevlar vest that had weighed me down. He bagged the watch that recorded the conversation between Kerry and me. I frowned. "Did you run out for donuts?"

"You weren't supposed to go to the edge of the forest. We had to evacuate three homes."

"I intended to go to hole number seven as planned, but she had a gun. Sheesh. You people will give them to anyone."

"Why provoke an attack? You could be missing half your head."

"I knew she'd aim for my heart." I knew no such thing. "I timed the jump well." That too was truly miraculous. I half expected him to ruffle my hair or offer a compliment and was a smidge disappointed he didn't. "I'm confused. Why did she encourage me to investigate Ella's death? Seems counter-intuitive for a guilty person."

Boynton spoke slowly. "Immunity."

I gave him a slow owl-like blink.

"Everyone who knows you knew you'd be dissatisfied and get involved. Ms. Blaine couldn't take that chance. She cheered you on to avoid becoming a suspect. It's a working theory."

"More like to steer me in the wrong direction, continuously."

"No sense you getting too close to the truth." Boynton pulled himself to his feet. "Make way. She's coming."

Two paramedics and a uniformed officer kicked up rocks trudging with their heavy burden. Kerry was belted to a backboard with an IV bag on her chest. What wasn't covered with sopping red bandages was blanketed.

"It's imperative that she lives. I'm not saying that to be kind."

Boynton grunted. "I know."

"Is it finished?"

"For now."

"Good. I need a rest."

Chapter 36

C hristmas Eve and all was not merry and bright. I drew my legs onto the porch glider and rearranged the quilt to insulate them against the frosty night air. The diamond sparkle of distant suns in the vacuum of space fit with my mood in ways the boisterous holiday party could not. Muriel earned good karma points for trying and rose to honorary mother in my esteem. We trimmed a fir tree with my collection of antique glass ornaments and spiraled twinkling lights around the porch columns. Muriel encouraged me to craft paper chains and snowflake cutouts to hang from the fireplace mantle. It gave me something simple to do and reminded me of doing the same with my grandparents so very long ago. Mulled wine simmered in the crockpot and puff pastries were fresh from the oven when the first guests arrived. My friends populated the guest list, but the Pastafarians were proving to be the life of the party. Their voices raised in song blotted out all accompanying music. Boynton now occupied the spot of grumpy uncle in my affections; though, he wouldn't have joined us even if Muriel had invited him.

Much agonizing could've been spared had Boynton focused his efforts exclusively on Kerry Blaine, the Janus-faced individual in our midst. Joan Doyle and her son Mike were brought in for questioning, as were the Faheys, the DeMarcos, and the Norellis. Louis and Cheryl reached out to express their outrage when a report of Kerry's capture made the front page of the Globe. Both demanded apologies for the indignity of being caught up in the sweep of police interrogations during my seaside vacation. Ridiculous that I did indeed apologize given they commissioned the Salted Stone protest video as a way to coerce me into engaging Leo Everson. I was ninety-nine percent sure.

Ella's killer, the person most likely responsible for Evelyn Pallotta's death, was chained to a bedrail in an intensive care unit. We still didn't know who hired Kerry and it'd be some time before she was able to communicate coherently, assuming she survived. I raised my lukewarm hot toddy to that image and wished Kerry a long and stunningly miserable life.

Six vapor rings floated above my head before breaking apart. No new revelations were forthcoming. I found Boynton's number and worked bare fingers over my phone's screen.

Danni: Kerry Blaine was Raymond Semple's fifth target. He covered for her as a professional courtesy. Didn't matter in the slightest that her license had been revoked. Her arrest would reflect poorly on his training. Go pound the snot out of him. Get some answers, please.
Happy holidays!
Charles: Merry Christmas, Danni! Say hello to your family from me.
Semple lawyered up too. We'll talk after New Year. Give your brain a rest.

A crash of drums and a wailing guitar trampled on my despair. Muriel closed the door behind her and snugged the belt of her jacket. "Why are you out here all alone?"

Emotion surged in my chest and leaked out of my eyes. "It's not over. It'll never be over. I failed Ella. What am I to do?"

Muriel squeezed in next to me on the glider and wrapped her arms around my shoulders. She pressed her forehead to mine. "Somethings you hang on tightly to. Other things you have to let go of. Wisdom is knowing what's what. I'm not there yet either, my love."

I sobbed into her shoulder while she rubbed warmth into my back. The clap of a car door turned our heads. Muriel whispered, "Merry Christmas."

Russell stepped into the light spilling off the porch with a gift bag in each hand. "Happy holidays. Miss me?"

I blotted my eyes with the back of my hands and pinched snot from my nose in a most unladylike manner. Wait till he sees my new collection of bruises.

K.J. Serafin

K.J. Serafin resides in New England with her husband and two sons. They are owned and cared for by two rescued mutts, Belle and Davi. The author is passionate about innovative cuisine, craft brews, animals of all kinds, and this wondrous planet we all call home. When she isn't experimenting with new recipes, biking and hiking with her family, or working on her next novel, she's watching her favorite NHL team compete and shouting out the bad calls.

Printed in Great Britain
by Amazon

47026014R00195